THE NEW
MYSTERY

THE NEW
MYSTERY

The International Association of Crime Writers'
Essential Crime Writing of the Late 20th Century

A BYRON PREISS BOOK

EDITED BY

JEROME CHARYN

A DUTTON BOOK

DUTTON
Published by the Penguin Group
Penguin Books USA Inc., 375 Hudson Street,
New York, New York 10014, U.S.A.
Penguin Books Ltd, 27 Wrights Lane, London W8 5TZ, England
Penguin Books Australia Ltd, Ringwood, Victoria, Australia
Penguin Books Canada Ltd, 10 Alcorn Avenue,
Toronto, Ontario, Canada M4V 3B2
Penguin Books (N.Z.) Ltd, 182–190 Wairau Road,
Auckland 10, New Zealand

Penguin Books Ltd, Registered Offices:
Harmondsworth, Middlesex, England

First published by Dutton, an imprint of New American Library,
a division of Penguin Books USA Inc.
Distributed in Canada by McClelland & Stewart Inc.

First Printing, February, 1993
10 9 8 7 6 5 4 3 2 1

 REGISTERED TRADEMARK—MARCA REGISTRADA

LIBRARY OF CONGRESS CATALOGING IN PUBLICATION DATA:
The New mystery / edited by Jerome Charyn.
    p. cm.
  ISBN 0-525-93516-9
  I. Charyn, Jerome.
PS3553.H33N4   1993
808.83'87208—dc20   92-22027
                                                              CIP

Printed in the United States of America

PUBLISHER'S NOTE

Special thanks to John Silbersack.

Contents

Introduction

Jerome Charyn

During the dark years of World War II, Edmund Wilson wrote two essays in the *New Yorker*, "Why Do People Read Detective Stories?" and "Who Cares Who Killed Roger Ackroyd?", that condemned mystery writing as a worthless mountain of rubbish. Wilson was very clear about his complaints. He attacked most mysteries for their "meagreness of imagination." The modern crime novel didn't seem to have Conan Doyle's "wit and fairy-tale poetry of hansom cabs, gloomy London lodgings, and lonely country estates." In fact, it had no poetry at all; it was only adding to a wartime paper shortage.

For Wilson, Dashiell Hammett was simply a former Pinkerton detective who happened to write novels. Wilson singled out *The Maltese Falcon* as being "not much above those newspaper picture strips in which you follow from day to day the ups and downs of a strong-jawed hero and a hardboiled but beautiful adventuress." And after dismissing *The Maltese Falcon*, Wilson dismissed the whole genre. "As a department of imaginative writing, it looks to me completely dead."

Wilson was the foremost literary critic of his time, perhaps the best reader of modern texts we've ever had. He introduced Kafka, Joyce, and Proust to an American audience, and was one of the first critics to comprehend the deceptively simple *and* complex style of Ernest Hemingway, but he did not understand Hammett at all. His own prejudice to the very idea of the detective story prevented him from seeing the relentless, muscular rhythm of Hammett's prose. Like Hemingway, Hammett was a master of the untold—it is the space between the sentences that tells most of the story. Hammett invented a kind of hard-rock poetry that had no real equal in America. It took a French surrealist poet like Louis Aragon to realize the nature of Hammett's gifts. Hammett was our first poet of crime. Aragon believed that one could learn more about the meanness of modern life from Hammett than from any other American writer, including Hemingway, Faulkner, and Fitzgerald.

Yet the damage was done. Crime writing couldn't seem to recover from "Who Cares Who Killed Roger Ackroyd?" Edmund Wilson's final conclusion was that "the reading of detective stories is simply a kind of vice that, for silliness and minor harmfulness, ranks somewhere between crossword puzzles and smoking."

In a letter to his British publisher, Raymond Chandler wrote that as a writer in the United States he "ranked slightly above a mulatto." He was his own invisible man. And for years most of America danced to Wilson's song about Roger Ackroyd and Dashiell Hammett. Crime writers lived in some neglected bordertown of the imagination. But while America disregarded Hammett and Chandler, the French, Germans, and English idolized them, and understood that they had revealed a much more convincing portrait of America than most "serious" writers ever could. And today festivals have mushroomed all over the world, honoring Hammett and Chandler and the *roman noir*. "Hammett took murder out of the Venetian vase and dropped it in the alley," wrote Raymond Chandler. And more than that, Hammett unmasked the "red harvest" behind America's deeply democratic dream.

Edmund Wilson couldn't seem to grasp that America itself had become a culture of crime. And Wilson, who lived through that culture, seemed blind to it *and* the uniqueness of Hammett's voice. Hammett's forebears aren't Poe and Conan Doyle. They're Baudelaire and Rimbaud, poets who understood the surreal nature of city life.

"Now is the time of the *Assassins*," Rimbaud declared as a boy of seventeen. For Rimbaud (and Hammett), the world was filled with "savage gentlemen who hunt their own histories in the light they create."

Wilson, who called Raymond Chandler an inferior ghost of Gra-

ham Greene, should have searched for the poetics of Chandler and
writers such as Horace McCoy, the author of *They Shoot Horses, Don't
They?*, one of the great nihilistic novels of the 1930s. Hammett, Chandler, and McCoy sang about the mindless brutality of modern life
and our own "big sleep," the quality of amnesia that haunts us all.
The best crime novels often solve no crimes, but lead us into the maze
of our very own lives, the masks we wear in an age of masks. And
it's no surprise that crime fiction is one of the few international "languages" we have, a language that cuts across cultures and stereotypes,
that wounds us and delights us. In the last decade of a brutal, murderous century, one might even argue that God himself is a crime
novelist.

Our best crime writers of this decade, such as James Ellroy, Paco
Taibo, and Didier Daeninckx, have created their own howling whirl-
wind inside the mouth of God. They've invented a new *noir* tradition,
a new "black bite." Daeninckx, France's most important crime novelist, writes about the suburbs of Paris, a no-man's-land where the
real danger is a constant grayness that breeds violence and sucks at
the soul. Paco Taibo's Mexico is the shadow of a shadow, where
everything is possible and nothing ever happens. Zapata appears in
modern dress, like a ghost who can comfort no one, not even himself.
And James Ellroy's Los Angeles of the forties and fifties is where
myth collides with the macabre of everyday life.

One of the first "modern" crime novels was *Fantômas*, by Marcel
Allain and Pierre Souvestre. Published in 1911, *Fantômas* was an immediate hit among ordinary readers as well as an entire crop of poets,
novelists, and painters. Picasso loved *Fantômas*, so did Cocteau and
Colette, Aragon and Magritte. "Everyone who could read, and even
those who could not, shivered at posters of a masked man in impecc-
able evening clothes, dagger in hand, looming over Paris like a somber
Gulliver," writes John Ashbery.

Apollinaire founded the Society of the Friends of Fantômas a year
after the novel was first published. The surrealists would adopt Fantômas as their own cult hero. And years later, the French filmmaker
Louis Malle said: "Fantômas has scared me and thrilled me since
childhood. He is one of the greatest characters of French popular
culture."

Allain and Souvestre wrote twenty-one sequels to *Fantômas*, and after Souvestre died, Allain continued the series on his own, writing eleven more Fantômas novels. Only what was *Fantômas?* A kind of crude children's story for adults, written with an "absurd and magnificent lyricism," according to Jean Cocteau. Fantômas, the emperor of crime, lived on the roofs of Paris and loved to murder people. Like Melville's Confidence Man, he assumes different disguises and personalities. Sometimes he seems like "a colossal figure with bestial face and muscular shoulders; sometimes a wan, thin creature, with strange and piercing eyes; sometimes a vague form, a phantom—Fantômas!"

He's a phantom with a crazy cutting edge. He has a daughter, a mistress, and a police inspector who chases after him. But they are only other phantoms who belong to the "king of the night." The books are filled with an explosive anarchy, with the wonderful dream of children who don't give a damn about redemption. Fantômas is the ur-child who has a daughter without ever bothering to have a wife; and Fantômas never cries. In his own peculiar way he anticipates Sam Spade, who "looked rather pleasantly like a blond Satan." Neither Spade nor the Continental Op ever cared much about "morality." They don't carry Fantômas's knife, or live around roofs, or wear a mask, but they toy with people and the law, as Fantômas does.

The anarchic play that is found in Fantômas (one almost thinks of him as the author of his own work—Fantômas begetting Fantômas) is also found in Faulkner and Flannery O'Connor, other writers who loved to tell murderous tales. There was an outcry in the American press when Faulkner won the Nobel Prize: he was treated like a Mississippi bumpkin who wrote crime stories.

But in the sixties, as America careened crazily toward the Vietnam War, a whole generation of writers, including Donald Barthelme, Norman Mailer, John Hawkes, William Burroughs, Thomas Pynchon, and Susan Sontag, would find a striking vocabulary for the violence around them and within themselves. In the last fifteen years, our best writers, including Don DeLillo, Robert Coover, Robert Stone, Joyce Carol Oates, and William Kennedy, have written crime novels with their own unique lexicon and poetic pull. And more traditional crime writers, such as Tony Hillerman, Roger Simon, James Crumley, Sara Paretsky, Joe Gores, Ross Thomas, Lawrence Block, George Chesbro, Stuart M. Kaminsky, Mickey Friedman, Andrew Vachss, Sue Grafton, William Bayer, and Walter Mosley, bring a bitter music and a deep melodic line to their novels and stories that propel them beyond the graveyard of any genre.

Throughout the world writers such as Paco Taibo of Mexico, Didier Daeninckx and Daniel Pennac of France, Manuel Vásquez Montalbán and Francisco Gonzales Ledesma of Spain, Julian Semionov of the Soviet Union, Pieke Biermann of Germany, Ryo Hara and Yumiko Kurahashi of Japan, Xu Yaya of the People's Republic of China, Janwillem van de Wetering of Holland and the United States, Howard Engel and Eric Wright of Canada, Julian Rathbone, John Le Carré, Julian Symons, Ruth Rendell, and P. D. James of Great Britain, Clarice Lispector of Brazil, and Laura Grimaldi and Marco Tropea of Italy, have created a literature that exists outside any ghetto, with an utterly different face, filled with violence and a morbid sexuality that often breaks the skin of a sentence to reveal a universe where men, women, and children play their own drugged games and dream of murder all the time.

It was in recognition of this "new face" that the International Association of Crime Writers was formed in 1987. Once or twice a year, writers from more than fifteen countries, including Canada, Cuba, Italy, Mexico, Bulgaria, the Soviet Union, Sweden, and the United States, meet to discuss the state of the mystery novel . . . and simply to talk, to break open absurd barrier of East and West, of continental drifts, of artificial borders and border patrols, particularly at a time when the notion of a "communist bloc" seems to vanish in front of our eyes. We have to wonder at the secret services involved in a constant dance of death. Vast spy networks which seemed imperative a few years ago now seem like one more grotesque "border patrol."

It is in the spirit of breaking *all* border patrols that we have prepared *The New Mystery*, an anthology which will, I hope, push the genre of crime writing to the very edge of its own possibilities and even beyond, to present a genuine literature of crime, a poetics that cannot be put into a box.

The IACW has been instrumental in creating an international "brotherhood and sisterhood of crime," a milieu in which the best crime writing can flourish. Paco Taibo, the IACW's international president, Julian Semionov, its former president, William Bayer, president of IACW's North American branch, and eight of its officers, including Roger L. Simon, Lawrence Block, Joe Gores, Stuart Kaminsky, Laura Grimaldi, Ross Thomas (current president of the Mystery Writers of America), Eric Wright, and myself, are represented in this anthology. Yet it is not a showcase for IACW writers, but rather a vision of where we think crime writing has come from and where it will be going.

I have included earlier masters, such as Isaac Babel and Jorge Luis Borges, because they write about violence and myth with a precision that makes them seem more and more like our own contemporaries; they share the "gift" of language, the ability to startle and delight, to invent images that can scratch our eyeballs. Didier Daeninckx and Laura Grimaldi write about murderous children who are much more caring than the adults around them. Joyce Carol Oates writes about a delinquent girl who breaks our heart even while she distances herself from us with her own controlled, frightening song. Walter Mosley writes about a black "detective" in post-World War II L.A. who has his own particular ethics in a world that has excluded him. Stuart M. Kaminsky writes a funny, sad tale about a unique kind of serial killer. Roger L. Simon takes us to Cuba with the misadventures of Moses Wine. Donald Barthelme reveals a bumbling Captain Blood. Raymond Carver portrays the spooky, magical touch of a blind man. Flannery O'Connor introduces us to the Misfit, a "religious" murderer with pale, red-rimmed eyes. Clarice Lispector shows us the terrible tricks of a young English teacher protecting herself from rapists on a train ride to Rio. Sara Paretsky invents her own new voice for Philip Marlowe. Don DeLillo delivers a sympathetic portrait of young Lee Harvey Oswald. Angela Carter lets us have a look at a cowardly werewolf. Gabriel García Márquez takes us on the last voyage of a ghost ship that may or may not exist. I can only wish you a wondrous journey through the stories in *The New Mystery*, with all the "meagreness of imagination" that Edmund Wilson had ever dared dream about. The stories create their own vertigo and labyrinthian dreams, with images of women and men falling into and out of different dangers, pulling us closer and closer to that rough edge of the world we inhabit, the irrevocable world of crime.

The Watts Lions

Walter Mosley

"If you don't help, Mr. Rawlins, that RayJohn gonna kill us all," Bigelow said. He was the largest of the men sitting before us.

"That's right!" Mr. Mink shouted. "We gotta have us some p'otection from that crazy man!" He wore white painter's overalls and smelled strongly of turpentine.

Bledsoe, the third man, said nothing.

At the desk next to mine Mofass lit a match on a piece of sandpaper nailed to the wall behind. In the flare his fat, black and deeply lined face shone like a hideous tiki mask.

"You mean Raymond Johns?" I asked.

"He's gonna kill us, Mr. Rawlins. He already got Ornin." Mr. Mink spoke loudly enough to be heard across a football field.

"He means Ornin Levesque," Mofass said. The cool smoke of his cigar broke in a wave across my desk.

I nodded. Mofass stifled a cough.

"Well?" Bigelow asked.

"Well what?"

"What can you do to help us?"

I took a beat-up Lucky from my breast pocket.

"Gimme a light, Mofass," I said. And while he struck another match and leaned across the span of our desks, I asked, "Why would RayJohn wanna kill Ornin Levesque?"

1

" 'Cause he crazy, that's why!" Mr. Mink shouted.

"So go to the po-lice. It's they job t'catch killers. They do that kinda work fo' free."

"They been to the police, Mr. Rawlins," Mofass said. "But RayJohn moved out his house an' all the police said was that if he come around botherin' them again that they should call back then."

It was 1955 and the police weren't too worried about colored murders.

"Why would RayJohn wanna kill anybody? He ain't all that crazy," I said, but I knew that he was.

"He is now!" Mr. Mink squealed.

"Now I'm gonna ask you boys again," I said. "Why would this man wanna kill you?"

"We sinned against him," Bledsoe whispered. His quiet eyes were focused on a point far behind my head.

"Don't listen to him, Easy." Bigelow put up his hand like a boy in school. "He's so upset over this killin' that he's a li'l crazy hisself."

"That's alright," I said. "*You* tell me."

"We was mindin' our own business, man. We was at the Lions when he come bustin' in there . . ."

The Watts Lions was a social club that some colored "professionals" had formed. Electricians, plumbers, real estate men (like Mofass) and other tradesmen. They didn't want to hear from *street niggers* like me. Of course they didn't know that I owned more property than the three of them combined. Mofass represented my apartment buildings but I still pretended to be his "assistant."

". . . it was that Olson-Turpin fight," Bigelow was saying. "RayJohn said that he laid a bet on Olson wit' Ornin. Three hundred dollars at four to one."

"An' you didn't pay?" I asked.

"We thought he was lyin' at first!" Mr. Mink screamed. Maybe he thought that if he yelled loud enough I'd believe his lies. "An' then we thought that it was Ornin's bet! Why should we pay just 'cause Ornin lost a bet?"

I was wondering whether or not to call him a liar when the coughing started. Mofass had developed a smoker's cough over the years. I told him that all that smoke was going to kill him but he blamed his health on the smog. He hacked long and loud, sounding like an engine that wouldn't turn over.

"He intends t'kill them," Mofass whispered after a long while.

I motioned my head at Bigelow. "Who says?"

"He told us hisself when he come over to the Lions. Then they found Ornin . . ." Bigelow paused. He put his thumbs in the pockets of his vest and stared at the floor.

I knew what he saw there.

On page fourteen the *Examiner* had reported that Ornin Levesque was found tied up, naked and spread-eagled, on his own bed. His mouth was stuffed full with cotton balls and taped shut. The flesh from his belly had been stripped off while he was still alive and plastered to the wall over his head. I could imagine RayJohn, the Louisiana halfbreed, stripping off a patch of Ornin's stomach and then walking to the head of the bed where he held the flesh tight until the blood scabbed up enough to hold. All the while Ornin, in pain and fear, trying to rip free of the knots at his wrists and ankles.

Then RayJohn would pick up his straight razor and go back to his grisly revenge. The report said that Ornin died from a heart attack and not his wounds. Just another way of saying that he was scared to death.

"So what do you want from me?" I asked.

"Save us, man!" Mr. Mink begged. "Save my life. You know I got fam'ly t'look after."

"We know that you do . . ." Bigelow moved his hands around as if he were trying to pick words out of the air. "Things. Things to help people out when the cops cain't . . ."

"They need protection, Mr. Rawlins," Mofass wheezed. "An' they willin' t'pay off the bet now even if they didn't know 'bout it."

I shook my head and said, "I don't know. T'get me t'go up against RayJohn would cost you boys sumpin'."

"How much?" Bigelow said. He reached for his back pocket to show me that he was serious.

"I don't know." I rubbed my chin. "Maybe a lifetime membership in the Lions."

The Watts Lions were all middle-class craftsmen and minor professionals. They could look at me, or the hundred thousand men just like me, and feel that they were better—superior.

They wore gold-plated rings with platinum-embossed onyx emblems of a roaring lion. They had the respect of churches and white businessmen. As a group they had climbed to a higher social level than any black people I'd known.

Everybody wanted something. Bigelow and Mink wanted to live a little longer. Bledsoe looked like he wanted his mother to slap his face and tell him that everything was okay. I wanted to share the knowledge of my success among the company of my peers.

"I thought you wanted money," Bigelow said.

"I don't need money that bad, man. Shit! Raymond Johns' one'a the baddest men in L.A. If you want me t'stop him you gotta be willin' to get up off'a that membership."

"Let's do it," Mr. Mink whispered.

"Okay," Bigelow answered. I could barely hear him.

Bledsoe didn't say a word.

"An' maybe you could come across wit' five hundred dollars too," I said.

"Fi'e hunnert!" Mr. Bigelow roared.

"Listen, man, I need a li'l stake t'pay my dues."

They both agreed. They weren't happy though. I wasn't either.

My friends would have called me a fool. Three men in mortal danger, telling me what anybody could see was a lie and there I was blinded by the offer of their company.

I made a few calls and then invited my clients to come downstairs. We left Mofass hucking phlegm and wiping his tongue with a stained handkerchief. Mofass' office was on Hooper at the time. The street was empty at two o'clock on a Tuesday afternoon.

It was a glorious November day. The clouds were piled high on a mild desert wind. All the smoke and smog had blown away. The mountains were so clear that I could almost see the craggy valleys and pointy pines. I imagined that I could even hear a branch cracking . . .

"Get'own! Get'own!" I shouted.

The shots were weak echoes in the air. They sounded harmless, like a car backfiring down a country road. Mr. Mink shouted in fear and then, again, in pain. A sliver of granite, or maybe a ricochet, whizzed past my face.

"Goddammit!" Bigelow yelled and suddenly there was a .44-

caliber pistol in his outstretched hand. He was behind Mofass' Pontiac, firing blindly in any direction the shots might have come from.

Mr. Mink was holding his calf. Thick blood oozed between his fingers. I tried to squeeze behind a bright yellow fire hydrant. It wasn't much, but it was all I could do.

Bledsoe didn't jump or try to hide. He just fell to his knees and let his head sag down.

Bigelow had shot all his cartridges and wasn't moving to reload. The streets were quiet except for Mr. Mink's moaning.

I got up into a crouch and sidled behind the Pontiac with Bigelow.

"You think I got 'im?" the fat man asked.

"Only if he gonna laugh to death; lookin' at you shootin' at shadows."

I hugged the side of Mofass' green car and caught a distorted glimpse of myself in the chrome. I looked like a grounded fish sucking at air. My eyes were big enough to see behind my head.

After a minute I stood up, cautiously. Bledsoe got up too. His navy blue pants were torn. His sad expression and raggedy knees made him look more like a boy than a man.

"You okay?" I asked him.

He just looked at me, the tears brimming in his sad eyes.

People were peeping out of their windows by then. A few brave souls ventured to their front doors. I hustled my future club brothers into my car and drove off before RayJohn came back to finish the job.

"What are we gonna do, Easy?" Mr. Mink cried. "That crazy man must be followin' us."

"Don't worry, Mink. I got places for all y'all." I drove on wondering how RayJohn knew to stake out Mofass' place.

I took Mr. Mink out to Primo Pena's house in the barrio. Primo's wife Flower knew how to dress a flesh wound.

I left Bigelow with Andre Lavender who had moved to Compton with his wife Juanita and their five-year-old boy.

I kept Bledsoe with me till last because I was worried about him and because I thought he was the one of them who might tell me the truth.

"What's wrong with you, man?" I asked Bledsoe. We were going down Avalon, to the safest place I knew.

"Nuthin'." With his knees hidden under the shadow of the dashboard and his dark blue suit and tie, Bledsoe almost looked like the notary public he was supposed to be.

"Then why didn't you hide when RayJohn shot at us?"

"Lord'll call me when I suffered enough to his will."

Bledsoe was a slight man. His dark blue suit seemed to be draped over wire. The bones of his eyebrows and cheeks protruded while the rest of his face drew back; black parchment stretched on a skull. He tried to smile at me but that failed.

"You wanna tell me why RayJohn is after you boys, Bled?"

"I'd like to thank you, Mr. Easy Rawlins, for he'pin' us brothers," he answered, then he nodded to himself. "Yes, I'd like to thank you, Mr. Easy Rawlins."

"Are you okay, Bled?"

He nodded in answer.

It was five-thirty by the time we made it to John Mckenzie's bar.

The side entrance to Targets was in an alley off of Cyprus. I led Bledsoe by the arm into the crowded bar. When I pushed open the swinging door that led to the private part of John's place the stony-eyed bartender looked up, but when he saw me he just waved.

Bledsoe and I went up to the second floor where we came to a small room that was adorned with an army cot, a straight-backed wooden chair and a sink.

"You stay here," I told the sad-eyed man. "John will bring you anything you need. Just ask'im when he comes up." I pointed in his face. "Now I don't want you to go nowhere, an' don't call nobody neither. Just sit in this room. Do you understand me?"

He sat down on the bed and nodded. It felt like I was talking to a dog.

Targets was a small bar but it was popular among my crowd: immigrants from southern Texas and Louisiana. The room, built to hold ninety, was populated by at least two hundred and fifty souls. People were drinking and shouting, blowing smoke and swaying to the tinny phonograph sounds of Billie Holiday. A woman yelled as I pushed open the swinging door. John was in the center of the room forcing Cedric Waters back by the lapels of his jacket.

"I'm'a kill the mothahfuckah, John! Ain't nobody gonna stop me!"

"You ain't gonna kill'im here, Cedric," John said firmly.

I noticed Jackson Blue leaning at the far end of the bar. Even though Jackson was a small man he stood out because he was blacker than waxed coal.

"Yes I will!" Cedric shouted and at the same time he threw a wild punch at John's jaw. Unluckily for Cedric that blow landed true. John cocked his head with almost the look of surprise on his stone face. Then he hit Cedric with a short left jab.

Cedric collapsed as if some great magician had suddenly snatched the bones from his body.

"Get this man outta here!" John shouted. Cedric's friends dragged the comatose man away. John strode through the crowd back toward his place behind the bar.

I stopped him before he got back to work. I put my arm around his shoulder, restraining him in a friendly fashion, and spoke into his ear, "I need a li'l help fo'a couple'a days, John. I put Nathaniel Bledsoe in yo' extra room upstairs."

"What you want me to do with'im?"

"Give'im some food if he need it. An' if he leaves tell me 'bout it. I think Raymond Johns wanna kill'im."

John nodded and made back toward his bar. The prospect of RayJohn didn't scare him. He faced death nearly every day in his trade.

After John was situated behind the bar I went over to Jackson Blue. I pointed at Jackson's empty glass and John filled it with sour mash.

"Obliged to ya, Easy," Jackson said after he'd downed the shot.

I pointed again and John poured.

"You know anything 'bout Raymond Johns?" I asked.

"You don't wanna mess wit' that boy, Easy. RayJohn on the warpath."

"Over what?"

"Easy, you just bought me a drink. Why I wanna send you into pain?"

When John saw that we were talking he went away.

"I take care'a myself, Jackson. Just tell me what you know."

"Alright," the little man shrugged. "They sayin' RayJohn kilt Ornin Levesque. They say Ray ain't gonna rest till he get a couple'a more'a them Watts Lions."

"Anybody know why he killed Ornin?"

"One story is that he didn't pay on a bet."

"That true?"

"I don't hardly think so."

"No?"

"Uh-uh," Jackson shook his head. "The word is that RayJohn found out that them boys took advantage of his daughter, Reba. Raped her pretty good, I hear."

"That the truth, Jackson?"

"Well I don't rightly know, but I do know that it would take sumpin' like that t'get RayJohn that mad."

"You know where I can find Raymond?"

Jackson stuck out his bottom lip and shook his head. "Don't know, Easy. He's hidin'. But he's pretty well known down in the hobo jungle. When he ain't got no place t' stay, they say he gets a box down there."

"Where's Reba then?"

"She wit' Selma. They got a place down on Crenshaw." Jackson laughed. "You know Ray ain't lived wit' them in ten years, since Reba was five. I guess it takes a tragedy to bring a fam'ly back together."

The hobo jungle was a big empty lot behind Metropolitan High School, downtown. It was about four square blocks in area and undeveloped so the earth was soft enough for a man's back. The unfortunates who stayed there would go to the nearby Sears-Roebuck and find a cardboard box from a refrigerator or other large appliance and use that for their home.

I stood at the edge of the jungle at about midnight. Here and there faint lights outlined the cardboard structures but, by and large, the lot was dark.

"Hello, mister," someone said. It was a little man with a blanket wrapped around his shoulders. When he looked up his face was revealed in the faint light. He was a brown man. Not a Negro but a white man who had spent so much time outside that he had weathered. He was hunched over and barefoot. His left eye winked at odd intervals and a coarse dank odor hung around him.

"Got a quarter for an old soldier?" he asked and winked.

"Maybe," I said. That got him to smile. "I might even have a dollar."

That got him grinning, winking and smelling like a pig in shit.

"I'm lookin' fo' somebody," I said.

"No girls down here, mister. An' if there was you wouldn't want 'em."

"Lookin' for a man. A Negro, halfbreed. Raymond Johns is his name."

The derelict grinned. He had a full set of teeth. They were as brown as his skin.

"RayJohn's a regular down here," he said. "He stays over on the colored side mostly. I could show you."

He held his hand out courteously and I went before him.

We made our way between the tents and flat beds of cardboard. Here and there a hand or foot stuck out. The smell of urine was everywhere. I could hear men scratching and moaning, snoring and talking. One man must have had a woman in his box, either that or he was dreaming pretty good about one.

The brown man kept talking about RayJohn and what a nice guy he was and how much he could use that dollar.

"Yeah, I sure could, sure could use a little Tokay right now," he said. "Eighty-nine cents buys you a whole quart. Bet you RayJohn would like that. Yeah, I sure . . ."

It was because he stopped talking that I turned around. I saw a man to my left throw something that looked like a brass globe. Somebody shouted, "Get 'im!" I ducked under the missile and heard the groan of a man on the other side of me. Two hands grabbed my ankles. I swung my fist downward but I don't know if I hit him because a board split itself on my back right then. There were at least five men on me. I kept swinging but they were at close quarters with me so the blows I threw were pretty much useless. Then there came a bright pain in the middle of my forehead and, for a moment, darkness.

"I got it," the brown man shouted. Suddenly I could see him running toward the outskirts of the jungle. I moved to run after him but tripped over the box that the sounds of love came from. The box ripped open and an angry, naked white man swarmed out at me. I grabbed half the plank I'd been hit with and brandished it. That slowed his pace.

I said, "Hey, man, listen, I'm sorry."

The torn crate revealed a slim brown girl. The white man hesitated and then crawled back into the box with her, pulling the tatters of cardboard over them.

The thieves were gone. So was my wallet. Sixteen dollars, a social security card and my driver's license. I wasn't mad at being robbed. I was mad because I was a fool to be out there in the first place. I was a fool to protect rapists, to look for RayJohn. I was a fool to want to be a Watts Lion. Shit! I was a fool to be a black man in a white man's world.

Fool though I was I still rummaged around looking for the killer. I carried two half-pound stones, one in either hand, in case I was attacked again. But I went unmolested. I found the colored side of the jungle but RayJohn hadn't been there in weeks.

The next morning I checked on Bledsoe. He was in the same position he'd been in the night before; sitting on the cot and nodding. John told me he hadn't eaten but I didn't care if a rapist wanted to starve.

I drove out to Primo's next.

By then Primo and Flower had their dreamhouse. It was a two-story wood-frame house with a fake Victorian facade. Everywhere there were flowers. Roses, begonias, dahlias, asters, sweet pea vines on a trellis. Row after row of flowering bushes and trees.

I knew when I saw the police car parked across the street that Mr. Mink was dead. The policemen and a few civilians were in the Jewish graveyard that sat across from Primo's house. It was an old graveyard reflecting how the neighborhood had changed.

I walked in like the other curiosity seekers. Primo and I saw each other but we didn't talk. The short, stout Mexican looked at me apologetically.

Behind a great stone at the top of a hill they'd found Mr. Mink. His throat was slashed so terribly that the ligaments in his neck were severed. His head lay back from the open neck like the hinged lid of a trash can.

His clothes were torn and there were bruises on his face from the beating he got before he was killed. Flower's bandage was still wrapped around his calf.

The man climbing into the side window of the Lavender house wasn't tall but his short sleeves revealed the arms of a titan. I saw him reach to lift the window silently as I opened the car door. He raised his foot into the window as I raced as quietly as I could across Andre's lawn. It was just when RayJohn turned, his legs already in the house, that he saw me.

I grabbed his shirt and skin and yanked him from the house. He fell to the ground like a cat, rolling into his crouch. Then I hit RayJohn with a solid right hand.

I could have just as well socked a tree.

I saw RayJohn's fist coming but I didn't feel it. I was just opening my eyes, flat on my back, when I saw three things. The first was Ray standing over me still crouching, but this time he had the second thing I saw in his hand. That was a vicious-looking hunter's knife. Just when I knew that that knife would be my end I saw a big, fat, jiggly belly come running down the path to the side of the house. Then a yell full of fear and the belly collided with my death stroke.

RayJohn rolled away and kept on running. I watched him go down the street but I didn't go after him. We'd had our duel and I was a dead man. I even waved him good-bye.

"I'm cut!" Andre yelled. He stood there above me, nude to the waist and bleeding pretty well from his left forearm. Skinny little Juanita and porky Andre Jr. came to him and wrapped his wound in their own shirts. I wanted to get up and help but the strength had gone out of me.

When I knocked there was no answer so I began to work the lock with my pocket knife.

"Who's that?" a woman shouted when I almost had the door open.

"It's me, Selma, Easy Rawlins."

"Why you breakin' in my house, Easy?"

It wasn't really a house. It was a renovated storeroom above the rear of a pawnshop on Crenshaw Boulevard, but I said, "I'm tryin' t'keep some men from gettin' killed by that crazy old man'a yours."

The door opened a crack. Selma put her face there and I pushed my way in. She didn't fight it, just backed away hanging her head. Selma was a big woman. Rose-brown in color, she had Ethiopian features.

Reba was spread out on the couch. Her face bore the same marks as Mr. Mink. Bruises and cuts. Her hands were wrapped in blood-soaked gauze. Both eyes were swollen to slimy slits.

"Huh huh huh," she cried, a blind salamander dropped into the sun's harsh light.

"Shush now," Selma said, going to the girl, stroking her hair. "It's just Easy Rawlins. It's okay."

"They do this?" I asked.

"What you want, Easy?" Selma asked. I noticed that she had a mouse under her own eye.

"What happened to her?"

"Why? You wanna do sumpin' 'bout it? You wanna save her?"

"What happened?"

Reba moaned. She had her father's buff skin color and she was slight. I wondered that the violence perpetrated on that slim body didn't kill her.

"Shut up!" Selma said. She was talking to Reba. "Women get beat! Women get fucked! An' cryin' just make it worse!"

She kept stroking the girl tenderly as she ranted.

"You kept t'home wouldn't none'a this happened in the first place!" she cried. "But ain't no use in cryin' now!"

I noticed that the furniture in the house was overturned and that shards of broken plates littered the floor. On the far wall to my left someone had flung a plate of spaghetti. The red stain was scrawled over by drying pasta worms.

"Just shut up!" Selma told her daughter.

"Those men at the Lions do this?" I asked again.

"They did worse than that," a voice said.

I can't say that I was scared at that moment. I only feel fear when there is some chance that I might survive.

"I didn't know, RayJohn," I said to the man behind me.

"Daddy, no!" Reba cried.

"Get yo' ass outta here!" Selma stood in front of her daughter. She pushed her shoulders forward and put her hands behind her, wrapped in the folds of her house coat.

"Calm down now, baby. I'm just here fo' Easy. He's gonna take me into Targets so I can have a talk with Nathaniel Bledsoe."

"No, Daddy. Please . . ." Reba got up from the couch holding her hands in front of her.

Selma went right up to RayJohn and started shouting.

"Get the fuck outta my house, niggah! Get out! Ain't you hurt her enough!"

It came clear to me that RayJohn had somehow found out about what happened to his daughter and he'd beaten her for being raped.

"Get outta my way, Selma." RayJohn sounded calm, but it was the kind of calm that preceded violence.

She bulled against him with her chest and shouted curses in his face.

I was hoping that she'd back off because I felt pretty sure that I could get the help I needed to stop the maniac at Targets. But I had no desire to take him on trying to save Selma's life.

"I say get yo' ass outta here!" Selma yelled.

"I'm'a have t'hurt you girl. Stand back now."

"Hurt me! Okay! Yeah, hurt me! Put yo' coward's fist there!" Selma pointed at her own jaw. RayJohn obliged with a solid slap that would have killed a smaller woman, or man. But Selma simply listed to the side. She drove her hand deep into the pocket of her house coat. Reba cried, "Momma!" The flash of the steak knife disappeared instantly, deeply into RayJohn's chest. The surprise on his face would have been comical in the movies. Maybe if he wasn't surprised, if he had believed that a woman could fight to save her own, he might have survived. But while RayJohn was gaping that blade flashed four times, five, six. When he fell to the floor he was already dead. I didn't see any reason to pull her off.

Bledsoe sat with his back against the wall on the cot. He hugged his knees to his chest and nodded slightly.

I asked him, "Why?"

He smiled.

The police didn't take Selma to jail. When they saw Reba they figured that it was self-defense. I didn't argue with them.

"Why, man?" I asked again.

"What?" He grinned at me.

"You know, Bled. You the one called RayJohn an' told him 'bout Reba. You the one told'im where t'find Biggs and Mink too. You the one had him waitin' outside Mofass' place. Had to be you."

"I told 'em when that girl started t'fightin' that it was wrong."

"They raped her, really?"

"She was playin' at first. It was late an' they had some drinks. But when Ornin started to pull at her dress she got scared. Then Bigelow

exposed hisself . . . That ain't right." Bledsoe stared off into space
again.

I don't know if they would have ever let me join the Watts Lions.
I never asked. I went to the funerals though. Ornin Levesque and
Gregory Mink were buried at the same service.

Raymond Johns was interred the next day. There were only four
people there. Selma was dressed in a nice blue two-piece suit. Reba's
eyes had opened like a newborn kitten's. I stayed in the back and
watched Nathaniel Bledsoe with his arms around both ladies. I remember wondering which one he would marry.

How I Contemplated the World from the Detroit House of Correction and Began My Life Over Again

Joyce Carol Oates

*Notes for an Essay for an English Class at Baldwin
Country Day School; Poking Around in Debris;
Disgust and Curiosity; A Revelation of the Meaning of Life;
A Happy Ending . . .*

I. EVENTS

The girl (myself) is walking through Branden's, that excellent store.
Suburb of a large famous city that is a symbol for large famous American cities. The event sneaks up on the girl, who believes she is herding
it along with a small fixed smile, a girl of fifteen, innocently experienced. She dawdles in a certain style by a counter of costume jewelry.
Rings, earrings, necklaces. Prices from $5 to $50, all within reach.
All ugly. She eases over to the glove counter, where everything is
ugly too. In her close-fitted coat with its black fur collar she contemplates the luxury of Branden's, which she has known for many years:

15

its many mild pale lights, easy on the eye and the soul, its elaborate tinkly decorations, its women shoppers with their excellent shoes and coats and hairdos, all dawdling gracefully, in no hurry.

Who was ever in a hurry here?

2. The girl seated at home. A small library, paneled walls of oak. Some one is talking to me. An earnest, husky, female voice drives itself against my ears, nervous, frightened, groping around my heart, saying, "If you wanted gloves, why didn't you say so? Why didn't you ask for them?" That store, Branden's, is owned by Raymond Forrest who lives on Du Maurier Drive. We live on Sioux Drive. Raymond Forrest. A handsome man? An ugly man? A man of fifty or sixty, with gray hair, or a man of forty with earnest, courteous eyes, a good golf game; who is Raymond Forrest, this man who is my salvation? Father has been talking to him. Father is not his physician; Dr. Berg is his physician. Father and Dr. Berg refer patients to each other. There is a connection. Mother plays bridge with . . . On Mondays and Wednesdays our maid Billie works at . . . The strings draw together in a cat's cradle, making a net to save you when you fall. . . .

3. *Harriet Arnold's.* A small shop, better than Branden's. Mother in her black coat, I in my close-fitted blue coat. Shopping. Now look at this, isn't this cute, do you want this, why don't you want this, try this on, take this with you to the fitting room, take this also, what's wrong with you, what can I do for you, why are you so strange . . . ? "I wanted to steal but not to buy," I don't tell her. The girl droops along in her coat and gloves and leather boots, her eyes scan the horizon, which is pastel pink and decorated like Branden's, tasteful walls and modern ceilings with graceful glimmering lights.

4. Weeks later, the girl at a bus stop. Two o'clock in the afternoon, a Tuesday; obviously she has walked out of school.

5. The girl stepping down from a bus. Afternoon, weather changing to colder. Detroit. Pavement and closed-up stores; grillwork over the windows of a pawnshop. What is a pawnshop, exactly?

II. CHARACTERS

1. The girl stands five feet five inches tall. An ordinary height. Baldwin Country Day School draws them up to that height. She dreams along the corridors and presses her face against the Thermoplex glass. No frost or steam can ever form on that glass. A smudge of grease from her forehead . . . could she be boiled down to grease? She wears her hair loose and long and straight in suburban teen-age style, 1968. Eyes smudged with pencil, dark brown. Brown hair. Vague green eyes. A pretty girl? An ugly girl? She sings to herself under her breath, idling in the corridor, thinking of her many secrets (the thirty dollars she once took from the purse of a friend's mother, just for fun, the basement window she smashed in her own house just for fun) and thinking of her brother who is at Susquehanna Boys' Academy, an excellent preparatory school in Maine, remembering him unclearly . . . he has long manic hair and a squeaking voice and he looks like one of the popular teen-age singers of 1968, one of those in a group, *The Certain Forces*, *The Way Out*, *The Maniacs Responsible*. The girl in her turn looks like one of those fieldsful of girls who listen to the boys' singing, dreaming and mooning restlessly, breaking into high sullen laughter, innocently experienced.

2. The mother. A Midwestern woman of Detroit and suburbs. Belongs to the Detroit Athletic Club. Also the Detroit Golf Club. Also the Bloomfield Hills Country Club. The Village Women's Club at which lectures are given each winter on Genet and Sartre and James Baldwin, by the Director of the Adult Education Program at Wayne State University. . . . The Bloomfield Art Association. Also the Founders Society of the Detroit Institute of Arts. Also . . . Oh, she is in perpetual motion, this lady, hair like blown-up gold and finer than gold, hair and fingers and body of inestimable grace. Heavy weighs the gold on the back of her hairbrush and hand mirror. Heavy heavy the candlesticks in the dining room. Very heavy is the big car, a Lincoln, long and black, that on one cool autumn day split a squirrel's body in two unequal parts.

3. The father. Dr. ——. He belongs to the same clubs as #2. A player of squash and golf; he has a golfer's umbrella of stripes. Candy

stripes. In his mouth nothing turns to sugar, however; saliva works
no miracles here. His doctoring is of the slightly sick. The sick are
sent elsewhere (to Dr. Berg?), the deathly sick are sent back for more
tests and their bills are sent to their homes, the unsick are sent to Dr.
Coronet (Isabel, a lady), an excellent psychiatrist for unsick people
who angrily believe they are sick and want to do something about it.
If they demand a male psychiatrist, the unsick are sent by Dr. ———
(my father) to Dr. Lowenstein, a male psychiatrist, excellent and
expensive, with a limited practice.

4. Clarita. She is twenty, twenty-five, she is thirty or more? Pretty,
ugly, what? She is a woman lounging by the side of a road, in jeans
and a sweater, hitchhiking, or she is slouched on a stool at a counter
in some roadside diner. A hard line of jaw. Curious eyes. Amused
eyes. Behind her eyes processions move, funeral pageants, cartoons.
She says, "I never can figure out why girls like you bum around down
here. What are you looking for anyway?" An odor of tobacco about
her. Unwashed underclothes, or no underclothes, unwashed skin,
gritty toes, hair long and falling into strands, not recently washed.

5. Simon. In this city the weather changes abruptly, so Simon's
weather changes abruptly. He sleeps through the afternoon. He sleeps
through the morning. Rising, he gropes around for something to get
him going, for a cigarette or a pill to drive him out to the street, where
the temperature is hovering around 35°. Why doesn't it drop? Why,
why doesn't the cold clean air come down from Canada; will he have
to go up into Canada to get it? will he have to leave the Country of
his Birth and sink into Canada's frosty fields . . . ? Will the F.B.I.
(which he dreams about constantly) chase him over the Canadian
border on foot, hounded out in a blizzard of broken glass and
horns . . . ?
    "Once I was Huckleberry Finn," Simon says, "but now I am
Roderick Usher." Beset by frenzies and fears, this man who makes
my spine go cold, he takes green pills, yellow pills, pills of white and
capsules of dark blue and green . . . he takes other things I may not
mention, for what if Simon seeks me out and climbs into my girl's
bedroom here in Bloomfield Hills and strangles me, what then . . . ?
(As I write this I begin to shiver. Why do I shiver? I am now sixteen

and sixteen is not an age for shivering.) It comes from Simon, who is always cold.

III. WORLD EVENTS

Nothing.

IV. PEOPLE AND CIRCUMSTANCES CONTRIBUTING TO THIS DELINQUENCY

Nothing.

V. SIOUX DRIVE

George, Clyde G. 240 Sioux. A manufacturer's representative; children, a dog, a wife. Georgian with the usual columns. You think of the White House, then of Thomas Jefferson, then your mind goes blank on the white pillars and you think of nothing. Norris, Ralph W. 246 Sioux. Public relations. Colonial. Bay window, brick, stone, concrete, wood, green shutters, sidewalk, lantern, grass, trees, black-top drive, two children, one of them my classmate Esther (Esther Norris) at Baldwin. Wife, cars. Ramsey, Michael D. 250 Sioux. Colonial. Big living room, thirty by twenty-five, fireplaces in living room, library, recreation room, paneled walls wet bar five bathrooms five bedrooms two lavatories central air conditioning automatic sprinkler automatic garage door three children one wife two cars a breakfast room a patio a large fenced lot fourteen trees a front door with a brass knocker never knocked. Next is our house. Classic contemporary. Traditional modern. Attached garage, attached Florida room, attached patio, attached pool and cabana, attached roof. A front door mail slot through which pour *Time* magazine, *Fortune*, *Life*, *BusinessWeek*, the *Wall Street Journal*, the *New York Times*, the *New Yorker*, the *Saturday Review*, *M.D.*, *Modern Medicine*, *Disease of the Month* . . . and also. . . . And in addition to all this, a quiet sealed letter from Baldwin saying: *Your daughter is not doing work compatible with her performance on the Stanford-Binet.* . . . And your son is not doing well, not well at all, very sad. Where is your son anyway? Once he stole trick-and-treat candy from some six-year-old kids, he himself being a robust ten. The beginning. Now your daughter steals. In the Village Pharmacy she made off with, yes she did, don't deny it, she made off with a copy of *Pageant Magazine* for no reason, she swiped a roll of Life Savers in a green wrapper and was in no need of saving her life or even in need of sucking candy; when she was no more than eight years old she stole, don't blush, she stole a package of Tums only because it was out on the counter and available, and the nice lady behind the counter (now dead) said nothing. . . . Sioux Drive. Maples, oaks, elms. Diseased elms cut down. Sioux Drive runs into Roosevelt Drive. Slow, turning lanes, not streets, all drives and lanes and ways and passes. A private police force. Quiet private police, in unmarked cars. Cruising on Saturday evenings with paternal smiles for the residents who are streaming in and out of houses, going to and from parties, a thousand parties, slightly staggering, the women in their furs alighting from automobiles bought of Ford and General Motors and Chrysler, very heavy automobiles. No foreign cars. Detroit. In 275 Sioux, down the block in that magnificent French-Normandy mansion, lives —— himself, who has the C—— account itself, imagine that! Look at where he lives and look at the enormous trees and chimneys, imagine his many fireplaces, imagine his wife and children, imagine his wife's hair, imagine her fingernails, imagine her bathtub of smooth clean glowing pink, imagine their embraces, his trouser pockets filled with odd coins and keys and dust and peanuts, imagine their ecstasy on Sioux Drive, imagine their income tax returns, imagine their little boy's pride in his experimental car, a scaled down C——, as he roars round the neighborhood on the sidewalks frightening dogs and Negro maids, oh imagine all these things, imagine everything, let your mind roar out all over Sioux Drive and Du Maurier Drive and Roosevelt Drive and Ticonderoga Pass and Burning Bush Way and Lincolnshire Pass and Lois Lane.

When spring comes, its winds blow nothing to Sioux Drive, no odors of hollyhocks or forsythia, nothing Sioux Drive doesn't already possess, everything is planted and performing. The weather vanes, had they weather vanes, don't have to turn with the wind, don't have to contend with the weather. There is no weather.

VI. DETROIT

There is always weather in Detroit. Detroit's temperature is always
32°. Fast-falling temperatures. Slow-rising temperatures. Wind from
the north-northeast four to forty miles an hour, small-craft warnings,
partly cloudy today and Wednesday changing to partly sunny through
Thursday . . . small warnings of frost, soot warnings, traffic warnings,
hazardous lake conditions for small craft and swimmers, restless Negro
gangs, restless cloud formations, restless temperatures aching to fall
out the very bottom of the thermometer or shoot up over the top and
boil everything over in red mercury.

Detroit's temperature is 32°. Fast-falling temperatures. Slow-rising
temperatures. Wind from the north-northeast four to forty miles an
hour. . . .

VII. EVENTS

1. The girl's heart is pounding. In her pocket is a pair of gloves!
In a plastic bag! Airproof breathproof plastic bag, gloves selling for
twenty-five dollars on Branden's counter! In her pocket! Shoplifted!
. . . In her purse is a blue comb, not very clean. In her purse is a
leather billfold (a birthday present from her grandmother in Phila-
delphia) with snapshots of the family in clean plastic windows, in the
billfold are bills, she doesn't know how many bills. . . . In her purse
is an ominous note from her friend Tykie *What's this about Joe H. and
the kids hanging around at Louise's Sat. night? You heard anything?* . . .
passed in French class. In her purse is a lot of dirty yellow Kleenex,
her mother's heart would break to see such very dirty Kleenex, and
at the bottom of her purse are brown hairpins and safety pins and a
broken pencil and a ballpoint pen (blue) stolen from somewhere forgotten and a purse-size compact of Cover Girl Make-Up, Ivory Rose.
. . . Her lipstick is Broken Heart, a corrupt pink; her fingers are
trembling like crazy; her teeth are beginning to chatter; her insides
are alive; her eyes glow in her head; she is saying to her mother's
astonished face *I want to steal but not to buy.*

2. At Clarita's. Day or night? What room is this? A bed, a regular
bed, and a mattress on the floor nearby. Wallpaper hanging in strips.

Clarita says she tore it like that with her teeth. She was fighting a
barbaric tribe that night, high from some pills; she was battling for
her life with men wearing helmets of heavy iron and their faces no
more than Christian crosses to breathe through, every one of those
bastards looking like her lover Simon, who seems to breathe with
great difficulty through the slits of mouth and nostrils in his face.
Clarita has never heard of Sioux Drive. Raymond Forrest cuts no ice
with her, nor does the C—— account and its millions; Harvard Business School could be at the corner of Vernor and Twelfth Street for
all she cares, and Vietnam might have sunk by now into the Dead
Sea under its tons of debris, for all the amazement she could show
. . . her face is overworked, overwrought, at the age of twenty (thirty?)
it is already exhausted but fanciful and ready for a laugh. Clarita says
mournfully to me *Honey somebody is going to turn you out let me give you
warning*. In a movie shown on late television Clarita is not a mess like
this but a nurse, with short neat hair and a dedicated look, in love
with her doctor and her doctor's patients and their diseases, enamored
of needles and sponges and rubbing alcohol. . . . Or no: she is a private
secretary. Robert Cummings is her boss. She helps him with fantastic
plots, the canned audience laughs, no, the audience doesn't laugh
because nothing is funny, instead her boss is Robert Taylor and they
are not boss and secretary but husband and wife, she is threatened
by a young starlet, she is grim, handsome, wifely, a good companion
for a good man. . . . She is Claudette Colbert. Her sister too is
Claudette Colbert. They are twins, identical. Her husband Charles
Boyer is a very rich handsome man and her sister, Claudette Colbert,
is plotting her death in order to take her place as the rich man's wife,
no one will know because they are *twins*. . . . All these marvelous
lives Clarita might have lived, but she fell out the bottom at the age
of thirteen. At the age when I was packing my overnight case for a
slumber party at Toni Deshield's she was tearing filthy sheets off a
bed and scratching up a rash on her arms. . . . Thirteen is uncommonly
young for a white girl in Detroit, Miss Brock of the Detroit House
of Correction said in a sad newspaper interview for the *Detroit News*;
fifteen and sixteen are more likely. Eleven, twelve, thirteen are not
surprising in colored . . . they are more precocious. What can we do?
Taxes are rising and the tax base is failing. The temperature rises
slowly but falls rapidly. Everything is falling out the bottom, Wood-
ward Avenue is filthy, Livernois Avenue is filthy! Scraps of paper

flutter in the air like pigeons, dirt flies up and hits you right in the eye, oh Detroit is breaking up into dangerous bits of newspaper and dirt, watch out. . . .

Clarita's apartment is over a restaurant. Simon her lover emerges from the cracks at dark. Mrs. Olesko, a neighbor of Clarita's, an aged white wisp of a woman, doesn't complain but sniffs with contentment at Clarita's noisy life and doesn't tell the cops, hating cops, when the cops arrive. I should give more fake names, more blanks, instead of telling all these secrets. I myself am a secret; I am a minor.

3. My father reads a paper at a medical convention in Los Angeles. There he is, on the edge of the North American continent, when the unmarked detective put his hand so gently on my arm in the aisle of Branden's and said, "Miss, would you like to step over here for a minute?"

And where was he when Clarita put her hand on my arm, that wintry dark sulphurous aching day in Detroit, in the company of closed-down barber shops, closed-down diners, closed-down movie houses, homes, windows, basements, faces . . . she put her hand on my arm and said, "Honey, are you looking for somebody down here?"

And was he home worrying about me, gone for two weeks solid, when they carried me off . . . ? It took three of them to get me in the police cruiser, so they said, and they put more than their hands on my arm.

4. I work on this lesson. My English teacher is Mr. Forest, who is from Michigan State. Not handsome, Mr. Forest, and his name is plain, unlike Raymond Forrest's, but he is sweet and rodentlike, he has conferred with the principal and my parents, and everything is fixed . . . treat her as if nothing has happened, a new start, begin again, only sixteen years old, what a shame, how did it happen?— nothing happened, nothing could have happened, a slight physiological modification known only to a gynecologist or to Dr. Coronet. I work on my lesson. I sit in my pink room. I look around the room with my sad pink eyes. I sigh, I dawdle, I pause. I eat up time. I am limp and happy to be home, I am sixteen years old suddenly, my head hangs heavy as a pumpkin on my shoulders, and my hair has just been cut by Mr. Faye at the Crystal Salon and is said to be very becoming.

(Simon too put his hand on my arm and said, "Honey, you have got to come with me," and in his six-by-six room we got to know each other. Would I go back to Simon again? Would I lie down with him in all that filth and craziness? Over and over again.

Clarita is being betrayed as in front of a Cunningham Drug Store. She is nervously eying a colored man who may or may not have money, or a nervous white boy of twenty with sideburns and an Appalachian look, who may or may not have a knife hidden in his jacket pocket, or a husky red-faced man of friendly countenance who may or may not be a member of the Vice Squad out for an early twilight walk.)

I work on my lesson for Mr. Forest. I have filled up eleven pages. Words pour out of me and won't stop. I want to tell everything . . . what was the song Simon was always humming, and who was Simon's friend in a very new trench coat with an old high school graduation ring on his finger . . . ? Simon's bearded friend? When I was down too low for him, Simon kicked me out and gave me to him for three days, I think, on Fourteenth Street in Detroit, an airy room of cold cruel drafts with newspapers on the floor. . . . Do I really remember that or am I piecing it together from what they told me? Did they tell the truth? Did they know much of the truth?

VIII. CHARACTERS

1. Wednesdays after school, at four; Saturday mornings at ten. Mother drives me to Dr. Coronet. Ferns in the office, plastic or real, they look the same. Dr. Coronet is queenly, an elegant nicotine-stained lady who would have studied with Freud had circumstances not prevented it, a bit of a Catholic, ready to offer you some mystery if your teeth will ache too much without it. Highly recommended by Father! Forty dollars an hour, Father's forty dollars! Progress! Looking up! Looking better! That new haircut is so becoming, says Dr. Coronet herself, showing how normal she is for a woman with an I.Q. of 180 and many advanced degrees.

2. Mother. A lady in a brown suede coat. Boots of shiny black material, black gloves, a black fur hat. She would be humiliated could

she know that of all the people in the world it is my ex-lover Simon who walks most like her . . . self-conscious and unreal, listening to distant music, a little bowlegged with craftiness. . . .

3. Father. Tying a necktie. In a hurry. On my first evening home he put his hand on my arm and said, "Honey, we're going to forget all about this."

4. Simon. Outside, a plane is crossing the sky, in here we're in a hurry. Morning. It must be morning. The girl is half out of her mind, whimpering and vague; Simon her dear friend is wretched this morning . . . he is wretched with morning itself . . . he forces her to give him an injection with that needle she knows is filthy, she had a dread of needles and surgical instruments and the odor of things that are to be sent into the blood, thinking somehow of her father. . . . This is a bad morning, Simon says that his mind is being twisted out of shape, and so he submits to the needle that he usually scorns and bites his lip with his yellowish teeth, his face going very pale. *Ah baby!* he says in his soft mocking voice, which with all women is a mockery of love, *do it like this—Slowly—*And the girl, terrified, almost drops the precious needle but manages to turn it up to the light from the window . . . is it an extension of herself then? She can give him this gift then? *I wish you wouldn't do this to me*, she says, wise in her terror, because it seems to her that Simon's danger—in a few minutes he may be dead—is a way of pressing her against him that is more powerful than any other embrace. She has to work over his arm, the knotted corded veins of his arm, her forehead wet with perspiration as she pushes and releases the needle, staring at that mixture of liquid now stained with Simon's bright blood. . . . When the drug hits him she can feel it herself, she feels that magic that is more than any woman can give him, striking the back of his head and making his face stretch as if with the impact of a terrible sun. . . . She tries to embrace him but he pushes her aside and stumbles to his feet. *Jesus Christ*, he says. . . .

5. Princess, a Negro girl of eighteen. What is her charge? She is closed-mouthed about it, shrewd and silent, you know that no one had to wrestle her to the sidewalk to get her in here; she came with

dignity. In the recreation room she sits reading *Nancy Drew and the Jewel Box Mystery*, which inspires in her face tiny wrinkles of alarm and interest: what a face! Light brown skin, heavy shaded eyes, heavy eyelashes, a serious sinister dark brow, graceful fingers, graceful wrist-bones, graceful legs, lips, tongue, a sugar-sweet voice, a leggy stride more masculine than Simon's and my mother's, decked out in a dirty white blouse and dirty white slacks; vaguely nautical is Princess' style. . . . At breakfast she is in charge of clearing the table and leans over me, saying, *Honey you sure you ate enough?*

6. The girl lies sleepless, wondering. Why here, why not there? Why Bloomfield Hills and not jail? Why jail and not her pink room? Why downtown Detroit and not Sioux Drive? What is the difference? Is Simon all the difference? The girl's head is a parade of wonders. She is nearly sixteen, her breath is marvelous with wonders, not long ago she was coloring with crayons and now she is smearing the landscape with paints that won't come off and won't come off her fingers either. She says to the matron *I am not talking about anything*, not because everyone has warned her not to talk but because, because she will not talk; because she won't say anything about Simon, who is her secret. And she says to the matron, *I won't go home*, up until that night in the lavatory when everything was changed. . . . "No, I won't go home I want to stay here," she says, listening to her own words with amazement, thinking that weeds might climb everywhere over that marvelous $180,000 house and dinosaurs might return to muddy the beige carpeting, but never never will she reconcile four o'clock in the morning in Detroit with eight o'clock breakfasts in Bloomfield Hills. . . . oh, she aches still for Simon's hands and his caressing breath, though he gave her little pleasure, he took everything from her (five-dollar bills, ten-dollar bills, passed into her numb hands by men and taken out of her hands by Simon) until she herself was passed into the hands of other men, police, when Simon evidently got tired of her and her hysteria. . . . *No, I won't go home, I don't want to be bailed out.* The girl thinks as a *Stubborn and Wayward Child* (one of several charges lodged against her), and the matron understands her crazy white-rimmed eyes that are seeking out some new violence that will keep her in jail, should someone threaten to let her out. Such children try to strangle the matrons, the attendants, or one another

. . . they want the locks locked forever, the doors nailed shut . . . and this girl is no different up until that night her mind is changed for her. . . .

IX. THAT NIGHT

Princess and Dolly, a little white girl of maybe fifteen, hardy however as a sergeant and in the House of Correction for armed robbery, corner her in the lavatory at the farthest sink and the other girls look away and file out to bed, leaving her. God, how she is beaten up! Why is she beaten up? Why do they pound her, why such hatred? Princess vents all the hatred of a thousand silent Detroit winters on her body, this girl whose body belongs to me, fiercely she rides across the Midwestern plains on this girl's tender bruised body . . . revenge on the oppressed minorities of America! revenge on the slaughtered Indians! revenge on the female sex, on the male sex, revenge on Bloomfield Hills, revenge revenge. . . .

X. DETROIT

In Detroit, weather weighs heavily upon everyone. The sky looms large. The horizon shimmers in smoke. Downtown the buildings are imprecise in the haze. Perpetual haze. Perpetual motion inside the haze. Across the choppy river is the city of Windsor, in Canada. Part of the continent has bunched up here and is bulging outward, at the tip of Detroit; a cold hard rain is forever falling on the expressways. . . . Shoppers shop grimly, their cars are not parked in safe places, their windshields may be smashed and graceful ebony hands may drag them out through their shatterproof smashed windshields, crying, *Revenge for the Indians!* Ah, they all fear leaving Hudson's and being dragged to the very tip of the city and thrown off the parking roof of Cobo Hall, that expensive tomb, into the river. . . .

XI. CHARACTERS WE ARE FOREVER ENTWINED WITH

1. Simon drew me into his tender rotting arms and breathed gravity into me. Then I came to earth, weighed down. He said, *You are such a little girl*, and he weighed me down with his delight. In the palms

of his hands were teeth marks from his previous life experiences. He was thirty-five, they said. Imagine Simon in this room, in my pink room: he is about six feet tall and stoops slightly, in a feline cautious way, always thinking, always on guard, with his scuffed light suede shoes and his clothes that are anyone's clothes, slightly rumpled ordinary clothes that ordinary men might wear to not-bad jobs. Simon has fair long hair, curly hair, spent languid curls that are like . . . exactly like the curls of wood shavings to the touch, I am trying to be exact . . . and he smells of unheated mornings and coffee and too many pills coating his tongue with a faint green-white scum. . . . Dear Simon, who would be panicked in this room and in this house (right now Billie is vacuuming next door in my parents' room; a vacuum cleaner's roar is a sign of all good things), Simon who is said to have come from a home not much different from this, years ago, fleeing all the carpeting and the polished banisters . . . Simon has a deathly face, only desperate people fall in love with it. His face is bony and cautious, the bones of his cheeks prominent as if with the rigidity of his ceaseless thinking, plotting, for he has to make money out of girls to whom money means nothing, they're so far gone they can hardly count it, and in a sense money means nothing to him either except as a way of keeping on with his life. *Each Day's Proud Struggle*, the title of a novel we could read at jail. . . . Each day he needs a certain amount of money. He devours it. It wasn't love he uncoiled in me with his hollowed-out eyes and his courteous smile, that remnant of a prosperous past, but a dark terror that needed to press itself flat against him, or against another man . . . but he was the first, he came over to me and took my arm, a claim. We struggled on the stairs and I said, *Let me loose, you're hurting my neck, my face*, it was such a surprise that my skin hurt where he rubbed it, and afterward we lay face to face and he breathed everything into me. In the end I think he turned me in.

2. Raymond Forrest. I just read this morning that Raymond Forrest's father, the chairman of the board at ——, died of a heart attack on a plane bound for London. I would like to write Raymond Forrest a note of sympathy. I would like to thank him for not pressing charges against me one hundred years ago, saving me, being so generous . . . well, men like Raymond Forrest are generous men, not like Simon.

I would like to write him a letter telling of my love, or of some other emotion that is positive and healthy. Not like Simon and his poetry, which he scrawled down when he was high and never changed a word . . . but when I try to think of something to say, it is Simon's language that comes back to me, caught in my head like a bad song, it is always Simon's language:

> *There is no reality only dreams*
> *Your neck may get snapped when you wake*
> *My love is drawn to some violent end*
> *She keeps wanting to get away*
> *My love is heading downward*
> *And I am heading upward*
> *She is going to crash on the sidewalk*
> *And I am going to dissolve into the clouds*

XII. EVENTS

1. Out of the hospital, bruised and saddened and converted, with Princess' grunts still tangled in my hair . . . and Father in his overcoat, looking like a prince himself, come to carry me off. Up the expressway and out north to home. Jesus Christ, but the air is thinner and cleaner here. Monumental houses. Heartbreaking sidewalks, so clean.

2. Weeping in the living room. The ceiling is two stories high and two chandeliers hang from it. Weeping, weeping, though Billie the maid is *probably listening*. I will never leave home again. Never. Never leave home. Never leave this home again, never.

3. Sugar doughnuts for breakfast. The toaster is very shiny and my face is distorted in it. Is that my face?

4. The car is turning in the driveway. Father brings me home. Mother embraces me. Sunlight breaks in movieland patches on the roof of our traditional-contemporary home, which was designed for the famous automotive stylist whose identity, if I told you the name of the famous car he designed, you would all know, so I can't tell you because my teeth chatter at the thought of being sued . . . or having

someone climb into my bedroom window with a rope to strangle me.
. . . The car turns up the blacktop drive. The house opens to me like
a doll's house, so lovely in the sunlight, the big living room beckons
to me with its walls falling away in a delirium of joy at my return,
Billie the maid is *no doubt* listening from the kitchen as I burst into
tears and the hysteria Simon got so sick of. Convulsed in Father's
arms, I say I will never leave again, never, why did I leave, where
did I go, what happened, my mind is gone wrong, my body is one
big bruise, my backbone was sucked dry, it wasn't the men who hurt
me and Simon never hurt me but only those girls . . . my God, how
they hurt me . . . I will never leave home again. . . . The car is
perpetually turning up the drive and I am perpetually breaking down
in the living room and we are perpetually taking the right exit from
the expressway (Lahser Road) and the wall of the rest room is perpetually banging against my head and perpetually are Simon's hands
moving across my body and adding everything up and so too are
Father's hands on my shaking bruised back, far from the surface of
my skin on the surface of my good blue cashmere coat (dry-cleaned
for my release). . . . I weep for all the money here, for God in gold
and beige carpeting, for the beauty of chandeliers and the miracle of
a clean polished gleaming toaster and faucets that run both hot and
cold water, and I tell them. *I will never leave home, this is my home, I
love everything here. I am in love with everything here.* . . .

I am home.

The Snail Watcher

Patricia Highsmith

When Mr. Peter Knoppert began to make a hobby of snail-watching, he had no idea that his handful of specimens would become hundreds in no time. Only two months after the original snails were carried up to the Knoppert study, some thirty glass tanks and bowls, all teeming with snails, lined the walls, rested on the desk and windowsills, and were beginning even to cover the floor. Mrs. Knoppert disapproved strongly, and would no longer enter the room. It smelled, she said, and besides she had once stepped on a snail by accident, a horrible sensation she would never forget. But the more his wife and friends deplored his unusual and vaguely repellent pastime, the more pleasure Mr. Knoppert seemed to find in it.

"I never cared for nature before in my life," Mr. Knoppert often remarked—he was a partner in a brokerage firm, a man who had devoted all his life to the science of finance—"but snails have opened my eyes to the beauty of the animal world."

If his friends commented that snails were not really animals, and their slimy habitats hardly the best example of the beauty of nature, Mr. Knoppert would tell them with a superior smile that they simply didn't know all that he knew about snails.

And it was true. Mr. Knoppert had witnessed an exhibition that was not described, certainly not adequately described, in any encyclopedia or zoology book that he had been able to find. Mr. Knoppert had wandered into the kitchen one evening for a bite of something before dinner, and had happened to notice that a couple of snails in the china bowl on the draining board were behaving very oddly. Standing more or less on their tails, they were weaving before each other for all the world like a pair of snakes hypnotized by a flute player. A moment later, their faces came together in a kiss of voluptuous intensity. Mr. Knoppert bent closer and studied them from all angles. Something else was happening: a protuberance like an ear was appearing on the right side of the head of both snails. His instinct told him that he was watching a sexual activity of some sort.

The cook came in and said something to him, but Mr. Knoppert silenced her with an impatient wave of his hand. He couldn't take his eyes from the enchanted little creatures in the bowl.

When the ear-like excrescences were precisely together rim to rim, a whitish rod like another small tentacle shot out from one ear and arched over toward the ear of the other snail. Mr. Knoppert's first surmise was dashed when a tentacle sallied from the other snail, too. Most peculiar, he thought. The two tentacles withdrew, then came forth again, and as if they had found some invisible mark, remained fixed in either snail. Mr. Knoppert peered intently closer. So did the cook.

"Did you ever see anything like this?" Mr. Knoppert asked.

"No. They must be fighting," the cook said indifferently and went away. That was a sample of the ignorance on the subject of snails that he was later to discover everywhere.

Mr. Knoppert continued to observe the pair of snails off and on for more than an hour, until first the ears, then the rods, withdrew, and the snails themselves relaxed their attitudes and paid no further attention to each other. But by that time, a different pair of snails had begun a flirtation, and were slowly rearing themselves to get into a position for kissing. Mr. Knoppert told the cook that the snails were not to be served that evening. He took the bowl of them up to his study. And snails were never again served in the Knoppert household.

That night, he searched his encyclopedias and a few general science books he happened to possess, but there was absolutely nothing on snails' breeding habits, though the oyster's dull reproductive cycle was described in detail. Perhaps it hadn't been a mating he had seen after all, Mr. Knoppert decided after a day or two. His wife, Edna, told him either to eat the snails or get rid of them—it was at this time that she stepped upon a snail that had crawled out on to the floor— and Mr. Knoppert might have, if he hadn't come across a sentence in Darwin's *Origin of Species* on a page given to gastropoda. The sentence was in French, a language Mr. Knoppert did not know, but the word *sensualité* made him tense like a bloodhound that has suddenly found the scent. He was in the public library at that time, and laboriously he translated the sentence with the aid of a French-English dictionary. It was a statement of less than a hundred words, saying that snails manifested a sensuality in their mating that was not to be found elsewhere in the animal kingdom. That was all. It was from the notebooks of Henri Fabre. Obviously Darwin had decided not to translate it for the average reader, but to leave it in its original language for the scholarly few who really cared. Mr. Knoppert considered himself one of the scholarly few now, and his round, pink face beamed with self-esteem.

He had learned that his snails were the freshwater type that laid their eggs in sand or earth, so he put moist earth and a little saucer of water into a big wash-bowl and transferred his snails into it. Then he waited for something to happen. Not even another mating happened. He picked up the snails one by one and looked at them, without seeing anything suggestive of pregnancy. But one snail he couldn't pick up. The shell might have been glued to the earth. Mr. Knoppert suspected the snail had buried its head in the ground to die. Two more days went by, and on the morning of the third, Mr. Knoppert found a spot of crumbly earth where the snail had been. Curious, he investigated the crumbles with a match stem, and to his delight discovered a pit full of shiny new eggs. Snail eggs! He hadn't been wrong. Mr. Knoppert called his wife and the cook to look at them. The eggs looked very much like big caviar, only they were white instead of black or red.

"Well, naturally they have to breed some way," was his wife's comment. Mr. Knoppert couldn't understand her lack of interest. He had to go and look at the eggs every hour that he was at home. He looked at them every morning to see if any change had taken place, and the eggs were his last thought every night before he went to bed. Moreover, another snail was now digging a pit. And another pair of snails was mating! The first batch of eggs turned a grayish color, and minuscule spirals of shells became discernible on one side of each egg. Mr. Knoppert's anticipation rose to a higher pitch. At last a morning arrived—the eighteenth after laying, according to Mr. Knoppert's careful count—when he looked down into the egg pit and saw the first tiny moving head, the first stubby little antennae uncertainly exploring the nest. Mr. Knoppert was as happy as the father of a new child. Every one of the seventy or more eggs in the pit came miraculously to life. He had seen the entire reproductive cycle evolve to a successful conclusion. And the fact that no one, at least no one that he knew of, was acquainted with a fraction of what he knew, lent his knowledge a thrill of discovery, the piquancy of the esoteric. Mr. Knoppert made notes on successive matings and egg hatchings. He narrated snail biology to fascinated, more often shocked, friends and guests, until his wife squirmed with embarrassment.

"But where is it going to stop, Peter? If they keep on reproducing at this rate, they'll take over the house!" his wife told him after fifteen or twenty pits had hatched.

"There's no stopping nature," he replied good-humoredly. "They've only taken over the study. There's plenty of room there."

So more and more glass tanks and bowls were moved in. Mr. Knoppert went to the market and chose several of the more lively-looking snails, and also a pair he found mating, unobserved by the rest of the world. More and more egg pits appeared in the dirt floors of the tanks, and out of each pit crept finally from seventy to ninety baby snails, transparent as dewdrops, gliding up rather than down the strips of fresh lettuce that Mr. Knoppert was quick to give all the pits as edible ladders for the climb. Mating went on so often that he no longer bothered to watch them. A mating could last twenty-four hours. But the thrill of seeing the white caviar become shells and start to move—that never diminished however often he witnessed it.

His colleagues in the brokerage office noticed a new zest for life in Peter Knoppert. He became more daring in his moves, more brilliant in his calculations, became in fact a little vicious in his schemes, but he brought money in for his company. By unanimous vote, his basic salary was raised from forty to sixty thousand dollars per year. When anyone congratulated him on his achievements, Mr. Knoppert gave all the credit to his snails and the beneficial relaxation he derived from watching them.

He spent all his evenings with his snails in the room that was no longer a study but a kind of aquarium. He loved to strew the tanks with fresh lettuce and pieces of boiled potato and beet, then turn on the sprinkler system that he had installed in the tanks to simulate natural rainfall. Then all the snails would liven up and begin eating, mating, or merely gliding through the shallow water with obvious pleasure. Mr. Knoppert often let a snail crawl on to his forefinger— he fancied his snails enjoyed this human contact—and he would feed it a piece of lettuce by hand, would observe the snail from all sides, finding as much aesthetic satisfaction as another man might from contemplating a Japanese print.

By now, Mr. Knoppert did not allow anyone to set foot in his study. Too many snails had the habit of crawling around on the floor, of going to sleep glued to chair bottoms, and to the backs of books on the shelves. Snails spent much of their time sleeping, especially the older snails. But there were enough less indolent snails who preferred love-making. Mr. Knoppert estimated that about a dozen pairs of snails must be kissing all the time. And certainly there was a multitude of baby and adolescent snails. They were impossible to count. But Mr. Knoppert did count the snails sleeping and creeping on the ceiling alone, and arrived at something between eleven and twelve hundred. The tanks, the bowls, the underside of his desk and the bookshelves must surely have held fifty times that number. Mr. Knoppert meant to scrape the snails off the ceiling one day soon. Some of them had been up there for weeks, and he was afraid they were not taking in enough nourishment. But of late he had been a little too busy, and too much in need of the tranquility that he got simply from sitting in the study in his favorite chair.

During the month of June he was so busy he often worked late into the evening at his office. Reports were piling in at the end of the fiscal year. He made calculations, spotted a half-dozen possibilities of gain, and reserved the most daring, the least obvious moves for his private operations. By this time next year, he thought, he should be three or four times as well off as now. He saw his bank account multiplying as easily and rapidly as his snails. He told his wife this, and she was overjoyed. She even forgave him the ruination of the study, and the stale, fishy smell that was spreading throughout the whole upstairs.

"Still, I do wish you'd take a look just to see if anything's happening, Peter," she said to him rather anxiously one morning. "A tank might have overturned or something, and I wouldn't want the rug to be spoilt. You haven't been in the study for nearly a week, have you?"

Mr. Knoppert hadn't been in for nearly two weeks. He didn't tell his wife that the rug was pretty much gone already. "I'll go up to-night," he said.

But it was three more days before he found time. He went in one evening just before bedtime and was surprised to find the floor quite covered with snails, with three or four layers of snails. He had difficulty closing the door without mashing any. The dense clusters of snails in the corners made the room look positively round, as if he stood inside some huge, conglomerate stone. Mr. Knoppert cracked his knuckles and gazed around him in astonishment. They had not only covered every surface, but thousands of snails hung down into the room from the chandelier in a grotesque clump.

Mr. Knoppert felt for the back of a chair to steady himself. He felt only a lot of shells under his hand. He had to smile a little: there were snails in the chair seat, piled up on one another, like a lumpy cushion. He really must do something about the ceiling, and immediately. He took an umbrella from the corner, brushed some of the snails off it, and cleared a place on his desk to stand. The umbrella point tore the wallpaper, and then the weight of the snails pulled down a long strip that hung almost to the floor. Mr. Knoppert felt suddenly frustrated and angry. The sprinklers would make them move. He pulled the lever.

The sprinklers came on in all the tanks, and the seething activity of the entire room increased at once. Mr. Knoppert slid his feet along the floor, through tumbling snails' shells that made a sound like pebbles on a beach, and directed a couple of the sprinklers at the ceiling. This was a mistake, he saw at once. The softened paper began to tear, and he dodged one slowly falling mass only to be hit by a swinging festoon of snails, really hit quite a stunning blow on the side of the head. He went down on one knee, dazed. He should open a window, he thought, the air was stifling. And there were snails crawling over his shoes and up his trouser legs. He shook his feet irritably. He was just going to the door, intending to call for one of the servants to help him, when the chandelier fell on him. Mr. Knoppert sat down heavily on the floor. He saw now that he couldn't possibly get a window open, because the snails were fastened thick and deep over the windowsills. For a moment, he felt he couldn't get up, felt as if he were suffocating. It was not only the musty smell of the room, but everywhere he looked long wallpaper strips covered with snails blocked his vision as if he were in a prison.

"Edna!" he called, and was amazed at the muffled, ineffectual sound of his voice. The room might have been soundproof.

He crawled to the door, heedless of the sea of snails he crushed under hands and knees. He could not get the door open. There were so many snails on it, crossing and recrossing the crack of the door on all sides, they actually resisted his strength.

"Edna!" A snail crawled into his mouth. He spat it out in disgust. Mr. Knoppert tried to brush the snails off his arms. But for every hundred he dislodged, four hundred seemed to slide upon him and fasten to him again, as if they deliberately sought him out as the only comparatively snail-free surface in the room. There were snails crawling over his eyes. Then just as he staggered to his feet, something else hit him—Mr. Knoppert couldn't even see what. He was fainting! At any rate, he was on the floor. His arms felt like leaden weights as he tried to reach his nostrils, his eyes, to free them from the sealing, murderous snail bodies.

"Help!" He swallowed a snail. Choking, he widened his mouth for air and felt a snail crawl over his lips on to his tongue. He was in hell! He could feel them gliding over his legs like a glutinous river, pinning his legs to the floor. "Ugh!" Mr. Knoppert's breath came in feeble gasps. His vision grew black, a horrible, undulating black. He could not breathe at all, because he could not reach his nostrils, could not move his hands. Then through the slit of one eye, he saw directly in front of him, only inches away, what had been, he knew, the rubber plant that stood in its pot near the door. A pair of snails were quietly making love in it. And right beside them, tiny snails as pure as dewdrops were emerging from a pit like an infinite army into their widening world.

Just Say No

Roger L. Simon

One thing you don't want to do is get busted for possession in Havana. They strip search you, interrogate you and put you in this greasy holding tank that looks like the basement bathroom of a bad fast-food joint that ran out of light bulbs. They leave you there all by yourself for thirty-six hours with nothing to eat but two slices of the local Spam. No one seems to speak English and they get impatient with your Spanish if it's not perfect, and whose is. That is if you see anyone at all, because mostly you just sit there in the dark. After a while, you begin to think no one knows you're alive and you can't call the State Department for help. In fact, you better not even mention the State Department or you're likely to end up at a reeducation camp on the Isle of Youth.

At least that's the way it was for me in 1978. And I was, I might add, someone who had always been a supporter of *"La Revolucion."* When I was thirteen years old I had even gone to the Hotel Theresa in Harlem with my friend Andy to try to interview our new hero *Commandante* Castro for the school paper. Later, in the early seventies, I had raised money for the *"Venceremos"* brigades that went down to help with the sugar crop and one time I had appeared on a Los Angeles television talk show to "correct the distortions" of the local Cuban *"gusanos"* who accused Fidel of being a fascist dictator.

And it wasn't just politics. I was a freak for Cuban music too, listening to Tito Puente's big band on the *Symphony Sid* radio show in New York when I was a kid—not to mention the great Chano Pozzo, conga drummer extraordinaire behind Dizzy Gillespie on "Night in Tunisia" and "Cubana Be, Cubana Bop." But none of this Cubanophilia stopped them from busting me.

It all happened because Edith Zussman needed a date. Well, not a date, exactly, more a companion. Edith was a filmmaker, the director of an agitprop documentary called *Flint*. The film, which showed unemployed auto workers being ripped off by union organizers in cahoots with General Motors, had created a small scandal at the New York Film Festival and caused her to be invited to open the first Festival of the New Latin American Cinema in Havana. Edith was thrilled, but being, at heart, a Jewish girl from Long Guyland, she didn't want to go alone.

Now I had always had a thing about Edith. She was smart, she was intense and she had black, black eyes that gave me an instant buzz in the gonads. I had gone out with her a couple of times and we even had gone to bed after a particularly romantic evening listening to Coltrane at Shelly's Manne Hole, although she took it, I suspect less seriously than I did. So when she called me up to accompany her to Cuba, I jumped at the chance. And I spent the next week fantasizing about it.

In those days you got to Havana by flying to Miami and chartering a plane with an outfit called Air South. The planes were usually six-seater Cessnas and the pilots were beefy cracker-types with names like Hank and Willy. Ours was named "John-o," or that's what he said anyway, and he spent most of his time talking about " 'Nam" and why didn't we nuke the V.C. and suspiciously scrutinizing his passengers, wondering who we were, these weird characters from the Left Coast and why they could possibly be visiting the Commie version of Mañanaland.

Besides Edith, my cabin mates, it turned out, were a somewhat famous blacklisted screenwriter and his wife—a fading actress—and an overweight executive from Paramount Studios whose claim to fame as a revolutionary was that back in the sixties he had charged airplane tickets for the Black Panthers on phony credit cards. Now his primary concern was how many Havana cigars he was going to be able to smuggle back into the States after his trip.

As a private eye, I decided to keep my mouth shut in this august

company. It was only a short hop to Cuba and it wasn't long before
we were cruising over deep green tobacco fields crisscrossed by dirt
roads dotted with what looked like prewar pickup trucks. Our pilot
pressed his radio.

"Flight forty-three twenty out of Miami requests permission to
land in Havana."

Something garbled came back in Spanish.

John-o looked as if he had been slapped. He sat there with a
stunned look for a moment, then glanced before talking to the box
again. "Speak English, will you?"

More Spanish. Some squeaks. Then a squawk.

John-o just sat there stunned again. Then he said: "Fuckin' V.C.
Commie spics—What the fuck they want us to do? What the fuck
we doin' anyway?"

"We're landing," said Artemis Levine, the blacklisted writer.

"No way. We're goin' back," insisted John-o.

"What do you mean?" said Danny Frankel, the Paramount exec,
incensed. "You're taking us down. We paid for this flight."

"What do you expect me to do?" said John-o, clearly agitated. He
looked around exaggeratedly. "I can't find the fucking airport. And
these commies don't even speak English." He leaned out the window
for emphasis, gesticulating at a field of mangy sugarcane. "You want
me to land *there*."

"Moses speaks Spanish," said Edith, nodding toward me.

The pilot looked at me as if I were some sort of freak who had
been consorting with the devil.

"Only a little," I said, to reassure him I wasn't completely the
antichrist.

"I'm not gonna land in this shithole," he replied.

"Listen, pallie, you cooperate with Mr. Wine over here," said
Frankel, "or we're going to report you to the FAA . . . Moses,"—he
gestured to the radio—"speak to these people. We're not going to let
this reactionary asshole ruin our trip."

So I climbed into the cockpit and talked to those people. Best I
could make out we were heading in the opposite direction from our
destination, so I got us turned around and flying in the right direction.
Then I guided us down into the small, almost rural-looking Havana
airport with its sprinkling of military aircraft and one Aeroflot jetliner

parked by the main gate. All the while I was thinking: Am I cool—this has *got* to be impressing Edith.

But I was wrong. The minute we hit the ground I meant about as much to Edith as a fly on the nearest banana tree. Right at the airport she was introduced to our interpreter, a bearded *guerrillero* named Esteban who looked like a cross between Che Guevara and Marlon Brando in *The Fugitive Kind*. He wore a red beret, a Cuban army shirt and a bamboo button on his lapel with a black silhouette of El Che himself. The only thing he lacked was an eye patch. Edith climbed in next to him in the van into town and that was the last I saw of her until breakfast.

We sat opposite each other over stale sweet rolls and coffee at the restaurant of the old neocolonial Hotel Nacional, where we were all staying. She was mildly apologetic and very hung over.

"Don't have such a long face," she said.

"You seem to be having a good time."

"Well . . . Jorge has been very nice."

"That's his name—Jorge?"

"Great name, isn't it?"

"It's just George to me."

"Don't be snotty, Moses . . . Listen,"—she touched my sleeve—"You know what I'd do if I were you . . . You love Afro-Cuban jazz—I'd try to find some. There must be some great underground clubs and stuff."

"Why don't you ask George?"

"Moses!"

Fortunately for both of us, that was the end of the discussion.

Not being a filmmaker and not, therefore, an *invitado* of the festival with my own guide and translator and Cuban intelligence agent—and not being wildly intrigued by the latest *vérité* documentary from the Uruguayan resistance movement in the first place, I was left to my own devices to wander the streets of Havana. For a while I was amused by the vintage DeSotos and Studebakers—the kind people would have killed for back in L.A., or mortgaged their homes for at the very least—sputtering exhaust as they cruised the tattered city streets, and by the aging fifties modern hotels that dominated the downtown area, a remnant of Batista and Meyer Lansky. Most of them were now office buildings or collectives, but some were still functioning hotels for party cadre from other parts of the island or visiting apparatchiks from Bulgaria come to cut loose in the sun. These buildings looked like some weird decayed version of Collins Avenue in Miami Beach caught in a time warp. One of them even had a cigar shop in the lobby, where I ran into Danny Frankel loading up on boxes of Monte Cruz Number 4's.

"Power to the People," he said, offering me one. I caught a glimpse of irony in his eyes and liked him instantly. He turned back to pay his bill, reaching for a well-stuffed wallet while whistling a riff of "Night in Tunisia."

"You're into Cuban jazz?" I said.

"Absolutely. Fantastic."

"So am I. Want to go find some?"

"I wish we could." He paid the salesgirl and took his boxes. "Fuckin' Revolution destroyed that with everything else . . . Not that I'm not in favor of the Revolution," he quickly added.

"Me too," I said, wanting to keep my leftie credentials intact as well as we exited the store. "But are you sure?"

"Completely. I put the studio research department on it before I left. It's a lock—no real Cuban music for foreigners. Unless you want to see the girlie show at the Tropicana which I'm told is just a hard-currency rip-off." His alarm wristwatch went beep. "Oh, shit, I promised this Czech director I'd see his documentary on collective farming on Slovenia. Why do I do these things? . . . Interested?"

"Thanks anyway," I said.

Frankel nodded and headed off up the street.

I walked up the other way to the city park and sat down on a bench. I smoked the cigar, watching local kids play and eat ice cream and thought again of when I was a kid and what Cuba had meant to me. I remembered seeing some television news show in the fifties, maybe it was Edward R. Murrow or the young Mike Wallace, and they were up in the Sierra Maestra interviewing the young Fidel. Even now I could see him, beard and bandana, crouching in the jungle, a machine gun over his shoulder. What a hero I thought he was, overthrowing the dictator and saving the poor. Robin fucking Hood. And now this.

I thought of those days and tried to decide if I could ever be truly idealistic again. And all this time there was some guy observing me and I wondered if, indeed, I did have my own Cuban intelligence agent after all. I had read that they had them on every block, watching the people in the neighborhood. This one was short and furtive and wore a baseball jacket that said "*Cienfuegos*" on the back. But I didn't study him carefully because, frankly, by then I was already feeling too sorry for myself to care.

It was still Edith. No doubt I had let my emotions run way ahead of reality and there I was carrying a torch in some public park in Havana with no place to go and nothing to do. It was starting to get dark and the local citizenry had begun their promenade, the evening's *paseo*. I sat down on a bench and sank deeper in depression.

I'm not sure how long he was there, but soon I was aware of the man in the baseball jacket seated beside me.

"*Yanqui?*" he said, averting his eyes when I looked at him. I nodded, shrugged. "How you like Havana?" he asked.

"It's okay," I said. "I like the cars."

"They betray the revolution, huh?"

What was this about? What did he expect me to say? This was definitely a time to be discreet. "That's for the Cubans to decide," I allowed.

"My sister, she is in Orlando. Maria Luisa Espinosa . . . You know her?"

"I don't know anybody in Orlando. I've never been there."

"Ah," he said. "How much you want for those shoes?"

"Sorry. They're the only pair I have with me."

He looked at me, frowned. "What you do here in *La Habana?*"

"I'm here with the film festival."

"Ah, a movie star."

"Actually, I'm not. I came down with this woman who was invited."

"Where is she?"

My silence spoke reams.

"You look sad," he said.

"Yeah, well . . ." I gestured.

"In Cuba, life is shit, but nobody sad. Not too much sad anyway. We know how make ourselves feel better. What you do feel better? You want lady? I get you nice Cuban girl—*mestiza*."

"Not now."

"What you want? You want something, right?" He seemed irritated. "You smoke?"

"What do you mean?"

He pursed his lips, sucking hard. It wasn't difficult to imagine what he meant. In truth, I hadn't had a joint in about six months. I had quit earlier in the year to help lose some weight and when the pounds fell off I just hadn't started again. It didn't bother me particularly. It felt like another in the long line of equivocal aspects of growing up. Or maybe it was just a precursor of the Reagan Years. In any case, I nodded and said, "Why not?"

"Okay, okay," said the man in the baseball jacket. "Good. Follow me."

I followed him down this side street in front of a hardware store that didn't seem to have anything in the window. And all the time I was thinking: Man, you have got to be an idiot. This is the most self-destructive move you have ever made. Or close to it.

And I was right. Because we walked through a door straight into the hands of State Security.

As I said, all my possessions were taken and I was strip-searched. A few minutes after that I was in a small room in the aforementioned basement being interrogated, through a translator, by a man who identified himself as Colonel Gomez. It didn't take long. When I said I was a private investigator he immediately summoned two guards who locked me in an even smaller room for a day and a half.

That was plenty of time to meditate on three things: If I had been set up and, if I had been, why on this not-so-green Earth they had decided to do it. And finally, and perhaps paranoically, whether I would ever get out of there alive.

I also thought about my children, tried to imagine every woman I had ever slept with, did squat jumps, push-ups and sit-ups, tried to eat their food, shouted for the guards, slept with my back against the wall and my butt on cold concrete, had nightmares, got a hacking cough and swore never ever to smoke marijuana again so-help-me-God.

Then, somewhere during the middle of the next day, I met *Commandante* N. He was gray-haired and imposing with the tall, trim look of a Spanish aristocrat.

He marched into my room without announcing himself and stared at me without saying a word for close to a full minute. Then he signaled for me to follow him.

We ended up in the same interrogation room where I had met Gomez. But this time there was no translator. N. nodded for me to sit and spoke to me directly in English.

"Why did you come to Cuba?" he asked.

"I was the guest of this woman who was invited. Edith Zussman."

"Guest?"

"She wanted company."

"And you had nothing better to do."

"I like to travel."

"Are you a member of the CIA?"

"No."

"Are you sure?"

"Yes, I'm sure. Why wouldn't I be sure?"

"What do you do?"

"I'm a private detective. I told Colonel Gomez."

"Why do you come to Cuba?"

"I just said. I was the guest of a woman."

"She does not seem very interested in you."

"What does that have to do with anything?"

"Do you know John McNally?"

"Never heard of him."

"Yes, you have. Don't lie. Are you a member of the CIA?"

"Look, I'm not a member of the CIA. I wouldn't want to be. And if I did, they wouldn't have me."

He looked at me for a moment without giving the slightest indication whether he believed me or not.

"How do you know John McNally?"

"What do you mean 'How do I know John McNally?' I don't even know who he is. How should I—" I was starting to get angry but I suddenly stopped myself. "Wait a minute," I said. "A day or two ago . . . it's hard for me to keep track . . . you guys busted me for possession of marijuana and not once have you asked me why I bought it, where I bought it, or who I bought it from. Kinda makes you wonder . . . unless your police procedure is *that* different from ours."

N. did not respond. I took a flyer.

"You wouldn't mean John-o, would you? John-o the pilot. Is that your John McNally?"

N. didn't answer right away. Then he said: "How do you know him?"

"I flew here in his plane. That's all I know about him."

N. cracked his fingers and sighed. He pressed a buzzer and two soldiers entered.

Minutes later I was in another room with the door locked behind me. It seemed my status had gone up because it had a cot and a window covered with wire mesh. Outside some kids were playing baseball in a vacant lot. It could've been anywhere in the Southern U.S., except the black and white kids were playing together without the slightest self-consciousness.

Exhausted, I sat down on the cot, listening to the reassuring child-hood sound of leather cracking on hardwood. Before I knew it, I had fallen asleep. But when I awoke again, it wasn't with any sense of reassurance. Someone was screaming in the next room. I heard a sound like a slap across the face and then a thud and another scream and then a brutal slamming noise and then an unbelievably blood-curdling shriek like a banshee cry from the depths of the soul. Someone was taking a horrendous beating. I imagined the worst torture sequences out of *Darkness at Noon*. I started to feel sick.

I held my stomach and leaned against the wall thinking about my situation. I wasn't sure what time it was, but it must have been somewhere around two in the morning. Sometime in the not too distant future someone would be coming to get me. That was certain. They wanted to know something about John McNally, but what? If I'd had anything to tell them, at this point I would have been delighted. But I didn't know anything. I was depressed before, but now I had good reason to be. It was like the old story of the guy who had the headache and then you broke his arm. That took care of the headache.

It couldn't have been more than a half hour when my door opened and two soldiers were standing there. They took me by the arms and started escorting me down the corridor. I felt my muscles loosen and my knees buckle. I struggled to stay erect, walking with them. This was it. Torture in Castro's Cuba. To hold myself together, I thought of the *Bridge on the River Kwai* and decided to whistle the "Colonel Bogie March," but for some reason "Cubana Be, Cubana Bop" came out instead. It was as if I were a little kid again, listening to *Symphony Sid*.

The soldiers didn't seem to react. I whistled louder and louder, heading down the stairs into the interrogation room. I could hear Chano Pozzo drumming in my ears—bopbopbip, bopbopbip. Cubans sitting on a park bench across from my apartment when I was seven, playing the congas. Please don't beat me. Please, please, please.

The door swung open and the soldiers pushed me into the interrogation room. *Commandante* N. was sitting there. I stumbled onto a chair, breathless. But I still kept whistling—"Cubana Be, Cubana Bop."

N. stared at me, but I didn't stop. I continued to whistle . . . sixteen bars . . . thirty-two . . . refrain and bridge. Then I started drumming on the table—one, two, three, four and kick . . . one, two, three, four and kick. Just like the great Chano himself.

N. started laughing. "Where'd you learn that?" he said.

"That's what I came here for, the jazz."

"I thought you came here for a girl."

"What girl?" I replied, without missing a beat on the tabletop. "A woman is a woman, but Cuban jazz is even better than a Cuban cigar." And then, I don't know where the memory came from, I began to scat the chorus of "Cubana Be, Cubana Bop," just the way Chano and Dizzy used to do it.

N. watched, smiling in amazement. Gradually, almost imperceptibly, his smile widened and curled into this great grin. He began to scat along with me. Oobopshebam . . . oobopshebe . . . Cubana Be, Cubana Bop." The soldiers stared at us nonplussed. I guess they didn't know the tune.

Then N. stopped, looked at me and shook his head. There was a long silence. Two hours later I was on an unmarked Cuban military plane bound for Mexico City Airport.

It was ten years later when I finally realized what had happened. I was dozing heavy-lidded in bed in the small hours of the morning, watching CNN, trying to decide whether to zap the news and switch over to Letterman, when a familiar face came on the screen.

It was *Commandante* N. He was heading up the tribunal that was trying the officers of Castro's military charged with running drugs with the Colombians and, presumably, those CIA fellow-travelers from 'Nam like John-o McNally. Back then, I could have been one of them, in cahoots with McNally, who, I remembered well, had suddenly wanted to turn tail for some reason as we approached Havana. My guess is his Spanish was better than he let on, better than mine, certainly.

And they had arrested me so N. could find out if I was his ally. N. must have been sentimental. He couldn't believe I could know those songs and be that kind of guy.

I wasn't so sure. History corrupts everyone. At the time of the news report, I was still a private dick, but trying hard to get out of it. Edith Zussman was making eight hundred thousand a year, shooting commercials.

In the Bronx*

Don DeLillo

This was the year he rode the subway to the ends of the city, two hundred miles of track. He liked to stand at the front of the first car, hands flat against the glass. The train smashed through the dark. People stood on local platforms staring nowhere, a look they'd been practicing for years. He kind of wondered, speeding past, who they really were. His body fluttered in the fastest stretches. They went so fast sometimes he thought they were on the edge of no-control. The noise was pitched to a level of pain he absorbed as a personal test. Another crazy-ass curve. There was so much iron in the sound of those curves he could almost taste it, like a toy you put in your mouth when you are little.

Workmen carried lanterns along adjacent tracks. He kept a watch for sewer rats. A tenth of a second was all it took to see a thing complete. Then the express stations, the creaky brakes, people bunched like refugees. They came wagging through the doors, banged against the rubber edges, inched their way in, were quickly pinned, looking out past the nearest heads into that practiced oblivion.

It had nothing to do with him. He was riding just to ride.

One forty-ninth, the Puerto Ricans. One twenty-fifth, the Ne-

* From *Libra*.

groes. At Forty-second Street, after a curve that held a scream right out to the edge, came the heaviest push of all, briefcases, shopping bags, school bags, blind people, pickpockets, drunks. It did not seem odd to him that the subway held more compelling things than the famous city above. There was nothing important out there, in the broad afternoon, that he could not find in purer form in these tunnels beneath the streets.

They watched TV, mother and son, in the basement room. She'd bought a tinted filter for their Motorola. The top third of the screen was permanently blue, the middle third was pink, the band across the bottom was a wavy green. He told her he'd played hooky again, ridden the trains out to Brooklyn, where a man wore a coat with a missing arm. Playing the hook, they called it here. Marguerite believed it was not so awful, missing a day now and then. The other kids ragged him all the time and he had problems keeping up, a turbulence running through him, the accepted fact of a fatherless boy. Like the time he waved a penknife at John Edward's bride. Not that Marguerite thought her daughter-in-law was worth getting into a famous feud about. She was not a person of high caliber and it was just an argument over whittling wood, over scraps of wood he'd whittled onto the floor of her apartment, where they were trying to be a family again. So there it was. They were not wanted anymore and they moved to the basement room in the Bronx, the kitchen and the bedroom and everything together, where blue heads spoke to them from the TV screen.

When it got cold they banged the pipes to let the super know. They had a right to decent heat.

She sat and listened to the boy's complaints. She couldn't fry him a platter of chops any time he wanted but she wasn't tight with the lunch money and even gave him extra for a funnybook or subway ride. All her life she'd had to deal with the injustice of these complaints. Edward walked out on her when she was pregnant with John Edward because he didn't want to support a child. Robert dropped dead on her one steamy summer day on Alvar Street, in New Orleans, when she was carrying Lee, which meant she had to find work. Then there was grinning Mr. Ekdahl, the best, the only hope, an older man who earned nearly a thousand dollars a month, an engineer. But he committed cunning adulteries, which she finally caught him out at,

recruiting a boy to deliver a fake telegram and then opening the door
on a woman in a negligee. This didn't stop him from scheming a
divorce that cheated her out of a decent settlement. Her life became
a dwindling history of moving to cheaper places.

Lee saw a picture in the *Daily News* of Greeks diving off a pier for
some sacred cross, downtown. Their priests have beards.

"Think I don't know what I'm supposed to be around here."

"I've been all day on my feet," she said.

"I'm the one you drag along."

"I never said any such."

"Think I like making my own dinner."

"I work. I work. Don't I work?"

"Barely finding food."

"I'm not a type that sits around boo-hoo."

Thursday nights he watched the crime shows. *Racket Squad, Drag-
net*, etc. Beyond the barred window, snow driving slantwise through
the streetlight. Northern cold and damp. She came home and told
him they were moving again. She'd found three rooms on one hundred
and something street, near the Bronx Zoo, which might be nice for
a growing boy with an interest in animals.

"Natures spelled backwards," the TV said.

It was a railroad flat in a red-brick tenement, five stories, in a
street of grim exhibits. A retarded boy about Lee's age walked around
in a hippity-hop limp, carrying a live crab he'd stolen from the Italian
market and pushing it in the faces of smaller kids. This was a routine
sight. Rock fights were routine. Guys with zip guns they'd made in
shop class were becoming routine. From his window one night he
watched two boys put the grocery store cat in a burlap sack and swing
the sack against a lamppost. He tried to time his movements against
the rhythm of the street. Stay off the street from noon to one, three
to five. Learn the alleys, use the dark. He rode the subways. He spent
serious time at the zoo.

There were older men who did not sit on the stoop out front until
they spread their handkerchiefs carefully on the gray stone.

His mother was short and slender, going gray now just a little.
She liked to call herself petite in a joke she really meant. They watched
each other eat. He taught himself to play chess, from a book, at the
kitchen table. Nobody knew how hard it was for him to read. She

bought figurines and knickknacks and talked on the subject of her life. He heard her footsteps, heard her key in the lock.

"Here is another notice," Marguerite said, "where they threaten a hearing. Have you been hiding these? They want a truancy hearing, which it says is the final notice. It states you haven't gone to school at all since we moved. Not one day. I don't know why it is I have to learn these things through the U.S. mails. It's a blow, it's a shock to my system."

"Why should I go to school? They don't want me there and I don't want to be there. It works out just right."

"They are going to crack down. It is not like home. They are going to bring us into court."

"I don't need help going into court. You just go to work like any other day."

"I'd have given the world to stay home and raise my children and you know it. This is a sore spot with me. Don't you forget, I'm the child of one parent myself. I know the meanness of the situation. I worked in shops back home where I was manager."

Here it comes. She would forget he was here. She would talk for two hours in the high piping tone of someone reading to a child. He watched the DuMont test pattern.

"I love my United States but I don't look forward to a courtroom situation, which is what happened with Mr. Ekdahl, accusing me of uncontrollable rages. They will point out that they have cautioned us officially. I will tell them I'm a person with no formal education who holds her own in good company and keeps a neat house. We are a military family. This is my defense."

The zoo was three blocks away. There were traces of ice along the fringes of the wildfowl pond. He walked down to the lion house, hands deep in his jacket pockets. No one there. The smell hit him full-on, a warmth and a force, the great carnivore reek of raw beef and animal fur and smoky piss.

When he heard the heavy doors open, the loud voices, he knew what to expect. Two kids from P.S. 44. A chunky kid named Scalzo in a pea coat and clacking shoes with a smaller, runny-nose comedian Lee knew only by his street name, which was Nicky Black. Here to pester the animals, create the routine disturbances that made up their days. He could almost feel their small joy as they spotted him, a little jump of muscle in the throat.

Scalzo's voice banged through the high chamber.

"They call your name every day in class. But what kind of name is Lee? That's a girl's name or what?"

"His name is Tex," Nicky Black said.

"He's a cowpoke," Scalzo said.

"You know what cowpokes do, don't you? Tell him, Tex."

"They poke the cows," Scalzo said.

Lee went out the north door, a faint smile on his face. He walked down the steps and around to the ornate cages of the birds of prey. He didn't mind fighting. He was willing to fight. He'd fought with the kid who threw rocks at his dog, fought and won, beat him good, whipped him, bloodied his nose. That was on Vermont Street, in Covington, when he had a dog. But this baiting was a torment. They would get on him, lose interest, circle back fitfully, picking away, scab-picking, digging down.

Scalzo drifted toward a group of older boys and girls huddled smoking around a bench. Lee heard someone say, "A two-tone Rocket Olds with wire wheels."

The king vulture sat on its perch, naked head and neck. There is a vulture that breaks ostrich eggs by hurling stones with its beak. Nicky Black was standing next to him. The name was always used in full, never just Nicky or Black.

"Playing the hook is one thing. I say all right. But you don't show your face in a month."

It sounded like a compliment.

"You shoot pool, Tex? What do you do, you're home all day. Pocket pool, right? Think fast."

He faked a punch to Lee's groin, drew back.

"But how come you live in the North? My brother was stationed in Fort Benning, Georgia. He says they have to put a pebble in their hand down south so they know left face from right face. This is true or what?"

He mock-sparred, wagging his head, breathing rapidly through his nose.

"My brother's in the Coast Guard," Lee told him. "That's why we're here. He's stationed in Ellis Island. Port security it's called."

"My brother's in Korea now."

"My other brother's in the Marines. They might send him to Korea. That's what I'm worried about."

"It's not the Koreans you have to worry about," Nicky Black said. "It's the fucking Chinese."

There was reverence in his voice, a small note of woe. He wore torn Keds and a field jacket about as skimpy as Lee's windbreaker. He was runty and snuffling and the left half of his face had a permanent grimace.

"I know where to get some sweet mickeys off the truck. We go roast them in the lot near Belmont. They have sweet mickeys in the South down there? I know where to get these books where you spin the pages fast, you see people screwing. The kid knows these things. The kid quits school the minute he's sixteen. I mean look out."

He blew a grain of tobacco from the tip of his tongue.

"The kid gets a job in construction. First thing, he buys ten shirts with Mr. B collars. He saves his money, before you know it he owns a car. He simonizes the car once a month. The car gets him laid. Who's better than the kid?"

Scalzo was the type that sauntered over, shoulders swinging. The taps on his shoes scraped lightly on the rough asphalt.

"But how come you never talk to me, Tex?"

"Let's hear you drawl," Nicky Black said.

"I say all right."

"Talk to Richie. He's talking nice."

"But let's hear you drawl. No shit. I been looking forward."

Lee smiled, started walking past the group hunched over the park bench, lighting cigarettes in the wind, the fifteen-year-old girls with bright lipstick, the guys in pegged pants with saddle stitching and pistol pockets. He walked up to the main court and took the path that led to the gate nearest his street.

Scalzo and Nicky Black were ten yards behind.

"Hey fruit."

"He sucks Clorets."

"Bad-breath kissing sweet in seconds."

"One and a two."

"I say all right."

"One two cha cha cha."

"He don't know dick."

"I mean look out."

"But how come he won't talk to me?"

"But what do we have to do?"

"Smoke a Fag-a-teeeer."

"Ex-treeeem-ly mild."

"I say all right."

"But talk to us."

"We're talking bad or what?"

"But say something."

"Think fast, Tex."

"I say all right."

At the gate a man in a lumber jacket and necktie asked him his name. Lee said he didn't talk to Yankees. The man pointed to a spot on the pavement, meaning that's where you stand until we get this straight. Then he walked over to the other two boys, talked to them for a moment, gesturing toward Lee. Nicky Black said nothing. Scalzo shrugged. The man identified himself as a truant officer. Scalzo tugged at his crotch, looking the man right in the eye. Like so what, mister. Nicky Black did a little cold-day dance, hands in pockets, giving a buck-tooth grin.

Out on the street the man escorted Lee to a green-and-white squad car. Lee was impressed. There was a cop behind the wheel. He drove with one hand, keeping the hand that cupped a cigarette down between his knees.

Marguerite stayed up late watching the test pattern.

Lee purely loves animals so the zoo was a blessing but they sent him downtown to a building where the nut doctors pick at him twenty-four hours a day. Youth House. Puerto Ricans by the galore. He has to take showers in that jabber. John Edward tried to get him to talk to the nut doctor but Lee won't talk to John Edward ever since he opened the pocketknife on John Edward's bride. They have got him in an intake dormitory. They talk to him about is he a nail-biter. Does he have religious affiliation and whatnot? Is he disruptive in class? He doesn't know the slang, your honor. The place is full of New York-type boys. They see my son in Levis, with an accent. Well many boys wear Levis. What is strange about Levis? But they get on him

about does he think he's Billy the Kid. This is a boy who played
Monopoly with his brothers and had a normal report card when we
lived with Mr. Ekdahl, on Eighth Avenue, in Fort Worth. It is a
question of adjusting, judge. It was only a whittling knife and he did
not actually cut her and now they don't talk, brothers. This is a boy
who studies the lives of animals, the eating and sleeping habits of
animals, animals in their burrows and caves. What is it called, lairs?
He is advanced, your honor. I have said from early childhood he liked
histories and maps. He knows uncanny things without the normal
schooling. This boy slept in my bed out of lack of space until he was
nearly eleven and we have lived the two of us in the meanest of small
rooms when his brothers were in the orphans' home or the military
academy or the Marines and the Coast Guard. Most boys think their
daddy hung the moon. But the poor man just crashed to the lawn
and that was the end of the only happy part of my adult life. It is
Marguerite and Lee ever since. We are a mother and son. It has never
been a question of neglect. They say he is truanting is the way they
state it. They state to me he stays home all day to watch TV. They
are talking about a court clinic. They are talking about the Protestant
Big Brothers for working with. He already has big brothers. What
does he need more brothers for? There is the Salvation Army that is
mentioned. They take the wrappers off the candy bars I bring my
son. They turn my pocketbook all out. This treatment is downgrad-
ing. It is not my fault if he dresses below the level. What is the fuss
about? A boy playing hooky in Texas is not a criminal who is put
away for study. They have made my boy a matter on the calendar.
They expect me to ask their permission to go back home. We are not
the common drifters they paint us out to be. How on God's earth,
and I am a Christian, does a neglectful mother make such a decent
home, which I am willing to show as evidence, with bright touches
and not a thing out of place. I am not afraid to make food last. This
is no disgrace, to cook up beans and cornbread and make it last. The
tightfisted one was Mr. Ekdahl, on Granbury Road, in Benbrook,
when the adulteries started. But I am the one accused of excesses and
rages. I took back my name, your honor. Marguerite Claverie Oswald.
We moved to Willing Street then, by the railroad tracks.

He did Human Figure Drawings, which were judged impover-
ished.

The psychologist found him to be in the upper range of Bright Normal Intelligence.

The social worker wrote, "Questioning elicited the information that he feels almost as if there is a veil between him and other people through which they cannot reach him, but he prefers this veil to remain intact."

The schoolteacher reported that he sailed paper planes around the room.

He returned to the seventh grade until classes ended. In summer dusk the girls lingered near the benches on Bronx Park South. Jewish girls, Italian girls in tight skirts, girls with ankle bracelets, their voices murmurous with the sound of boys' names, with song lyrics, little remarks he didn't always understand. They talked to him when he walked by, making him smile in his secret way.

Oh a woman with beer on her breath, on the bus coming home from the beach. He feels the tired salty sting in his eyes of a day in the sun and water.

"The trouble leaving you with my sister," Marguerite said, "she had too many children of her own. Plus the normal disputes of family. That meant I had to employ Mrs. Roach, on Pauline Street, when you were two. But I came home one day and saw she whipped you, raising welts on your legs, and we moved to Sherwood Forest Drive."

Heat entered the flat through the walls and windows, seeped down from the tar roof. Men on Sundays carried pastry in white boxes. An Italian was murdered in a candy store, shot five times, his brains dashing the wall near the comic-book rack. Kids trooped to the store from all around to see the traces of grayish spatter. His mother sold stockings in Manhattan.

A woman on the street, completely ordinary, maybe fifty years old, wearing glasses and a dark dress, handed him a leaflet at the foot of the El steps. *Save the Rosenbergs*, it said. He tried to give it back, thinking he would have to pay for it, but she'd already turned away. He walked home, hearing a lazy radio voice doing a ballgame. Plenty of room, folks. Come on out for the rest of this game and all of the second. It was a Sunday, Mother's Day, and he folded the leaflet neatly and put it in his pocket to save for later.

There is a world inside the world.

He rode the subway up to Inwood, out to Sheepshead Bay. There were serious men down there, rocking in the copper light. He saw chinamen, beggars, men who talked to God, men who lived on the trains, day and night, bruised, with matted hair, asleep in patient bundles on the wicker seats. He jumped the turnstiles once. He rode between cars, gripping the heavy chain. He felt the friction of the ride in his teeth. They went so fast sometimes. He liked the feeling they were on the edge. How do we know the motorman's not insane? It gave him a funny thrill. The wheels touched off showers of blue-white sparks, tremendous hissing bursts, on the edge of no-control. People crowded in, every shape face in the book of faces. They pushed through the doors, they hung from the porcelain straps. He was riding just to ride. The noise had a power and a human force. The dark had a power. He stood at the front of the first car, hands flat against the glass. The view down the tracks was a form of power. It was a secret and a power. The beams picked out secret things. The noise was pitched to a fury he located in the mind, a satisfying wave of rage and pain.

Never again in his short life, never in the world, would he feel this inner power, rising to a shriek, this secret force of the soul in the tunnels under New York.

Goldfish

Didier Daeninckx

I would never have thought you could feel so calm after killing your father. Or stepfather . . . I have never known the other one, so it comes to the same thing! *No great loss!* . . . I heard this a thousand times . . .

Mum was pregnant again, with me, when he went away. He left me only his first name, Albert . . . which I have been dragging around for twenty-three years. He is not responsible for it, Mum is, she still loved him in spite of everything, but it wasn't a reason to impose "Albert" on me for my entire life.

I slept normally, without pills, eight hours in a row and if they hadn't banged at the door to bring the coffee, I would still be at it. I didn't want to think about the whole thing before going to sleep. I clenched my teeth, so hard as to almost break them, and the ideas flew out of my head.

I am alone in a cell, a privilege they say! You can see that they live on the other side of the bars. You hit the wall with your knees just trying to sit down. At least, if we were two, we wouldn't be so cold. And you can talk to each other, even if you don't say everything.

They had me deposit all my belongings when I arrived. A sort of bundle of clothes tied up with my belt, sitting among all the others, with my registration number, in an unoccupied cell crammed with lockers.

It's the first time I sleep anywhere other than in my own bed. At "the three days" *, I stayed only in the morning and the afternoon; they discharged me before the Morse test, along with a guy who had trouble recovering from a motorbike accident. No one held it against me at home, not even Grandma who just was a little sad about it.

The lawyer was there and he is the one who asked the warder about the notebook and the pen, if I could take them with me. The warder started to say that he didn't want any problems, that one would see later, and then he shrugged and waved me to go ahead.

You don't escape with a pen and paper!

It's a big seamstress's log-book of the year 1973, two pages per day, hour by hour, pressed in a thick black binding. For almost fifteen years, I had been recording the summary of each of my weeks, a week a page, numbering them all. My writing remained almost the same, tiny, bent on one side when I write by the window and on the other when I sit by the lamp. Tomorrow will be week 730, there is only one more page to fill up.

Week 1, April 2–8, 1974
The weather wasn't nice and I didn't go to the zoo with my class. I pretended I was sick, that I had a cough. On Wednesday, Mum took me to the townhall market. I dragged her to the back, behind the hall. There were dwarf rabbits, hamsters and a whole litter of little dogs, nicer than poodles, Labrit sheepdogs. I managed to come back with two goldfish (because they don't make dirty), promising to look after them for their food.

Week 18, July 29–August 4, 1974
I don't like it when they fight. Quarrels are not the same thing. I could hear her shriek in her bedroom. When I came in, he was on top of her and held her arms. Mum gave a start when she saw me. He sprang up, a hand between his legs that hid nothing, and slapped me. He has plenty of hair on his chest and a big belly with a wrinkled belly button. I didn't cry.

---

* Three days: a period of examination before being formally enlisted in the military service.

Week 31, November 30–December 6, 1974

Again, I got bad marks at school. I am left-handed so, of course, as soon as I write a word with my inkpen, my hand brushes against it before it's dry. It looks dirty and the schoolmistress doesn't want to understand because she herself uses the right hand. Mum gave me a test at home: she threw a ball at me and I hit it. It always was the left foot that kicked, so I am a genuine left-hander, except that she doesn't dare go and tell the schoolmistress. She is too ashamed.

Week 40, January 23–29, 1975

The little remote control car is broken. He wouldn't stop playing with it and it kept hitting the legs of the table. Of course, I am the one who breaks everything! He thinks he's smarter but I watched him drinking his wine at dinner . . . He clicked his tongue against his palate, saying: *"This Gamay is really good, for the price . . . We should think of getting some more . . . Don't you want to taste it?"* I know that Mum never drinks alcohol otherwise I wouldn't have pissed in the bottle . . . Not much, five or six drops, I wanted to do more but I pulled my weeny out of the neck of the bottle when I heard his steps.

Week 47, March 13–19, 1975

My goldfish have vanished! As soon as I am back, at lunchtime, I put down my satchel and go look for them but the aquarium wasn't in its place on top of the refrigerator. At first, I thought it was in the sink in order to change the water. Nothing. I found it on top of the kitchen cabinet among empty jars. I caused some of the jars to fall down. *He* came out of the bathroom, half-shaved, upon hearing the rattle. Looked uneasy. Every other week, he works very early in the morning and now it was the week of "the afternoons." I burst into tears. He put on a sad face to tell me that I hadn't rinsed the bowl properly after washing it with detergent. The fish were in the garbage can beneath the coffee grinds. I buried them in the big flower pot on the balcony, putting little Indian figurines on top.

Week 48, March 20–26, 1975

I don't know if one can die at nine years old, if the heart can stop all of a sudden from sorrow. It's the downstairs neighbor who started it all because the water had come down through her ceiling, dripping, and caused a short-circuit in her TV set. She was hammering at the door and her shouts reverberated in the staircase. *He* went to open up, in his pajamas. Mum was in the bathtub, her head propped against the enameled edge with half-closed eyes. Water was pouring from the showerhead and running over the top in many little trickles. At first, I thought she was playing a trick on us. He said: *"Don't touch anything"* and cut the electricity at the meter. And then he removed the hairdryer that floated in front of Mum's breasts.

Week 50, April 3–9, 1975

Since Monday, she is alone in the cemetery. I met many people in the family that I didn't know. We went to eat together in a restaurant at the gate of Pantin cemetery and I cried during the whole meal. They asked me a lot of questions, a man from the police and another from the insurance, to do with the hairdryer, but nothing about the goldfish. It has nothing to do with detergent.

Week 354, February 7–13, 1981

He could be more discreet, that asshole! Or take his bitches to some other place . . . If I put the music on at full blast, it's so as not to hear them! He speaks again of apprenticing me in a carpentry school near Lamastre, down in the Ardèche, where he knows someone. With the pretext that I don't want to learn anything. For him it's just like that! The bungling carpenter. Give me Mum back and I'd learn, I'd learn a lot.

Week 553, November 5–11, 1984

They didn't keep me long, at Vincennes! Not even a half-day. It was just like a classroom except that the teacher was in uniform. Loads of tests, each one stupider than the other such as: *What do you use to hit the nail on the head? Scissors, speech, or hammer* . . . Make your choice! I answered just anything and in the end I didn't even read the questions. When we started the Morse code deciphering, one long, two shorts, an examiner came in and called me, me and a guy who had his head all bandaged up from a motorbike accident. Straight to the psychiatrist. He talked to me about my mother and it was as if I could see the tub again. Grandma came home but she can't bear him either.

Week 726, January 24–30, 1988

For months he has been coughing like a cavern. In the morning he couldn't keep down his breakfast anymore. It spurted out into the sink with the toothpaste. Good morning! He had a nasty thing beneath the throat, in the esophagus. The ambulance came over to fetch him, with all the neighbors on the staircase. I slammed the door on them when they started commiserating, I don't care about their sick people so let them just do the same.

Week 727, January 31–February 6, 1988

No wonder he wouldn't leave me at home alone! All kids happen to play with ether and matches. First of all, I was eleven years old and the flaming liquid started to run on the tile floor. I poured water over it, only too late. It had already slipped under the door. Hardly burned the hall linoleum . . . Since then he thinks I am an arsonist! Just a pretext! I was looking for the letters I had sent Mum from summer camp, when I hit upon a large shoebox in their bedroom closet. A box for boots, but in their place, wrapped in rags, there was a hairdryer, the same one that had killed Mum, with the ventilator showing in its hole above the handle, except that it was pink instead of blue. I unscrewed it. It was all rusty inside as if it had been plunged into water.

Week 728, February 7–15, 1988

For three nights, I kept thinking of that hairdryer, and how he had managed it. It flashed into my mind when I recalled the goldfish! I flicked back in my diary to March 1975 and realized that they had disappeared only a few days before Mum electrocuted herself in her bath.

I can see him as if it was happening right in front of my eyes, filling up the tub, pouring the aquarium water and the fish into it, turning on the hairdryer and throwing it into the tub to check whether the current killed them . . .

Week 729, February 14–20, 1988

He tried to smile when he saw me enter his bedroom. With his finger, he motioned me to come closer. The operation had left him with a hole in his throat and a big bandage that vibrated with his breathing. He opened his eyes wide when I pressed the gauze with my fist.

It didn't even last a minute. I rang for the nurse.

There I was, in front of the blank last page of the seamstress's book, when the door of my cell opened. The cop to whom I had explained everything at the police station came in, my stepfather's brother on his heels.

"You remember the date . . . for your mother?"

The brother was staring at me.

"March 21, 1975, the first day of spring, why?"

He pointed to the hairdryer with his chin.

"Because your story doesn't hold up: I sent the machine back to the manufacturer to have a look. They're positive, this model didn't go into production until September 1975, six months after your mother's death . . ."

The brother felt like meddling in.

"Why didn't you say anything? If you had asked me, I would have explained to you that Jean and your mother loved each other . . . as few people would dare to imagine . . . He never quite got over it . . . I knew he had tried to do something foolish at that time . . ."

I started to chuckle. Him, love? What a joke! There is only one who loves her. I started to shout.

"Liars! liars! You're making it all up as you go along . . ."

The cop came to my rescue. "Unfortunately, it's the truth . . . Your father tried to commit suicide the same way your mother died . . . electrocuting himself. You killed him for nothing . . ."

At last they left, they couldn't bear to hear me sing anymore . . . I opened my notebook at the last page, the one before the 1974 calendar and I wrote my title:

Week 730, February 21–27, 1988

and found only one sentence to write. "They say that to make me have regrets."

Translated by Cécile Bloc-Rodot

Cathedral

Raymond Carver

This blind man, an old friend of my wife's, he was on his way to spend the night. His wife had died. So he was visiting the dead wife's relatives in Connecticut. He called my wife from his in-laws'. Arrangements were made. He would come by train, a five-hour trip, and my wife would meet him at the station. She hadn't seen him since she worked for him one summer in Seattle ten years ago. But she and the blind man had kept in touch. They made tapes and mailed them back and forth. I wasn't enthusiastic about his visit. He was no one I knew. And his being blind bothered me. My idea of blindness came from the movies. In the movies, the blind moved slowly and never laughed. Sometimes they were led by seeing-eye dogs. A blind man in my house was not something I looked forward to.

That summer in Seattle she had needed a job. She didn't have any money. The man she was going to marry at the end of the summer was in officers' training school. He didn't have any money, either. But she was in love with the guy, and he was in love with her, etc. She'd seen something in the paper: HELP WANTED—*Reading to Blind Man*, and a telephone number. She phoned and went over, was hired on the spot. She'd worked with this blind man all summer. She read stuff to him, case studies, reports, that sort of thing. She helped him organize his little office in the county social-service department.

They'd become good friends, my wife and the blind man. How do I know these things? She told me. And she told me something else. On her last day in the office, the blind man asked if he could touch her face. She agreed to this. She told me he touched his fingers to every part of her face, her nose—even her neck! She never forgot it. She even tried to write a poem about it. She was always trying to write a poem. She wrote a poem or two every year, usually after something really important had happened to her.

When we first started going out together, she showed me the poem. In the poem, she recalled his fingers and the way they had moved around over her face. In the poem, she talked about what she had felt at the time, about what went through her mind when the blind man touched her nose and lips. I can remember I didn't think much of the poem. Of course, I didn't tell her that. Maybe I just don't understand poetry. I admit it's not the first thing I reach for when I pick up something to read.

Anyway, this man who'd first enjoyed her favors, the officer-to-be, he'd been her childhood sweetheart. So okay. I'm saying that at the end of the summer she let the blind man run his hands over her face, said goodbye to him, married her childhood etc., who was now a commissioned officer, and she moved away from Seattle. But they'd kept in touch, she and the blind man. She made the first contact after a year or so. She called him up one night from an Air Force base in Alabama. She wanted to talk. They talked. He asked her to send him a tape and tell him about her life. She did this. She sent the tape. On the tape, she told the blind man about her husband and about their life together in the military. She told the blind man she loved her husband but she didn't like it where they lived and she didn't like it that he was a part of the military-industrial thing. She told the blind man she'd written a poem and he was in it. She told him that she was writing a poem about what it was like to be an Air Force officer's wife. The poem wasn't finished yet. She was still writing it. The blind man made a tape. He sent her the tape. She made a tape. This went on for years. My wife's officer was posted to one base and then another. She sent tapes from Moody AFB, McGuire, McConnell, and finally Travis, near Sacramento, where one night she got to feeling lonely and cut off from people she kept losing in that moving-around life. She got to feeling she couldn't go it another step. She went in and swallowed all the pills and capsules in the medicine chest and washed them down with a bottle of gin. Then she got into a hot bath and passed out.

But instead of dying, she got sick. She threw up. Her officer— why should he have a name? he was the childhood sweetheart, and what more does he want?—came home from somewhere, found her, and called the ambulance. In time, she put it all on a tape and sent the tape to the blind man. Over the years, she put all kinds of stuff on tapes and sent the tapes off lickety-split. Next to writing a poem every year, I think it was her chief means of recreation. On one tape, she told the blind man she'd decided to live away from her officer for a time. On another tape, she told him about her divorce. She and I began going out, and of course she told her blind man about it. She told him everything, or so it seemed to me. Once she asked me if I'd like to hear the latest tape from the blind man. This was a year ago. I was on the tape, she said. So I said okay, I'd listen to it. I got us drinks and we settled down in the living room. We made ready to listen. First she inserted the tape into the player and adjusted a couple of dials. Then she pushed a lever. The tape squeaked and someone began to talk in this loud voice. She lowered the volume. After a few minutes of harmless chitchat, I heard my own name in the mouth of this stranger, this blind man I didn't even know! And then this: "From all you've said about him, I can only conclude—" But we were interrupted, a knock at the door, something, and we didn't ever get back to the tape. Maybe it was just as well. I'd heard all I wanted to.

Now this same blind man was coming to sleep in my house.

"Maybe I could take him bowling," I said to my wife. She was at the draining board doing scalloped potatoes. She put down the knife she was using and turned around.

"If you love me," she said, "you can do this for me. If you don't love me, okay. But if you had a friend, any friend, and the friend came to visit, I'd make him feel comfortable." She wiped her hands with the dish towel.

"I don't have any blind friends," I said.

"You don't have *any* friends," she said. "Period. Besides," she said, "goddamn it, his wife's just died! Don't you understand that? The man's lost his wife!"

I didn't answer. She'd told me a little about the blind man's wife.

Her name was Beulah. Beulah! That's a name for a colored woman.

"Was his wife a Negro?" I asked.

"Are you crazy?" my wife said. "Have you just flipped or something?" She picked up a potato. I saw it hit the floor, then roll under the stove. "What's wrong with you?" she said. "Are you drunk?"

"I'm just asking," I said.

Right then my wife filled me in with more detail than I cared to know. I made a drink and sat at the kitchen table to listen. Pieces of the story began to fall into place.

Beulah had gone to work for the blind man the summer after my wife had stopped working for him. Pretty soon Beulah and the blind man had themselves a church wedding. It was a little wedding— who'd want to go to such a wedding in the first place?—just the two of them, plus the minister and the minister's wife. But it was a church wedding just the same. It was what Beulah had wanted, he'd said. But even then Beulah must have been carrying the cancer in her glands. After they had been inseparable for eight years—my wife's word, *inseparable*—Beulah's health went into a rapid decline. She died in a Seattle hospital room, the blind man sitting beside the bed and holding on to her hand. They'd married, lived and worked together, slept together—had sex, sure—and then the blind man had to bury her. All this without his having ever seen what the goddamned woman looked like. It was beyond my understanding. Hearing this, I felt sorry for the blind man for a little bit. And then I found myself thinking what a pitiful life this woman must have led. Imagine a woman who could never see herself as she was seen in the eyes of her loved one. A woman who could go on day after day and never receive the smallest compliment from her beloved. A woman whose husband could never read the expression on her face, be it misery or something better. Someone who could wear makeup or not—what difference to him? She could, if she wanted, wear green eye-shadow around one eye, a straight pin in her nostril, yellow slacks and purple shoes, no matter. And then to slip off into death, the blind man's hand on her hand, his blind eyes streaming tears—I'm imagining now—her last thought maybe this: that he never even knew what she looked like, and she on an express to the grave. Robert was left with a small insurance policy and half of a twenty-peso Mexican coin. The other half of the coin went into the box with her. Pathetic.

So when the time rolled around, my wife went to the depot to pick him up. With nothing to do but wait—sure, I blamed him for that—I was having a drink and watching the TV when I heard the car pull into the drive. I got up from the sofa with my drink and went to the window to have a look.

I saw my wife laughing as she parked the car. I saw her get out of the car and shut the door. She was still wearing a smile. Just amazing. She went around to the other side of the car to where the blind man was already starting to get out. This blind man, feature this, he was wearing a full beard! A beard on a blind man! Too much, I say. The blind man reached into the back seat and dragged out a suitcase. My wife took his arm, shut the car door, and, talking all the way, moved him down the drive and then up the steps to the front porch. I turned off the TV. I finished my drink, rinsed the glass, dried my hands. Then I went to the door.

My wife said, "I want you to meet Robert. Robert, this is my husband. I've told you all about him." She was beaming. She had this blind man by his coat sleeve.

The blind man let go of his suitcase and up came his hand.

I took it. He squeezed hard, held my hand, and then he let it go.

"I feel like we've already met," he boomed.

"Likewise," I said. I didn't know what else to say. Then I said, "Welcome. I've heard a lot about you." We began to move then, a little group, from the porch into the living room, my wife guiding him by the arm. The blind man was carrying his suitcase in his other hand. My wife said things like, "To your left here, Robert. That's right. Now watch it, there's a chair. That's it. Sit down right here. This is the sofa. We just bought this sofa two weeks ago."

I started to say something about the old sofa. I'd liked that old sofa. But I didn't say anything. Then I wanted to say something else, small-talk, about the scenic ride along the Hudson. How going *to* New York, you should sit on the right-hand side of the train, and coming *from* New York, the left-hand side.

"Did you have a good train ride?" I said. "Which side of the train did you sit on, by the way?"

"What a question, which side!" my wife said. "What's it matter which side?" she said.

"I just asked," I said.

"Right side," the blind man said. "I hadn't been on a train in nearly forty years. Not since I was a kid. With my folks. That's been a long time. I'd nearly forgotten the sensation. I have winter in my beard now," he said. "So I've been told, anyway. Do I look distinguished, my dear?" the blind man said to my wife.

"You look distinguished, Robert," she said. "Robert," she said. "Robert, it's just so good to see you."

My wife finally took her eyes off the blind man and looked at me. I had the feeling she didn't like what she saw. I shrugged.

I've never met, or personally known, anyone who was blind. This blind man was late forties, a heavy-set, balding man with stooped shoulders, as if he carried a great weight there. He wore brown slacks, brown shoes, a light-brown shirt, a tie, a sports coat. Spiffy. He also had this full beard. But he didn't use a cane and he didn't wear dark glasses. I'd always thought dark glasses were a must for the blind. Fact was, I wished he had a pair. At first glance, his eyes looked like anyone else's eyes. But if you looked close, there was something different about them. Too much white in the iris, for one thing, and the pupils seemed to move around in the sockets without his knowing it or being able to stop it. Creepy. As I stared at his face, I saw the left pupil turn in toward his nose while the other made an effort to keep in one place. But it was only an effort, for that eye was on the roam without his knowing it or wanting it to be.

I said, "Let me get you a drink. What's your pleasure? We have a little of everything. It's one of our pastimes."

"Bub, I'm a Scotch man myself," he said fast enough in this big voice.

"Right," I said. Bub! "Sure you are. I knew it."

He let his fingers touch his suitcase, which was sitting alongside the sofa. He was taking his bearings. I didn't blame him for that.

"I'll move that up to your room," my wife said.

"No, that's fine," the blind man said loudly. "It can go up when I go up."

"A little water with the Scotch?" I said.

"Very little," he said.

"I knew it," I said.

He said, "Just a tad. The Irish actor, Barry Fitzgerald? I'm like that fellow. When I drink water, Fitzgerald said, I drink water. When

I drink whiskey, I drink whiskey." My wife laughed. The blind man brought his hand up under his beard. He lifted his beard slowly and let it drop.

I did the drinks, three big glasses of Scotch with a splash of water in each. Then we made ourselves comfortable and talked about Robert's travels. First the long flight from the West Coast to Connecticut, we covered that. Then from Connecticut up here by train. We had another drink concerning that leg of the trip.

I remembered having read somewhere that the blind didn't smoke because, as speculation had it, they couldn't see the smoke they exhaled. I thought I knew that much and that much only about blind people. But this blind man smoked his cigarette down to the nubbin and then lit another one. This blind man filled his ashtray and my wife emptied it.

When we sat down at the table for dinner, we had another drink. My wife heaped Robert's plate with cube steak, scalloped potatoes, green beans. I buttered him up two slices of bread. I said, "Here's bread and butter for you." I swallowed some of my drink. "Now let us pray," I said, and the blind man lowered his head. My wife looked at me, her mouth agape. "Pray the phone won't ring and the food doesn't get cold," I said.

We dug in. We ate everything there was to eat on the table. We ate like there was no tomorrow. We didn't talk. We ate. We scarfed. We grazed that table. We were into serious eating. The blind man had right away located his foods, he knew just where everything was on his plate. I watched with admiration as he used his knife and fork on the meat. He'd cut two pieces of meat, fork the meat into his mouth, and then go all out for the scalloped potatoes, the beans next, and then he'd tear off a hunk of buttered bread and eat that. He'd follow this up with a big drink of milk. It didn't seem to bother him to use his fingers once in a while, either.

We finished everything, including half a strawberry pie. For a few moments, we sat as if stunned. Sweat beaded on our faces. Finally, we got up from the table and left the dirty plates. We didn't look back. We took ourselves into the living room and sank into our places again. Robert and my wife sat on the sofa. I took the big chair. We had us two or three more drinks while they talked about the major things that had come to pass for them in the past ten years. For the

most part, I just listened. Now and then I joined in. I didn't want
him to think I'd left the room, and I didn't want her to think I was
feeling left out. They talked of things that had happened to them—
to them!—these past ten years. I waited in vain to hear my name on
my wife's sweet lips: "And then my dear husband came into my
life"—something like that. But I heard nothing of the sort. More talk
of Robert. Robert had done a little of everything, it seemed, a regular
blind jack-of-all-trades. But most recently he and his wife had had an
Amway distributorship, from which, I gathered, they'd earned their
living, such as it was. The blind man was also a ham radio operator.
He talked in his loud voice about conversations he'd had with fellow
operators in Guam, in the Philippines, in Alaska, and even in Tahiti.
He said he'd have a lot of friends there if he ever wanted to go visit
those places. From time to time, he'd turn his blind face toward me,
put his hand under his beard, ask me something. How long had I
been in my present position? (Three years.) Did I like my work? (I
didn't.) Was I going to stay with it? (What were the options?) Finally,
when I thought he was beginning to run down, I got up and turned
on the TV.

My wife looked at me with irritation. She was heading toward a
boil. Then she looked at the blind man and said, "Robert, do you
have a TV?"

The blind man said, "My dear, I have two TVs. I have a color
set and a black-and-white thing, an old relic. It's funny, but if I turn
the TV on, and I'm always turning it on, I turn on the color set. It's
funny, don't you think?"

I didn't know what to say to that. I had absolutely nothing to say
to that. No opinion. So I watched the news program and tried to
listen to what the announcer was saying.

"This is a color TV," the blind man said. "Don't ask me how,
but I can tell."

"We traded up a while ago," I said.

The blind man had another taste of his drink. He lifted his beard,
sniffed it, and let it fall. He leaned forward on the sofa. He positioned
his ashtray on the coffee table, then put the lighter to his cigarette.
He leaned back on the sofa and crossed his legs at the ankles.

My wife covered her mouth, and then she yawned. She stretched.
She said, "I think I'll go upstairs and put on my robe. I think I'll

change into something else. Robert, you make yourself comfortable," she said.

"I'm comfortable," the blind man said.

"I want you to feel comfortable in this house," she said.

"I am comfortable," the blind man said.

After she'd left the room, he and I listened to the weather report and then to the sports roundup. By that time, she'd been gone so long I didn't know if she was going to come back. I thought she might have gone to bed. I wished she'd come back downstairs. I didn't want to be left alone with a blind man. I asked him if he wanted another drink, and he said sure. Then I asked if he wanted to smoke some dope with me. I said I'd just rolled a number. I hadn't, but I planned to do so in about two shakes.

"I'll try some with you," he said.

"Damn right," I said. "That's the stuff."

I got our drinks and sat down on the sofa with him. Then I rolled us two fat numbers. I lit one and passed it. I brought it to his fingers. He took it and inhaled.

"Hold it as long as you can," I said. I could tell he didn't know the first thing.

My wife came back downstairs wearing her pink robe and her pink slippers.

"What do I smell?" she said.

"We thought we'd have us some cannabis," I said.

My wife gave me a savage look. Then she looked at the blind man and said, "Robert, I didn't know you smoked."

He said, "I do now, my dear. There's a first time for everything. But I don't feel anything yet."

"This stuff is pretty mellow," I said. "This stuff is mild. It's dope you can reason with," I said. "It doesn't mess you up."

"Not much it doesn't, bub," he said, and laughed.

My wife sat on the sofa between the blind man and me. I passed her the number. She took it and toked and then passed it back to me. "Which way is this going?" she said. Then she said, "I shouldn't be smoking this. I can hardly keep my eyes open as it is. That dinner did me in. I shouldn't have eaten so much."

"It was the strawberry pie," the blind man said. "That's what did it," he said, and he laughed his big laugh. Then he shook his head.

"There's more strawberry pie," I said.

"Do you want some more, Robert?" my wife said.

"Maybe in a little while," he said.

We gave our attention to the TV. My wife yawned again. She said, "Your bed is made up when you feel like going to bed, Robert. I know you must have had a long day. When you're ready to go to bed, say so." She pulled his arm. "Robert?"

He came to and said, "I've had a real nice time. This beats tapes, doesn't it?"

I said, "Coming at you," and I put the number between his fingers. He inhaled, held the smoke, and then let it go. It was like he'd been doing it since he was nine years old.

"Thanks, bub," he said. "But I think this is all for me. I think I'm beginning to feel it," he said. He held the burning roach out for my wife.

"Same here," she said. "Ditto. Me, too." She took the roach and passed it to me. "I may just sit here for a while between you two guys with my eyes closed. But don't let me bother you, okay? Either one of you. If it bothers you, say so. Otherwise, I may just sit here with my eyes closed until you're ready to go to bed," she said. "Your bed's made up, Robert, when you're ready. It's right next to our room at the top of the stairs. We'll show you up when you're ready. You wake me up now, you guys, if I fall asleep." She said that and then she closed her eyes and went to sleep.

The news program ended. I got up and changed the channel. I sat back down on the sofa. I wished my wife hadn't pooped out. Her head lay across the back of the sofa, her mouth open. She'd turned so that her robe had slipped away from her legs, exposing a juicy thigh. I reached to draw her robe back over her, and it was then that I glanced at the blind man. What the hell! I flipped the robe open again.

"You say when you want some strawberry pie," I said.

"I will," he said.

I said, "Are you tired? Do you want me to take you up to your bed? Are you ready to hit the hay?"

"Not yet," he said. "No, I'll stay up with you, bub. If that's all right. I'll stay up until you're ready to turn in. We haven't had a chance to talk. Know what I mean? I feel like me and her monopolized the evening." He lifted his beard and he let it fall. He picked up his cigarettes and his lighter.

"That's all right," I said. Then I said, "I'm glad for the company."

And I guess I was. Every night I smoked dope and stayed up as long as I could before I fell asleep. My wife and I hardly ever went to bed at the same time. When I did go to sleep, I had these dreams. Sometimes I'd wake up from one of them, my heart going crazy.

Something about the church and the Middle Ages was on the TV. Not your run-of-the-mill TV fare. I wanted to watch something else. I turned to the other channels. But there was nothing on them, either. So I turned back to the first channel and apologized.

"Bub, it's all right," the blind man said. "It's fine with me. Whatever you want to watch is okay. I'm always learning something. Learning never ends. It won't hurt me to learn something tonight. I got ears," he said.

We didn't say anything for a time. He was leaning forward with his head turned at me, his right ear aimed in the direction of the set. Very disconcerting. Now and then his eyelids drooped and then they snapped open again. Now and then he put his fingers into his beard and tugged, like he was thinking about something he was hearing on the television.

On the screen, a group of men wearing cowls was being set upon and tormented by men dressed in skeleton costumes and men dressed as devils. The men dressed as devils wore devil masks, horns, and long tails. This pageant was part of a procession. The Englishman who was narrating the thing said it took place in Spain once a year. I tried to explain to the blind man what was happening.

"Skeletons," he said. "I know about skeletons," he said, and he nodded.

The TV showed this one cathedral. Then there was a long, slow look at another one. Finally, the picture switched to the famous one in Paris, with its flying buttresses and its spires reaching up to the clouds. The camera pulled away to show the whole of the cathedral rising above the skyline.

There were times when the Englishman who was telling the thing would shut up, would simply let the camera move around over the cathedrals. Or else the camera would tour the countryside, men in fields walking behind oxen. I waited as long as I could. Then I felt I had to say something. I said, "They're showing the outside of this cathedral now. Gargoyles. Little statues carved to look like monsters. Now I guess they're in Italy. Yeah, they're in Italy. There's paintings on the walls of this one church."

"Are those fresco paintings, bub?" he asked, and he sipped from his drink.

I reached for my glass. But it was empty. I tried to remember what I could remember. "You're asking me are those frescoes?" I said. "That's a good question. I don't know."

The camera moved to a cathedral outside Lisbon. The differences in the Portuguese cathedral compared with the French and Italian were not that great. But they were there. Mostly the interior stuff. Then something occurred to me, and I said, "Something has occurred to me. Do you have any idea what a cathedral is? What they look like, that is? Do you follow me? If somebody says cathedral to you, do you have any notion what they're talking about? Do you know the difference between that and a Baptist church, say?"

He let the smoke dribble from his mouth. "I know they took hundreds of workers fifty or a hundred years to build," he said. "I just heard the man say that, of course. I know generations of the same families worked on a cathedral. I heard him say that, too. The men who began their life's work on them, they never lived to see the completion of their work. In that wise, bub, they're no different from the rest of us, right?" He laughed. Then his eyelids drooped again. His head nodded. He seemed to be snoozing. Maybe he was imagining himself in Portugal. The TV was showing another cathedral now. This one was in Germany. The Englishman's voice droned on. "Cathedrals," the blind man said. He sat up and rolled his head back and forth. "If you want the truth, bub, that's about all I know. What I just said. What I heard him say. But maybe you could describe one to me? I wish you'd do it. I'd like that. If you want to know, I really don't have a good idea."

I stared hard at the shot of the cathedral on the TV. How could I even begin to describe it? But say my life depended on it. Say my life was being threatened by an insane guy who said I had to do it or else.

I stared some more at the cathedral before the picture flipped off into the countryside. There was no use. I turned to the blind man and said, "To begin with, they're very tall." I was looking around the room for clues. "They reach way up. Up and up. Toward the sky. They're so big, some of them, they have to have these supports. To help hold them up, so to speak. These supports are called buttresses. They remind me of viaducts, for some reason. But maybe you don't know viaducts, either? Sometimes the cathedrals have devils and such carved into the front. Sometimes lords and ladies. Don't ask me why this is," I said.

He was nodding. The whole upper part of his body seemed to be moving back and forth.

"I'm not doing so good, am I?" I said.

He stopped nodding and leaned forward on the edge of the sofa. As he listened to me, he was running his fingers through his beard. I wasn't getting through to him, I could see that. But he waited for me to go on just the same. He nodded, like he was trying to encourage me. I tried to think what else to say. "They're really big," I said. "They're massive. They're built of stone. Marble, too, sometimes. In those olden days, when they built cathedrals, men wanted to be close to God. In those olden days, God was an important part of everyone's life. You could tell this from their cathedral-building. I'm sorry," I said, "but it looks like that's the best I can do for you. I'm just no good at it."

"That's all right, bub," the blind man said. "Hey, listen. I hope you don't mind my asking you. Can I ask you something? Let me ask you a simple question, yes or no. I'm just curious and there's no offense. You're my host. But let me ask if you are in any way religious? You don't mind my asking?"

I shook my head. He couldn't see that, though. A wink is the same as a nod to a blind man. "I guess I don't believe in it. In anything. Sometimes it's hard. You know what I'm saying?"

"Sure, I do," he said.

"Right," I said.

The Englishman was still holding forth. My wife sighed in her sleep. She drew a long breath and went on with her sleeping.

"You'll have to forgive me," I said. "But I can't tell you what a cathedral looks like. It just isn't in me to do it. I can't do any more than I've done."

The blind man sat very still, his head down, as he listened to me.

I said, "The truth is, cathedrals don't mean anything special to me. Nothing. Cathedrals. They're something to look at on late-night TV. That's all they are."

It was then that the blind man cleared his throat. He brought something up. He took a handkerchief from his back pocket. Then he said, "I get it, bub. It's okay. It happens. Don't worry about it," he said. "Hey, listen to me. Will you do me a favor? I got an idea. Why don't you find us some heavy paper? And a pen. We'll do something. We'll draw one together. Get us a pen and some heavy paper. Go on, bub, get the stuff," he said.

So I went upstairs. My legs felt like they didn't have any strength in them. They felt like they did after I'd done some running. In my wife's room, I looked around. I found some ballpoints in a little basket on her table. And then I tried to think where to look for the kind of paper he was talking about.

Downstairs, in the kitchen, I found a shopping bag with onion skins in the bottom of the bag. I emptied the bag and shook it. I brought it into the living room and sat down with it near his legs. I moved some things, smoothed the wrinkles from the bag, spread it out on the coffee table.

The blind man got down from the sofa and sat next to me on the carpet.

He ran his fingers over the paper. He went up and down the sides of the paper. The edges, even the edges. He fingered the corners.

"All right," he said. "All right, let's do her."

He found my hand, the hand with the pen. He closed his hand over my hand. "Go ahead, bub, draw," he said. "Draw. You'll see. I'll follow along with you. It'll be okay. Just begin now like I'm telling you. You'll see. Draw," the blind man said.

So I began. First I drew a box that looked like a house. It could have been the house I lived in. Then I put a roof on it. At either end of the roof, I drew spires. Crazy.

"Swell," he said. "Terrific. You're doing fine," he said. "Never thought anything like this could happen in your lifetime, did you, bub? Well, it's a strange life, we all know that. Go on now. Keep it up."

I put in windows with arches. I drew flying buttresses. I hung great doors. I couldn't stop. The TV station went off the air. I put down the pen and closed and opened my fingers. The blind man felt around over the paper. He moved the tips of his fingers over the paper, all over what I had drawn, and he nodded.

"Doing fine," the blind man said.

I took up the pen again, and he found my hand. I kept at it. I'm no artist. But I kept drawing just the same.

My wife opened up her eyes and gazed at us. She sat up on the sofa, her robe hanging open. She said, "What are you doing? Tell me, I want to know."

I didn't answer her.

The blind man said, "We're drawing a cathedral. Me and him are working on it. Press hard," he said to me. "That's right. That's good," he said. "Sure. You got it, bub. I can tell. You didn't think you could. But you can, can't you? You're cooking with gas now. You know what I'm saying? We're going to really have us something here in a minute. How's the old arm?" he said. "Put some people in there now. What's a cathedral without people?"

My wife said, "What's going on? Robert, what are you doing? What's going on?"

"It's all right," he said to her. "Close your eyes now," the blind man said to me.

I did it. I closed them just like he said.

"Are they closed?" he said. "Don't fudge."

"They're closed," I said.

"Keep them that way," he said. He said, "Don't stop now. Draw."

So we kept on with it. His fingers rode my fingers as my hand went over the paper. It was like nothing else in my life up to now.

Then he said, "I think that's it. I think you got it," he said. "Take a look. What do you think?"

But I had my eyes closed. I thought I'd keep them that way for a little longer. I thought it was something I ought to do.

"Well?" he said. "Are you looking?"

My eyes were still closed. I was in my house. I knew that. But I didn't feel like I was inside anything.

"It's really something," I said.

Dealer's Choice

Sara Paretsky

1942

She was waiting in the outer office when I came in, sitting with a stillness that made you think she'd been planted there for a decade or two and could make it to the twenty-first century if she had to. She didn't move when I came in except to flick a glance at me under the veil of the little red hat that had built a nest in her shiny black hair. She was all in red; she'd taken the May's company's advertisers to heart and was wearing victory red. But I doubted if she'd ever seen the inside of May's. This was the kind of shantung number that some sales clerk acting like the undertaker for George V pulled from a back room and whispered to madam that it might suit if madam would condescend to try it on. The shoes and gloves and bag were black.

"Mr. Marlowe?" Her voice was soft and husky with a hint of a lisp behind it.

I acknowledged the fact.

She got to her feet. Perched on top of her boxy four-inch heels she just about cleared my armpit.

"I've been hoping to see you, Mr. Marlowe. Hoping to interest you in taking a case for me. If you have the time, that is."

She made it sound as though her problem, whatever it was, was just a bit on the dull side, and that if I didn't have time for it the two of us could forget it and move on to something more interesting. I grunted and unlocked the inner door. The muffled tapping on the rug behind me let me know she was following me in.

The April sunshine was picking up the dust motes dancing on the edge of my desk. I dumped the morning paper onto the blotter and reached into my desk drawer for my pipe. My visitor settled herself in the other chair with the same composure she'd shown in the outer office. Whatever little problem she had didn't make her twitch or catch her heels in her rosy silk stockings.

While I was busy with my pipe she leaned forward in her chair, looking at the paper; something on the front page had caught her eye. Maybe the Red Army bashing the Krauts along the Caspian, or the U.S. carving a few inches out of Milne Bay. Or Ichuro Kimura eluding the U.S. Army right here at home, or maybe the lady whose twin daughters were celebrating their first birthday without ever having seen their daddy. He was interned by the Japs in Chungking.

When she caught me watching her she settled back in her chair. "Do you think the war will end soon, Mr. Marlowe?"

"Sure," I said, tamping the tobacco in. "Out of the trenches by Christmas." We'd missed Easter by a day already.

The girl nodded slightly to herself, as if I'd confirmed her opinion of the war. Or maybe me. The bright sunlight let me see her eyes now, despite the little veil. The irises were large and dark, looking black against the clear whites. She was watching me calmly enough but those eyes gave her away—they could light up the whole Trojan backfield if she wanted to use them that way. But something in her manner and that hint of a lisp made me think they didn't play much football where she came from.

"I need some help with a man," she finally said.

"You look as though you do just fine without help." I struck a match against the side of the desk.

She ignored me. "He's holding some of my brother's markers."

"Your brother lose them in fair play?"

She gave a shrug that moved like a whisper through the shantung. "I wouldn't know, Mr. Marlowe. All I know is that my brother staked a—an item that didn't belong to him. My brother has gone into hiding, since he knows he can't pay up and he's afraid they'll break his legs, or whatever it is they do when you can't pay your gambling losses."

"Then I don't see you have a problem. All you have to do is keep supplying your brother with food and water and everyone will be happy. Your gambler will go after easier prey by and by. What's his name?"

I thought I saw a faint blush, but it was such a phantom wave of color I couldn't be sure. It made me think she knew where her brother was all right.

"Dominick Bognavich. And if it were just my brother I wouldn't mind, not so much I mean, since he was gambling and he has to take his chances. But they're threatening my mother. And that's where I need your help. I thought perhaps you could explain to Mr. Bognavich—get him to see that—he should leave my mother alone."

I busied myself with my pipe again. "Your brother shouldn't bet with Bognavich unless he can stake the San Joaquin Valley. I believe that's all Dominick doesn't own at this point. What did your brother put up?"

She watched me consideringly. I knew that look. It was the kind I used when I wondered if a chinook would accept my bait.

"A ring," she finally said. "An old diamond and sapphire ring that had been in Mother's family for a hundred years. My brother knows he'll get it when she's dead, and she could die tomorrow—I don't know—she's very ill and in a nursing home. So he anticipated events."

Anticipated events. I like that. It showed a certain thoughtfulness with the language and the people. "And what about your brother. I mean, does he have a name, or do we do this whole thing incognito."

She studied me again. "No, I can see you need his name. It's— uh—Richard."

"Is that his first or his last name? And do you have the same last name or should I call you something else?"

"You can call me Miss Felstein. Naomi Felstein. And that would be Richard's last name, too."

"And your mother is Mrs. Felstein, and your father is Mr. Felstein."

"Was." She gave a tight little smile, the first I'd seen and not any real sample of what she could do if she were in the mood. "He's been dead for some years now."

"And what is it you want me to do for you, Miss Felstein? Shoot

Dominick Bognavich? He's got a lot of backups and I might run out of bullets before he ran out of people to send after me."

One black-gloved finger traced a circle on the arm of the chair. "Maybe you could see Mr. Bognavich and explain to him. About my brother not owning the ring, I mean. Or—or maybe you could talk my brother into coming out of hiding. He won't listen to me."

Sure I could talk to Bognavich. He and I were good pals, sure we were, and my words carried a lot of weight with him, about as much as maggots listening to protests from a dead body. I didn't like it, any of it. I didn't believe her story and I didn't believe in her brother. I was pretty sure she didn't have a brother, or if she did Bognavich had never heard of him. But it was the day after Easter and I'd been too savvy to let myself get suckered by the Easter bunny, so I owed the rubes one.

I gave her my usual rate, twenty-five dollars a day and expenses, and told her I'd need some up-front money. She opened the little black bag without a word and lifted ten twenties from a stash in the zipper compartment with the ease of a dealer sliding off queens to send you over the top in twenty-one.

She gave another ghostly smile. "I'll wait for you here. In case you have no success with Mr. Bognavich and want me to take you to my brother."

"I'll call you, Miss Felstein."

That seemed to confuse her a little. "I may—I don't—"

"I'd rather you didn't wait in my office. I'll call you."

Reluctantly she wrote a number on a piece of paper and handed it to me. Her script was bold and dark, the writing of a risk taker. Oh, yeah, her brother lost some big ones to Dominick Bognavich all right.

A guy like Bognavich doesn't start his rounds until the regular working stiffs are heading home for a drink. If I was lucky I'd make it to his place before he went to bed for the day. But when I'd wound my way up Laurel Canyon to Ventura, where Bognavich had a modest mansion on a cul-de-sac, I found he'd become the kind of guy who doesn't make rounds any time of day.

He was slumped against the door leading from the garage to the house. He looked as though he'd felt tired getting out of the car and decided to sit down for a minute to catch his breath but had fallen asleep instead. It was just that he had taken the kind of nap where six small-caliber bullets give you a permanent hangover.

I felt his face and wrists. He'd been dead a while; if I had a look around without calling the cops it wasn't going to halt the wheels of justice any. The door behind him was unlocked, an invitation for fools to go dancing in and chase the angels out. I listened for a while but didn't hear anything, not even Dominick's blood congealing on the floor.

The kitchen was a white-tiled affair that looked like the morgue after a good scrubdown. I gave it a quick once-over, but Bognavich wasn't the kind of guy who hid his secrets in the granulated sugar. I passed on through to the main part of the house.

The gambler had employed a hell of a housekeeper. She'd left sofa cushions torn apart with their stuffing spread all over the pale gold on the living room floor. White tufts clung to my trouser legs like cottontails. Marlowe the Easter bunny hunting for eggs the other kids hadn't been able to find.

Bognavich's study was where he'd kept his papers. He'd been a gambler, not a reader, and most of the books dealt with the finer points of cards and horses. They lay every which way, their backs breaking, loose pages lying nearby like pups trying to get close enough to suckle their dam.

I did the best I could with the papers and the ledger. There were I.O.U.'s for the asking if I'd been inclined to go hustling for bread, but nothing that looked like a Felstein. I didn't feel like lingering for a detailed search. Whoever had put those six holes into Dominick might be happy for the cops to find an unwelcome peeper fingering the gambler's papers. I gave the rest of the house a quick tour, admired Bognavich's taste in silk pajamas, and slid back through the kitchen.

He was still sitting where I'd left him. He seemed to sigh as I passed. I patted him on the shoulder and went back to the Chrysler. Miss Felstein could have put six rounds into Bognavich without wrinkling her silk dress, let alone her smooth little forehead. It was the kind of shooting a dame might do—six bullets where one or two would do the job. Wasteful, with a war on.

I pulled the pint from the glove compartment and swallowed a mouthful just on principle, a farewell salute to Dominick. He hadn't been a bad guy, he just had a lousy job.

I half expected to find Miss Naomi Felstein, if that was who she was, not just what I could call her, planted in my waiting room like a well-kept jacaranda. I expected her because I wanted her to be there. I wanted to see if I could shake a little fire into those cool dark eyes and get her to tell me why she'd come to me after finding Dominick's dead body lying in front of his kitchen door this morning.

She wasn't there, though. I wondered if she ever had been there, if perhaps she was just an Easter vision, in red the way these visions always appear, leaving the faintest whiff of Chanel behind to undercut the tobacco fumes. I had a drink from the office bottle and the Chanel disappeared.

I didn't have much hope for the number the mirage had left, and my hope began to dwindle after fifteen rings. But I didn't have anything else to do so I sat at my desk with the phone in my ear looking at the front page of the paper, trying again to figure out which of the stories had caught my phantom's attention.

I finished the details of Errol Flynn's cruelty to his wife and why she had to get his entire estate as a settlement and started on why the army thought Ichuro Kimura was an enemy spy. I'd gotten to the part where he'd thrown empty sake bottles at the soldiers who came to arrest him for not reporting for deportation at Union Station last Wednesday when I realized someone was talking to me.

It was a querulous old man who repeated that he was the Boylston Ranch and who was I calling. Without much interest I asked for Miss Felstein.

"No one here by that name. No women here at all." His tone demanded congratulations for having rid Eden of all temptresses.

"Five feet tall, lots of glossy black hair, dark eyes that could bring a guy back from the grave if she wanted them to."

He hung up on me. Just like that. I stuck the bottle of rye neatly in the middle of the drawer and stared at nothing for a while. Then I got up and locked the office behind me. Oh, yes, Marlowe's a very methodical guy. Very orderly. He always tidies up his whiskey bottle when he's been drinking and locks up behind himself. You can tell he came from a good home.

The army had a roadblock set up just outside Lebec. I guess they were trying to make sure no one was smuggling empty sake bottles in for Ichuro Kimura. They made me get out of my car while they looked under the seats and in the trunk. Then they checked my I.D. and made me tell them I was looking for a runaway girl and that I had a hot tip she was hiding out on the Boylston place. That made them about as happy as a housewife seeing her cat drag a dead bird into the kitchen. They started putting me through my paces until the sergeant who was running the block came over and told them to let me through. He was bored: he wanted to be killing Japs at Milne Bay instead of looking for old men in Lebec.

The sun had had all it could take of Kern County by the time I got to the turnoff for the Boylston Ranch. It was easing itself down behind the Sierra Madres, striking lightning bolts from the dashboard that made it hard for me to see. I was craning my neck forward, shielding my eyes with my left hand, when I realized I was about to go nose to nose with a pickup.

I pulled over to the side to let the truck go by, but it stopped and a lean, dusty man jumped down. He had on a cowboy hat and leather leggings, in case the gearshift chafed his legs, and his face was young and angry, with a jutting upper lip trying to dominate the uncertain jaw beneath it.

"Private property here, mister. You got any reason to be here?"

"Yup," I said.

"Then let's have it."

I got out of the Chrysler to be on eye level with him, just in case being alone with the cows all day made him punch happy.

"You got any special reason for asking, son? Other than just nosiness, I mean?"

His fists clenched reflexively and he took half a step nearer. "I'm Jay Boylston. That good enough for you?"

"You own this spread?"

"My old man does, but I'm in charge of the range. So spill it, and make it fast. Time is money here and I don't have much to waste of either."

"An original sentiment. Maybe you could get it engraved on your tombstone. If your old man owns the place I'd better talk to him. It's kind of a delicate matter. Involves a lady's reputation, you might say."

At that he did try to swing at me. I grabbed his arm. It was a bit tougher than his face but not much.

"What's going on here?"

The newcomer had ridden up behind us on horseback. The horse stopped in its tracks at a short command and the rider jumped down. He was an older, stockier edition of Jay. His face held the kind of arrogance men acquire when they own a big piece of land and think it means they own all the people around them as well.

"Man's trespassing and he's giving kind of smart answers when I ask him to explain himself," Jay said sullenly.

"Mr. Boylston?" I asked. The older man nodded fractionally, too calm to give anything to a stranger, even the movement of his head.

"Philip Marlowe. I'm a private detective from Los Angeles and I'm up here on a case."

"A case involving my ranch is something I would know about," Boylston said. His manner was genial but his eyes were cold.

"I didn't say it involved your ranch. Except as a hiding place for a runaway. Big place, lot of places to hide. Am I right?"

"The army's been all through here in the last week looking for a runaway Jap," Boylston said. "I don't think there's too much those boys missed. You're a long way from L.A. if you hope to sleep in your own bed tonight."

"This is a recent case," I said doggedly, Marlowe the intrepid, fighting on where others would have turned tail and run. "This is a woman who only recently disappeared. And she's attractive enough that someone might be persuaded to hide her from the army."

Boylston had headed back to his horse, but at the end of my speech he turned back to me. He exchanged a glance with his son. When Jay shook his head the father said, "Who's the girl?"

"I don't have a name. But she's five feet tall, glossy black hair, probably a lot of it but she wears it in kind of a roll or chignon or whatever they're calling them this year. Very well dressed—lots of money in the background someplace."

"If you don't know her name how do you know she's missing or even what she looks like?"

I smiled a little. "I can't tell you all my secrets, Mr. Boylston. But I will tell you she's wanted for questioning about a murder down in L.A."

Boylston swung himself back onto his horse. "I haven't seen anyone like that. I can account for all the women around here: my two daughters, and three of the hands are married, and none of 'em has black hair. But if you want to look around, be my guest. There's an abandoned farmhouse on up the road about five miles. We just acquired the land so we only have one hand living out there so far; he can't keep an eye on the house and cover the range, too. That'd be the only place I know of. If you don't see her there you'd best get off my land. Now move your truck, Jay, and let Mr. Marlowe get by."

Jay got into the truck and moved it with an ill will that knocked little pebbles into the side of the Chrysler. I climbed back in and headed on up the track. In the rearview mirror I could see Boylston on his horse watching me, standing so still he might have been a knight on a chessboard.

The road petered out for a while into a couple of tire marks in the grass, but after four miles it turned into a regular road again. Not too long after that I came to the house.

It was a single-story, trim ranch, built like a U with short arms. It was made of wood and painted white, fresh as the snow on the Sierras, with green trim like pine trees. Whoever used to live here had loved the place and kept it up. Or the hand who was watchdogging was a homebody who kept the shrubs trimmed and weeded the begonias.

I rang the bell set into the front door, waited a few minutes, and rang again. It was sunset, not too unreasonable to think the man was done with his chores for the day. But he might be in the shower and not able to hear me ringing. I tried the door and found it unlocked. I pushed it open and went on in with a cloud of virtue wrapped around my shoulders. After all, I wasn't even housebreaking—I had Boylston's permission to search the place.

The hall floor was tiled in brown ceramic with a couple of knotted rugs floating on it. The tiles were covered with a film of dust—the hand who lived there didn't have time for the finer points of housekeeping. Opposite the front door, sliding glass doors led to a garden, a place which the previous owner had tended with care. I stared through the glass at the trim miniature shrubs and flowering bushes. There even seemed to be a pond in the middle.

I turned left and found myself in the kitchen wing. No one was hiding in the stove or under the sink. The other wing held the bedrooms. In one you could see the cowboy's obvious presence, several pairs of jeans, a change of boots, another of regular shoes. The other two bedrooms had been stripped of their furnishings. No one was in the closets or hiding in the two bathtubs.

The only thing that gave me hope was the telephone. It sat next to the kitchen stove, and pasted to it, in neat printing, not my mirage's bold script, was the number I had called. The number where the querulous man had hung up on me after I'd described her.

When I'd finished with the bedrooms I went back to the sliding door leading into the small garden. Sure enough, a pool stood in the middle, bigger than it had appeared from inside the house. I climbed onto a bridge that crossed it and looked down. Immediately a trio of giant goldfish popped to the surface. They practically stood on their tails begging for bread.

"Go work for a living like the regular fish," I admonished them. "There's a war on. No one has time to pamper goldfish."

The fish swam under the bridge. I turned and looked down at them. They'd taken my words to heart—they were hard at work on the face and hands of a man who was staring up at me in the shallow water. In the fading light I couldn't make out his features, but he still had all of them so he couldn't have been in the water long. His dark hair waved like silk seaweed in the little eddies the carp stirred up.

What a detective that Marlowe is. Someone strews bodies all over Southern California and Marlowe finds them with the ease and derring-do of a bloodhound. I wanted a flashlight so I could get a closer look at the face. I wanted a drink and a cigarette, and I was beginning to think I shouldn't stray too far from my gun. All these useful items were in the Chrysler's glove compartment. I headed back through the house, skating on the lily pads on the tile floor, and climbed into the passenger seat. I had just unscrewed the bottle cap when I detected something else—a grand display of pyrotechnics exploding in my retinas. I didn't even feel the blow, just saw the red stabbing lights riding on a wave of nausea before I fell into deep blackness.

My head was a seventy-eight on a turntable that had automatic reset. Every time I thought I'd come to the end of the song and could stop spinning around someone would push the button and start me turning again. Someone had tied a couple of logs behind my back but when I reached around to cut them loose I discovered they were my arms bound behind me. I reeked of gasoline.

The time had come to open my eyes. Come on, Marlowe, you can get your eyelids up, it's only a little less horrible than the old bamboo shoots under the fingernails trick.

I was in the driver's seat of the Chrysler. Someone had moved me over, but otherwise the scene was just the way I'd left it. The glove compartment was open. I could see my gun and the bottle of rye and I wanted both of them in the kind of detached fashion a man lost in the desert wants an oasis, but I couldn't see my way clear to getting them.

Footsteps scrabbled on the gravel behind me. "You can't set fire to him here," someone said impatiently. "You may own the valley, but the U.S. Army is camped on the road and they will certainly investigate a big gasoline fire up here."

I knew that voice. It was husky, with a hint of a lisp behind it. I'd heard it a century or so ago in my office.

"Well, you're such a damned know-it-all, what do you suggest? That we leave him here until morning when the hands will find him?" The sulky tones of the kid, Jay Boylston.

"No," the woman said coolly, "I think you should let me drive him into the mountains. He can go over a ravine there and no one will be surprised."

"Kitty's right," Boylston senior said authoritatively.

Kitty? She was a kitty all right, the kind that you usually like a good solid set of iron bars around before you toss raw meat to her twice a day. There was a bit more backchat about who would do the driving, but they agreed in the end that the kitten could do it so that no one would wonder where Jay and his daddy were.

"You fired his gun?" Daddy asked.

"Yes," Jay said sulkily. "I shot Richard twice with it. When they find him they'll think Marlowe did it."

"Right. Kitty, just see that his gun falls clear of the car before you set it off. We want to make sure the law doesn't have any loose ends to tie up."

So she did have a brother named Richard. Or had had. That wavy black hair in the goldfish pond, that was what her dark leopard tresses would look like if she undid that bun.

"Sure, Kurt," the husky voice drawled.

Kurt and Jay shoved me roughly back into the passenger seat and Miss Kitty took my spot behind the wheel. I tried to sniff the Chanel, but the gasoline fumes were too strong. She drove rapidly up the track, bouncing the Chrysler's tire from rock to rock as though she was driving a mountain goat.

Things looked bad for Marlowe. I wondered if it was worth trying any of my winsome charms, or if I should just roll over on top of her and force both of us flaming into a ditch. It was worth a try. At least it would change the situation—give those cool black eyes something to look surprised about. I was getting ready to roll when she stopped the car.

Her next move took me utterly by surprise: she reached behind me and hacked my arms loose with an efficient woodsman's knife.

"You're kind of pushing your luck, Kitty." I moved my arms cautiously in front of me. They felt like someone had just forced the Grand Coulee's overflow through them. "I've been concussed before. I'm not feeling so sorry for myself that I couldn't take that knife from you and get myself out of here. You'd have to explain it to Kurt and Jay as best you can."

"Yes," the husky voice agreed coolly. "I'll tell them something if I have to—if I ever see them again, that is. But I need your help."

"Right, Miss Kitty. You lure me to Dominick Bognavich's body. You bring me into the mountains and set the sweetest sucker trap I've ever seen, including planting bullets from my gun in what I assume is your brother's body, and now you want my help. You want me to drive my car over a cliff for you so you don't have to chip those bright red nails of yours?"

She drew a sharp breath. "No. No. I didn't know they were going to knock you out. And I didn't know they had killed Richard until I got here. He—he was the weak link. He always was, but I never thought he would betray me."

The quiver of emotion in her voice played on my heart like a thousand violin strings. "The gambler. I know. He gambled away your mother's whoosis and so you had Kurt Boylston drown him in the goldfish pond."

"It didn't happen quite like that. But I don't blame you for being angry."

"Gee, sister. That's real swell of you. I'm not angry, though—I love being hit on the head. I came up from L.A. just to get knocked out. And then have gasoline poured on me so I couldn't miss the cars."

"That was never supposed to happen," she said quickly. "I was trying to get to Grandfather—to the ranch—before Jay did but I couldn't—there were reasons. . . ." Her voice trailed away.

"Maybe you could tell me what was supposed to happen. If it wouldn't strain your brain too much to tell the truth. Maybe you could even start with who you really are."

In the dark I couldn't tell if she was blushing or not. "My real name is Kathleen Moloney. Kathleen Akiko Moloney. My mother married an Irishman, but her father was Ichuro Kimura. I know I look Jewish to many people, and in this climate today it is helpful to let them think so. Dominick—Dominick is the one who suggested it. He suggested the name Felstein. And when I pretended to lose the title to my grandfather's land to him, he kept it under the name of Felstein." Her voice trailed away. "I needed help and I was so afraid you wouldn't help me . . ."

"If I knew you were Nisei." I finished for her. "And what makes you so sure I will help you now?"

"I don't know." She leaned close to me and I could smell her perfume again, mixed with the gasoline and a faint tinge of ladylike sweat. "I saved your life, but that wouldn't count with you, would it, if you thought it was your duty to turn me in and force me to go to Manzanar."

"You're not in any danger. A girl like you knows how to fight her way out of trouble."

"Yes. I have to use the gifts I have, just as you do, Mr. Marlowe. But we can argue about that later. Let me finish because we must move quickly. If you agree to help me, I mean."

In the moonlight all I could see was her shape. She'd shed the hat and the suit and was wearing trousers and cowboy boots. I couldn't see her features to tell if she was spinning me another long yarn into which she had somehow appropriated the tale of Ichuro Kimura from the morning paper. I shook a large portion of rye into me to give my brain a fighting edge.

"Don't drink," she said sharply to me. "It's the worst thing for a man in your condition."

"On the contrary," I said, tilting the bottle a second time. The first swallow had settled the nausea in my stomach and sharpened the pain in my head, but the second one went clear to the base of my spine and worked its way into the brain. "I think I can stand to hear your tale of woe now. Tell me about Richard, the weakling."

"Kurt Boylston has wanted to own my grandfather's land for a long time. It's a small ranch, only nine hundred acres, nothing compared to the Boylston spread, but it has the best water. My grandfather worked it as a field hand when he came here from Japan in 1879 and gradually came to own it.

"Boylston has tried everything to get his hands on it. Then, with the internments and the anti-Japanese scare, he saw his chance. He announced that Kimura was a Japanese spy and that his land should be confiscated. Boylston said he would farm it as a service to the government. Of course, in times like these, frightened men will believe anything."

Her husky voice was shaky with passion. I wanted a cigarette very badly but didn't want to send us up in flames lighting it.

"My grandfather would not go. Why should he? He is no spy. And he knew it was only a ruse, a trick by Kurt Boylston to get his land. I'm sure you saw in the paper how he fought the army and then disappeared. I took the title and gave it to Dominick, but I had to tell Richard. And Richard was weak. Kurt must have bought him. I saw—I saw when I got to Dominick's house this morning, how he had been shot, and knew it was Richard, shooting him six times out of fright, then tearing the house up to find the title. After he turned it over to Kurt, the Boylstons drowned him in my grandfather's goldfish pond. I pretended all along to be in love with Kurt, to be supporting him against my grandfather, but after tonight even he will be able to understand."

I wondered if even now she was telling the truth. She sure believed in it, but did I? "Why didn't you tell me this this morning?"

The moonlight caught leopard sparks dancing from her eyes. "I didn't think you'd believe me. A Japanese spy, written up in all the papers? I thought I would get here ahead of you and explain it all to you, but then I saw Richard's body in the pond and knew that Kurt would figure out my true involvement before long. I had—had to go back to his ranch and—" Her voice broke off as she shuddered. "I used my special gifts, that's all, and took the title from his pocket while he slept."

I put one of my gasoline-soaked hands on her soft leopard paw. Why not? She'd told a good tale, she deserved a little applause.

"Bravo. You got your paper back. You don't need me. You want a lift someplace on my way back to L.A.?"

She sucked her breath in again and pulled her hand back. "I do need you. To smuggle my grandfather into the city. The army knows my car, and they know my face. They would stop me, but they won't stop you."

I rubbed the bottle a few times, wondering if her grandfather would pop out of it, a wizened Japanese genie.

"He's been hiding here in an old well, but it's bad for him, bad for his rheumatism, and it's hard for me to sneak him food. And now, he could climb down into the well, but not up, not by himself, but you—you are strong enough for two."

She was the genie in the bottle, or maybe she just had a little witch blood mixed in with the leopard. I found myself walking across the jagged ground to where a well cover lay hidden beneath the sage. I pried it loose according to the enchantress's whispered instructions. She knelt down on the rim and called softly, "It's Akiko, Grandfather. Akiko and a friend who will bring you to Los Angeles."

It wasn't as simple as Miss Moloney thought it would be, driving around to pick up Route Five from the north, but then these things never are. In the first place Kimura wouldn't travel without a little shrine to the Buddha that he'd been keeping in the well with him, and it was a job packing the two of them in the trunk under some old blankets. And in the second place we ran into Kurt and Jay because the only way to Route Five was along the trail that led past the Kimura Place. And in the confusion I put a bullet through Kurt Boylston's head—purely by mistake, as I explained to the sheriff, but Miss Moloney had hired me to look for rustlers on her grandfather's old place and when Kurt had started to shoot at us I didn't know what else to do. The sheriff liked it about as well as a three-day hangover, but he bought it in the end.

What with one thing and another the sun was poking red fingers up over the San Gabriels by the time we coasted past Burbank and into the city.

I dropped Miss Moloney and her grandfather at a little place she owned in Beverly Hills, just ten rooms and a pool in the back. I figured Dominick had been a pretty good friend, all right. Or maybe the Irishman who married her mother—I was willing to keep an open mind.

She invited me in for a drink, but I didn't think gasoline and rye went too well with the neighborhood or the decor, so I just left the two of them to the ministrations of a tearful Japanese maid and lowered myself by degrees through the canyons back to the city. The concrete looked good to me. Even the leftover drunks lying on the park benches looked pretty good. I've never been much of an outdoors man.

When I got to my office I tried the air to see if there was any perfume left, but I couldn't detect it. I wondered what kind of detective I was, anyway. There wasn't anything for me in the office. I didn't know why I'd come here instead of finding my shower and bed—that was the kind of thing I could detect all right.

I put the office bottle back in the drawer and locked it. I put yesterday's paper tidily in the trash can and looked around for a minute. There was a scrap of black on the floor underneath the visitor's chair. I bent over to pick it up. It was a little square of lace, the kind of thing a lady with the poise of a dealer would have tucked in her black bag, the kind of thing even the most sophisticated lady might drop when she was peeling off twenties. It smelled faintly of Chanel. I put it in my breast pocket and locked the door.

The Summer of '37

Julian Semionov

There were three of us left on Spaso-Palikovsky Street then, Vitek, Talka, and I. Mornings we gathered near the sixth entrance, read some bits of *Pionerskaya pravda*, played some potsie or dodge-ball, and then went through the apartment building, to look at the apartments the secret police had sealed up. Every night in our building a few apartments were sealed. Sometimes they were sealed with proper sealing wax, then they used candle wax or modeling clay to seal the doors. We would pick that off carefully to model little soldiers that we dunked in the puddles, so they came out just like tin soldiers.

"I hear they arrested Marshal Budyennyi yesterday," I said, "because he had a Japanese ballerina living at his dacha."

"Where did you hear that?" Talka asked angrily. He hated it when one of us was the first to have the most important news.

"That's what people are saying," I answered evasively, because my mother had strictly forbidden me to talk about what I heard at home. "You're a big boy," she said. "You should know that we have to remain silent now." I asked "Why?" and she began to tell me about the enemies of the people who now, because of our successes, had entirely surrounded the motherland, as if I hadn't read the same thing myself in *Pionerskaya*. My parents had gotten strange in general, ever since my father had begun taking me with him during the day. Before that he used to be driven to his office at the newspaper in a car; he had two gorgeous secretaries there who used to let me type. One of them, Rosa, was incredibly beautiful, and I used to dream that she would become my mother. I always dreamed about a beautiful mother, though I also loved my real mother. Then I rarely saw my father, and now he and I went about the streets together while he pasted up theater posters. One time I got badly shaken. Lately I had been hearing how my father talked quietly to my mother late at night.

"They picked up Krasnoshchekov, and put Kurochkin against the wall."

At first I didn't understand what "against the wall" meant. When we played dodge-ball we also were up against the wall in order to make it easier to throw tennis balls at the loser. But when my father mentioned that our friend Sasha Kurochkin had been "put to the wall," my mother had sighed and asked quietly, "They didn't really shoot Sasha too?"

So "shoot" and "put to the wall" must mean the same thing, I understood. So one Sunday when my father and I were going to Gorky Park on the metro, there was a drunk in our car, wearing ski pants with brown foot straps that he kept getting his heels tangled in. When we were leaving the car at Komintern Station the drunk hit my father on the head.

My father shouted, "Quit that hooliganism! I'm calling the militia!"

A crowd gathered. A militiaman came over and told my father, "Citizen, don't block the way for people. Stand against the wall."

I began to howl with fear, thinking that my father was going to be shot right then. I grabbed his hand and tried to drag him up the stairs, toward the street, where there was sunshine and cars and none of the horrible half-dark of the tiled station. My father's hands got cold and I could see how his knees trembled when the militiaman asked for his passport. Out on the street my father picked me up and hugged me, as though I were a baby. I hugged his neck, which was shaking; that made me ashamed and I was frightened that everyone would notice he was shaking.

. . . Now Vitek drew a new potsie with a big hell and began to jump first. He was a terrific jumper. He could do four-corners and snake and every-other and even eyes-closed. He was the best dodge-ball player too, and never put dirt on the ball when he threw it at someone. He was the only one of us who wouldn't tease girls, and he didn't hide the fact that he was in love with Alka Blat. Alka was awfully serious for her age and knew the whole story about family life. When I told her that the leaders didn't pee-pee, she laughed until tears came.

"Want to know something?" she whispered, coming over to us. "But you have to give your word of honor as an October Scout that you won't tell anyone . . ."

We gave our October Scout word.

"I have learned where children come from," she said. "They are born."

"We know that," Vitek said. "But how?"

"It's easy," Alka Blat said. "You have to hug each other very hard, then kiss."

Talka and I began to laugh derisively, but Vitek went over to Alka and said, "I want you to have a baby for me."

"Happy to," Alka Blat replied.

Vitka hugged her, then kissed her. Talka and I were dumbfounded. Then Talka cleared his throat, leafed through *Pionerskaya*, and said, "I want a baby too."

Alka looked inquiringly at Vitka. Vitka was concentrating on potsie hops and wasn't looking at anyone.

"He's my friend," Talka said convincingly. "He'll let you."

"All right," Vitek sighed, "just be quick."

However, just as soon as Talka hugged Alka Blat and began to take aim for his kiss, Vitek threw his potsie stone, hitting Talka in the leg. Talka began to howl, because the stone had hit a funny bone, so he almost fainted with the pain. Talka hopped around on one leg crying. Alka laughed, then crossed her hands on her middle just like her grandmother and said, "What kind of a man are you, crying like that?! Only us women can stand pain, that's for sure!"

. . . In the evening, after Mama had given me tea with raspberry preserves, I fell asleep immediately. I woke up though because a dog was howling in our apartment. I was surprised at first, because we didn't have a dog, no matter how hard I had begged my parents for one. I dreamed of training one, then sending it to the border, for Comrade Karatsup. Then, however, between the howls, I heard my mother's rapid voice. I decided that my parents had got me a dog as a present, and were bringing a German shepherd in at night. I got out of bed, put on the pretty fur slippers that Nikolai Ivanovich (Bukharin) had brought me from abroad, and crept down to the bathroom, where the dog was howling and my mother was saying softly, "Don't do that, don't, come on, calm down . . . don't, please don't, I beg you . . ."

I opened the door a crack and saw that my father was sitting on a stool and howling, holding his head in long bony hands, while Mama was stroking his face with one hand, with the other clutching Papa's Mauser that was usually locked in the desk.

I went back to my room, leaving the door open a little, and scrunched myself into a ball under the blankets so that I wouldn't shake. Then I saw Mama go to the front door, where she listened for a long time, her ear to the crack. She unlocked the door carefully, went out onto the landing, and knocked at the apartment opposite. That was where Vitka's father lived, Vasya, my father's friend and a friend of the family. I heard their door open, and immediately I wasn't scared anymore. I listened to Mama whispering something to Vasya, but then he interrupted her, to say very loudly:

"Spare me your provocational favors! I'm not going to have any pistols in this house! And if your husband wants to leave this life because he got himself mixed up with enemies of the people, I'm not going to stop him!"

He slammed the door.

Mama came back into the apartment and began to cry. Then Father came out of the bathroom and began to stroke her head. Mama cried very quietly and piteously.

Nodding his head at me, Father said, "If it hadn't been for him, I'd have known what to do."

"Shhh," Mama whispered, "please, shhh . . ."

"I'm sorry for the boy," Father repeated, "otherwise I'd have known what to do."

"Shhh," my mother repeated. "How come you can't talk in a whisper?"

"I would have done what has to be done!" my father suddenly shouted, his voice breaking. "I would have done it!"

"What are you saying?" my mother was horrified. "You want to destroy the baby?"

"I'm not asleep, Mommy," I said in a sleepy voice. "I just woke up."

Mother ran in to me. Her cheeks were wet, but her lips were dry and swollen.

"What does 'leave this life' mean?" I asked carefully. She began to tremble, and then began to rock me. Father got up and laughed cruelly.

"It's a whorehouse, and inside the whorehouse there's another whorehouse."

There was a knock at the door. Mother froze, and I could feel how chill her face became. Father laughed, like he used to laugh before they began sealing up apartments in our building.

"Who is it?" he asked loudly.

"Me," our friend Fedya, Talka's father, answered just as loudly. He was a *chekist*, a commisar of the state security.

Father opened the door. Fedya came into the apartment. He was in full uniform, with gold braid sewn to his jacket.

"Show me the warrant first," my father said.

"Fool," Fedya said. "How is it you're not ashamed of yourself, Semion? Let me take the gun, Galya."

Mother gave him the Mauser, which he put in his pocket.

"You'd better leave immediately," he told my father. "Go to a village somewhere, or camp out, cut some hay maybe . . ."

He sniffed at something, clapped Papa on the shoulder, and left.

. . . The next morning Vitek told me, "My papa told me not to play with you anymore."

"Why?" I was astonished.

"Because you are the son of someone who helped an enemy of the people."

"You're a fool," I said. "My father is Charlie Chaplin's assistant."

(That was the truth. My father had told me himself while we were pasting up notices. I kept badgering him with the question "What are you now, Papa?" All of us in the building, the preschoolers and October Scouts, gave a good deal of weight to the posts that our parents occupied, which was important because it determined the role you got when you played war. So then father told me about Charlie Chaplin.)

Vitek laughed contemptuously. "Don't lie to me. They put Chaplin to the wall a long time ago."

"But he's an artist," I objected.

"So what? Artists get put to the wall too. Anyone can get put against the wall."

Alka Blat came over, her nose red from crying.

"What's wrong?" Vitek asked.

"Talka tattled that I'm going to give you babies."

"That right?" Vitek asked, not looking at anyone.

"No," Talka said. "I didn't tattle to anybody. I just said that we were going to have a baby soon."

"Who did you say it to?"

"My grandma."

Vitek punched Talka sharply in the chest, then kicked him in the butt.

"Get out of here," he said. "I'm not going to play potsie with you anymore."

So three of us began to play potsie alone, while Talka sat near the courtyard entrance on a bench, whimpering but not saying anything, because he was afraid of Vitek.

A green car rolled up to our entrance and three men got out, wearing high-peaked military caps. The driver didn't turn the engine off, so the exhaust pipes sputtered bluish smoke. The sunlight glistened on the well-waxed roof and the nickeled bumpers and the blinding hubcaps that said in red, "Molotov Auto Factory."

The three men in hats went quickly into the entrance. We were amazed; where were they going so early? Talka's father, Fedya the security man, left at twelve, when a car with license plates MA 12-41 came for him. Nobody lived on the sixth floor, because they'd all been arrested; on the fifth there was a trumpeter from the military orchestra, but people said he was "a relative" and tuberculosis besides, and only played the trumpet late at night. Vitka and I lived on the fourth, everyone on three had been arrested, Talka lived on two, and the apartment manager had moved onto one after they had taken away Vinter and his wife, who had turned out to be Japanese spies. They were always throwing us candies when we played potsie or war under their windows. After Nadezhda Konstantinovna Krupskaia came to see them, as a sign of our especial respect, we began to say "Guten abend!" to the Vinters, but we didn't say "Guten abend" for long, because they were soon arrested. The morning after their apartment was sealed up Talka said, "I thought my stomach felt funny."

"So what?" Vitek asked.

"Nothing," Talka sighed. "If you don't get it, think about it for a moment."

We thought about it, but couldn't think of anything.

"Whose candies were we eating?" Talka finally gave us a hint.

"The Vinters," we answered.

"The enemy's," Talka corrected us. "Enemy trotskyite-bukharinist candies."

"Nonsense," Vitek said, after a moment's thought. "The writing on them was Soviet."

"Camouflage," Talka laughed sadly. "Believe me or not, but those candies were obviously poisoned by those damned Vinters."

The three men in hats came out of the entrance with Vitka's father and mother.

"Vitka!" His father Vasya shouted. "Son!"

"My baby boy!" his mother shrieked. "Son, come let me kiss you! Vitka, come give me a kiss!"

"The boy's alone!" Vitek's father shouted, when they put him in the car. "The boy's completely alone! Comrades, can't you understand, the boy's entirely alone!"

The driver stepped on the gas and the car disappeared. Vitek stood rooted to the spot where he stood. Talka winked significantly at me. A window opened on the first floor, and the wife of the building administrator looked us over carefully. Then our window opened and Mama shouted for me.

"Come upstairs immediately!"

"Coming!" I answered.

A window opened in Talka's apartment too.

"Talka, home!" his grandmother shouted. "Quick!"

"Alka!" Grandmother Blat boomed from the fifth entryway. "Home!"

And we all went home. Vitka stayed where he was, standing.

Their apartment was sealed with candle wax. I took a bit off to make a soldier later. The wax was still very warm and workable.

Translated by Anthony Olcott

No Radio

Mickey Friedman

1

"Miranda? Miranda?"

"No. Wrong number." She spoke softly. Her husband was asleep beside her.

"Miranda—"

"My name isn't Miranda. Wrong—"

"Don't hang up," the man said.

Silence.

"Are you still there?"

"Yes."

"Don't hang up. I want to talk to you."

"I told you, I'm not Miranda."

"I made up a name. I dialed some number, I don't even know what number. Are you listening?"

"Yes."

"I want to talk to you."

The digital clock said 2:00 A.M. Her husband hadn't moved. "Just a minute," she said. She muffled the telephone receiver under her pillow, and walked through the dark apartment to the extension in the kitchen.

That was her introduction to Jaime.

2

Jaime glanced at his watch as she walked toward him across the atrium at the Winter Garden. Cold, early-spring light off the Hudson filled the soaring room. She wore dark glasses, jeans, a black leather jacket, high heels. "I haven't got all day to wait for you," he said.

"I had trouble getting out." She glanced around at the tourist-filled tables. "I don't even know why I came."

"Sure you do, Miranda." Jaime wore tortoise-shell glasses, a gray pinstripe suit.

"My name isn't Miranda." She pulled a cigarette out of her bag. "He asked where I was going, and everything." Jaime made no move to light the cigarette. She took out a book of matches and lit it herself, with shaking hands.

Jaime suppressed a yawn. "You're not quite what I expected."

Her eyes were invisible behind the glasses. "Yeah."

"So you had trouble getting out? What did you tell him?"

"To go fuck himself." The smoke dispersed in whorls, weaving in and out of the beams of light.

Jaime checked his watch again. "Let's go."

Later, in the room, she pressed her clenched fist to her mouth. Tears slid out of her eyes and moistened the crumpled, anonymous pillow. "I hate you," she said.

Jaime picked up his watch from the bedside table. "I've got a meeting in half an hour."

"No, you don't."

3

She came out of an apartment building on Fifth Avenue, not far from the Metropolitan Museum. Her heels made sharp, determined *tac*s on the sidewalk. She crossed the street, gazing uptown as if searching for a taxi. She wore a navy blue suit, and carried a leather portfolio under her arm.

Jaime was sitting on one of the benches next to Central Park. "Hey, Miranda," he said.

Tac tac tac.

"Miranda."

She stopped. "Oh, Jesus," she said.

Jaime grinned at her, his arms folded across his chest. He wore a cerise tank top, sweatpants, running shoes. "How are you, Miranda?"

She glanced at her watch. "Late."

He patted the bench beside him. "Sit down for a minute."

She shook her head. "Are you crazy?" She glanced across the street. "The doorman is watching."

"Come on, babe. I've missed you." Jaime's hand, lying on his upper thigh, moved suggestively.

She laughed. "Don't be ridiculous. I've got a meeting in half an hour."

Jaime pouted. "I've been waiting a long time."

"You're pathetic." She glanced up the avenue again. A free cab was approaching. She walked to the curb and signaled.

As the taxi slid to a stop, Jaime bounded across the pavement to open the door for her. He gave a mocking bow as she stepped inside, then got in after her.

4

"It's my father. He watches every move I make," she said.

"You're pathetic," said Jaime.

They were having afternoon tea at a midtown hotel. The room was filled with enormous bouquets of flowers: yawning lilies, spidery chrysanthemums, drooping mimosa. "He would never approve of you," she said. She wore pearl earrings, and a high-necked white dress with insets of lace.

"So what?" Jaime dug into the pocket of his denim jacket and brought out a package of cigarettes and a lighter.

She coughed when he lit up. "I'm allergic to smoke."

He leaned back on the peach-colored banquette. "Get to the point, Miranda."

"I'm not a little girl anymore."

"Sure you are."

She winced. "Why are you so cruel?"

He sipped tea. "So your father watches your every move, eh?"

"Yes." She looked over her shoulder. "He's probably got somebody watching now."

Jaime glanced around languidly, incuriously. He inhaled his cigarette, pressing his hand over his mouth like a gag. "He has a lot of money, your old man?"

"Of course he does, stupid."

In the room, she pressed against him. "I've been waiting a long time," she said.

Jaime felt her throat pulsing under his lips. You're pathetic.

5

She was already dancing when Jaime arrived, but she caught sight of him and waved across the bobbing heads. The lights were dim, the noise was outrageously loud. Jaime wore a navy blue sport coat, white shirt, striped tie. He pinched the bridge of his nose and ordered a mineral water at the bar. When she joined him, her hair drenched, droplets of sweat dampening her metallic halter, he said, "Am I supposed to pay for your time tonight?"

She laughed a silly, dazed laugh.

"Whore," he said.

Standing next to him, close, she brushed her hand across the front of his trousers.

"Why are you so cruel?" he said tonelessly.

"My husband has a lot of money." She leaned against him. "Give me a cigarette."

"I'm allergic to smoke."

The bartender gave her a cigarette. She smoked without speaking, moving to the beat of the music. Jaime leaned over his mineral water, his eyes fixed on the pulpy lime slice floating in it. "What's next?" he said.

"Who cares?"

"Priest? Nun? Cop? Nurse?"

"It's boring. Stupid and boring."

Jaime pushed himself upright. "Let's go, then."

She shook her head. "I'm not going. I want to stay here."

"No, you don't." He took her arm and dragged her through the crowd. She writhed and fought, but nobody seemed to notice.

6

The car was a white Chevrolet with a "No Radio" sign in a side window. It was six o'clock, time for the alternate-side-of-the-street parking to change over. Other people, as well as the three men in the white Chevrolet, were sitting in their cars, all apparently waiting for the legal hour.

She approached, wearing jeans and a baggy T-shirt, carrying a canvas gym bag. Her hair was wet, combed back. One of the men got out of the car and spoke to her briefly. She shook her head and tried to walk past him, but he blocked her way. She strode to the car and bent down to look in the window. The man in the backseat opened the door, and the man on the sidewalk may have pushed her in, although she did not really struggle.

As they drove away she said to Jaime, in the backseat, "This is as stupid as the rest."

Jaime also wore a T-shirt and jeans. "Hello, Miranda," he said.

"Don't call me that."

Jaime crossed his arms and settled against the seat. She gestured at the two men in the front. "Who are they?"

"Kidnappers," Jaime said. He laughed. "Do you like this one?"

Looking out the window, her head turned away from him, she didn't answer. The city rushed by. The "No Radio" sign was dog-eared, the tape that held it to the glass yellowed. "Maybe," she said at last.

7

They drove across the Brooklyn Bridge, and soon were in a maze of streets she had never seen before. She had been pale at first, but now her cheeks were flushed. She ran her fingers through her hair and watched the unfamiliar streets glide across the window.

"How much longer?" she asked.

Jaime caressed her shoulder blades. "Not much."

"Good." She leaned back. Her eyes were bright.

They stopped at a yellow-brick low-rise apartment building. Laundry hung on some of its balconies. They parked in a small, weedy lot in the rear, and the two men in the front seat got out. The driver tossed the car keys to Jaime. They walked away without a word.

"Goodbye," she called after them.

"Come on," Jaime said. He pulled her up the fire escape to a third-floor window that was cracked at the bottom. He pushed the window up and they climbed in.

They were in a bedroom. Yellowish light filtered through open-weave curtains. Twin beds with plaid bedspreads stood against opposite walls. She put down her gym bag and sat on one of the beds. "So I'm the victim," she said.

"That's right." He sat beside her, pulling her backward.

8

When she woke up, he was rehearsing the telephone call. The bedroom door was half open. He was mumbling, as if he were reading aloud.

She put on her jeans and shirt. The air in the room was stuffy. She could hear, an undercurrent beneath Jaime's voice, the rush and whine of traffic outside. She picked up her bag. "If you want to see her alive again—" Jaime was mumbling.

She walked into the living room, which was bare except for a sagging sofa, a console television set, and a dinette table where Jaime sat, the phone by his elbow still on the hook, reading words written on a piece of lined yellow paper. He glanced up at her. "He should be worried by now, right?"

"Very."

"How much will he give for you, Miranda?"

She lifted her shoulders. "Don't you have an amount in mind?"

Jaime's hands were shaking, the yellow paper vibrating in the harsh ceiling light. "Screw this," he said.

She laughed. "Go on, call. Be a sport."

She sat on the arm of the sofa, her bag in her lap, and waited while he made the call. He read the words from the sheet, then listened for a few seconds. "No, you can't," he said. "You'll talk to her when I get the money." She played with the zipper on her bag, which made a faint whir as she zipped it back and forth.

Jaime hung up. Neither of them spoke for a minute. He dropped the paper on the table and ran a hand through his hair. He said, "He didn't sound so old."

"I never said he was old."

"I thought he was some old rich guy."

The zipper made its rhythmic rasp. "I never said he was old. He isn't old."

"He was upset. I couldn't tell for sure."

She unzipped the gym bag, reached in, and brought out a revolver. Jaime blinked, or almost blinked, and she shot him. He didn't try to say anything, but buckled and tumbled to the floor.

She picked up the car keys from the table. "I don't go around unprotected, you fool," she said.

9

Downstairs in the parking lot, she unlocked the car with the "No Radio" sign. She put the key in the ignition, started the engine, drove out into the unfamiliar streets. A few blocks away, she pulled into the parking lot of a McDonald's and looked in the glove compartment for a map. There wasn't one. She felt under the front seat. No map, but she found the disconnected car radio. She spent a moment or two reconnecting it and turned it on, loud, before she started off again.

10

Back in Manhattan, she left the car in a No Parking zone and walked the rest of the way. As she put her key in the apartment door she heard footsteps on the other side. When she opened the door, her husband stood there. "Welcome home. Welcome home, Miranda," her husband said.

Mafia Western

Leonardo Sciascia

A big town, almost the size of a city, on the border between the provinces of Palermo and Trapani. The First World War is in progress. And, as if that were not enough, there is another, internal one being waged: no less bloody, with a death-toll from assassination comparable to the death-toll of its citizens falling at the Front. Two Mafia cells are engaged in a long-standing feud. A monthly average of two deaths. And every time, everyone knows whose hand was on the trigger and who will answer for it with his life. Even the carabinieri know. It's almost a game, played by the rules of a game. Young mafiosi avid for promotion on the one side, old mafiosi defending their positions on the other. The death of a henchman from one faction is followed by the death of a henchman from the other. The leaders are unruffled: they are awaiting negotiations. Possibly, when peace has been restored, one of the leaders, the old one or the young one, will die in the internecine maelstrom of friendship.

But now something strange happens: the feud intensifies, involving ever higher ranks in the hierarchy. In the normal course of events, this is a sign that the side promoting the violence wants peace. This is the moment when the patriarchs bestir themselves from their neighboring villages and come into town to interview both factions, to unite them, to convince the young ones that they can't have everything and

110

the old ones that they can't keep it all to themselves. There is an armistice, a treaty. And, when the reunification has been accomplished, one of the leaders will be eliminated by emigration, superannuation or death. But this time is different. The patriarchs arrive, delegations of the two factions meet, but meanwhile, contrary to custom and expectation, the rhythm of the executions continues unabated, becomes, indeed, even more frenetic, more implacable. Each faction, in the presence of the patriarchs, accuses the other of treachery. The town can make neither head nor tail of what is happening. Nor can the carabinieri. By great good fortune, the patriarchs are men of cool, clear judgment. They bring the two delegations together again, present them with a list of all those who have been assassinated over the past six months and from the resultant dialogue—"This one we killed," "This was ours," "This was nothing to do with us," "Nor with us,"—arrive at the disconcerting conclusion that two thirds of the deaths can be attributed to neither side and must therefore be the work of an outsider. Can it be that there is a third cell, secret and invisible, dedicated to the extermination of both the quasi-official ones? Or is there some avenger working on his own, a lone wolf, a madman making a hobby of slaying mafiosi on both sides? The consternation is great. Even among the carabinieri, who, although they have been collecting the corpses with a certain degree of satisfaction (the bullets having nailed criminals where convictions had failed), have nevertheless got to the point, their hands already full with the problem of deserters, where they would like to see an end to this civic feud.

The patriarchs, having put their finger accurately on the problem, left it up to the two cells to resolve it as quickly as possible. They then made themselves scarce, because in the circumstances, neither of the two factions, nor both acting collectively, was in a position to guarantee them safe conduct. The mafiosi of the town began to make their own investigations; but fear, the sense of being the objects of an inscrutable vendetta or homicidal whim, and finding themselves suddenly in exactly the same position in which they themselves had placed honest people for so long, left them bewildered and robbed of much of their will to act. They were reduced to imploring their political members in their turn to implore the carabinieri to mount a real, thorough-going and efficient investigation—even though they suspected that the carabinieri themselves, having failed to smoke them out by legal methods, might have resorted to this shadier, more secure one. After all, if the government could arrange for a cholera epidemic every now and then to solve the problem of over-population, why should one not suppose that the carabinieri might adopt this secret method of extermination against the Mafia?

The hunt for the unknown man, or men, goes on. The leader, or *capo*, of the older Mafia faction also falls a victim. There is a sense of liberation throughout the town as well as of alarm. The carabinieri are completely nonplussed. The mafiosi are terrified. But immediately after the funeral of the old *capo* (attended by the entire town with a great show of assumed grief), the mafiosi cease to give the impression of being bewildered and frightened. The conviction spreads that they know the identity of the assassin and that his days are numbered. A *capo* is a *capo* even in death, and somehow, as the old man lay dying, he managed to convey some hint, to point the finger in some way. And his friends have now succeeded in identifying the assassin. He is a man whom no one would ever have suspected, a professional man of good character and well respected; though of a somewhat taciturn disposition and given to a solitary life-style, there is no one in the entire town (apart from the mafiosi, who know) who would ever have dreamed that he was capable of conducting that long drawn out, pitiless and deadly vendetta that had already consigned to the autopsy-bench a fair number of those men that the carabinieri had never succeeded in holding for more than a few hours. And the mafiosi had also remembered why, after so many years, this man's hatred of them should have issued with such cold and deadly calculation in this series of executions. There was, needless to say, a woman involved.

Since his student days, he had been romantically attached to a girl who came from a doubtfully noble, but certainly wealthy family. After graduating, he approached her family with the confidence inspired by the strength of their mutual feelings, and formally asked for her hand. He was rejected; because he was poor and because his professional future, given the poverty of his origins, was insecure. But he and the girl continued to see each other, and the feeling between them became even more profound by reason of the difficulties that lay ahead. So the noble and wealthy relatives of the girl appealed to the Mafia for assistance. The *capo*, the old and much feared *capo*, summoned the young man and attempted, with much quoting of proverb and precept, to persuade him to give up the girl. When this failed, he had recourse to open threats. The young man shrugged it off, but the impression made upon the girl was dire. Fearing that the terrible threats would be carried out, and perhaps finally convinced that their love was in any case impossible, she hastily married one of her own set. The young man became gloomy and withdrawn but showed no signs of being desperate or even excessively angry. Evidently, he began to plot his revenge from that moment.

Now the Mafia had discovered his identity and he was a marked man. The sentence was to be executed by the son of the dead *capo*: his was the right, by virtue of his bereavement and the rank held by his late father. The habits of the condemned man, the topography of the district in which he lived and that of the house itself, were studied carefully. The point was overlooked, however, that by now everyone had realized that the Mafia knew: their habitual arrogance had returned and their fear of the unknown danger had obviously vanished. And the very first person to realize all this had been the condemned man himself.

The youthful avenger slipped out of his house one night with the viaticum of the maternal blessing, and made his way to the house of the pharmacist, which was quite close by. There he hid himself to await the other man's return; or he tried to enter the house in order to surprise the man as he slept; or he knocked, expecting him to come to this window or to step on to that balcony. All that is certain is that his intended victim had anticipated him and now turned the tables upon him. The widow of the *capo* and mother of the young man heard a shot. Imagining the vendetta safely accomplished, she awaited her son's return with an anxious heart that became ever more alarmed as the minutes ticked away. At last, the appalling truth dawned upon her. She went out and found her son lying dead outside the house of the man who, according to all the plans and the promises, should have died that night. She picked up the body, carried it home and laid it upon the bed. The next morning she let it be known that her son had died of a wound there upon his bed, but that she knew neither where nor by whom he had been wounded. No word did she utter to the carabinieri about the man who might have killed him. But her friends understood—they knew—and they now set about very careful preparations.

Towards the end of a summer's day, when the piazza was filled with people enjoying the first cool evening breezes seated outside their clubs, cafés and shops (and the man who had eluded the Mafia's revenge was also there, sitting in front of the chemist's shop), a man tried to start up his car. He swung the starting handle and the engine burst into life with a violent grinding of metal parts and a volley of crackles that sounded like machine-gun fire. When the noise had died away, there, sprawled upon a chair in front of the chemist's shop, his heart pierced by a rifle bullet, lay the body of the man who had succeeded in sowing death and fear among the ranks of one of the most battle-hardened Mafia cells in the whole of Sicily.

Translated by Avril Bardoni

Manufacture of a Legend

Paco Ignacio Taibo II

This dude with his face all eaten up by smallpox or something walks up to you and says:

"You the *Mister* with the funny name? You M. Limas. Ain't that so? M. Limas, lick my dick, *que nombre más pendejo.*"

You almost killed him right there, stuck a blade between his ribs but the knife busted off at the point. Hell, you thought, the motherfucker's gone and ruined a good blade, but then once you got to thinking about it, maybe not, maybe now it was better than before, whoever got that busted-off knife shoved in his face from now on would be able to see right off it'd been used before, busted off on bone, like the sword of some rookie matador.

You were a real mean somebitch, Rolando, no doubt about it, nickel 'n' diming it in third-rate bars full of whores, where even the lottery ticket sellers wouldn't go, sleeping on top of your own puke from one day to the next and with the same goddam case of syphilis that no matter how much penicillin you pumped into your veins always came back like a Gypsy curse. But all that somebitchedness wasn't any more real to you than a dream, one day you'd be selling weed in Acapulco, the next day passing stolen cars in McAllen, Texas, one day drunk off your ass in Matamoros, and the next tying it on with a bad-ass pair of *judiciales* in TJ.

You knew all along it was just part of your apprenticeship, you had your eye on the big money and you knew once you got it all down real good you were gonna reap what you had sown. When was it, Rolando, those big fat cows let you milk them for the first time? When was it the almighty decided to give out the word: "Lay off that somebitch some and let him go on and make that stash of green he's been waiting for, with all this shit he's had to swallow for so long." I guess it all started when you got in good with the Chihuahua boys and they put you in charge of rustling up hookers for the peons on the poppy harvest. They had about 200 grunts up there in the hills working for them like slaves in Egypt long before Moses ever made prince. They had them up there two months running so they'd bring in a bunch of whores to do double duty as cooks and washerwomen when they weren't flat on their backs. You brought in those sweet mommas from the Jalisco hill country, emptying out maybe half a dozen whorehouses and loading all the girls onto a flatbed truck. I guess it must have started back then because when the army came in and busted the whole thing up, the only somebitch knew where the airstrip and the warehouse was was you, and you had the smarts to go sell it all to Milton for 50 thousand bucks.

That was only the beginning. A year later you were the same dude, Rolando, only with money like leaves on the trees. And when it came time to pick the Spring Festival Queen in Ciudad Obregón you made up your mind that this one was yours and you sent the boys out to sell tickets at a thousand pesos a piece. They'd lay their iron on the counter top and start in with the sales pitch: "That Enriqueta sure is a good looker, isn't she, boss, I just knew you'd want to buy ten of these here tickets . . ." In the end Enriqueta won the elections fair and square, with every vote counted and no dirty tricks. Not like this shit the government tries to pull all the time.

After a while the right sort of people started to sit up and take notice and they called you in. And you, Rolando, you played it smart like you always did, none of this crap of walking in in a Day-Glo red sport coat, flashing your .45 and a whole gang of bodyguards sweeping the dust off your boottops. What you had going for you was know-how, high tech all the way, man. You were fast on your way to being the baddest dude on the border. You were going to get all the queers south of the Río Bravo to walk across the line with 200 grams of coke stuck up their ass, wrapped in plastic so they wouldn't blow it all with one fart and get a free trip out of it, flying high on their ass. Your operation was going to be so big that all those motherfuckers in L.A. were going to get crazy from smoking so much of your weed. After all, you were the same somebitch who went and got a degree in public accounting at the University of Mexico before he ever started crawling around all those low-down bars and stinking whorehouses. And before long that same somebitch was going to be sitting at the table with bankers and governors.

When do you sleep, Rolando? 'Cause in the last few years you spend all your time doing *biznis* and fucking and hustling and dressing up in your gringo clothes or learning shit from this junkie grade school teacher who gives you classes in geography and English when he isn't shooting up, who you've got to handcuff to the foot of the bed at night to make him stay put, quizzing you on what's the capital of Malaysia, how many pesos to the pound sterling, how to say racehorse in English. Everybody knows the most you ever do at night is rest, but you never sleep, Rolando. It's been two years now since you had any sleep. Two years. And that's the most important thing of all. Here on the border, shit-ass full of bad dudes who have to sleep sometime, there's one somebitch, the somebitch of all the somebitches, Rolando M. Limas, born in Toluca, who never ever goes to sleep.

It's too much, it knocks a normal man off his stride, shrivels up his balls to have to do *biznis* with some somebitch never closes his eyes. A dude who doesn't know what sleep means. A dude who you know, when you're just about to drift off and catch a few z's laying in bed and stroking up against your old lady, that he's out there somewhere in the middle of the night walking around like a vampire, his eyes wide open. Watching.

You were only one guy before, but now you're someone else, a bunch of someone elses, on the road to becoming one of the all-time dark legends of Mexico. Was a time when you could have laundered your dough and gone straight. Set up a legal racket, started in stealing from inside the law like any honest man. But that's not your style. Better to make a million bucks in a single week with three truckloads of dope and waste half of it buying blind men, the blindest men in the world, guys who can't see a truck driving by in front of their face because they've got that 20 thousand peso blindfold over their eyes. Better that than running a dairy farm in Coahuila.

You've had to go through some changes to stay in shape. You used to be the dude that didn't sleep, now you're the dude who isn't even there, the fucking invisible man, the dude who goes in through the door and then isn't anywhere inside, the dude who never left because he never arrived. You're like one of those sixteen-wheelers driving across the border and not even kicking up the dust because it doesn't even exist.

They say you changed your face, they say you got rid of the scar on your chin from when they cut you with that Tecate can in Hermosillo, that you dyed your hair, that you've got sunglasses for eyeballs that change color when you walk through the neon cities at night. Word on the street is you change your face once a week, that you keep a plastic surgeon waiting in the back of a limousine and that the dude doesn't do nothing but face jobs for you and you only.

You've got a house on the beach in Tecate, but the furniture's all covered with sheets and the sheets are covered with dust an inch thick. You've got a house in Mexico City that doesn't even have any furniture in it. Those're the houses of the dude that doesn't exist. You've only got them so the cops who say they're out looking for you will have something to do. The man pays them to hunt you down, you pay them to watch over your houses where you never go. It's a square deal and everybody wins. They work hard and get paid double for it besides.

You built a hospital for the honorable, heroic, honest dirt-poor families of El Rosario in Toluca. So they could get sick in style. Except that someone forgot to hire the doctors. I guess you forgot too. Now the dogs go there to piss and howl in the night and teenage sweethearts fuck on the cold floors. It isn't just that you never sleep and don't have no face, you've got ghost hospitals and abandoned houses too.

But you're still the same old somebitch Rolando. You watch, you see, you stay on top. Like a vulture flying over the borderline, checking in on every deal, on your hidden labs reeking of sulfuric acid, all the little fields in the middle of the sierra where your men come to plant and harvest in phantom trucks. You're always there, a ghost floating in the air, the million-dollar skydiver. You're only twenty-seven years old and there's already been a *corrido* written about you, a song the Mexicali radio stations aren't allowed to play. But every now and then, in the middle of some hot Tijuana night, a mariachi band shows up in one of the plazas, hired by nobody knows who, playing "El

Corrido de la Mota," a wailing druggy-drag northern Mexico blues, and without anyone having to say a word, without even a whisper, everyone knows you're around there somewhere, listening to your song, each note from the out-of-tune trumpets, unsleeping, wearing another man's face.

They say that after the shootout on the highway you disappeared, took off North to have a word with the *Mister Bigs*, make them sweat a little to get a look at the somest somebitch on the border. But around here we know better, because that *corrido* keeps on getting played in the plazas around Juárez and Reynosa, and just the other day the bells rang for half an hour in the cathedral in Hermosillo because somebody left the priest a million pesos in the sacristy.

These days you're not just the dude who never sleeps, you're not just the invisible man, you're totally immune, there ain't nobody can touch you, man. The word in Juarez is you were driving the third rig yourself, the one that ran up against Aguilar's rat *judiciales*, the ones that sold you out after you'd bought them off fair and square, but the bullets bounced off you. You were the invisible man at the wheel of a big rig the bullets passed right by, a rig that didn't even stir up the dust by the side of the road, running down phantom dogs that didn't even howl when they died. Leaning on that air horn like a ship moving through the fog.

What they say is that before someone cut off Aguilar's hands with a machete he emptied the barrel of his .45 into your belly and put the last bullet through your face, same way you'd kill a ghost, five bullets in the belly and one in the face, and all you did was stand there and laugh at him. Pretty funny, I guess. Now he's walking around with no hands and you've gone and changed your face again so only the whores in the crummiest Ensenada fuckhouses know who you are, because they can smell you coming.

Now you're the dude that fucks the whores and the queers and leaves the rubbers at home, no AIDS ever gonna touch you, man, you blow five lines of coke and never feel a thing, you're the dude goes into the Caballo Bar in Ciudad Obregón or the Lobo in Mexicali and tells all the meanest motherfuckers you'll pay his weight in gold to the man with balls enough to off you, but they all just kind of sit tight with a cramp in their asses looking for the signs, like to see if you're not the one-handed dude they've heard about (round here they say someone cut your hand off and nailed it to a door), or to see if they can't spot that old scar on your chin that your face changer never 100% erased because you like to show it off so much, or to see if your name might just not happen to be Rolando M. Limas. And even though none of them is ever completely sure, they don't never have the guts to ask you for your *biznis* card and find out. They all just sit and squirm for a while and you go out looking for action somewhere else.

The dogs and the chickens run away when they see you and even the cats, that haven't never been afraid of nothing, slink into the alleys when you walk by. Same as the *judiciales* when your trucks ride the line.

Some of these assholes say you're bored of living, that's why you go around looking for someone to kill you. But no one's got balls enough to do you the favor.

What I think is that you went up North to do a little *biznis* with the asshole gringos. To give them a few lessons, an education, Balls and Dope 101: how to live without sleeping, how to wear a different face every day, how to walk so the bullets don't see you.

And if you never come back, brother . . .

We'll still be here, the last of the real dudes, the shitkickers, the baddest motherfuckers ever was and ever will be, we're just going to sit right here, keeping on, watching over the border for you while you're away, just like if it was our own little baby girl, our own *mamacita santa*, making sure and watching out that no one comes along to take away the line and leave us out of a job.

Us dudes, man, the meanest, the motherfuckingest, the assholest of them all, we kiss your shadow, man, Rolando M. Limas.

Translated by William I. Neuman

The King

Isaac Babel

When the wedding ceremony was over, the Rabbi sat for a while in an armchair. Then, going outside, he viewed the tables arrayed all down the courtyard. There were so many of them that those right at the end even poked out into Hospital Street. Velvet-spread, they wound their way down the yard like so many serpents with variegated patches on their bellies, and they sang full-throatedly, those patches of velvet, orange and red.

The living quarters had been turned into kitchens. A sultry flame beat through the soot-swathed doorways, a flame drunken and puffy-lipped. The faces of the old crones broiled in its smoky rays—old women's tremulous chins and beslobbered bosoms. Sweat with the pinkness of fresh blood, sweat as pink as the slaver of a mad dog, streamed this way and that over those mounds of exorbitant and sweetly pungent flesh. Not counting the dishwashers, three old cooks were preparing the wedding feast, and supreme over all the cooks and dishwashers reigned the octogenarian Reisl, tiny and humpbacked, as patinated with tradition as a roll of the Torah.

Before the feast began a young man unknown to the guests made his dim and elusive way into the yard. Wanted a word with Benya Krik. Led Benya Krik unobtrusively aside.

"Listen here, King," said the young man. "A word in your ear. I'm from Aunt Hannah in Kostetskaya Street."

"Right," said Benya Krik, alias The King. "Out with it."

"Aunt Hannah told me to tell you that there's a new police captain down at the station."

"Knew that much day before yesterday," said Benya Krik. "Go on."

"The captain's gone and gathered the whole lot together and speechified."

"New brooms," said Benya Krik. "He's planning a raid. Go on."

"Suppose you know, King, when the raid will be."

"It's scheduled for tomorrow."

"For today, King."

"Who said so, young man?"

"Aunt Hannah. You know Aunt Hannah?"

"I do. Go on."

"The captain, I say, assembled all his men and made a speech. We must settle Benya Krik's hash, he said, seeing that where there's an emperor there's no room for a king. Today, when Krik's sister's getting married and they'll all be together, is just the day. We can nab the lot."

"Go on."

"Well, the cops began to worry. If we raid 'em today, they said, on a day when Krik is celebrating, he'll see red, and then blood will flow. So the captain said, Duty before everything."

"Right. Off you go," said the King.

"What shall I tell Aunt Hannah?"

"Tell her: Benya knows all about the raid."

And so the young man departed. After him went three of Benya's pals. Said they'd be back in half an hour. And so they were.

Not according to their years did the wedding guests take their seats. Foolish old age is no less pitiable than timorous youth. Nor according to their wealth. Heavy purses are lined with tears.

In the place of honor sat the bride and groom. Today was their day. In the next place sat Zender Eichbaum, father-in-law of the King. Such was his right. One should know the story of Zender Eichbaum, for it is no ordinary story.

How had Benya Krik, gangster and king of gangsters, become Eichbaum's son-in-law? Become son-in-law of a man who owned sixty milk cows, all save one? The answer lay in a raid. About a year before, Benya had written Eichbaum a letter.

"Monsieur Eichbaum," he had written, "have the goodness to deposit, tomorrow morning, in the entrance to No. 17 Sofievskaya Street, the sum of twenty thousand roubles. If you fail to comply with this request, something unheard of will happen to you, and you will be the talk of Odessa. Yours respectfully, Benya the King."

Three letters, each one more to the point than the preceding, had remained unanswered. Then Benya took steps. They came in the night, nine of them, bearing long poles in their hands. The poles were wrapped about with pitch-dipped tow. Nine flaming stars flared in Eichbaum's cattle yard. Benya beat the locks from the door of the cowshed and began to lead the cows out one by one. Each was received by a lad with a knife. He would overturn the cow with one blow of the fist and plunge his knife into her heart. On the blood-flooded ground the torches bloomed like roses of fire. Shots rang out. With these shots Benya scared away the dairymaids who had come hurrying to the cowshed. After him other bandits began firing in the air. (If you don't fire in the air you may kill someone.) And now, when the sixth cow had fallen, mooing her death-moo, at the feet of the King, into the courtyard in his underclothes galloped Eichbaum, asking:

"What good will this do you, Benya?"

"If I don't have my money, Monsieur Eichbaum, you won't have your cows. It's as simple as that."

"Come indoors, Benya."

And indoors they came to terms. The slaughtered cows were divided fairly between them, and Eichbaum was guaranteed the integrity of his possessions, even receiving a written pledge with affixed seal. But the wonder came later.

During the raid, on that dreadful night when cows bellowed as they were slaughtered and calves slipped and slithered in the blood of their dams, when the torch-flames danced like dark-visaged maidens and the farm-women lunged back in horror from the muzzles of amiable Brownings—on that dread night there ran out into the yard wearing nought save her V-necked shift, Tsilya the daughter of old man Eichbaum. And the victory of the King was turned to defeat.

Two days later, without warning, Benya returned to Eichbaum all the money he had taken from him, and then one evening he paid the old man a social call. He wore an orange suit, beneath his cuff gleamed a bracelet set with diamonds. He walked into the room, bowed politely, and asked Eichbaum for his daughter's hand. The old man had a slight stroke, but recovered. He was good for another twenty years.

"Listen, Eichbaum," said the King. "When you die I will bury you in the First Jewish Cemetery, right by the entrance. I will raise you, Eichbaum, a monument of pink marble. I will make you an Elder of the Brody Synagogue. I will give up my own business and enter yours as a partner. Two hundred cows we will have, Eichbaum. I will kill all the other cow-keepers. No thief will walk the street you live in. I will build you a villa where the streetcar line ends. Remember, Eichbaum, *you* were no Rabbi in your young days. People have forged wills, but why talk about it? And the King shall be your son-in-law—no milksop, but the King."

And Benya Krik had his way, for he was passionate, and passion rules the universe. The newlyweds spent three months on the fat lands of Bessarabia, three months flooded with grapes, rich food, and the sweat of love's encounters. Then Benya returned to Odessa to marry off his sister Deborah, a virgin of forty summers who suffered from goiter. And now, having told the story of Zender Eichbaum, let us return to the marriage of Deborah Krik, sister of the King.

At the wedding feast they served turkey, roast chicken, goose, stuffed fish, fish-soup in which lakes of lemon gleamed nacreously. Over the heads of defunct geese, flowers swayed like luxuriant plumages. But does the foamy surge of the Odessa sea cast roast chicken on the shore?

All that is noblest in our smuggled goods, everything for which the land is famed from end to end, did, on that starry, that deep-blue night, its entrancing and disruptive work. Wines not from these parts warmed stomachs, made legs faint sweetly, bemused brains, evoked belches that rang out sonorous as trumpets summoning to battle. The Negro cook from the *Plutarch*, that had put in three days before from Port Said, bore unseen through the customs fat-bellied jars of Jamaica rum, oily Madeira, cigars from the plantations of Pierpont Morgan, and oranges from the environs of Jerusalem. That is what the foaming surge of the Odessa sea bears to the shore, that is what sometimes comes the way of Odessa beggars at Jewish weddings. Jamaica rum came their way at the wedding of Deborah Krik. And so, having sucked their fill like infidel swine, the Jewish beggars began to beat the ground deafeningly with their crutches. Eichbaum, his waistcoat unbuttoned, scanned with puckered eyes the tumultuous gathering, hiccuping lovingly the while. The orchestra played a fanfare. It was just like a divisional parade: a fanfare—nothing but. The gangsters, sitting in compact rows, were at first excessively embarrassed by the presence of outsiders. Later they loosened up. Lyova Rooski cracked a bottle of vodka on the head of his beloved, Monya Gunner fired a shot in the air. The rejoicings reached their pitch when, in accordance with the custom of olden times, the guests began bestowing their wedding presents. One shammes from the synagogue after another leaped on a table and there, to the stormy wailing of the fanfare, sang out how many roubles had been presented, how many silver spoons. And now the friends of the King showed what blue blood meant, and the chivalry, not yet extinct, of the Moldavanka district. On the silver trays, with ineffably nonchalant movements of the hand, they cast golden coins, rings, and threaded coral.

Aristocrats of the Moldavanka, they were tightly encased in raspberry waistcoats. Russet jackets clasped their shoulders and on their fleshy feet the azure leather cracked. Rising to their full height and thrusting out their bellies, they beat their palms in time with the music. With the traditional cry of "Bitter, bitter!" they called on the married couple to kiss, and showered the bride in blossoms. And she, Deborah of forty summers, sister of Benya Krik, distorted by her illness, with her swollen crop and her eyes bulging from their orbits, sat on a pile of cushions side by side with the feeble youth, now mute with misery, whom Eichbaum's money had purchased.

The bestowal of gifts was drawing to a close, one shammes after another was growing hoarse and croaky, and the double bass was at cross purposes with the fiddle. Over the courtyard there suddenly spread a faint smell of burning.

"Benya," said Papa Krik, famed among his fellow-draymen as a bully, "Benya, d'you know what I think? I think our chimney's on fire."

"Papa," said Benya to his inebriated parent, "eat and drink, and don't let such trifles bother you."

And Papa Krik took the filial advice. Drink and eat he did. But the smoke cloud grew more and more pungent. Here and there the edges of the sky were turning pink, and now there shot up, narrow as a sword blade, a tongue of flame. The guests, half rising from their seats, began to snuffle the air, and the womenfolk gave little squeaks of fear. The gangsters eyed one another. And only Benya Krik, aware of nothing, was disconsolate.

"The celebration's going all to pieces," he cried, filled with despair. "Good friends, I beg you, eat and drink!"

But now there appeared in the courtyard the same young man who had come earlier in the evening.

"King," he said, "I'd like a word in your ear."

"Out with it, then," said the King. "I've always a spare ear for a spare word."

"King," said the unknown young man, and giggled. "It's really comical: the police station's blazing like a house on fire!"

The shopkeepers were silent. The gangsters grinned. The sexagenarian Manka, ancestress of the suburban bandits, placed two fingers in her mouth and whistled so piercingly that her neighbors jerked away in fright.

"You're not on the job, Manka," observed Benya. "More *sang-frwa!*"

The young man who had brought these astounding tidings was still doubled up with laughter. He was chortling like a schoolgirl.

"They came out of the station, forty of them," he related, vigorously moving his jaws, "all set for the raid, and they hadn't hardly gone fifty yards when the whole place was on fire. Why don't you folks drop around and watch it burn?"

But Benya forbade his guests to go and view the conflagration. He set out himself with two comrades. The station was blazing away. Policemen, their buttocks waggling, were rushing up smoky staircases and hurling boxes out of windows, while the prisoners, unguarded, were making the most of their chance. The firemen were filled with zeal, but no water flowed when the nearest tap was turned. The police captain—the broom that was to have swept clean—was standing on the opposite pavement, biting the ends of his mustache that curled into his mouth. Motionless the new broom stood there. As he passed the captain, Benya gave him a military salute.

"Good health, Your Excellency," he said, deeply sympathetic. "What do you say to this stroke of bad luck? A regular act of God!"

He stared hard at the burning building and slowly shook his head.

"Tut-tut-tut!" he went.

When Benya got back home the little lamps in the courtyard were flickering out, and dawn was beginning to touch the sky. The guests had departed and the musicians were dozing, leaning their heads on their double basses. Deborah alone was not thinking of sleep. With both hands she was urging her fainthearted husband toward the door of their nuptial chamber, glaring at him carnivorously. Like a cat she was, that holding a mouse in her jaws tests it gently with her teeth.

Translated by Walter Morison

The Law of the Eye

Pieke Biermann

The thunderstorm was overdue, like a period, and the city contorted in a kind of premenstrual syndrome. High tension in the pit of the stomach, paired with catatonia on the outside. Streets and houses yearned for the great, cleansing downpour and the cool clarity that comes afterwards. Not to mention the inhabitants. For weeks. People no longer laughed at last season's joke: "Did you take your cancer sunbath today?" Most of those who live here probably were exposed to such a bath; for the first time in their lives they seem to sense that the sun may be a violent planet.

The old woman is well over seventy, and the way she sits makes her look wider than she's tall. She actually hangs, immobile, apathetic, on a kind of ledge that juts out in front of the store window of a Turkish agency for low-cost housing, insurance, and travel arrangements back to Turkey. Her right shoulder leans against the window frame, her hands are interlocked in her lap, her head droops forward. The eyes are half open. Or half shut. Clamped between lids that are too heavy. Her gaze is lost on the spot between her black oxfords, where a brownish dog sprawls on the pavement. His fat rump stretches the short-furred skin like the casing of a sausage. He is as immobile as the woman, only the unusually wide eyes are alive in the pointed face. With nervous attention. Riveted on her stony stare.

It's about six o'clock on a Saturday evening in July. Schöneberger Hauptstrasse is about to choke under the windowless dome of smog, formed by the heat, steaming pavement, and other big-city stenches. Whenever possible, people avoid the smallest movement, lie around the house, or in the shade, near some body of water. The buses that crawl along Schöneberger Hauptstrasse at regular intervals are almost empty, and, except for an occasional bicycle, the only means of transportation. In one of the old tenements on the opposite side of the street, above the wide-open door of an Italian pool parlor, the sturdy rear end of a man is wedged into an open window. In the room behind it, a flicker of colored lights. Every once in a while, a wave of low-rumbling male voices crests, then ebbs again to a low, lazy-mouthed mumble. From time to time the man raises a can of beer and shakes the contents into his throat, without taking his eyes off the game on the screen.

Not a breath of wind. The sun burns down on the side, where the old woman is sitting, but the store window with the ads for low-cost housing and the hand-painted poster "Biletleri Otobüs" are still in the shade. A delivery van is parked along the curb, blocking the sun. Somebody has scratched "partners in crime" on the panel, in Bronx-style graffiti. The old woman was taught Gothic script.

The sausage dog jumps up, as soon as the two young women park their Vespa next door on the sidewalk, directly outside the laundromat. Whining and tail wagging, he races toward them on spindly legs. They ignore him. They pull their helmets off their heads, and unstrap two travel bags from the luggage rack. The fat little dog shirks no danger. Like a marionette he jumps up against the women, licking their feet and legs.

"Fucking mutt! You'll get yaself a heart attack," hisses one of the women, and almost bashes him on the head with her bag.

Then she sees the old woman, notices her slightly disarrayed but proper dress, her sweat-soaked yet neat permanent curls, and gets the picture. Typical old biddy, probably a block warden fifty years ago, always finds something to kvetch about, especially about women with colored streaks in their hair, who smooch in the stairs.

"If ya can't learn ya mutt some manners before ya let him loose on humans, then move at least up a flight and put ya mutt in training school."

The other young woman looks at her, then looks at a sign on the first floor of the building. SPORTSTUDIO APOLLO. She grins. "Worse than a guy, a cur like that. I bet he's the spitting image of the dear departed."

"Yeah, but the old hag don't pick up his poop."

They disappear into the laundromat without wasting another glance on the old woman. And they don't see that the fat little dog pants back to lie down between her feet, with a look of resignation.

"Yuck! What a stench!" The woman with the bleached blond poodle cut and the greenish-yellow T-shirt wipes the sweat off her forehead.

"Ya mean them two?" The other woman with ash-blond streaks and olive-drab overalls points to two young men, sitting far apart on the wooden benches along the windowed street front.

"Naw," says Greenish-Yellow, "Right now it's the nerve gas in here that's getting to me."

"Ya ain't kidding! Fucking patriarchy. Sure makes ya puke."

One of the two young men is twenty at most, and visibly a student. He's reading a text with a yellow felt-tip marker. He is slight, very pretty, and quite aware of it. As evidenced by the casual ease with which his body sits inside his jeans and the short light shirt, his elegant posture, the half-laced-up Adidas, and the soft brown curls with blond streaks above his nut-brown face. However, his eyes, which went to the two women during their verbal exchange, without the slightest tilt of the head, tell a different story. They tell of a basic mistrust. Perhaps even fear, although it is well hidden. He checks out a situation for potential danger signals. Now the eyes wander without attracting attention: from the two women to the other man, back and forth among the three, from detail to overall picture. After that he focuses on one of the nineteen washing machines along the lateral wall to his right, with a decisive turn of the head. Thereupon the black kid reimmerses himself in his text with equal determination; he lowers his head, underlines, turns pages. But his ears remain on the alert. Like cat's ears. Except that his ears don't rotate.

The two young women ignore him. They drop their bags, and throw their helmets down on the dryer by the entrance. On the wall hangs a pegboard with want ads: Apartments, jobs, stray roommates. The weekly display of the Women's Hotline almost disappears under a hand-painted sign: WARNING TO ALL WOMEN! DESCRIPTIONS OF PERPETRATORS ARE SLOWLY BECOMING SUPERFLUOUS, WE KEEP HEARING ABOUT RAPES/MOLESTATIONS ALL AROUND NOLLENDORF/WINTERFELD PLATZ. WOMEN, DON'T COUNT ON HELP FROM ANYONE! RELY ONLY ON YOURSELVES! BAND TOGETHER! DON'T LET YOURSELVES BE INTIMIDATED! DON'T BE TRUSTING! The greenish-yellow woman is digging through her pants for her wallet, while she stands reading.

"Did ya read that? Still the same notice. And the pigs keep napping."

"What do ya mean: napping? They're no better. Or do ya think there's a shortage of motherfuckers in the ranks?" Olive-Drab hoists her bag from the floor onto the dryer. The service notice falls off: "When the red light goes off, drying time has expired."

The other man is about thirty, and the prototype of the eternal adolescent. He's visibly straining to look relaxed in the Here and Now, inside his heavy black motorcycle jacket, as though it were an air-conditioned loggia, rather than a leather wall coated with detergent stench and machine exudations in an airtight summer. Even the simply casual just-sitting-there does not come easy to him. He's constantly tapping one foot on the floor, and keeps wriggling his behind on the bench, as though readjustment might give credence to something contained inside his skintight jeans. The zipper is adorned with a safety pin. Wet, thin, mouse-brown curlicues are plastered above his ultra-white, pasty face with the in-look three-day stubble.

His eyes are very light, and set far apart; since the arrival of the two women in the laundromat, his eyes have strayed from them only once. A brief glance to check out the other male. All further glances hang on the two women, eager for the slightest chance to attract attention to his ultra-white prototype. To be looked at. To be among the noticed.

The two women casually look him over. "Eyes like a mina boyd," Olive Drab sums him up.

"Yep, and the same kinda neck," adds Greenish-Yellow.

"Since when do mina boyds have necks?"

"Precisely."

Greenish-Yellow sparkles an aggressive glance in Ultra-White's direction, casts a probing eye on the other man, then turns to the coin machine, to get tokens for the washing machine, the tumbler, and the dryer. She's about to turn around, when she finds Prototype glued to her shoulder blades.

"So, what were you two just saying?" Unmistakably West German.

At the same instant, Olive-Drab materializes beside him, Greenish-Yellow completes her turn sideways, so that she flanks him on the other side. Prototype's eyes race back and forth from one to the other with joyful excited anticipation, as though watching a highly professional Ping-Pong match; he clicks his tongue, briefly sinks his upper teeth into the lower lip, slowly opens his mouth to engineer the pickup of the millennium—but he has missed his chance.

"Watch it, Buster! With eyes like that I'd get myself a sunglass transplant!" Olive-Drab's eyes slowly travel from his head to his toes, and up again.

"Aw, what's the matter with you two. You were talking about me. So I thought I'd take a look . . ."

"There's nothing to be looked at here!"

"Aw, to hell with his eye fucking. He don't get it." Olive-Drab hands Greenish-Yellow her helmet. They walk around the long laundry-folding table and the tumblers to the washing machine. Prototype goes the opposite way. The black kid imperceptibly raises his head, takes in the scene.

The two women exchange a look, simultaneously drop their bags and helmets, and menacingly take a step toward Prototype. "Are ya goin to beat it, or do ya want them gawkers colored a shade darker?" Olive-Drab's voice already is a shade darker. Prototype looks surprised, steps back an inch and attempts to start an argument, at which he's even worse than at trading glances.

"Is that how bad it has gotten in Berlin? Can't anyone even look at women anymore?"

"That's right, Mushhole. That's how it is. And now get lost!"

"But why? Don't *you* like to look at something beautiful? That's only human."

"We women have had it up to here with ya gawkin. Ya only see one thing anyway." Greenish-Yellow is enjoying herself. Olive-Drab pushes the sleeves of her overalls a little higher, smugly inspects each bicep, spreads her legs a little wider, provocatively taps her right foot, and prepares for her turn. "Don't bother with him. We don't need to give his kind of babypuss from Paderborn* an education vacation."

"From Bielefeld," proffers Prototype, confident that he has at last hit upon a subject to strike up a conversation.

"And"—Greenish-Yellow is pulling dirty laundry from the bag —"because the way a man looks at a woman is in itself an insult!" She stuffs the laundry into the machine, glances over to the black student, who, at a three-yard distance, seems to be studying his text, slams the door shut, and inserts a token into the slot.

"And because it reduces women to an object. A sex object, that is. And we've had that up to here. And that's that!" She grabs the second bag. Olive-Drab is still standing in front of Prototype, ready for combat. "Did ya hear me!" Greenish-Yellow can't put the brakes on. "And you're just another hicktown voyeur. Who come into the city to gawk at women. Just what we've been waitin for." She slams the second machine door shut, and throws the money into the slot.

The student sits studying.

"Am I nuts? Is everybody turning prudish around here, or what are you talking about?" It gradually dawns on Prototype that his carefully chosen defense tactic is making no impression; he considers a more aggressive maneuver. He puts his hands in his jacket pockets, hunches his shoulders, pumps himself up, and tries for a superior look. "Or did you just take an attack course with the militant Auntie Panthers?"

Before anything else can dawn on him, Olive-Drab has jumped him, her hands have gripped the collar of his leather jacket, and her right knee is in his groin. "With assholes like you, attack is the best defense."

Prototype lets out a yelp, and doubles over. "But I didn't even . . . Man . . ."

"Right, and we're not goin to wait around for ya ta, either." Greenish-Yellow has put her arm around his neck from behind, and presses, before he can sink under. Then she abruptly lets go, and hits him in the kidneys with the edge of her hand. He screams again, his arms blindly hitting air. Disjointed words spill from his wide-open mouth, until Olive-Drab rams her knee under his chin. "Because ya jerks see nothing in a woman. Nothing. Nothing. Nothing." Greenish-Yellow

* A small town in West Germany, symbolic of conservative behavior.

is rhythmically pulling at his hair. Each "nothing" comes with hair pulling and chin ramming.

"All ya can do is gawk. And think that that's what we're here for. So that ya can get off. So that ya can jerk off over it. But ya see nothing. Nothing. Nothing."

They continue to kick and beat him after he has sunk to the floor. He's bleeding from several wounds on the head and in the face. They stand over him, and stare down at him. They don't see that the student has taken his wet laundry out of the machine and stuffed it into a bag. Nor do they see the blood-red imprints his shoes leave on the terrazzo floor, as he soundlessly, furtively walks out of the laundromat. They see the safety pin on Prototype's zipper.

"Look at that!" shouts Olive-Drab triumphantly. "Bragging about his prowess. I wonder if he's already blacklisted on the Women's Hotline, or if he's new in the neighborhood."

Greenish-Yellow contentedly wipes her forehead.

"That's just because of his fat hips," grins Olive-Drab.

"Huh?" Greenish-Yellow is distracted. One of the bags is caught under Prototype's thighs.

"That he needs a safety pin on his fly."

Then they focus on pulling the bag out from under him without dragging it through the blood puddles that are all over the floor, and on leaving the scene of their triumph with all their dirty laundry.

On the opposite side of the street, the sturdy rear end is no longer hanging out the window. The total man is now standing in its frame, a fresh can of beer in his hand, watching the scene across the street. A fat old woman is lying motionless on the sidewalk; a fat little dog frantically swooshes around her, yaps, jumps up the legs of a black kid who is hurrying toward the street with a large, dripping bag; he stops, glances at the woman, then at the laundromat behind him, bends down and pets the dog's head as though to reassure him, hastily straightens up and continues running as a green and white bus with blue lights comes into view.

Sweat is running down the forehead and into the eyes of the man in the tenement window. It drops onto his chest. He cracks open the can of beer, and grunts something. Then he goes to fetch a pillow, and settles himself comfortably to watch the live show in the street below.

A police van brakes, tires screeching, in front of the store window of the low-cost housing agency. A woman and a man in uniform jump down; the dog instantly races toward them, wagging his tail. The policewoman walks over to the old woman on the ground. The policeman checks the streets and houses, in search of possible eyewitnesses. Five yards in front of him, a Vespa starts up on the sidewalk, and trundles away. In the hot, smelly cloud, two women can be seen; the one in the back is holding two bags in one hand in her lap, and two helmets in the other at her side.

"Stop!" he roars. But they're already too far away; he can't make out their license plate number. "Helmets belong on the head, even in hot weather!"

"She's dead." The policewoman is crouched next to the old woman. "And you're going to give yourself a heart attack, too, if you don't stop futzing around like this."

The fat little dog obediently lies down on the sidewalk, making himself as flat as possible; he's panting.

"I'll call the ambulance," says the policeman. "Why don't you ask that man up there in the window?"

She stands up: "Scuse me, did you see what happened down here?"

"So, what should be happening. Nothing exciting. With this heat. I was watching the game."

"And did you see anything else?"

"A black guy came bolting out of that laundromat. You should go in there and take a look. Who called you? Somebody musta seen something."

"The bus driver, over his radio. Thanks for the suggestion. We'll be right up."

"Naw, naw, don't bother. I'll come down." The stocky man disappears from the window. The policewoman disappears into the laundromat.

She reappears just as an ambulance-and-paramedics van rumbles onto the sidewalk. The policeman jumps off the little wall behind the old woman. "Well?"

Five men, two in firemen's uniforms, three in white, jump from the van. "Paramedics into the laundromat," says the policewoman. "There's a guy in there on the floor, bleeding from every pore."

Translated by Ursule Molinaro

The Merciful Angel of Death

Lawrence Block

"People come here to die, Mr. Scudder. They check out of hospitals, give up their apartments, and come to Caritas. Because they know we'll keep them comfortable here. And they know we'll let them die."

Carl Orcott was long and lean, with a long sharp nose and a matching chin. Some gray showed in his fair hair and his strawberry-blond mustache. His facial skin was stretched tight over his skull, and there were hollows in his cheeks. He might have been naturally spare of flesh, or worn down by the demands of his job. Because he was a gay man in the last decade of a terrible century, another possibility suggested itself. That he was HIV-positive. That his immune system was compromised. That the virus that would one day kill him was already within him, waiting.

"Since an easy death is our whole reason for being," he was saying, "it seems a bit much to complain when it occurs. Death is not the enemy here. Death is a friend. Our people are in very bad shape by the time they come to us. You don't run to a hospice when you get the initial results from a blood test, or when the first purple K-S lesions show up. First you try everything, including denial, and everything works for a while, and finally nothing works, not the AZT, not the pentamidine, not the Louise Hay tapes, not the crystal healing. Not even the denial. When you're ready for it to be over, you come

136

here and we see you out." He smiled thinly. "We hold the door for you. We don't boot you through it."

"But now you think—"

"I don't know what I think." He selected a briar pipe from a walnut stand that held eight of them, examined it, sniffed its bowl. "Grayson Lewes shouldn't have died," he said. "Not when he did. He was doing very well, relatively speaking. He was in agony, he had a CMV infection that was blinding him, but he was still strong. Of course he was dying, they're all dying, everybody's dying, but death certainly didn't appear to be imminent."

"What happened?"

"He died."

"What killed him?"

"I don't know." He breathed in the smell of the unlit pipe. "Someone went in and found him dead. There was no autopsy. There generally isn't. What would be the point? Doctors would just as soon not cut up AIDS patients anyway, not wanting the added risk of infection. Of course most of our general staff are seropositive, but even so you try to avoid unnecessary additional exposure. Quantity could make a difference, and there could be multiple strains. The virus mutates, you see." He shook his head. "There's such a great deal we still don't know."

"There was no autopsy."

"No. I thought about ordering one."

"What stopped you?"

"The same thing that keeps people from getting the antibody test. Fear of what I might find."

"You think someone killed Lewes."

"I think it's possible."

"Because he died abruptly. But people do that, don't they? Even if they're not sick to begin with. They have strokes or heart attacks."

"That's true."

"This happened before, didn't it? Lewes wasn't the first."

He smiled ruefully. "You're good at this."

"It's what I do."

"Yes." His fingers were busy with the pipe. "There have been a few unexpected deaths. But there would be, as you've said. So there was no real cause for suspicion. There still isn't."

"But you're suspicious."

"Am I? I guess I am."

"Tell me the rest of it, Carl."

"I'm sorry," he said. "I'm making you drag it out of me, aren't I? Grayson Lewes had a visitor. She was in his room for twenty minutes, perhaps half an hour. She was the last person to see him alive. She may have been the first person to see him dead."

"Who is she?"

"I don't know. She's been coming here for months. She always brings flowers, something cheerful. She brought yellow freesias the last time. Nothing fancy, just a five-dollar bunch from the Korean on the corner, but they do brighten a room."

"Had she visited Lewes before?"

He shook his head. "Other people. Every week or so she would turn up, always asking for one of our residents by name. It's often the sickest of the sick that she comes to see."

"And then they die?"

"Not always. But often enough so that it's been remarked upon. Still, I never let myself think that she played a causative role. I thought she had some instinct that drew her to your side when you were circling the drain." He looked off to the side. "When she visited Lewes, someone joked that we'd probably have his room available soon. When you're on staff here, you become quite irreverent in private. Otherwise you'd go crazy."

"It was the same way on the police force."

"I'm not surprised. When one of us would cough or sneeze, another might say, 'Uh-oh, you might be in line for a visit from Mercy.' "

"Is that her name?"

"Nobody knows her name. It's what we call her among ourselves. The Merciful Angel of Death. Mercy, for short."

A man named Bobby sat up in bed in his fourth-floor room. He had short gray hair and a gray brush mustache and a gray complexion bruised purple here and there by Kaposi's sarcoma. For all the ravages of the disease, he had a heartbreakingly youthful face. He was a ruined cherub, the oldest boy in the world.

"She was here yesterday," he said.

"She visited you twice," Carl said.

"Twice?"

"Once last week and once three or four days ago."

"I thought it was one time. And I thought it was yesterday." He frowned. "It all seems like yesterday."

"What does, Bobby?"

"Everything. Camp Arrowhead. *I Love Lucy.* The moon shot. One enormous yesterday with everything crammed into it, like his closet. I don't remember his name but he was famous for his closet."

"Fibber McGee," Carl said.

"I don't know why I can't remember his name," Bobby said languidly. "It'll come to me. I'll think of it yesterday."

I said, "When she came to see you—"

"She was beautiful. Tall, slim, gorgeous eyes. A flowing dove-gray robe, a blood-red scarf at her throat. I wasn't sure if she was real or not. I thought she might be a vision."

"Did she tell you her name?"

"I don't remember. She said she was there to be with me. And mostly she just sat there, where Carl's sitting. She held my hand."

"What else did she say?"

"That I was safe. That no one could hurt me anymore. She said—"

"Yes?"

"That I was innocent," he said, and he sobbed and let his tears flow.

He wept freely for a few moments, then reached for a Kleenex. When he spoke again his voice was matter-of-fact, even detached. "She *was* here twice," he said. "I remember now. The second time I got snotty, I really had the rag on, and I told her she didn't have to hang around if she didn't want to. And she said *I* didn't have to hang around if *I* didn't want to.

"And I said, right, I can go tap-dancing down Broadway with a rose in my teeth. And she said, no, all I have to do is let go and my spirit will soar free. And I looked at her, and I knew what she meant."

"And?"

"She told me to let go, to give it all up, to just let go and go to the light. And I said—this is strange, you know?"

"What did you say, Bobby?"

"I said I couldn't see the light and I wasn't ready to go to it. And she said that was all right, that when I was ready the light would be there to guide me. She said I would know how to do it when the time came. And she talked about how to do it."

"How?"

"By letting go. By going to the light. I don't remember everything she said. I don't even know for sure if all of it happened, or if I dreamed part of it. I never know anymore. Sometimes I have dreams and later they feel like part of my personal history. And sometimes I look back at my life and most of it has a veil over it, as if I never lived it at all, as if it were nothing but a dream."

Back in his office Carl picked up another pipe and brought its blackened bowl to his nose. He said, "You asked why I called you instead of the police. Can you imagine putting Bobby through an official interrogation?"

"He seems to go in and out of lucidity."

He nodded. "The virus penetrates the blood-brain barrier. If you survive the K-S and the opportunistic infections, the reward is dementia. Bobby is mostly clear, but some of his mental circuits are beginning to burn out. Or rust out, or clog up, whatever it is that they do."

"There are cops who know how to take testimony from people like that."

"Even so. Can you see the tabloid headlines? 'MERCY STRIKES AIDS HOSPICE.' We have a hard enough time getting blood as it is. You know, whenever the press happens to mention how many dogs and cats the SPCA puts to sleep, donations drop to a trickle. Imagine what would happen to us."

"Some people would give you more."

He laughed. " 'Here's a thousand dollars—kill ten of 'em for me.' You could be right."

He sniffed at the pipe again. I said, "You know, as far as I'm concerned you can go ahead and smoke that thing."

He stared at me, then at the pipe, as if surprised to find it in his hand. "There's no smoking anywhere in the building," he said. "Anyway, I don't smoke."

"The pipes came with the office?"

He colored. "They were John's," he said. "We lived together. He died . . . God, it'll be two years in November. It doesn't seem that long."

"I'm sorry, Carl."

"I used to smoke cigarettes, Marlboros, but I quit ages ago. But I never minded his pipe smoke, though. I always liked the aroma. And now I'd rather smell one of his pipes than the AIDS smell. Do you know the smell I mean?"

"Yes."

"Not everyone with AIDS has it but a lot of them do, and most sickrooms reek of it. You must have smelled it in Bobby's room. It's an unholy musty smell, a smell like rotted leather. I can't stand the smell of leather anymore. I used to love leather, but now I can't help associating it with the stink of gay men wasting away in fetid airless rooms.

"And this whole building smells that way to me. There's the stench of disinfectant over everything. We use tons of it, spray and liquid. The virus is surprisingly frail, it doesn't last long outside the body, but we leave as little as possible to chance, and so the rooms and halls all smell of disinfectant. But underneath it, always, there's the smell of the disease itself."

He turned the pipe over in his hands. "His clothes were full of the smell. John's. I gave everything away. But his pipes held a scent I had always associated with him, and a pipe is such a personal thing, isn't it, with the smoker's toothmarks in the stem." He looked at me. His eyes were dry, his voice strong and steady. There was no grief in his tone, only in the words themselves. "Two years in November, though I swear it doesn't seem that long, and I use one smell to keep another at bay. And, I suppose, to bridge the gap of years, to keep him a little closer to me." He put the pipe down. "Back to cases. Will you take a careful but unofficial look at our Angel of Death?"

I said I would. He said I'd want a retainer, and opened the top drawer of his desk. I told him it wouldn't be necessary.

"But isn't that standard for private detectives?"

"I'm not one, not officially. I don't have a license."

"So you told me, but even so—"

"I'm not a lawyer, either," I went on, "but there's no reason why I can't do a little *pro bono* work once in a while. If it takes too much of my time I'll let you know, but for now let's call it a donation."

The hospice was in the Village, on Hudson Street. Rachel Book-span lived five miles north in an Italianate brownstone on Claremont Avenue. Her husband, Paul, walked to work at Columbia University, where he was an associate professor of political science. Rachel was a free-lance copy editor, hired by several publishers to prepare man-uscripts for publication. Her specialties were history and biography.

She told me all this over coffee in her book-lined living room. She talked about a manuscript she was working on, the biography of a woman who had founded a religious sect in the late nineteenth cen-tury. She talked about her children, two boys, who would be home from school in an hour or so. Finally she ran out of steam and I brought the conversation back to her brother, Arthur Fineberg, who had lived on Morton Street and worked downtown as a librarian for an investment firm. And who had died two weeks ago at the Caritas Hospice.

"How we cling to life," she said. "Even when it's awful. Even when we yearn for death."

"Did your brother want to die?"

"He prayed for it. Every day the disease took a little more from him, gnawing at him like a mouse, and after months and months and months of hell it finally took his will to live. He couldn't fight anymore. He had nothing to fight with, nothing to fight *for*. But he went on living all the same."

She looked at me, then looked away. "He begged me to kill him," she said.

I didn't say anything.

"How could I refuse him? But how could I help him? First I thought it wasn't right but then I decided it was his life, and who had a better right to end it if he wanted to? But how could I do it? How?

"I thought of pills. We don't have anything in the house except Midol for cramps. I went to my doctor and said I had trouble sleeping. Well, that was true enough. He gave me a prescription for a dozen Valium. I didn't even bother getting it filled. I didn't want to give Artie a handful of tranquilizers. I wanted to give him one of those cyanide capsules the spies always had in World War Two movies. You bite down and you're gone. But where do you go to get something like that?"

She sat forward in her chair. "Do you remember that man in the Midwest who unhooked his kid from a respirator? The doctors wouldn't let the boy die and the father went into the hospital with a gun and held everybody at bay until his son was dead. I think that man was a hero."

"A lot of people thought so."

"God, I wanted to be a hero! I had fantasies. There's a Robinson Jeffers poem about a crippled hawk and the narrator puts it out of its misery. 'I gave him the lead gift,' he says. Meaning a bullet, a gift of lead. I wanted to give my brother that gift. I don't have a gun. I don't even believe in guns. At least I never did. I don't know what I believe in anymore.

"If I'd had a gun, could I have gone in there and shot him? I don't see how. I have a knife, I have a kitchen full of knives, and believe me, I thought of going in there with a knife in my purse and waiting until he dozed off and then slipping the knife between his ribs and into his heart. I visualized it, I went over every aspect of it, but I didn't do it. My God, I never even left the house with a knife in my bag."

She asked if I wanted more coffee. I said I didn't. I asked her if her brother had had other visitors, and if he might have made the same request of one of them.

"He had dozens of friends, men and women who loved him. And yes, he would have asked them. He told everybody he wanted to die. As hard as he fought to live, for all those months, that's how determined he became to die. Do you think someone helped him?"

"I think it's possible."

"God, I hope so," she said. "I just wish it had been me."

"I haven't had the test," Aldo said. "I'm a forty-four-year-old gay man who led an active sex life since I was fifteen. I don't *have* to take the test, Matthew. I assume I'm seropositive. I assume everybody is."

He was a plump teddy bear of a man, with black curly hair and a face as permanently buoyant as a smile button. We were sharing a small table at a coffeehouse on Bleecker, just two doors from the shop where he sold comic books and baseball cards to collectors.

"I may not develop the disease," he said. "I may die a perfectly respectable death due to overindulgence in food and drink. I may get hit by a bus or struck down by a mugger. If I do get sick I'll wait until it gets really bad, because I love this life, Matthew, I really do. But when the time comes I don't want to make local stops. I'm gonna catch an express train out of here."

"You sound like a man with his bags packed."

"No luggage. Travelin' light. You remember the song?"

"Of course."

He hummed a few bars of it, his foot tapping out the rhythm, our little marble-topped table shaking with the motion. He said, "I have pills enough to do the job. I also have a loaded handgun. And I think I have the nerve to do what I have to do, when I have to do it." He frowned, an uncharacteristic expression for him. "The danger lies in waiting too long. Winding up in a hospital bed too weak to do anything, too addled by brain fever to remember what it was you were supposed to do. Wanting to die but unable to manage it."

"I've heard there are people who'll help."

"You've heard that, have you?"

"One woman in particular."

"What are you after, Matthew?"

"You were a friend of Grayson Lewes. And of Arthur Fineberg. There's a woman who helps people who want to die. She may have helped them."

"And?"

"And you know how to get in touch with her."

"Who says?"

"I forget, Aldo."

The smile was back. "You're discreet, huh?"

"Very."

"I don't want to make trouble for her."

"Neither do I."

"Then why not leave her alone?"

"There's a hospice administrator who's afraid she's murdering people. He called me in rather than start an official police inquiry. But if I don't get anywhere—"

"He calls the cops." He found his address book, copied out a number for me. "Please don't make trouble for her," he said. "I might need her myself."

I called her that evening, met her the following afternoon at a cocktail lounge just off Washington Square. She was as described, even to the gray cape over a long gray dress. Her scarf today was canary yellow. She was drinking Perrier, and I ordered the same.

She said, "Tell me about your friend. You say he's very ill."

"He wants to die. He's been begging me to kill him but I can't do it."

"No, of course not."

"I was hoping you might be able to visit him."

"If you think it might help. Tell me something about him, why don't you."

I don't suppose she was more than forty-five, if that, but there was something ancient about her face. You didn't need much of a commitment to reincarnation to believe she had lived before. Her facial features were pronounced, her eyes a graying blue. Her voice was pitched low, and along with her height it raised doubts about her sexuality. She might have been a sex change, or a drag queen. But I didn't think so. There was an Eternal Female quality to her that didn't feel like parody.

I said, "I can't."

"Because there's no such person."

"I'm afraid there are plenty of them, but I don't have one in mind." I told her in a couple of sentences why I was there. When I'd finished she let the silence stretch, then asked me if I thought she could kill anyone. I told her it was hard to know what anyone could do.

She said, "I think you should see for yourself what it is that I do."

She stood up. I put some money on the table and followed her out to the street.

We took a cab to a four-story brick building on Twenty-second Street west of Ninth. We climbed two flights of stairs, and the door opened when she knocked on it. I could smell the disease before I was across the threshold. The young black man who opened the door was glad to see her and unsurprised by my presence. He didn't ask my name or tell me his.

"Kevin's so tired," he told us both. "It breaks my heart."

We walked through a neat, sparsely furnished living room and down a short hallway to a bedroom, where the smell was stronger. Kevin lay in a bed with its head cranked up. He looked like a famine victim, or someone liberated from Dachau. Terror filled his eyes.

She pulled a chair up to the side of his bed and sat in it. She took his hand in hers and used her free hand to stroke his forehead. You're safe now, she told him. You're safe, you don't have to hurt anymore, you did all the things you had to do. You can relax now, you can let go now, you can go to the light.

"You can do it," she told him. "Close your eyes, Kevin, and go inside yourself and find the part that's holding on. Somewhere within you there's a part of you that's like a clenched fist, and I want you to find that part and be with that part. And let go. Let the fist open its fingers. It's as if the fist is holding a little bird, and if you open up the hand the bird can fly free. Just let it happen, Kevin. Just let go."

He was straining to talk, but the best he could do was make a sort of cawing sound. She turned to the black man, who was standing in the doorway. "David," she said, "his parents aren't living, are they?"

"I believe they're both gone."

"Which one was he closest to?"

"I don't know. I believe they're both gone a long time now."

"Did he have a lover? Before you, I mean."

"Kevin and I were never lovers. I don't even know him that well. I'm here 'cause he hasn't got anybody else. He had a lover."

"Did his lover die? What was his name?"

"Martin."

"Kevin," she said, "you're going to be all right now. All you have to do is go to the light. Do you see the light? Your mother's there, Kevin, and your father, and Martin—"

"Mark!" David cried. "Oh, God, I'm sorry, I'm so stupid, it wasn't Martin, it was Mark, Mark, that was his name."

"That's all right, David."

"I'm so damn stupid—"

"Look into the light, Kevin," she said. "Mark is there, and your parents, and everyone who ever loved you. Matthew, take his other hand. Kevin, you don't have to stay here anymore, darling. You did everything you came here to do. You don't have to stay. You don't have to hold on. You can let go, Kevin. You can go to the light. Let go and reach out to the light—"

I don't know how long she talked to him. Fifteen, twenty minutes, I suppose. Several times he made the cawing sound, but for the most part he was silent. Nothing seemed to be happening, and then I realized that his terror was no longer a presence. She seemed to have talked it away. She went on talking to him, stroking his brow and holding his hand, and I held his other hand. I was no longer listening to what she was saying, just letting the words wash over me while my mind played with some tangled thought like a kitten with yarn.

Then something happened. The energy in the room shifted and I looked up, knowing that he was gone.

"Yes," she murmured. "Yes, Kevin. God bless you, go on, you rest. Yes."

"Sometimes they're stuck," she said. "They want to go but they can't. They've been hanging on so long, you see, that they don't know how to stop."

"So you help them."

"If I can."

"What if you can't? Suppose you talk and talk and they still hold on?"

"Then they're not ready. They'll be ready another time. Sooner or later everybody lets go, everybody dies. With or without my help."

"And when they're not ready—"

"Sometimes I come back another time. And sometimes they're ready then."

"What about the ones who beg for help? The ones like Arthur Fineberg, who plead for death but aren't physically close enough to it to let go?"

"What do you want me to say?"

"The thing you want to say. The thing that's stuck in your throat, the way his own unwanted life was stuck in Kevin's throat. You're holding on to it."

"Just let it go, eh?"

"If you want."

We were walking somewhere in Chelsea, and we walked a full block now without either of us saying a word. Then she said, "I think there's a world of difference between assisting someone verbally and doing anything physical to hasten death."

"So do I."

"And that's where I draw the line. But sometimes, having drawn that line—"

"You step over it."

"Yes. The first time I swear I acted without conscious intent. I used a pillow, I held it over his face and—" She breathed deeply. "I swore it would never happen again. But then there was someone else, and he just needed help, you know, and—"

"And you helped him."

"Yes. Was I wrong?"

"I don't know what's right or wrong."

"Suffering is wrong," she said, "unless it's part of His plan, and how can I presume to decide if it is or not? Maybe people can't let go because there's one more lesson they have to learn before they move on. Who the hell am I to decide it's time for somebody's life to end? How dare I interfere?"

"And yet you do."

"Just once in a while, when I just don't see a way around it. Then I do what I have to do. I'm sure I must have a choice in the matter, but I swear it doesn't feel that way. It doesn't feel as though I have any choice at all." She stopped walking, turned to look at me. She said, "Now what happens?"

"Well, she's the Merciful Angel of Death," I told Carl Orcott. "She visits the sick and dying, almost always at somebody's invitation. A friend contacts her, or a relative."

"Do they pay her?"

"Sometimes they try to. She won't take any money. She even pays for the flowers herself." She'd taken Dutch iris to Kevin's apartment on Twenty-second Street. Blue, with yellow centers that matched her scarf.

"She does it *pro bono*," he said.

"And she talks to them. You heard what Bobby said. I got to see her in action. She talked the poor sonofabitch straight out of this world and into the next one. I suppose you could argue that what she does comes perilously close to hypnosis, that she hypnotizes people and convinces them to kill themselves psychically, but I can't imagine anybody trying to sell that to a jury."

"She just talks to them."

"Uh-huh. 'Let go, go to the light.' "

" 'And have a nice day.' "

"That's the idea."

"She's not killing people?"

"Nope. Just letting them die."

He picked up a pipe. "Well, hell," he said, "that's what we do. Maybe I ought to put her on staff." He sniffed the pipe bowl. "You have my thanks, Matthew. Are you sure you don't want some of our money to go with it? Just because Mercy works *pro bono* doesn't mean you should have to."

"That's all right."

"You're certain?"

I said, "You asked me the first day if I knew what AIDS smelled like."

"And you said you'd smelled it before. Oh."

I nodded. "I've lost friends to it. I'll lose more before it's over. In the meantime I'm grateful when I get the chance to do you a favor. Because I'm glad this place is here, so people have a place to come to."

Even as I was glad she was around, the woman in gray, the merciful angel of death. To hold the door for them, and show them the light on the other side. And, if they really needed it, to give them the least little push through it.

Ishmael

Joe Gores

On my feet, shouting, when the screen door of the radio shack banged open and the Arab bastard ran out.

The AR bucked against my hands, stitching him from navel to forehead: AR's on full auto climb with the burst. He grabbed himself with both hands and spun around like an actor in the American action cinemas.

I already was by him, into the transmitting room. The European bastard was backed up against the wall with his arms raised and sweat splotches on his shirt. He was balding and wore a small mustache. On his desk was a framed photo of a woman and a child.

Say widow and orphan, rather, I thought as I gave him my favorite, a burst in the gut. Gut-shot men die slowly, their screams serving to demoralize others who might seek to oppose us.

The wireless station was ours. Other bands were securing the cable office, the police headquarters, government buildings. I had led *this* assault because the wireless was the most important. To tell the People that the Oppressors had been ground to flour, that we Africans now held the Republic in our palms.

From town came the even pounding of a machine gun, like a fist upon a hotel room door.

A voice called, *"Chai, Bwana Osoko."*

150

I rolled over and sat up in the soft bed, soaked in sweat. Silk pajamas really are too hot for our climate. I massaged my head with stiffened fingers.

The servant outside the hotel room door called again. *"Chai, bwana."*

I needed tea. The night had been full of dreams and portents, as a rotted beam is full of termites. Dreams of the Republic, my first triumph. Of Kambule, my first Betrayer. Barefoot on the thick carpet, I reached for the door, checked, then opened it with a shrug. Africa is full of Oppressors, even now, but here in the land of my birth—I had been born only 200 miles to the north—the Prime Minister was a weak man, a frightened man, an indecisive man.

The *mtumishi* came in with the tea tray.

"Unalala boma mtu aliyebufa," he said, a big grin on his black face.

For such as he, serving Field Marshal Maccabeus Osoko was a great honor indeed. I have done much for my people. But he angered me by saying I slept like one who is dead. There are too many Oppressors who would wish it so.

"Sasa ondoka hapa," I snapped at him.

He put the tea tray on the bedside table and fled from my wrath. I added milk and two heaping spoons of sugar, and got out of my pajamas while sipping the tea. The mirror gave me back a lean and muscular black, not tall but well-proportioned. Black. The color of freedom. Under the driving shower I reflected that when I was a child only the *wazungu*, with their grub-white hides, could have had a room with a private bath here in central Africa. That has changed now, because of Patriots such as I.

It was God Who told my parents to name me after Judas Maccabeus, the Hammer of God. It was God Who, when I was at the mission school, led me to the story of the Maccabees, and thus revealed my destiny to me.

And he pursued the wicked and sought them out, and them that troubled his people he burnt with fire.

I toweled off vigorously, then from my pigskin luggage selected a fresh khaki shirt, khaki shorts, and long socks. On the shirt collar I pinned the polished brass insignia I had bought in Dar to go with the gold braid of my officer's hat.

The dining room was only half filled, but no one came up to me as I waited in the doorway. I tapped my swagger stick on my thigh in frustration: The maître d' was seating some damned European with an over-trussed wife. As I waited, the images floated out from behind my eyes, where the headaches come from . . .

I moved toward the cockpit of the commercial airliner over the strip of coastal water that separates the Republic from the mainland. The stewardess, knowing who I was, stood aside. I took my hand from the flap of my holster. Beyond the connecting door I could see the plane's bare metal ribs.

"Contact the Republic."

The pilot's white moon face. "Yes, sir, Mr. Osoko—"

"Field Marshal!" The words ripped from my throat at that hateful white countenance. "You will address me by rank!"

"Yes sir, Field Marshal, sir."

European swine. Your usefulness is at an end, soon not even South Africa will be ruled by you anymore. Patriots such as I are cleansing our continent of you in the name of the People.

"Airport tower."

I took the microphone to answer the static-crackling voice. "It is I, Field Marshal Osoko, who arrives. Have my Army and the press waiting to receive me."

But there was no Army, no waiting press. Only Kambule, President of the new Republic whom *I* had put in power, standing bareheaded on the tarmac in the gently falling rain.

"This way, please, Field Marshal."

I followed the black maître d' to my table, striding like a lion with all eyes upon me, a ripple of whispers following my progress. I ordered pineapple, corn flakes, kippers, fried eggs and bacon, toast and coffee.

Why did I wait while some European jackal was seated? I began to eat. Next time it would be very different. Next time I would not relinquish to the Oppressors of the People the power I had won. The Oppressors are now more often black than white. Like Kambule. Like those who had ruled in the countries blurred behind my eyes since I had liberated the Republic. Yes, and like the Prime Minister here in the land of my birth. Oppressors and Betrayers, all of them, and many such have died. The blood of dead men against the dust is red, no matter what color their punctured hides.

I thrust my fork savagely into my second egg so I could watch the yolk flow sluggishly across my plate. *Black* Oppressors. Kambule. The Prime Minister—another Oppressor but also a fool, one who would soon join the others in the dust. I knew now why I had returned: to thrust the Oppressor from the seat of power here in the land of my birth.

"Maccabeus Osoko?"

I narrowed my eyes against the aggressive voice which jerked my head up. A slim black man in khaki shorts and shirt was standing before me, flanked by two black *askaris*—themselves, in their Colonialist uniforms, symbols of the Oppressors. The slim man had a lean cool stubborn black face and faint tired lines at the corners of his eyes and broad mouth.

"*Field Marshal* Osoko," I told him angrily.

He did not react to the title. Instead, he sat down unbidden across from me. He said, "Inspector Wakamula, Immigration."

From the corners of my eyes I could see his *askaris* ground the butts of their old-fashioned Enfields. They shifted nervously from foot to foot. Of course. They were aware of being in the presence of the Field Marshal, even if Wakamula pretended not to be. The headache jabbed at the backs of my eyes like needles.

"What do you want, Wakamula?"

He already was unfolding a paper on the tablecloth. He looked up at me, his eyes totally without expression. "An order for your immediate expulsion as an undesirable alien. Or if you choose to remain, your detention in the north. Your choice, Osoko."

The red particles danced before my eyes, but I knew this was the time to be cool. The Prime Minister had acted first—when I had not thought he would act at all. Who could have foreseen it? He was a soft man of a soft tribe whose lands and women my own fierce tribe once took at spearpoint. A weakling, a gullible fool who spoke of schools and budgets and tourism and game parks instead of fire and steel and blood and death.

So it had to be the man before me, Wakamula, who had arranged for this public humiliation. Obviously, he was jealous of my strength, fearful of my power, and had used his access to the ear of the Prime Minister for his own traitorous ends.

"You cannot deport me," I said icily. "I was born here."

"Do you have any documentation to support that?"

I shrugged. "Up-country records are notoriously poor. But everyone knows that Field Marshal Osoko was born in—"

"No records." He tapped the order with a lean black finger, so that it jiggled against the fork I had laid on the table. The tines left a tiny smear of congealing yolk on the paper. "Your unsupported statement against an order personally signed by the Prime Minister."

"An Oppressor of his People . . ."

He leaned forward almost violently, his face alive for the first time. "You have your options, Osoko. Out. Or remain in detention in the Northern District. Myself, I would rather put a dum-dum in your gut and leave you singing in the bush until the hyenas come. The Prime Minister is an idealist, he believes in human decency, even yours, but I know the *real* body counts in the Republic and in the countries since then. The counts that don't reach the newsmen."

" 'When two elephants fight, it is the grass which is trampled,' " I sneered, quoting the Swahili proverb.

It only seemed to make him more rigidly steel. "Human beings, Osoko, not the grasses of the field. Your own people. Not foreigners. Not Arabs. Blood of your blood."

My hands were knots. The pain behind my eyes was intense. I knew how to deal with this Betrayer of the People, him and his threats of soft-nosed bullets under the table! I would say I had to pack my luggage, get my Webley from the suitcase. The *askaris* would support my actions . . .

"Your bags have been packed and brought down to the lobby, Osoko. And your account with the hotel has been paid."

The pain was lessening behind my eyes. Withdraw and regroup, as the Advisers had taught at the Republic. Tactics.

I stalked from the room with immense dignity, slapping my swagger stick against my palm impatiently so it would seem to be I who led, rather than they who herded. Outside, I wanted to recoil from the sunlight glaring off the hotel's whitewashed facade, but Wakamula would be watching and I would not give him the satisfaction. I strode down the broad steps to my waiting Jaguar. An African servant in a bright green *kanzu* held the door for me.

"My luggage?" I demanded.

"It is in the boot, Field Marshal."

At least *he* knew to address me by my proper title. I laid a coin on his pale callused palm and slid behind the wheel. The leather of the seat was cool against the backs of my bare legs. I found my sunglasses in the side pocket and put them on. They served to lessen the pain that had returned behind my eyes.

The main street was lined with tightly packed *dukas* that had once belonged to the Asians. These shops were crowded with shrill black market-morning crowds so it was difficult to thread my way through in the big red car.

Why was it always like this? The Oppressors victorious while I was driven forth? The Prime Minister. Wakamula. Kambule. *Kambule* . . .

Kambule's heavy black face was grave. "To future generations, Osoko, you might well be the father of the Revolution here in the Republic. They probably will put you in the history books, I probably will be a footnote. But it shall be I—*I*—who shall shape this nation."

"Without me?" I sneered. "Together we could—"

Kambule sighed patiently. He was a bulky man built like a stevedore, as pedantic of speech as the secondary-school teacher he once had been.

"Together, Osoko? We had the slogans—*Africa for the Africans, blackenization, negritude*—but we needed someone like you. A Robespierre to follow a Rousseau, a Trotsky to follow a Marx. Men of action. Fanatics—"

"You do not understand! I am no fanatic! I am a patriot!"

He went right on as if he had not heard me, or, hearing, held what I said of little value.

"But what do you do with your revolutionary, your fanatic, once the revolution has been won and it is time to build? I have to create a nation now out of chaos, Osoko, have to extinguish tribal enmities that a week ago I was fanning into flame just so our sacred revolution could succeed. Now all that is over, now is the time of creating—but what does such a one as you know of creating? You understand only foments, destructions, extremes, cruelties . . ."

"You fat fool, without me—"

The suddenly cold, hooded eyes stopped me in mid-sentence.

There was death in those eyes. I remembered seeing Kambule shoot kneeling men in the back of the head when it had been necessary.

"I have deposited twenty thousand pounds to your account at the bank in Nairobi, Osoko. The plane leaves in five minutes. Be on it."

Two miles beyond the outskirts of the Capital the tarmac ended. I stopped my Jaguar at the roundabout. The road north led to the village of my birth: the road west led toward the interior and the nations beyond the mountains.

Straight ahead to the north would mean detention for a time, but that soon would pass. I had money, an auto, I could return to my trade, take wives, loom large in tribal matters.

It was the way of my people. I had only to go north.

But left, west toward the mountains, that would mean . . .

What had Kambule said? Foments, he had said. Extremes. Destructions. Cruelties. What do I know of such things? I know only necessities. I know that when it is necessary to shoot a kneeling man, unlike Kambule *I* shoot him in the forehead. I am not afraid to see the bone chips fly, I am not afraid to watch his eyes die.

Leave you in the bush to die, Wakamula had said.

Shauri ya Mungu. That is God's affair.

Wakamula and his talk of my people, blood of my blood. All about me lay the sun-scorched red earth of my native country, the land of my birth, but what did those words signify? Nothing. Two hundred miles to the north lay my tribal home but there is no one of my blood. There are no people I call my own.

For I am the Hammer of God. Who is my mother? And who are my brethren?

But a scant hundred miles to the west, beyond the mountains, lay the border and beyond that the ten million square miles of Africa. A vast land of opportunity where there were only the Oppressors and the poor fools they oppressed.

For I am come to set a man at variance against his father, and the daughter against her mother.

Of course I turned left, toward the mountains, toward the countries of the Oppressors which lay beyond. Shadows from the tall gum trees flanking the road dappled the red skin of my flashing auto as I passed, giving it the momentary illusion of being blood-spattered.

Somewhere they will need me.

The Last Voyage
of the Ghost Ship

Gabriel García Márquez

Now they're going to see who I am, he said to himself in his strong
new man's voice, many years after he had first seen the huge ocean
liner without lights and without any sound which passed by the village
one night like a great uninhabited palace, longer than the whole village
and much taller than the steeple of the church, and it sailed by in the
darkness toward the colonial city on the other side of the bay that
had been fortified against buccaneers, with its old slave port and the
rotating light, whose gloomy beams transfigured the village into a
lunar encampment of glowing houses and streets of volcanic deserts
every fifteen seconds, and even though at that time he'd been a boy
without a man's strong voice but with his mother's permission to stay
very late on the beach to listen to the wind's night harps, he could
still remember, as if still seeing it, how the liner would disappear
when the light of the beacon struck its side and how it would reappear
when the light had passed, so that it was an intermittent ship sailing
along, appearing and disappearing, toward the mouth of the bay,
groping its way like a sleepwalker for the buoys that marked the harbor
channel until something must have gone wrong with the compass
needle, because it headed toward the shoals, ran aground, broke up,

and sank without a single sound, even though a collision against the reefs like that should have produced a crash of metal and the explosion of engines that would have frozen with fright the soundest-sleeping dragons in the prehistoric jungle that began with the last streets of the village and ended on the other side of the world, so that he himself thought it was a dream, especially the next day, when he saw the radiant fishbowl of the bay, the disorder of colors of the Negro shacks on the hills above the harbor, the schooners of the smugglers from the Guianas loading their cargoes of innocent parrots whose craws were full of diamonds, he thought, I fell asleep counting the stars and I dreamed about that huge ship, of course, he was so convinced that he didn't tell anyone nor did he remember the vision again until the same night on the following March when he was looking for the flash of dolphins in the sea and what he found was the illusory liner, gloomy, intermittent, with the same mistaken direction as the first time, except that then he was so sure he was awake that he ran to tell his mother and she spent three weeks moaning with disappointment, because your brain's rotting away from doing so many things backward, sleeping during the day and going out at night like a criminal, and since she had to go to the city around that time to get something comfortable where she could sit and think about her dead husband, because the rockers on her chair had worn out after eleven years of widowhood, she took advantage of the occasion and had the boatman go near the shoals so that her son could see what he really saw in the glass of the sea, the lovemaking of manta rays in a springtime of sponges, pink snappers and blue corvinas diving into the other wells of softer waters that were there among the waters, and even the wandering hairs of victims of drowning in some colonial shipwreck, no trace of sunken liners or anything like it, and yet he was so pig-headed that his mother promised to watch with him the next March, absolutely, not knowing that the only thing absolute in her future now was an easy chair from the days of Sir Francis Drake which she had bought at an auction in a Turk's store, in which she sat down to rest that same night, sighing, oh, my poor Olofernos, if you could only see how nice it is to think about you on this velvet lining and this brocade from the casket of a queen, but the more she brought back the memory of her dead husband, the more the blood in her heart bubbled up and turned to chocolate, as if instead of sitting down

she were running, soaked from chills and fevers and her breathing
full of earth, until he returned at dawn and found her dead in the
easy chair, still warm, but half rotted away as after a snakebite, the
same as happened afterward to four other women before the murderous chair was thrown into the sea, far away where it wouldn't
bring evil to anyone, because it had been used so much over the
centuries that its faculty for giving rest had been used up, and so he
had to grow accustomed to his miserable routine of an orphan who
was pointed out by everyone as the son of the widow who had brought
the throne of misfortune into the village, living not so much from
public charity as from the fish he stole out of boats, while his voice
was becoming a roar, and not remembering his visions of past times
anymore until another night in March when he chanced to look sea-
ward and suddenly, good Lord, there it is, the huge asbestos whale,
the behemoth beast, come see it, he shouted madly, come see it, raising
such an uproar of dogs' barking and women's panic that even the
oldest men remembered the frights of their great-grandfathers and
crawled under their beds, thinking that William Dampier had come
back, but those who ran into the street didn't make the effort to see
the unlikely apparatus which at that instant was lost again in the east
and raised up in its annual disaster, but they covered him with blows
and left him so twisted that it was then he said to himself, drooling
with rage, now they're going to see who I am, but he took care not
to share his determination with anyone, but spent the whole year with
the fixed idea, now they're going to see who I am, waiting for it to
be the eve of the apparition once more in order to do what he did,
which was steal a boat, cross the bay, and spend the evening waiting
for his great moment in the inlets of the slave port, in the human
brine of the Caribbean, but so absorbed in his adventure that he didn't
stop as he always did in front of the Hindu shops to look at the ivory
mandarins carved from the whole tusk of an elephant, nor did he make
fun of the Dutch Negroes in their orthopedic velocipedes, nor was
he frightened as at other times of the copper-skinned Malayans, who
had gone around the world enthralled by the chimera of a secret tavern
where they sold roast filets of Brazilian women, because he wasn't
aware of anything until night came over him with all the weight of
the stars and the jungle exhaled a sweet fragrance of gardenias and
rotten salamanders, and there he was, rowing in the stolen boat toward

the mouth of the bay, with the lantern out so as not to alert the customs police, idealized every fifteen seconds by the green wing flap of the beacon and turned human once more by the darkness, knowing that he was getting close to the buoys that marked the harbor channel, not only because its oppressive glow was getting more intense, but because the breathing of the water was becoming sad, and he rowed like that, so wrapped up in himself, that he didn't know where the fearful shark's breath that suddenly reached him came from or why the night became dense, as if the stars had suddenly died and it was because the liner was there, with all of its inconceivable size, Lord, bigger than any other big thing in the world and darker than any other dark thing on land or sea, three hundred thousand tons of shark smell passing so close to the boat that he could see the seams of the steel precipice, without a single light in the infinite portholes, without a sigh from the engines, without a soul, and carrying its own circle of silence with it, its own dead air, its halted time, its errant sea in which a whole world of drowned animals floated, and suddenly it all disappeared with the flash of the beacon and for an instant it was the diaphanous Caribbean once more, the March night, the everyday air of the pelicans, so he stayed alone among the buoys, not knowing what to do, asking himself, startled, if perhaps he wasn't dreaming while he was awake, not just now but the other times too, but no sooner had he asked himself than a breath of mystery snuffed out the buoys, from the first to the last, so that when the light of the beacon passed by the liner appeared again and now its compasses were out of order, perhaps not even knowing what part of the ocean sea it was in, groping for the invisible channel but actually heading for the shoals, until he got the overwhelming revelation that that misfortune of the buoys was the last key to the enchantment and he lighted the lantern in the boat, a tiny red light that had no reason to alarm anyone in the watchtowers but which would be like a guiding sun for the pilot, because, thanks to it, the liner corrected its course and passed into the main gate of the channel in a maneuver of lucky resurrection, and then all the lights went on at the same time so that the boilers wheezed again, the stars were fixed in their places, and the animal corpses went to the bottom, and there was a clatter of plates and a fragrance of laurel sauce in the kitchens, and one could hear the pulsing of the orchestra on the moon decks and the throbbing of the arteries of high sea lovers in the shadows of the staterooms, but he still carried so much leftover rage in him that he would not let himself be confused by emotion or be frightened by the miracle, but said to himself with more decision than ever, now they're going to see who I am, the cowards, now they're going to see, and instead of turning aside so that the colossal machine would not charge into him, he began to row in front of it, because now they really are going to see who I am, and he continued guiding the ship with the lantern until he was so sure of its obedience that he made it change course from the direction of the docks once more, took it out of the invisible channel, and led it by the halter as if it were a sea lamb toward the lights of the sleeping village, a living ship, invulnerable to the torches of the beacon, that no longer made it invisible but made it aluminum every fifteen seconds, and the crosses of the church, the misery of the houses, the illusion began to stand out, and still the ocean liner followed behind him, following his will inside of it, the captain asleep on his heart side, the fighting bulls in the snow of their pantries, the solitary patient in the infirmary, the orphan water of its cisterns, the unredeemed pilot who must have mistaken the cliffs for the docks, because at that instant the great roar of the whistle burst forth, once, and he was soaked with the downpour of steam that fell on him, again, and the boat belonging to someone else was on the point of capsizing, and again, but it was too late, because there were the shells of the shoreline, the stones of the streets, the doors of the disbelievers, the whole village illuminated by the lights of the fearsome liner itself, and he barely had time to get out of the way to make room for the cataclysm, shouting in the midst of the confusion, there it is, you cowards, a second before the huge steel cask shattered the ground and one could hear the neat destruction of ninety thousand five hundred champagne glasses breaking, one after the other, from stem to stern, and then the light came out and it was no longer a March dawn but the noon of a radiant Wednesday, and he was able to give himself the pleasure of watching the disbelievers as with open mouths they contemplated the largest ocean liner in this world and the other aground in front of the church, whiter than anything, twenty times taller than the steeple and some ninety-seven times longer than the village, with its name engraved in iron letters, *Haldlcsillag*, and the ancient and languid waters of the seas of death dripping down its sides.

Translated by Gregory Rabassa

Cain

Andrew Vachss

1

"Look at my Buster . . . look what they did to him."

The old man pointed a shaking finger at the dog, a big German shepherd. The animal was cowering in a corner of the kitchen of the railroad flat—his fine head was lopsided, a piece of his skull missing under the ragged fur. A deep pocket of scar tissue glowed white where one eye had been, the other was cataract-milky, fire-dotted with fear. The dog's tail hung behind him at a demented angle, one front paw hung useless in a plaster cast.

"Who did it?"

The old man wasn't listening, not finished yet. Squeezing the wound to get the pus out. "Buster guards out back, where the chicken wire is. They tormented him, threw stuff at him, made him crazy. Then they cut the lock. Two of them. One had a baseball bat, the other had a piece of pipe. My Buster . . . he wouldn't hurt anyone. They beat on him, over and over, laughing. I ran downstairs to stop them . . . they just slapped me, like I was a fly. They did my Buster so bad, it even hurts him when I try and rub him."

The old man sat crying at his kitchen table.

The dog watched me, a thin whine coming from his open mouth. Half his teeth were missing.

"You know who did it," I said. It wasn't a question. He didn't know, he wouldn't have called me—I'm no private eye.

"I called . . . I called the cops. 911. They never came. I went down to the precinct. The man at the desk, he said to call the ASPCA."

"You know who they are?"

"I don't know their names. Two men, young men. One has big muscles, the other's skinny."

"They're from around here?"

"I don't know. They're always together—I've seen them before. Everybody knows them. They have their heads shaved too."

"Everybody knows them?"

"Everybody. They beat other dogs too. They make the dogs bark at them, then they . . ." He was crying again.

I waited, watching the dog.

"They come back. I see them walking down the alley. Almost every day. I can't leave Buster outside anymore—can't even take him for a walk. I have to clean up after him now."

"What do you want?"

"What do I want?"

"You called me. You got my name from somewhere. You know what I do."

The old man got up, knelt next to his dog. Put his hand gently on the dog's head. "Buster used to be the toughest dog in the world —wasn't afraid of nothing. I had him ever since he was a pup. He won't even look out the back window with me now."

"What do you want?" I asked him again.

They both looked at me. "You know," the old man said.

2

A freestanding brick building in Red Hook, not far from the water-front, surrounded by a chain-link fence topped with razor wire. I rang the bell. A dog snarled a warning. I looked into the mirrored glass, knowing they could see me. The steel door opened. A man in a white T-shirt over floppy black trousers opened the door. He was barefoot, dark hair cropped close, body so smooth it might have been extruded from rubber. He bowed slightly. I returned his bow, followed him inside.

A rectangular room, roughened wood floor. A canvas-wrapped

heavy bag swung from the ceiling in one corner. In another, a car tire was suspended from a thick rope. A pair of long wood staves hung on hooks.

"I'll get him," the man said.

I waited, standing in one spot.

He returned, leading a dog by a chain. A broad-chested pit bull, all white except for a black patch over one eye. The dog watched me, cobra-calm.

"Here he is," the man said.

"You sure he'll do it?"

"Guaranteed."

"What's his name?"

"Cain."

I squatted down, said the dog's name, scratched him behind his erect ears when he came to me.

"You want to practice with him?"

"Yeah, I'd better. I know the commands you gave me, but . . ."

"Wait here."

I played with Cain, putting him through standard-obedience paces. He was a machine, perfect.

The trainer came back into the room. Two other men with him, dressed in full agitator's suits, leather-lined and padded. Masks on their faces, like hockey goalies wear.

"Let's do it," he said.

3

I walked down the alley behind the old man's building, Cain on a thin leather leash, held lightly in my left hand. The dog knew the route by now—it was our fifth straight day.

They turned the corner fifty feet from me. The smaller one had a baseball bat over his shoulder, the muscleman slapped a piece of lead pipe into one palm.

They closed in. I stepped aside to let them pass, pulling Cain close to my leg.

They didn't walk past. The smaller one planted his feet, looking into my eyes.

"Hey, man. That's a pit bull, right? Pretty tough dogs, I heard."

"No, he's not tough," I said, a catch in my voice. "He's just a pet."

"He looks like a bad dog to me," the big guy said, poking the lead pipe into the dog's face, stabbing. Cain stepped out of the way.

"Please don't hurt my dog," I begged them, pulling up on the leash.

Cain leaped into my arms, his face against my chest. I could feel the bunched muscles in his legs, all four paws flat against me.

"Aw, is your dog *scared*, man?" the big one sneered, stepping close to me, slapping the dog's back with the pipe.

"Leave us alone," I said, stepping back as they closed in.

"Put the dog down, faggot!"

I put my mouth close to Cain's ear, whispered "Go!" as I threw open my arms. The pit bull launched himself off my chest without a sound, his alligator teeth locking on the big guy's face. A scream bubbled out. The big man fell to the ground, clawing at Cain's back. Pieces of his face flew off, red and white. He spasmed like he was in the electric chair, but the dog held on, wouldn't drop the bite. The smaller guy stood there, rooted, mouth open, no sound coming out, his pants turning dark at the crotch.

"Out!" I snapped at the dog. Cain stepped away, his mouth foamy with bloody gristle.

"Your turn," I said to the smaller guy. He took off, running for his life. Cain caught him, running right up his spine, locking onto the back of his neck.

I called him off when I heard a snap.

As we turned to walk back down the alley, I glanced up.

The old man was at the window. Buster next to him, the plaster cast on his paw draped over the sill.

The Ultimate Caper

Donald E. Westlake

I. THE PURLOINED LETTER

"Yes," the fat man said, "I've spent the last 17 years in this pursuit. More armagnac, Mr. Staid?"

"Nice booze," Staid admitted. Adding a splash of Fresca, he said, "What is this dingus anyway, this purloined letter?"

"Ah," the fat man said. "It's quite a story, Mr. Staid. Have you ever heard of the Barony of Ueltenplotz?"

Staid sucked on his stogie. "Thuringian, isn't it? One of the prizes in the Carpathian succession, not settled till MCCLXIV."

"Very good, Mr. Staid! I like a man who knows his dates."

"These onions aren't bad either," Staid allowed.

"Well, sir," the fat man said, "if you know the history of the Barons Ueltenplotz, you know they've been the renegades of Mitteleuropa for a thousand years."

"Maupers and gapes," Staid grated.

"Exactly. And arrogant to a fault. What would you say, sir, if I told you the seventh Baron Ueltenplotz stole a letter from the European alphabet?"

"I'd say your brain was all funny."

"And yet, sir, that is precisely what happened. Yes, sir. The family name was originally one letter longer, beginning with that missing letter."

"Which letter was it?"

"No one knows," the fat man said. "In MXXIX, the seventh Baron, Helmut the Homicidal, having seen one of his personal monogrammed polo shirts being used as a horsewipe, determined to commandeer his initial letter for his own personal use. The Barony was wealthy in those days—carrots had been discovered in the territory —and so monks, scribes, delineators, transvestites and other civil servants were dispatched across Europe to excise that letter wherever it might appear. Illuminated manuscripts developed sudden unexplained fly specks and pen smears. Literate men—and they were few in the XIth century, Mr. Staid, I assure you—were bribed or threatened to forget that letter. The alphabet, which had been 27 letters in length—'Thrice nine' was a saying of the time, Mr. Staid, long since forgotten—was reduced to 26. The letter between K and L had been stolen! And what do you say to *that*, sir?"

"I say you've been staring at the light too long," Staid said. He puffed on his pipe.

"And yet these are facts, sir, facts. I first came across this remarkable story 17 years ago, in MCMLVIII, in conversation with a retired harpsichord tuner in Potsdam. The letter had been removed everywhere, Mr. Staid, except from the face of *one shield*, sir, one shield maintained for centuries in the deepest recesses of Schloss Ueltenplotz. During the Second World War, a technical sergeant from Bismarck, N.D., stumbling across the shield and mistaking it for a beer tray, sent it home to his father, an official in the Veterans of Foreign Wars. But the shield never arrived, sir, and what do you think of *that?*"

"Not much," Staid admitted, and dragged on his cigarette.

"It had been stolen, sir, yet again, by a Yugoslav general in Istanbul, one Brigadier Ueltehmitt. But he didn't know what he had, sir. He thought the mark on the shield was a typographical error, and believed it to be a 'Yield' sign from the Hungarian Highway Department."

"What's this dingus look like, anyway?"

"No one knows for certain," the fat man said. "Some think it's a ϕ, and some say a λ."

"φ seems more likely," Staid said. "What's it supposed to sound like?"

"No one has pronounced that letter," the fat man said, "in over a thousand years. Some think it's the sound in a man's throat on the third day of Asian flu when watching a rock record commercial during the 6 o'clock news."

"Guttural," said Staid.

The fat man, whose real name was Guttural, frowned at Staid through narrowed eyes. "It seems I've underestimated you," he said.

"Looks like," admitted Staid.

"Well, sir," the fat man said, "we'll put our cards on the table. I want that letter. Will you join me?"

"Where is this dingus, anyway?"

"Come along, sir!"

II. THE SHIELD OF UELTENPLOTZ

The Ueltehmitt Caper ran without a hitch. First, the three helicopters descended over the Bahnhof Boogie in Dusseldorf, released their grappling hooks and removed the building to Schwartzvogel Island in Lake Liebfraumilch, where the demolition team with the laser sliced through the sides of the vault. Eliminating the alarm system by squirting Redi-Whip into the air-conditioning ducts, they sprayed the guards with a sleep-inducing gas disguised as pocket packs of Propa PH, and lowered ropes to one another until exactly 6:27. Removing the lead-lined box containing the priceless Shield of Ueltenplotz, they placed it in the speedboat and sped away to the innocent-appearing minesweeper dawdling in the current. Waterline gates in the minesweeper yawned open, the speedboat entered, and before the minesweeper sank, the lead-lined box had been transferred to the catapult plane and launched skyward. Two hours later, the pilot parachuted over Loch Ness and was driven swiftly to Scotswa Hay, the ancestral retreat of Guttural's co-conspirator Hart in the highlands.

Staid, Guttural, Hart, Wilmer, Obloquy and the beauteous Laurinda synchronized their watches and crowded around the table where lay the package, now wrapped in yesterday's Dortmunder Zeitung Geblatt. Ripping off the wrappings, the fat man opened the box and took out the precious shield.

"Ahhhh," said the beauteous Wilmer.

"At last," commented Obloquy, and choked to death on his Russian cigarette.

The fat man turned over the shield. "No!" he cried. "No!"

Staid frowned at the shield. Rounder than most, it bore the figure π. It was a Frisbee.

"It's a Frisbee!" cried the fat man.

"You fool!" shrieked Laurinda, stamping her foot and mailing it. "Ueltehmitt tricked you!"

"Wrong dingus, huh?" Staid asked, and lit up a corncob.

"Seventeen years," the fat man said. "Well, I'll give it 17 more if need be." He flung the false shield out the window. "On to Istanbul! Will you join us, Staid?"

"No, thanks, fat man." Staid watched the Frisbee sail over the moors. "π in the sky," he said.

Chee's Witch

Tony Hillerman

Snow is so important to the Eskimos they have nine nouns to describe its variations. Corporal Jimmy Chee of the Navajo Tribal Police had heard that as an anthropology student at the University of New Mexico. He remembered it now because he was thinking of all the words you need in Navajo to account for the many forms of witchcraft. The word Old Woman Tso had used was "anti'l," which is the ultimate sort, the absolute worst. And so, in fact, was the deed which seemed to have been done. Murder, apparently. Mutilation, certainly, if Old Woman Tso had her facts right. And then, if one believed all the mythology of witchery told among the fifty clans who comprised The People, there must also be cannibalism, incest, even necrophilia.

On the radio in Chee's pickup truck, the voice of the young Navajo reading a Gallup used-car commercial was replaced by Willie Nelson singing of trouble and a worried mind. The ballad fit Chee's mood. He was tired. He was thirsty. He was sticky with sweat. He was worried. His pickup jolted along the ruts in a windless heat, leaving a white fog of dust to mark its winding passage across the Rainbow Plateau. The truck was gray with it. So was Jimmy Chee. Since sunrise he had covered maybe two hundred miles of half-graded gravel and unmarked wagon tracks of the Arizona–Utah–New Mexico border country. Routine at first—a check into a witch story at the Tsossie hogan north of Teec Nos Pos to stop trouble before it started. Routine and logical. A bitter winter, a sand storm spring, a summer of rainless, desiccating heat. Hopes dying, things going wrong, anger growing, and then the witch gossip. The logical. A bitter winter, a sand storm spring, a summer awry. The trouble at the summer hogan of the Tsossies was a sick child and a water well that had turned alkaline— nothing unexpected. But you didn't expect such a specific witch. The skinwalker, the Tsossies agreed, was the City Navajo, the man who had come to live in one of the government houses at Kayenta. Why the City Navajo? Because everybody knew he was a witch. Where had they heard that, the first time? The People who came to the trading post at Mexican Water said it. And so Chee had driven west-ward over Tohache Wash, past Red Mesa and Rabbit Ears to Mexican Water. He had spent hours on the shady porch giving those who came to buy, and to fill their water barrels, and to visit, a chance to know who he was until finally they might risk talking about witchcraft to a stranger. They were Mud Clan, and Many Goats People, and Stand-ing Rock Clan—foreign to Chee's own Slow Talking People—but finally some of them talked a little.

A witch was at work on the Rainbow Plateau. Adeline Etcitty's mare had foaled a two-headed colt. Hosteen Musket had seen the witch. He'd seen a man walk into a grove of cottonwoods, but when he got there an owl flew away. Rudolph Bisti's boys lost three rams while driving their flocks up into the Chuska high pastures, and when they found the bodies, the huge tracks of a werewolf were all around them. The daughter of Rosemary Nashibitti had seen a big dog both-ering her horses and had shot at it with her .22 and the dog had turned into a man wearing a wolfskin and had fled, half running, half flying. The old man they called Afraid of His Horses had heard the sound of the witch on the roof of his winter hogan, and saw the dirt falling through the smoke hole as the skinwalker tried to throw in his corpse powder. The next morning the old man had followed the tracks of the Navajo Wolf for a mile, hoping to kill him. But the tracks had faded away. There was nothing very unusual in the stories, except their number and the recurring hints that the City Navajo was the witch. But then came what Chee hadn't expected. The witch had killed a man.

The police dispatcher at Window Rock had been interrupting Willie Nelson with an occasional blurted message. Now she spoke directly to Chee. He acknowledged. She asked his location.

"About fifteen miles south of Dennehotso," Chee said. "Homeward bound for Tuba City. Dirty, thirsty, hungry, and tired."

"I have a message."

"Tuba City," Chee repeated, "which I hope to reach in about two hours, just in time to avoid running up a lot of overtime for which I never get paid."

"The message is FBI Agent Wells needs to contact you. Can you make a meeting at Kayenta Holiday Inn at eight P.M.?"

"What's it about?" Chee asked. The dispatcher's name was Virgie Endecheenie, and she had a very pretty voice and the first time Chee had met her at the Window Rock headquarters of the Navajo Tribal Police he had been instantly smitten. Unfortunately, Virgie was a born-into Salt Cedar Clan, which was the clan of Chee's father, which put an instant end to that. Even thinking about it would violate the complex incest taboo of the Navajos.

"Nothing on what it's about," Virgie said, her voice strictly business. "It just says confirm meeting time and place with Chee or obtain alternate time."

"Any first name on Wells?" Chee asked. The only FBI Wells he knew was Jake Wells. He hoped it wouldn't be Jake.

"Negative on the first name," Virgie said.

"All right," Chee said. "I'll be there."

The road tilted downward now into the vast barrens of erosion which the Navajos call Beautiful Valley. Far to the west, the edge of the sun dipped behind a cloud—one of the line of thunderheads forming in the evening heat over the San Francisco Peaks and the Cococino Rim. The Hopis had been holding their Niman Kachina dances, calling the clouds to come and bless them.

Chee reached Kayenta just a little late. It was early twilight and the clouds had risen black against the sunset. The breeze brought the faint smells that rising humidity carries across desert country—the perfume of sage, creosote brush, and dust. The desk clerk said that Wells was in room 284 and the first name was Jake. Chee no longer cared. Jake Wells was abrasive but he was also smart. He had the best record in the special FBI Academy class Chee had attended, a quick, tough intelligence. Chee could tolerate the man's personality for a while to learn what Wells could make of his witchcraft puzzle.

"It's unlocked," Wells said. "Come on in." He was propped against the padded headboard of the bed, shirt off, shoes on, glass in hand.

He glanced at Chee and then back at the television set. He was as tall as Chee remembered, and the eyes were just as blue. He waved the glass at Chee without looking away from the set. "Mix yourself one," he said, nodding toward a bottle beside the sink in the dressing alcove.

"How you doing, Jake?" Chee asked.

Now the blue eyes reexamined Chee. The question in them abruptly went away. "Yeah," Wells said. "You were the one at the Academy." He eased himself on his left elbow and extended a hand. "Jake Wells," he said.

Chee shook the hand. "Chee," he said.

Wells shifted his weight again and handed Chee his glass. "Pour me a little more while you're at it," he said, "and turn down the sound."

Chee turned down the sound.

"About thirty percent booze," Wells demonstrated the proportion with his hands. "This is your district then. You're in charge around Kayenta? Window Rock said I should talk to you. They said you were out chasing around in the desert today. What are you working on?"

"Nothing much," Chee said. He ran a glass of water, drinking it thirstily. His face in the mirror was dirty—the lines around mouth and eyes whitish with dust. The sticker on the glass reminded guests that the laws of the Navajo Tribal Council prohibited possession of alcoholic beverages on the reservation. He refilled his own glass with water and mixed Wells's drink. "As a matter of fact, I'm working on a witchcraft case."

"Witchcraft?" Wells laughed. "Really?" He took the drink from Chee and examined it. "How does it work? Spells and like that?"

"Not exactly," Chee said. "It depends. A few years ago a little girl got sick down near Burnt Water. Her dad killed three people with a shotgun. He said they blew corpse powder on his daughter and made her sick."

Wells was watching him. "The kind of crime where you have the insanity plea."

"Sometimes," Chee said. "Whatever you have, witch talk makes you nervous. It happens more when you have a bad year like this. You hear it and you try to find out what's starting it before things get worse."

"So you're not really expecting to find a witch?"

"Usually not," Chee said.

"Usually?"

"Judge for yourself," Chee said. "I'll tell you what I've picked up today. You tell me what to make of it. Have time?"

Wells shrugged. "What I really want to talk about is a guy named Simon Begay." He looked quizzically at Chee. "You heard the name?"

"Yes," Chee said.

"Well, shit," Wells said. "You shouldn't have. What do you know about him?"

"Showed up maybe three months ago. Moved into one of those U.S. Public Health Service houses over by the Kayenta clinic. Stranger. Keeps to himself. From off the reservation somewhere. I figured you federals put him here to keep him out of sight."

Wells frowned. "How long you known about him?"

"Quite a while," Chee said. He'd known about Begay within a week after his arrival.

"He's a witness," Wells said. "They broke a car-theft operation in Los Angeles. Big deal. National connections. One of those where they have hired hands picking up expensive models and they drive 'em right on the ship and off-load in South America. This Begay is one of the hired hands. Nobody much. Criminal record going all the way back to juvenile, but all nickel-and-dime stuff. I gather he saw some things that help tie some big boys into the crime, so Justice made a deal with him."

"And they hide him out here until the trial?"

Something apparently showed in the tone of the question. "If you want to hide an apple, you drop it in with the other apples," Wells said. "What better place?"

Chee had been looking at Wells's shoes, which were glossy with polish. Now he examined his own boots, which were not. But he was thinking of Justice Department stupidity. The appearance of any new human in a country as empty as the Navajo Reservation provoked instant interest. If the stranger was a Navajo, there were instant questions. What was his clan? Who was his mother? What was his father's clan? Who were his relatives? The City Navajo had no answers to any of these crucial questions. He was (as Chee had been repeatedly told) unfriendly. It was quickly guessed that he was a "relocation Navajo," born to one of those hundreds of Navajo families which the federal government had tried to reestablish forty years ago in Chicago, Los Angeles, and other urban centers. He was a stranger. In a year of witches, he would certainly be suspected. Chee sat looking at his boots, wondering if that was the only basis for the charge that City Navajo was a skinwalker. Or had someone seen something? Had someone seen the murder?

"The thing about apples is they don't gossip," Chee said.

"You hear gossip about Begay?" Wells was sitting up now, his feet on the floor.

"Sure," Chee said. "I hear he's a witch."

Wells produced a pro-forma chuckle. "Tell me about it," he said.

Chee knew exactly how he wanted to tell it. Wells would have to wait awhile before he came to the part about Begay. "The Eskimos have nine nouns for snow," Chee began. He told Wells about the variety of witchcraft on the reservations and its environs: about frenzy witchcraft, used for sexual conquests, of witchery distortions, of curing ceremonials, of the exotic two-heart witchcraft of the Hopi Fog Clan, of the Zuni Sorcery Fraternity, of the Navajo "chindi," which is more like a ghost than a witch, and finally of the Navajo Wolf, the anti'l witchcraft, the werewolves who pervert every taboo of the Navajo Way and use corpse powder to kill their victims.

Wells rattled the ice in his glass and glanced at his watch.

"To get to the part about your Begay," Chee said, "about two months ago we started picking up witch gossip. Nothing much, and you expect it during a drought. Lately it got to be more than usual." He described some of the tales and how uneasiness and dread had spread across the plateau. He described what he had learned today, the Tsossies's naming City Navajo as the witch, his trip to Mexican Water, of learning there that the witch had killed a man.

"They said it happened in the spring—couple of months ago. They told me the ones who knew about it were the Tso outfit." The talk of murder, Chee noticed, had revived Wells's interest. "I went up there," he continued, "and found the old woman who runs the outfit. Emma Tso. She told me her son-in-law had been out looking for some sheep, and smelled something, and found the body under some chamiso brush in a dry wash. A witch had killed him."

"How—"

Chee cut off the question. "I asked her how he knew it was a witch killing. She said the hands were stretched out like this." Chee extended his hands, palms up. "They were flayed. The skin was cut off the palms and fingers."

Wells raised his eyebrows.

"That's what the witch uses to make corpse powder," Chee explained. "They take the skin that has the whorls and ridges of the individual personality—the skin from the palms and the finger pads, and the soles of the feet. They take that, and the skin from the glans of the penis, and the small bones where the neck joins the skull, and they dry it, and pulverize it, and use it as poison."

"You're going to get to Begay any minute now," Wells said. "That right?"

"We got to him," Chee said. "He's the one they think is the witch. He's the City Navajo."

"I thought you were going to say that," Wells said. He rubbed the back of his hand across one blue eye. "City Navajo. Is it that obvious?"

"Yes," Chee said. "And then he's a stranger. People suspect strangers."

"Were they coming around him? Accusing him? Any threats? Anything like that, you think?"

"It wouldn't work that way—not unless somebody had someone in their family killed. The way you deal with a witch is hire a singer and hold a special kind of curing ceremony. That turns the witchcraft around and kills the witch."

Wells made an impatient gesture. "Whatever," he said. "I think something has made this Begay spooky." He stared into his glass, communing with the bourbon. "I don't know."

"Something unusual about the way he's acting?"

"Hell of it is I don't know how he usually acts. This wasn't my case. The agent who worked him retired or some damn thing, so I got stuck with being the delivery man." He shifted his eyes from glass to Chee. "But if it was me, and I was holed up here waiting, and the guy came along who was going to take me home again, then I'd be glad to see him. Happy to have it over with. All that."

"He wasn't?"

Wells shook his head. "Seemed edgy. Maybe that's natural, though. He's going to make trouble for some hard people."

"I'd be nervous," Chee said.

"I guess it doesn't matter much anyway," Wells said. "He's small potatoes. The guy who's handling it now in the U.S. Attorney's Office said it must have been a toss-up whether to fool with him at all. He said the assistant who handled it decided to hide him out just to be on the safe side."

"Begay doesn't know much?"

"I guess not. That, and they've got better witnesses."

"So why worry?"

Wells laughed. "I bring this sucker back and they put him on the witness stand and he answers all the questions with I don't know and it makes the USDA look like a horse's ass. When a U.S. Attorney looks like that, he finds an FBI agent to blame it on." He yawned. "Therefore," he said through the yawn, "I want to ask you what you think. This is your territory. You are the officer in charge. Is it your opinion that someone got to my witness?"

Chee let the question hang. He spent a fraction of a second reaching the answer, which was they could have if they wanted to try. Then he thought about the real reason Wells had kept him working late without a meal or a shower. Two sentences in Wells's report. One would note that the possibility the witness had been approached had been checked with local Navajo Police. The next would report whatever Chee said next. Wells would have followed Federal Rule One— Protect Your Ass.

Chee shrugged. "You want to hear the rest of my witchcraft business?"

Wells put his drink on the lamp table and untied his shoe. "Does it bear on this?"

"Who knows? Anyway there's not much left. I'll let you decide. The point is we had already picked up this corpse Emma Tso's son-in-law found. Somebody had reported it weeks ago. It had been collected, and taken in for an autopsy. The word we got on the body was Navajo male in his thirties probably. No identification on him."

"How was this bird killed?"

"No sign of foul play," Chee said. "By the time the body was brought in, decay and the scavengers hadn't left a lot. Mostly bone and gristle, I guess. This was a long time after Emma Tso's son-in-law saw him."

"So why do they think Begay killed him?" Wells removed his second shoe and headed for the bathroom.

Chee picked up the telephone and dialed the Kayenta clinic. He got the night supervisor and waited while the supervisor dug out the file. Wells came out of the bathroom with his toothbrush. Chee covered the mouthpiece. "I'm having them read me the autopsy report," Chee explained. Wilson began brushing his teeth at the sink in the dressing alcove. The voice of the night supervisor droned into Chee's ear.

"That all?" Chee asked. "Nothing added on? No identity yet? Still no cause?"

"That's him," the voice said.

"How about shoes?" Chee asked. "He have shoes on?"

"Just a sec," the voice said. "Yep. Size ten D. And a hat, and . . ."

"No mention of the neck or skull, right? I didn't miss that? No bones missing?"

Silence. "Nothing about neck or skull bones."

"Ah," Chee said. "Fine. I thank you." He felt great. He felt wonderful. Finally things had clicked into place. The witch was exorcised. "Jake," he said. "Let me tell you a little more about my witch case."

Wells was rinsing his mouth. He spit out the water and looked at Chee, amused. "I didn't think of this before," Wells said, "but you really don't have a witch problem. If you leave that corpse a death by natural causes, there's no case to work. If you decide it's a homicide, you don't have jurisdiction anyway. Homicide on an Indian reservation, FBI has jurisdiction." Wells grinned. "We'll come in and find your witch for you."

Chee looked at his boots, which were still dusty. His appetite had left him, as it usually did an hour or so after he missed a meal. He still hungered for a bath. He picked up his hat and pushed himself to his feet.

"I'll go home now," he said. "The only thing you don't know about the witch case is what I just got from the autopsy report. The corpse had his shoes on and no bones were missing from the base of the skull."

Chee opened the door and stood in it, looking back. Wells was taking his pajamas out of his suitcase. "So what advice do you have for me? What can you tell me about my witch case?"

"To tell the absolute truth, Chee, I'm not into witches," Wells said. "Haven't been since I was a boy."

"But we don't really have a witch case now," Chee said. He spoke earnestly. "The shoes were still on, so the skin wasn't taken from the soles of his feet. No bones missing from the neck. You need those to make corpse powder."

Wells was pulling his undershirt over his head. Chee hurried.

"What we have now is another little puzzle," Chee said. "If you're not collecting stuff for corpse powder, why cut the skin off this guy's hands?"

"I'm going to take a shower," Wells said. "Got to get my Begay back to L.A. tomorrow."

Outside the temperature had dropped. The air moved softly from the west, carrying the smell of rain. Over the Utah border, over the Cococino Rim, over the Rainbow Plateau, lightning flickered and glowed. The storm had formed. The storm was moving. The sky was black with it. Chee stood in the darkness, listening to the mutter of thunder, inhaling the perfume, exulting in it.

He climbed into the truck and started it. How had they set it up, and why? Perhaps the FBI agent who knew Begay had been ready to retire. Perhaps an accident had been arranged. Getting rid of the assistant prosecutor who knew the witness would have been even simpler—a matter of hiring him away from the government job. That left no one who knew this minor witness was not Simon Begay. And who was he? Probably they had other Navajos from the Los Angeles community stealing cars for them. Perhaps that's what had suggested the scheme. To most white men all Navajos looked pretty much alike, just as in his first years at college all Chee had seen in white men was pink skin, freckles, and light-colored eyes. And what would the imposter say? Chee grinned. He'd say whatever was necessary to cast doubt on the prosecution, to cast the fatal "reasonable doubt," to make—as Wells had put it—the U.S. District Attorney look like a horse's ass.

Chee drove into the rain twenty miles west of Kayenta. Huge, cold drops drummed on the pickup roof and turned the highway into a ribbon of water. Tomorrow the backcountry roads would be impassable. As soon as they dried and the washouts had been repaired, he'd go back to the Tsossie hogan, and the Tso place, and to all the other places from which the word would quickly spread. He'd tell the people that the witch was in custody of the FBI and was gone forever from the Rainbow Plateau.

Little Leo

Jerome Charyn

He was losing his marbles, one by one. He couldn't remember the names of his own adjutants. He was struggling against some swollen thing that swallowed up the different particles of his past. I'm Isaac Sidel, he had to tell himself. I'm the PC. My daughter's name is Marilyn. My mother used to be Sophie Sidel. My dad is a portrait painter in Paris. He panicked. He couldn't recall his brother's name. Leo, he said. Like Count Leo Tolstoy, the father of *War and Peace*. But Leo Sidel was no fucking count. His wife had rid herself of him. His children ran from Leo. He was in and out of alimony jail until Isaac settled a small allowance on him. Leo couldn't seem to hold a job even while his own brother was the big cop of New York City, a guy suffering from selective amnesia. What the hell was the name of Leo's two kids? A boy and a girl. He could imagine their faces, hear them call him "Uncle Isaac."

He was up on the fourteenth floor of One Police Plaza, where he would dream of crimes he might commit. The phone started to buzz. His chauffeur was waiting for him. Isaac went into the bowels of One PP and rode out of the commissioner's parking slot in his black Dodge, with Joe Barbarossa behind the wheel. Barbarossa was the most decorated cop in New York City. He was also an FBI informant. He had a rotten habit of ripping off drug dealers. He wore a white glove over his "shooting hand." He was a Ping-Pong player, like Isaac's dead angel, Manfred Coen. Barbarossa was a vagabond who lived at the same Ping-Pong club where Coen had died, and it was the ritual of Ping-Pong that bound him to Isaac. Joe was the Justice Department's private shadow at One PP. Half his coke deals must have been arranged by the Bureau. But Isaac preferred Barbarossa to any other spy. And he'd rather have him up close than in some rat's corner where Isaac couldn't see.

Isaac began to growl. "That actress, what the hell was her name? She was a calendar girl. She married DiMaggio."

Barbarossa didn't even prick up his ears. "Marilyn. Like your daughter . . . Marilyn Monroe. What's the matter, boss?"

"My fucking mind is going. I can't remember the names of my nephew and niece."

"You don't have a niece. You have two nephews. Davie and Michael. We visited them last month."

"That's impossible. I know I have a niece. I can picture her face."

"That's Caroline. Davie's girlfriend."

"Girlfriend? The kid's in kneepants."

"He's going to college, boss."

"I'm telling you, Joe. Time is fucking with my head. I wake up and I can't remember who I am."

"You're the PC. Your ass is always on the line. Somebody suffers. You suffer with them. It's hard to pull back . . . boss, a call came in while you were coming down. It's your brother."

"Brother?" Isaac said.

"Yeah, he was caught shoplifting. Some shit like that. They're holding him in a dinky lock-up at a department store. The store dick won't release him."

"Does that department store know who he is?"

"Yeah, boss. But the detective is a ballbreaker. He won't release Leo until you come for him."

"What's his name?"

"The dispatcher didn't say."

"And the store?"

"It's a big shoebox on Fordham Road. Fashion Town."

"Never heard of it."

"No one shops there."

"Except my brother Leo . . . what's my schedule like?"

"You have a three o'clock with Cardinal Jim on Gun Hill Road. Should I cancel?"

"No," Isaac said. "Let Leo sit. It will do him some good. The cardinal doesn't like cancellations. We'll go to him first. Then we'll collect fucking Leo."

Jim O'Bannon, the cardinal archbishop of New York, liked to rendezvous with Isaac in distant streets where he wouldn't be noticed. Isaac enjoyed these little cabals. And it gave him a chance to ride through the City like a random voyager. Joe would pick the most "scenic" route, where Isaac could observe one wasteland after the other.

They crossed into the Bronx, rode up the Grand Concourse, the borough's own blasted Champs Élysées, with broken courtyards, blighted trees, Art Deco palaces with ghostly, crumbling roofs. Isaac must have found some of his marbles. His fucking mind started to flash. He had an image of Leo in short pants. The image was forty-five years old. Isaac had been a bandit long before he became police commissioner. He robbed ration stamps in the middle of World War II. Leo was his courier, little Leo, who could run across lines of policemen with contraband in the pockets of his short pants . . .

They got to Gun Hill Road. The cardinal stood outside his big black Lincoln in an ancient shirt. He loved old clothes. He took a walk with Isaac, tore at the cigarette in his hand and toyed with the tobacco. But Isaac was spooked by that picture of Leo in short pants.

"There's a bit of a crisis, love."

"Tell me about it, Jim."

"I have a problem priest. He's been undressing little boys. And now we're being blackmailed."

"Who's the blackmailer?"

"One of your lads."

"A cop?" Isaac said. "I can't believe it."

"I didn't say 'cop,' did I? A lab technician. Broderick Swirl. He's one of your Crime Scene boys."

"I'll cripple him."

"Ain't that easy. I met the lad. Mentioned your name. He didn't blink. He'd like a monthly stipend from the Church. He has photographs, Isaac."

"Is he Catholic?"

"Indeed. A former friend of my priest. Our lawyers are against any sort of scandal. They've set up a discretionary fund. We wouldn't be involved. And we can always pounce on him at a later date."

"Don't," Isaac said. "Once you pay him, that's it. Lemme have a go at him."

"He's a devil. He won't scare."

"I'll run over to Crime Scene and nail him to a door."

"The lad's convalescing. He broke his leg. He lives right around the corner. That's why I brought you up here. Shall we visit him together? Sort of good cop, bad cop, eh? I could bash him around the ears."

"I'd have to arrest you for aggravated assault."

"You're a bloody civilian, like me."

"But I wear a badge with five blue stars. And I can still make a citizen's arrest. Goodbye, Jim."

The cardinal scribbled Swirl's address and the name and parish of the problem priest. Isaac hugged the old man. "Jim," he said, adopting his policeman's brogue. "I'll expect a bit of compensation."

The cardinal smiled. "Ah, now I have two blackmailers. What is it, Isaac?"

Both of them managed baseball teams for the Police Athletic League.

"I'm short a third baseman. I'd like to borrow one of yours."

"That's robbery," the cardinal said. But he loved to barter with Isaac Sidel. "I'll see what I can do."

The cardinal left and Isaac rode around the corner.

"Joe, do we have a mask in the glove compartment?"

"I think so," Barbarossa said.

"Give it here."

Barbarossa gave Isaac the old ski mask he often used as a rag.

"Can you tell me what it's about, boss?"

Isaac pointed to a private house. "I'm going in there. Just sit where you are."

"What about your brother Leo?"

"Leo will have to wait."

He should have gone through the files at Crime Scene and kidnapped Swirl's folder, but he was feeling reckless. He stepped out of the car, pranced onto a lawn, put on the ski mask, climbed a crooked porch, and knocked on the door. No one answered. Isaac tried the knob. The door wasn't locked. He entered Broderick's house.

The blackmailer was waiting for him in a miserable armchair. His right leg was in a cast. He looked about thirty years old. He was wearing a gold chain around his neck. His eyes didn't seem to startle at the sight of the mask. Where did a lousy lab technician get such a big pair of balls?

"Fuck it," Isaac said, and he tore off the mask.

"That's better," Broderick said. "That's much, much better. I work for you. Are you gonna waste me, chief?"

"No."

"I'm a pretty good photographer. Did the cardinal show you my snaps of Father Tom?"

Ah, Father Tom of St. Anne's parish. He'd already forgotten the name of the priest on Jim's slip of paper.

"You have a pension, Mr. Swirl. I can bring Internal Affairs right down on your back. Have you ever met Martin Malik? He's my trials commissioner. He'll tear your heart out. He's a Turk."

"I'm not a cop. You can fuck me or fire me, but you can't give me a departmental trial."

"Sonny, I can turn every one of your days into a living hell."

"I've already been there, Commissioner Isaac."

He had a cat's crazy grin.

Isaac heard an echo behind him. Barbarossa had come into the house with his white glove. The grin disappeared from Swirl's face.

"You know each other?"

"Sure, boss," Barbarossa said. "Brod's one of my customers. He buys dope from me. I recognized his fucking bungalow. I've been here before . . . right, Brod?"

The blackmailer shook his head like a little boy.

"And what happens to people who cross Uncle Joe?"

"They get lost," the blackmailer said. "I swear, Joey. I didn't know you were with the Commish."

"You're entitled to a mistake, Brod. But only one . . . don't worry, boss. He likes to do a little blackmail on the side. He's got a thing about priests. But it's all finished. Just go outside for a minute."

Isaac was like a drugged man. He walked out and stood on the porch. Barbarossa appeared with a thick envelope. "It's his whole inventory."

"Tear up the pictures. I don't want to look."

He sulked in the car. His own driver had more sway in the City of New York. He'd have to retire to an old people's home. He was fifty-six. But he was still a fox. He'd have a new third baseman for his Delancey Giants. And Cardinal Jim would have to hide his problem priest.

He started to dream. He had become a priest, Father Isaac. And his parish was a baseball field with broken red grass. The bleachers were filled with boys and girls. The girls all looked like Isaac. He couldn't tell what position he was meant to play. He was lost in that sea of red grass.

Boss.

Barbarossa had his hand on Isaac's shoulder. "Boss, we're here."

Isaac couldn't rouse himself from his own murderous sleep. "Here?"

"At the shoebox on Fordham Road."

"Why'd you wake me?"

"Boss, we have to get Leo."

It was a shoebox, like Barbarossa said. A bargain basement three floors high. Fashion Town. The clothier of Leo Sidel. The dummies in the window had a maddening, sunburnt look. Bronzed men who could have been white, black, Latino, or native American. Their nostrils, their eyes and ears looked like the holes of a mask. But the dummies were draped in shirts and vests that mocked Isaac, who had his own bargain basements on Orchard Street. Isaac loved to wear Orchard Street's best.

"Come with me, Joe."

"Boss, you'll get embarrassed about your brother. And you'll hate it if I see you cry."

"I won't cry," Isaac said. "I promise."

Barbarossa had become his fucking noble savage, Friday with a pink face. He moved in mysterious rings around Isaac, repairing his life.

The store was a bombed-out zone with racks of clothing that seemed to extend for half a mile, like Isaac's red grass. He asked for the security department and had to travel into the heart of the store with Joe Barbarossa. They went down a flight of stairs into the darkness. A light was switched on. And Isaac saw his brother Leo inside a cage with six black men. With them was the warden, wearing handcuffs around his belt and carrying a policeman's billy. He was an enormous man, this warden, like a thick, prehistoric creature that was beyond any of Isaac's baseball dreams.

"I'm Kronenberg," he said. "You must be the Commish. And your chum?"

"Detective Barbarossa," Isaac said.

Kronenberg laughed. "Your bodyguard and your babysitter."

"Yeah, something like that," Isaac said. He was going to beat Kronenberg's brains out. But he hadn't said hello to his brother, who skulked behind the warden. "Kronenberg, how come you're in that cage with all these men?"

"It's discipline," Kronenberg said. "They'd be biting their fingernails without me . . . and robbing each other."

Kronenberg came out of the cage. He had to duck under the narrow door. He was half a head taller than Isaac. He didn't even bother to lock the cage. Isaac had a much better view of Leo now. Leo had been stripped down to his underpants. Isaac shivered. Leo couldn't seem to shake his short pants.

"Kronenberg, I don't like it when my kid brother is obliged to stand half naked in the dark."

"He's a thief," Kronenberg said. "And he's not naked."

"A thief?" Isaac said. "Have you read him his rights? Are you a fucking police officer?"

"I have him on tape, Sidel. He stole three pairs of pants and a shirt. And I don't have to read him his rights. I interrogated him. That's my privilege. I'm a licensed security man. I can't keep going back and forth to the precinct all day. I collect the trash in this box and then I make a run to the precinct. It's strictly legal."

"Is it legal to let men live in the dark?"

"I'm saving electricity, that's all, and teaching them a lesson. They're all trash, including your brother. I checked him with our credit agency. He's a chronic shoplifter. You can't waltz him out of my jail, Sidel."

"I don't intend to waltz him anywhere. You're going to set him free."

"Not a chance."

Isaac peeked inside the cage, saw those seven unfortunate, masklike faces, and started to cry. He was thinking of Leo and the six black men cooped up in the cellar of a crazy department store. And he was thinking of Isaac, who'd sent his brother out on missions to protect his own supply of ration stamps.

The warden began to gloat. "Go on. Get out of here."

Isaac socked him on the side of the head. The warden crashed into the cage and Isaac socked him again, grabbed the warden's billy, dug it into the skin under his throat, and turned to Barbarossa. "Sorry, Joe. I didn't mean to cry."

"Boss, lemme talk to the clown."

Barbarossa stooped over Kronenberg. The warden was blubbering now. "I have friends. I can get to the mayor."

"Mr. Kronenberg, the mayor is Isaac's biggest fan."

"Then I'll shoot the Commish."

"With what? He can tear up your gun permit, revoke your license. Do yourself a favor. Sign a release form for Leo Sidel."

"And the other six," Isaac said. "I'm not leaving without them."

"Boss, you don't even know what they did. They could have swallowed a couple of babies."

"I don't care. Joe, I'll kill this fat fuck."

Barbarossa helped the warden to his feet, found the release forms, guided Kronenberg's hand, and helped him sign the forms. The six black men walked out of the cage, said goodbye to Leo, and left.

Barbarossa found Leo's clothes. He walked Leo out of the department store, with Isaac behind him, bewildered in that long, long corridor of clothes.

Isaac sat with Leo in back of the sedan, while Barbarossa drove across the ruins of the Grand Concourse and out to Indian Road, where Leo lived, at the very edge of Manhattan.

"You promised me you wouldn't steal."

"I can't help myself," Leo said. He seemed destined to sit or stand in tiny jails.

"Don't I pay your fucking bills? You want clothes, I'll buy them for you."

"I couldn't wear them," Leo said. "I need my own clothes. I'm fifty-two."

"You're crazy," Isaac said. "You're a fucking kid." He was crying again. "Leo, I shouldn't have made you my mule."

"I'm nobody's mule."

"But you carried my ration stamps . . . during the war."

"I don't remember."

"You walked in front of policemen with my stamps in your pockets. I couldn't have done it."

"Big deal," Leo said. "But at least I had a brother then, not some shit who plays God and punches people. Stop crying."

"Kill me. I'm a crier. Didn't I get you out of that closet? . . . next time I might not be able to save your ass."

"I know," Leo said, and disappeared into his apartment house on Indian Road.

Cities & the Dead

Italo Calvino

Never in all my travels had I ventured as far as Adelma. It was dusk
when I landed there. On the dock the sailor who caught the rope and
tied it to the bollard resembled a man who had soldiered with me and
was dead. It was the hour of the wholesale fish market. An old man
was loading a basket of sea urchins on a cart; I thought I recognized
him; when I turned, he had disappeared down an alley, but I realized
that he looked like a fisherman who, already old when I was a child,
could no longer be among the living. I was upset by the sight of a
fever victim huddled on the ground, a blanket over his head: my father
a few days before his death had yellow eyes and a growth of beard
like this man. I turned my gaze aside; I no longer dared look anyone
in the face.

I thought: "If Adelma is a city I am seeing in a dream, where you
encounter only the dead, the dream frightens me. If Adelma is a real
city, inhabited by living people, I need only continue looking at them
and the resemblances will dissolve, alien faces will appear, bearing
anguish. In either case it is best for me not to insist on staring at
them."

A vegetable vendor was weighing a cabbage on a scales and put
it in a basket dangling on a string a girl lowered from a balcony. The
girl was identical with one in my village who had gone mad for love

189

and killed herself. The vegetable vendor raised her face: she was my grandmother.

I thought: "You reach a moment in life when, among the people you have known, the dead outnumber the living. And the mind refuses to accept more faces, more expressions: on every new face you encounter, it prints the old forms, for each one it finds the most suitable mask."

The stevedores climbed the steps in a line, bent beneath demijohns and barrels; their faces were hidden by sackcloth hoods; "Now they will straighten up and I will recognize them," I thought, with impatience and fear. But I could not take my eyes off them; if I turned my gaze just a little toward the crowd that crammed those narrow streets, I was assailed by unexpected faces, reappearing from far away, staring at me as if demanding recognition, as if to recognize me, as if they had already recognized me. Perhaps, for each of them, I also resembled someone who was dead. I had barely arrived at Adelma and I was already one of them, I had gone over to their side, absorbed in that kaleidoscope of eyes, wrinkles, grimaces.

I thought: "Perhaps Adelma is the city where you arrive dying and where each finds again the people he has known. This means I, too, am dead." And I also thought: "This means the beyond is not happy."

Translated by William Weaver

Gravy Train

James Ellroy

Out of the Honor Farm and into the work force: managing the maintenance crew at a Toyota dealership in Koreatown. Jap run, a gook clientele, boogies for the shitwork and me, Stan "The Man" Klein, to crack the whip and keep on-duty loafing at a minimum. My probation officer got me the gig: Liz Trent, skinny and stacked, four useless Master's degrees, a bum marriage to a guy on methadone maintenance and the hots for yours truly. She knew I got off easy: three convictions resulting from the scams I worked with Phil Turkel—a phone sales racket that involved the deployment of hard core loops synced to rock songs and Naugahyde bibles embossed with glow-in-the-dark pictures of the Rev. Martin Luther King, Jr.—a hot item with the shvartzes. We ran a drug recovery crashpad as a front, suborned teenyboppers into prostitution, coerced male patients into phone sales duty and kept them motivated with Benzedrine-laced espresso—all of which peaked at twenty-four grand jury bills busted down to three indictments apiece. Phil had no prior record, was strung out on cocaine and got diverted to a drug rehab; I had two G.T.A. convictions and no chemical rationalizations—bingo on a year County time, Wayside Honor Rancho, where my reputation as a lackluster heavyweight contender got me a dorm boss job. My attorney, Miller Waxman, assured me a sentence reduction was in the works; he was

wrong—counting "good time" and "work time" I did the whole nine
and a half months. My consolation prize: Lizzie Trent, Waxman's ex-
wife, for my P.O.—guaranteed to cut me a long leash, get me soft
legitimate work and give me head before my probationary term was
a month old. I took two out of three: Lizzie had sharp teeth and an
overbite, so I didn't trust her on the trifecta. I was at my desk,
watching my slaves wash cars, when the phone rang.

I picked up. "Yellow Empire Imports, Klein speaking."

"Miller Waxman here."

"Wax, how's it hangin'?"

"A hard yard—and you still owe me money on my fee. Seriously,
I need it. I lent Liz some heavy coin to get her teeth capped."

The trifecta loomed. "Are you dunning me?"

"No, I'm a Greek bearing gifts at ten percent interest."

"Such as?"

"Such as this: a grand a week cash and three hots and a cot at a
Beverly Hills mansion, all legit. I take a tensky off the top to cover
your bill. The clock's ticking, so yes or no?"

I said, "Legit?"

"If I'm lyin', I'm flyin'. My office in an hour?"

"I'll be there."

Wax worked out of a storefront on Beverly and Alvarado—close
to his clientele—dope dealers and wetbacks hot to bring the family
up from Calexico. I doubleparked, put a "Clergyman on Call" sign
on my windshield and walked in.

Miller was in his office, slipping envelopes to a couple of Immigration Service goons—big guys with that hinky look indigenous to
bagmen worldwide. They walked out thumbing C-notes; Wax said,
"Do you like dogs?"

I took a chair uninvited. "Well enough. Why?"

"Why? Because Phil feels bad about lounging around up at the
Betty Ford Clinic while you went inside. He wants to play catch-up,
and he asked me if I had ideas. A plum fell into my lap and I thought
of you."

Weird Phil: facial scars and a line of shit that could make the Pope
go Protestant. "How's Phil doing these days?"

"Not bad. Do you like dogs?"

"Like I said before, well enough. Why?"

Wax pointed to his clients' wall of fame—scads of framed mug-shots. Included: Leroy Washington, the "Crack King" of Watts; Chester Hardell, a TV preacher indicted for unnatural acts against cats; the murderous Sanchez family—scores of inbred cousins foisted on L.A. as the result of Waxie's green card machinations. In a prominent spot: Richie "The Sicko" Sicora and Chick Ottens, the 7-Eleven Slayers, still at large. Picaresque: Sicora and Ottens heisted a convenience store in Pacoima and hid the salesgirl behind an upended Slurpee machine to facilitate their escape. The machine disgorged its contents: ice, sugar and carcinogenic food coloring: the girl, a diabetic, passed out, sucked in the goo, went into sugar shock and kicked. Sicora and Ottens jumped bail for parts unknown—and Wax got a commendation letter from the ACLU, citing his tenacity in defending the L.A. underclass.

I said, "You've been pointing for five minutes. Want to narrow it down?"

Wax brushed dandruff off his lapels. "I was illustrating a point, the point being that my largest client is not on that wall because he was never arrested."

I feigned shock. "No shit, Dick Tracy?"

"No shit, Sherlock. I'm referring, of course, to Sol Bendish, entrepreneur, bail bondsman supreme, heir to the late great Mickey Cohen's vice kingdom. Sol passed on recently, and I'm handling his estate."

I sighed. "And the punch line?"

Wax tossed me a keyring. "He left a twenty-five-million-dollar estate to his dog. It's legally inviolate and so well safeguarded that I can't contest it or scam it. You're the dog's new keeper."

My list of duties ran seven pages. I drove to Beverly Hills wishing I'd been born canine.

"Basko" lived in a mansion north of Sunset; Basko wore cashmere sweaters and a custom-designed flea collar that emitted minute amounts of nuclear radiation guaranteed not to harm dogs—a physicist spent three years developing the product. Basko ate prime steak, Beluga caviar, Häagen-Dazs ice cream and Fritos soaked in ketchup. Rats were brought in to sate his blood lust: rodent mayhem every

Tuesday morning, a hundred of them let loose in the back yard for Basko to hunt down and destroy. Basko suffered from insomnia and required a unique sedative: a slice of Velveeta cheese melted in a cup of hundred-year-old brandy.

I almost shit when I saw the pad; going in the door my knees went weak. Stan Klein enters the white-trash comfort zone to which he had so long aspired.

Deep-pile purple rugs everywhere.

A three-story amphitheater to accommodate a gigantic satellite dish that brought in four hundred TV channels.

Big-screen TVs in every room and a comprehensive library of porn flicks.

A huge kitchen featuring two walk-in refrigerators: one for Basko, one for me. Wax must have stocked mine—it was packed with the high-sodium, high-cholesterol stuff I thrive on. Rooms and rooms full of the swag of my dreams—I felt like Fulgencio Batista back from exile.

Then I met the dog.

I found him in the pool, floating on a cushion. He was munching a cat carcass, his rear paws in the water. I did not yet know that it was the pivotal moment of my life.

I observed the beast from a distance.

He was a white bull terrier—muscular, compact, deep in the chest, bowlegged. His short-haired coat gleamed in the sunlight; he was so heavily muscled that flea-nipping required a great effort. His head was perfect good-natured misanthropy: a sloping wedge of a snout, close-set beady eyes, sharp teeth and a furrowed brow that gave him the look of a teenaged kid scheming trouble. His left ear was brindled—I sighed as the realization hit me, an epiphany—like the time I figured out Annie "Wild Thing" Behringer dyed her pubic hair.

Our eyes met.

Basko hit the water, swam and ran to me and rooted at my crotch. Looking back, I recall those moments in slow motion, gooey music on the sound track of my life, like those frenchy films where the lovers never talk, just smoke cigarettes, gaze at each other and bang away.

Over the next week we established a routine.

Up early, roadwork by the Beverly Hills Hotel, Basko's A.M. dump on an Arab sheik's front lawn. Breakfast, Basko's morning nap; he kept his head on my lap while I watched porno films and read sci-fi novels. Lunch: blood-rare fillets, then a float in the pool on adjoining cushions. Another walk; an eyeball on the foxy redhead who strolled her Lab at the same time each day—I figured I'd bide my time and propose a double date: us, Basko and the bitch. Evenings went to introspection: I screened films of my old fights, Stan "The Man" Klein, feather-fisted, cannon fodder for hungry schmucks looking to pad their records. There I was: six-pointed star on my trunks, my back dusted with Clearasil to hide my zits. A film editor buddy spliced me in with some stock footage of the greats; movie magic had me kicking the shit out of Ali, Marciano and Tyson. Wistful might-have-been stuff accompanied by Basko's beady browns darting from the screen to me. Soon I was telling the dog the secrets I always hid from women.

When I shifted into a confessional mode, Basko would scrunch up his brow and cock his head; my cue to shut up was one of his gigantic mouth-stretching yawns. When he started dozing, I carried him upstairs and tucked him in. A little Velveeta and brandy, a little goodnight story—Basko seemed to enjoy accounts of my sexual exploits best. And he always fell asleep just as I began to exaggerate.

I could never sync my sleep to Basko's: his warm presence got me hopped up, thinking of all the good deals I'd blown, thinking that he was only good for another ten years on earth and then I'd be fifty-one with no good buddy to look after and no pot to piss in. Prowling the pad buttressed my sense that this incredible gravy train was tangible and would last—so I prowled with a vengeance.

Sol Bendish dressed antithetical to his Vegas-style crib: tweedy sports jackets, slacks with cuffs, Oxford-cloth shirts, wing tips and white bucks. He left three closets stuffed with Ivy League threads just about my size. While my canine charge slept, I transformed myself into his sartorial image. Jewboy Klein became Jewboy Bendish, wealthy contributor to the U.J.A., the man with the class to love a dog of supreme blunt efficacy. I'd stand before the mirror in Bendish's clothes—and my years as a pimp, burglar, car thief and scam artist would melt away—replaced by a thrilling and fatuous notion: finding *the* woman to compliment my new persona . . .

I attacked the next day.

Primping formed my prelude to courtship: I gave Basko a flea dip, brushed his coat and dressed him in his best spiked collar; I put on a spiffy Bendish ensemble: navy blazer, gray flannels, pink shirt and penny loafers. Thus armed, we stood at Sunset and Linden and waited for the Labrador woman to show.

She showed right on time; the canine contingent sniffed each other hello. The woman deadpanned the action; I eyeballed her while Basko tugged at his leash.

She had the freckled look of a rare jungle cat—maybe a leopard/ snow tiger hybrid indigenous to some jungleland of love. Her red hair reflected sunlight and glistened gold—a lioness's mane. Her shape was both curvy and svelte; I remembered that some female felines actually stalked for mates. She said, "Are you a professional dog walker?"

I checked my new persona for dents. My slacks were a tad too short; the ends of my necktie hung off kilter. I felt myself blushing and heard Basko's paws scrabbling on the sidewalk. "No, I'm what you might want to call an entrepreneur. Why do you ask?"

"Because I used to see an older man walking this dog. I think he's some sort of organized crime figure."

Basko and the Lab were into a mating dance—sniffing, licking, nipping. I got the feeling Cat Woman was stalking me—and not for love. I said, "He's dead. I'm handling his estate."

One eyebrow twitched and flickered. "Oh? Are you an attorney?"

"No, I'm working for the man's attorney."

"Sol Bendish was the man's name, wasn't it?"

My shit detector clicked into high gear—this bimbo was pumping me. "That's right, Miss?"

"It's Ms. Gail Curtiz, that's with a T, I, Z. And it's Mr.?"

"Klein with an E, I, N. My dog likes your dog, don't you think?"

"Yes, a disposition of the glands."

"I empathize. Want to have dinner some time?"

"I think not."

"I'll try again then."

"The answer won't change. Do you do other work for the Bendish estate? Besides walk the man's dog, I mean."

"I look after the house. Come over some time. Bring your Lab, we'll double."

"Do you thrive on rejections, Mr. Klein?"

Basko was trying to hump the Lab—but no go. "Yeah, I do."
"Well, until the next one, then. Good day."

The brief encounter was Weirdsville, U.S.A.—especially Cat
Woman's Strangeville take on Sol Bendish. I dropped Basko off at the
pad, drove to the Beverly Hills library and had a clerk run my dead
benefactor through their information computer. Half an hour later I
was reading a lapful of scoop on the man.
An interesting dude emerged.
Bendish ran loan-sharking and union protection rackets inherited
from Mickey Cohen; he was a gold star contributor to Israel bonds
and the U.J.A. He threw parties for underprivileged kids and operated
his bail bond business at a loss. He lost a bundle on a homicide bond
forfeiture: Richie "Sicko" Sicora and Chick Ottens, the 7-Eleven slayers, Splitsvilled for Far Gonesville, sticking him with a two-million-
dollar tab. Strange: the *L.A. Times* had Bendish waxing philosophical
on the bug-out, like two mill down the toilet was everyday stuff to
him.
On the personal front, Bendish seemed to love broads, and eschew
birth control: no less than six paternity suits were filed against him.
If the suit-filing mothers were to be believed, Sol had three grown
sons and three grown daughters—and the complainants were bought
off with chump change settlements—weird for a man so given to
charity for appearance's sake. The last clippings I scanned held another
anomaly: Miller Waxman said Bendish's estate came to twenty-five
mill, while the papers placed it at a cool forty. My scamster's brain
kicked into very low overdrive . . .

I went back to my routine with Basko and settled into days of
domestic bliss undercut with just the slightest touch of wariness. Wax
paid my salary on time; Basko and I slept entwined and woke up
simultaneously, in some kind of cross-species psychic sync. Gail Curtiz continued to give me the brush; I got her address from Information
and walked Basko by every night, curious: a woman short of twenty-
five living in a Beverly Hills mansion—a rental by all accounts—a
sign on the lawn underlining it: "For Sale. Contact Realtor. Please
Do Not Disturb Renting Tenant." One night the bimbo spotted me
snooping; the next night I spotted her strolling by the Bendish/Klein

residence. On impulse, I checked my horoscope in the paper: a bust, no mention of romance or intrigue coming my way.

Another week passed, business as usual, two late-night sightings of Gail Curtiz sniffing my turf. I reciprocated: late-night prowls by her place, looking for window lights to clarify my take on the woman. Basko accompanied me: the missions brought to mind my youth: heady nights as a burglar/panty raider. I was peeping with abandon, crouched with Basko behind a eucalyptus tree, when the shit hit the fan—a crap-o, non-Beverly Hills car pulled up.

Three shifty-looking shvartzes got out, burglar's tools gleamed in the moonlight. The unholy trio tiptoed up to Gail Curtiz's driveway.

I pulled a nonexistent gun and stepped out from hiding; I yelled, "Police officer! Freeze!" and expected them to run. They froze instead; I got the shakes; Basko yanked at his leash and broke away from me. Then pandemonium.

Basko attacked; the schmucks ran for their car; one of them whipped out a cylindrical object and held it out to the hot pursuing hound. A streetlamp illuminated the offering: a bucket of Kentucky Colonel ribs.

Basko hit the bucket and started snouting; I yelled "No!" and chased. The boogies grabbed my beloved comrade and tossed him in the back seat of their car. The car took off—just as I made a last leap and hit the pavement memorizing plate numbers, a partial read: P-L-blank-0016. BASKO BASKO BASKO NO NO—

The next hour went by in a delirium. I called Liz Trent, had her shake down an ex-cop boyfriend for a DMV runthrough on the plate and got a total of fourteen possible combinations. None of the cars were reported stolen; eleven were registered to Caucasians, three to southside blacks. I got a list of addresses, drove to Hollywood and bought a .45 automatic off a fruit hustler known to deal good iron—then hit darktown with a vengeance.

My first two addresses were losers: staid sedans that couldn't have been the kidnap car. Adrenaline scorched my blood vessels; I kept seeing Basko maimed, Basko's beady browns gazing at me. I pulled up to the last address seeing double: silhouettes in the pistol range of my mind. My trigger finger itched to dispense .45-caliber justice.

I saw the address, then smelled it: a wood-framed shack in the shadow of a freeway embankment, a big rear yard, the whole package reeking of dog. I parked and sneaked back to the driveway gun first.

Snarls, growls, howls, barks, yips—floodlights on the yard and two pit bulls circling each other in a ring enclosed by fence pickets. Spectators yipping, yelling, howling, growling and laying down bets—and off to the side of the action my beloved Basko being primed for battle.

Two burly shvartzes were fitting black leather gloves fitted with razor blades to his paws. Basko was wearing a muzzle embroidered with swastikas. I padded back and got ready to kill; Basko sniffed the air and leaped at his closest defiler. A hot second for the gutting: Basko lashed out with his paws and disemboweled him clean. The other punk screamed; I ran up and bashed his face in with the butt of my roscoe. Basko applied the *coup de grace*: left-right paw shots that severed his throat down to the windpipe. Punk number two managed a death gurgle; the spectators by the ring heard the hubbub and ran over. I grabbed Basko and hauled ass.

We made it to my sled and peeled rubber; out of nowhere a car broadsided us, fender to fender. I saw a white face behind the wheel, downshifted, brodied, fishtailed and hit the freeway doing eighty. The attack car was gone—back to the nowhere it came from. I whipped off Basko's muzzle and paw weapons and threw them out the window; Basko licked my face all the way to Beverly Hills.

More destruction greeted us: the Bendish/Klein/Basko pad had been ransacked, the downstairs thoroughly trashed: shelves over-turned, sections of the satellite dish ripped loose, velvet flocked Elvis paintings torn from the walls. I grabbed Basko again; we hotfooted it to Gail Curtiz's crib.

Lights were burning inside; the Lab was lounging on the lawn chomping on a Nylabone. She noticed Basko and started demurely wagging her tail; I sensed romance in the air and unhooked my side-kick's leash. Basko ran to the Lab; the scene dissolved into horizontal nuzzling. I gave the lovebirds some privacy, sneaked around to the rear of the house and started peeping.

Va Va Va Voom through a back window. Gail Curtiz, nude, was writhing with another woman on a tigerskin rug. The gorgeous bru-nette seemed reluctant: her face spelled shame and you could tell the perversity was getting to her. My beady eyes almost popped out of my skull; in the distance I could hear Basko and the Lab rutting like cougars. The brunette faked an orgasm and made her hips buckle— I could tell she was faking from twenty feet away. The window was cracked at the bottom; I put an ear to the sill and listened.

Gail got up and lit a cigarette; the brunette said, "Could you turn off the lights, please?"—a dead giveaway—you could tell she wanted to blot out the dyke's nudity. Basko and the Lab, looking sated, trotted up and fell asleep at my feet. The room inside went black; I listened extra hard.

Smutty endearments from Gail; two cigarette tips glowing. The brunette, quietly persistent: "But I don't understand why you spend your life savings renting such an extravagant house. You *never* spell things out for me, even though we're . . . And just who is this rich man who died?"

Gail, laughing. "My daddy, sweetie. Blood test validated. Momma was a carhop who died of a broken heart. Daddy stiffed her on the paternity suit, among many other stiffs, but he promised to take care of me—three million on my twenty-fifth birthday or his death, which-ever came first. Now, dear, would you care to hear the absurdist punch line? Daddy left the bulk of his fortune to his dog, to be overseen by a sharpie lawyer and this creep who looks after the dog. *But*— there has to be some money hidden somewhere. Daddy's estate was valued at twenty-five million, while the newspapers placed it as much higher. Oh, shit, isn't it all absurd?"

A pause, then the brunette. "You know what you said when we got back a little while ago? Remember, you had this feeling the house had been searched?"

Gail: "Yes. What are you getting at?"

"Well, maybe it *was* just your imagination, or maybe one of the other paternity suit kids has got the same idea, maybe that explains it."

"Linda, honey, I can't think of that just now. Right now I've got you on my mind."

Small talk was over—eclipsed by Gail's ardor, Linda's phony moans, I hitched Basko to his leash, drove us to a motel safe house and slept the sleep of the righteously pissed.

In the morning I did some brainwork. My conclusions: Gail Curtiz wanted to sink my gravy train and relegate Basko to a real dog's life. Paternity suit intrigue was at the root of the Bendish house trashing and the "searching" of Gail's place. The car that tried to broadside me was driven by a white man—a strange anomaly. Linda, in my eyes a non-dyke, seemed to be stringing the lust-blinded Gail along —could she also be a paternity suit kid out for Basko's swag? Sleazy Miller Waxman was Sol Bendish's lawyer and a scam artist bent from the crib—how did he fit in? Were the shvoogies who tried to break into Gail's crib the ones who later searched it—and trashed my place? Were they in the employ of one of the paternity kids? *What was going on?*

I rented a suite at the Bel-Air Hotel and ensconced Basko there, leaving a grand deposit and detailed instructions on his care and feeding. Next I hit the Beverly Hills Library and reread Sol Bendish's clippings. I glommed the names of his paternity suit complainants, called Liz Trent and had her give me DMV addresses. Two of Sol's playmates were dead; one was address unknown, two—Marguerita Montgomery and Jane Hawkshaw—were alive and living in Los Angeles. The Montgomery woman was out as a lead: a clipping I'd scanned two weeks ago quoted her on the occasion of Sol Bendish's death—she mentioned that the son he fathered had died in Vietnam. I already knew that Gail Curtiz's mother had died—and since none of the complainants bore the name Curtiz, I knew Gail was using it as an alias. That left Jane Hawkshaw: last known address 8902 Saticoy Street in Van Nuys.

I knocked on her door an hour later. An old woman holding a stack of *Watchtowers* opened up. She had the look of religious crackpots everywhere: bad skin, spaced-out eyes. She might have been hot stuff once—around the time man discovered the wheel. I said, "I'm Brother Klein. I've been dispatched by the Church to ease your conscience in the Sol Bendish matter."

The old girl pointed me inside and started babbling repentance. My eyes hit a framed photograph above the fireplace—two familiar faces smiling out. I walked over and squinted.

Ultra-paydirt: Richie "Sicko" Sicora and another familiar-looking dude. I'd seen pics of Sicora before—but in this photo he looked like

someone *else* familiar. The resemblance seemed very vague—but nig-
gling. The other man was easy—he'd tried to broadside me in darktown last night.

The old girl said, "My son Richard is a fugitive. He doesn't look
like that now. He had his face changed when he went on the run.
Sol was going to leave Richie money when he turned twenty-five, but
Richie and Chuck got in trouble and Sol gave it out in bail money
instead. I've got no complaint against Sol and I repent my unmarried
fornication."

I superimposed the other man's bone structure against photos I'd
seen of Chick Ottens and got a close match. I tried, tried, tried to
place Sicora's pre-surgery resemblance, but failed. Sicora pre-plastic,
Ottens already sliced—a wicked brew that validated non-dyke Linda's
theory straight down the line . . .

I gave the old woman a buck, grabbed a *Watchtower* and boogied
southside. The radio blared hype on the Watts homicides: the monster
dog and his human accomplice. Fortunately for Basko and myself,
eyewitnesses' accounts were dismissed and the deaths were attributed
to dope intrigue. I cruised the bad boogaloo streets until I spotted the
car that tried to ram me—parked behind a cinderblock dump circled
by barbed wire.

I pulled up and jacked a shell into my piece. I heard yips emanating
from the back yard, tiptoed around and scoped out the scene.

Pit Bull City: scores of them in pens. A picnic table and Chick
Ottens noshing bar-b-q'd chicken with his snazzy new face. I came
up behind him; the dogs noticed me and sent out a cacophony of
barks. Ottens stood up and wheeled around, going for his waistband.
I shot off his kneecaps—canine howls covered my gun blasts. Ottens
flew backwards and hit the dirt screaming; I poured bar-b-q sauce on
his kneeholes and dragged him over to the cage of the baddest-looking
pit hound of the bunch. The dog snapped at the blood and soul sauce;
his teeth tore the pen. I spoke slowly, like I had all the time in the
world. "I know you and Sicora got plastic jobs, I know Sol Bendish
was Sicora's daddy and bailed you and Sicko out on the 7-Eleven job.
You had your goons break into Gail Curtiz's place and the Bendish
pad and all this shit relates to you trying to mess with my dog and
screw me out of my gravy train. Now I'm beginning to think Wax
Waxman set me up. I think you and Sicora have some plan going to

get at Bendish's money, and Wax ties in. You got word that Curtiz was snouting around, so you checked out her crib. I'm a dupe, right? Wax's patsy? Wrap this up for me or I feed your kneecaps to Godzilla."

Pit Godzilla snarled an incisor out of the mesh and nipped Ottens where it counts. Ottens screeched; going blue, he got out, "Wax wanted . . . you . . . to . . . look after . . . dog . . . while him and . . . Phil . . . scammed a way to . . . discredit paternity . . . claims . . . I . . . I . . ."

Phil.

My old partner—I didn't know a thing about his life before our partnership.

Phil Turkel was Sicko Sicora, his weird facial scars derived from the plastic surgery that hid his real identity from the world.

"Freeze, suckah."

I looked up. Three big shines were standing a few yards away, holding Uzis. I opened Godzilla's cage; Godzilla burst out and went for Chick's face. Ottens screamed; I tossed the bucket of chicken at the gunmen; shots sprayed the dirt. I ate crabgrass and rolled, rolled, rolled, tripping cage levers, ducking, ducking, ducking. Pit bulls ran helter skelter, then zeroed in: three soul brothers dripping with soul sauce.

The feast wasn't pretty. I grabbed an Uzi and got out quicksville.

Dusk.

I leadfooted it to Wax's office, the radio tuned to a classical station—I was hopped up on blood, but found some soothing Mozart to calm me down, and highballed it to Beverly and Alvarado.

Waxman's office was stone silent; I picked the back door lock, walked in and made straight for the safe behind his playmate calendar—the place where I knew he kept his dope and bribery stash. Left-right-left: an hour of diddling the tumblers and the door creaked open. Four hours of studying memo slips, ledgers and little black book notations and I trusted myself on a reconstruction.

Labyrinthine, but workable:

Private eye reports on Gail Curtiz and Linda Claire Woodruff— the two paternity suit kids Wax considered most likely to contest the Bendish estate. Lists of stooges supplied by Wax contacts in the LAPD: criminal types to be used to file phony claims against the estate, whatever money gleaned to be kicked back to Wax himself. Address-book names circled: snuff artists I knew from jail, including the fearsome Angel "Fritz" Trejo. A note from Phil Turkel to Waxman: "Throw Stan a bone—he can babysit the dog until we get the money." A diagram of the Betty Ford Clinic, followed by an ominous epiphany: Wax was going to have Phil and the real paternity kids clipped. Pages and pages of notes in legalese—levers to get at the extra fifteen million Sol Bendish had stuffed in Swiss bank accounts.

I turned off the lights and raged in the dark; I thought of escaping to a nice deserted island with Basko and some nice girl who wouldn't judge me for loving a bull terrier more than her. The phone rang— and I nearly jumped out of my hide.

I picked up and faked Wax's voice. "Waxman here."

"Ees Angel Fritz. You know your man Phil?"

"Yeah."

"Ees history. You pay balance now?"

"My office in two hours, homeboy."

"Ees bonaroo, homes."

I hung up and called Waxman's pad; Miller answered on the second ring. "Yes?"

"Wax, it's Klein."

"Oh."

His voice spelled it out plain: he'd heard about the southside holocaust.

"Yeah, 'Oh.' Listen, shitbird, here's the drift. Turkel's dead, and I took out Angel Trejo. I'm at your office and I've been doing some reading. Be here in one hour with a cash settlement."

Waxman's teeth chattered; I hung up and did some typing: Stan Klein's account of the whole Bendish/Waxman/Turkel/Ottens/Trejo scam—a massive criminal conspiracy to bilk the dog I loved. I included everything but mention of myself and left a nice blank space for Wax to sign his name. Then I waited.

Fifty minutes later—a knock. I opened the door and let Wax in. His right hand was twitching and there was a bulge under his jacket. He said, "Hello, Klein," and twitched harder; I heard a truck rumble by and shot him point blank in the face.

Wax keeled over dead, his right eyeball stuck to his law school diploma. I frisked him, relieved him of his piece and twenty large in cash. I found some papers in his desk, studied his signature and forged his name to his confession. I left him on the floor, walked outside and pulled over to the pay phone across the street.

A taco wagon pulled to the curb; I dropped my quarter, dialed 911 and called in a gunshot tip—anonymous citizen, a quick hangup. Angel Fritz Trejo rang Wax's doorbell, waited, then let himself in. Seconds dragged; lights went on; two black-and-whites pulled up and four cops ran inside brandishing hardware. Multiple shots—and four cops walked out unharmed.

So in the end I made twenty grand and got the dog. The L.A. County Grand Jury bought the deposition, attributed my various dead to Ottens/Turkel/Trejo/Waxman *et al*—all dead themselves, thus unindictable. A superior court judge invalidated Basko's twenty-five mill and divided the swag between Gail Curtiz and Linda Claire Woodruff. Gail got the Bendish mansion—rumor has it that she's turning it into a crashpad for radical lesbian feminists down on their luck. Linda Claire is going out with a famous rock star—androgynous, but more male than female. She admitted, elliptically, that she tried to "hustle" Gail Curtiz—validating her dyke submissiveness as good old American fortune hunting. Lizzie Trent got her teeth fixed, kicked me off probation and into her bed. I got a job selling cars in Glendale—and Basko comes to work with me every day. His steak and caviar diet have been replaced by Gravy Train—and he looks even groovier and healthier. Lizzie digs Basko and lets him sleep with us. We're talking about combining my twenty grand with her life savings and buying a house, which bodes marriage: my first, her fourth. Lizzie's a blast: she's smart, tender, funny and gives great skull. I love her almost as much as I love Basko.

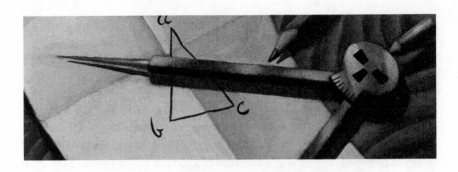

Death and the Compass

Jorge Luis Borges

Of the many problems which exercised the reckless discernment of
Lönnrot, none was so strange—so rigorously strange, shall we say—
as the periodic series of bloody events which culminated at the villa
of Triste-le-Roy, amid the ceaseless aroma of the eucalypti. It is true
that Erik Lönnrot failed to prevent the last murder, but that he foresaw
it is indisputable. Neither did he guess the identity of Yarmolinsky's
luckless assassin, but he did succeed in divining the secret morphology
behind the fiendish series as well as the participation of Red Scharlach,
whose other nickname is Scharlach the Dandy. That criminal (as
countless others) had sworn on his honor to kill Lönnrot, but the latter
could never be intimidated. Lönnrot believed himself a pure reasoner,
an Auguste Dupin, but there was something of the adventurer in him,
and even a little of the gambler.

The first murder occurred in the Hôtel du Nord—that tall prism
which dominates the estuary whose waters are the color of the desert.
To that tower (which quite glaringly unites the hateful whiteness of
a hospital, the numbered divisibility of a jail, and the general appearance of a bordello) there came on the third day of December the
delegate from Podolsk to the Third Talmudic Congress, Doctor Marcel Yarmolinsky, a gray-bearded man with gray eyes. We shall never
know whether the Hôtel du Nord pleased him; he accepted it with
the ancient resignation which had allowed him to endure three years

of war in the Carpathians and three thousand years of oppression and pogroms. He was given a room on Floor R, across from the suite which was occupied—not without splendor—by the Tetrarch of Galilee. Yarmolinsky supped, postponed until the following day an inspection of the unknown city, arranged in a *placard* his many books and few personal possessions, and before midnight extinguished his light. (Thus declared the Tetrarch's chauffeur who slept in the adjoining room.) On the fourth, at 11:03 A.M., the editor of the *Yidische Zaitung* put in a call to him; Doctor Yarmolinsky did not answer. He was found in his room, his face already a little dark, nearly nude beneath a large, anachronistic cape. He was lying not far from the door which opened on the hall; a deep knife wound had split his breast. A few hours later, in the same room amid journalists, photographers and policemen, Inspector Treviranus and Lönnrot were calmly discussing the problem.

"No need to look for a three-legged cat here," Treviranus was saying as he brandished an imperious cigar. "We all know that the Tetrarch of Galilee owns the finest sapphires in the world. Someone, intending to steal them, must have broken in here by mistake. Yarmolinsky got up; the robber had to kill him. How does it sound to you?"

"Possible, but not interesting," Lönnrot answered. "You'll reply that reality hasn't the least obligation to be interesting. And I'll answer you that reality may avoid that obligation but that hypotheses may not. In the hypothesis that you propose, chance intervenes copiously. Here we have a dead rabbi; I would prefer a purely rabbinical explanation, not the imaginary mischances of an imaginary robber."

Treviranus replied ill-humoredly:

"I'm not interested in rabbinical explanations. I am interested in capturing the man who stabbed this unknown person."

"Not so unknown," corrected Lönnrot. "Here are his complete works." He indicated in the wall-cupboard a row of tall books: a *Vindication of the Cabala; An Examination of the Philosophy of Robert Fludd*; a literal translation of the *Sepher Yezirah*; a *Biography of the Baal Shem*; a *History of the Hasidic Sect*; a monograph (in German) on the Tetragrammaton; another, on the divine nomenclature of the Pentateuch. The inspector regarded them with dread, almost with repulsion. Then he began to laugh.

"I'm a poor Christian," he said. "Carry off those musty volumes if you want; I don't have any time to waste on Jewish superstitions."

"Maybe the crime belongs to the history of Jewish superstitions," murmured Lönnrot.

"Like Christianity," the editor of the *Yidische Zaitung* ventured to add. He was myopic, an atheist and very shy.

No one answered him. One of the agents had found in the small typewriter a piece of paper on which was written the following unfinished sentence:

The first letter of the Name has been uttered

Lönnrot abstained from smiling. Suddenly become a bibliophile or Hebraist, he ordered a package made of the dead man's books and carried them off to his apartment. Indifferent to the police investigation, he dedicated himself to studying them. One large octavo volume revealed to him the teachings of Israel Baal Shem Tobh, founder of the sect of the Pious; another, the virtues and terrors of the Tetragrammaton, which is the unutterable name of God; another, the thesis that God has a secret name, in which is epitomized (as in the crystal sphere which the Persians ascribe to Alexander of Macedonia) his ninth attribute, eternity—that is to say, the immediate knowledge of all things that will be, which are and which have been in the universe. Tradition numbers ninety-nine names of God; the Hebraists attribute that imperfect number to magical fear of even numbers; the Hasidim reason that that hiatus indicates a hundredth name—the Absolute Name.

From this erudition Lönnrot was distracted, a few days later, by the appearance of the editor of the *Yidische Zaitung*. The latter wanted to talk about the murder; Lönnrot preferred to discuss the diverse names of God; the journalist declared, in three columns, that the investigator, Erik Lönnrot, had dedicated himself to studying the names of God in order to come across the name of the murderer. Lönnrot, accustomed to the simplifications of journalism, did not become indignant. One of those enterprising shopkeepers who have discovered that any given man is resigned to buying any given book published a popular edition of the *History of the Hasidic Sect*.

The second murder occurred on the evening of the third of January, in the most deserted and empty corner of the capital's western suburbs. Towards dawn, one of the gendarmes who patrol those solitudes on horseback saw a man in a poncho, lying prone in the shadow of an old paint shop. The harsh features seemed to be masked in blood; a deep knife wound had split his breast. On the wall, across the yellow and red diamonds, were some words written in chalk. The gendarme spelled them out . . . That afternoon, Treviranus and Lönnrot headed for the remote scene of the crime. To the left and right of the automobile the city disintegrated; the firmament grew and houses were of less importance than a brick kiln or a poplar tree. They arrived at their miserable destination: an alley's end, with rose-colored walls which somehow seemed to reflect the extravagant sunset. The dead man had already been identified. He was Daniel Simon Azevedo, an individual of some fame in the old northern suburbs, who had risen from wagon driver to political tough, then degenerated to a thief and even an informer. (The singular style of his death seemed appropriate to them: Azevedo was the last representative of a generation of bandits who knew how to manipulate a dagger, but not a revolver.) The words in chalk were the following:

The second letter of the Name has been uttered

The third murder occurred on the night of the third of February. A little before one o'clock, the telephone in Inspector Treviranus' office rang. In avid secretiveness, a man with a guttural voice spoke; he said his name was Ginzberg (or Ginsburg) and that he was prepared to communicate, for reasonable remuneration, the events surrounding the two sacrifices of Azevedo and Yarmolinsky. A discordant sound of whistles and horns drowned out the informer's voice. Then, the connection was broken off. Without yet rejecting the possibility of a hoax (after all, it was carnival time), Treviranus found out that he had been called from the Liverpool House, a tavern on the rue de Toulon, that dingy street where side by side exist the cosmorama and the coffee shop, the bawdy house and the bible sellers. Treviranus spoke with the owner. The latter (Black Finnegan, an old Irish criminal who was immersed in, almost overcome by, respectability) told him that the last person to use the phone was a lodger, a certain Gryphius, who had just left with some friends. Treviranus went immediately to Liverpool House. The owner related the following. Eight days ago

Gryphius had rented a room above the tavern. He was a sharp-featured man with a nebulous gray beard, and was shabbily dressed in black; Finnegan (who used the room for a purpose which Treviranus guessed) demanded a rent which was undoubtedly excessive; Gryphius paid the stipulated sum without hesitation. He almost never went out; he dined and lunched in his room; his face was scarcely known in the bar. On the night in question, he came downstairs to make a phone call from Finnegan's office. A closed cab stopped in front of the tavern. The driver didn't move from his seat; several patrons recalled that he was wearing a bear's mask. Two harlequins got out of the cab; they were of short stature and no one failed to observe that they were very drunk. With a tooting of horns, they burst into Finnegan's office; they embraced Gryphius, who appeared to recognize them but responded coldly; they exchanged a few words in Yiddish—he in a low, guttural voice, they in high-pitched, false voices—and then went up to the room. Within a quarter hour the three descended, very happy. Gryphius, staggering, seemed as drunk as the others. He walked—tall and dizzy—in the middle, between the masked harlequins. (One of the women at the bar remembered the yellow, red and green diamonds.) Twice he stumbled; twice he was caught and held by the harlequins. Moving off toward the inner harbor which enclosed a rectangular body of water, the three got into the cab and disappeared. From the footboard of the cab, the last of the harlequins scrawled an obscene figure and a sentence on one of the slates of the pier shed.

Treviranus saw the sentence. It was virtually predictable. It said:

The last of the letters of the Name has been uttered

Afterwards, he examined the small room of Gryphius-Ginzberg. On the floor there was a brusque star of blood, in the corners, traces of cigarettes of a Hungarian brand; in a cabinet, a book in Latin— the *Philologus Hebraeo-Graecus* (1739) of Leusden—with several manuscript notes. Treviranus looked it over with indignation and had Lönnrot located. The latter, without removing his hat, began to read while the inspector was interrogating the contradictory witnesses to the possible kidnapping. At four o'clock they left. Out on the twisted rue de Toulon, as they were treading on the dead serpentines of the dawn, Treviranus said:

"And what if all this business tonight were just a mock rehearsal?"

Erik Lönnrot smiled and, with all gravity, read a passage (which was underlined) from the thirty-third dissertation of the *Philologus: Dies Judacorum incipit ad solis occasu usque ad solis occasum diei sequentis.*

"This means," he added, " 'The Hebrew day begins at sundown and lasts until the following sundown.' "

The inspector attempted an irony.

"Is that fact the most valuable one you've come across tonight?"

"No. Even more valuable was a word that Ginzberg used."

The afternoon papers did not overlook the periodic disappearances. *La Cruz de la Espada* contrasted them with the admirable discipline and order of the last Hermetical Congress; Ernst Palast, in *El Mártir*, criticized "the intolerable delays in this clandestine and frugal pogrom, which has taken three months to murder three Jews"; the *Yidische Zaitung* rejected the horrible hypothesis of an anti-Semitic plot, "even though many penetrating intellects admit no other solution to the triple mystery"; the most illustrious gunman of the south, Dandy Red Scharlach, swore that in his district similar crimes could never occur, and he accused Inspector Franz Treviranus of culpable negligence.

On the night of March first, the inspector received an impressive-looking sealed envelope. He opened it; the envelope contained a letter signed "Baruch Spinoza" and a detailed plan of the city, obviously torn from a Baedeker. The letter prophesied that on the third of March there would not be a fourth murder, since the paint shop in the west, the tavern on the rue de Toulon and the Hôtel du Nord were "the perfect vertices of a mystic equilateral triangle"; the map demonstrated in red ink the regularity of the triangle. Treviranus read the *more geometrico* argument with resignation, and sent the letter and the map to Lönnrot—who, unquestionably, was deserving of such madnesses.

Erik Lönnrot studied them. The three locations were in fact equidistant. Symmetry in time (the third of December, the third of January, the third of February); symmetry in space as well . . . Suddenly, he felt as if he were on the point of solving the mystery. A set of calipers and a compass completed his quick intuition. He smiled, pronounced the word Tetragrammaton (of recent acquisition) and phoned the inspector. He said:

"Thank you for the equilateral triangle you sent me last night. It has enabled me to solve the problem. This Friday the criminals will be in jail, we may rest assured."

"Then they're not planning a fourth murder?"

"Precisely because they *are* planning a fourth murder we can rest assured."

Lönnrot hung up. One hour later he was traveling on one of the Southern Railway's trains, in the direction of the abandoned villa of Triste-le-Roy. To the south of the city of our story, flows a blind little river of muddy water, defamed by refuse and garbage. On the far side is an industrial suburb where, under the protection of a political boss from Barcelona, gunmen thrive. Lönnrot smiled at the thought that the most celebrated gunman of all—Red Scharlach—would have given a great deal to know of his clandestine visit. Azevedo had been an associate of Scharlach; Lönnrot considered the remote possibility that the fourth victim might be Scharlach himself. Then he rejected the idea . . . He had very nearly deciphered the problem; mere circumstances, reality (names, prison records, faces, judicial and penal proceedings) hardly interested him now. He wanted to travel a bit, he wanted to rest from three months of sedentary investigation. He reflected that the explanation of the murders was in an anonymous triangle and a dusty Greek word. The mystery appeared almost crystalline to him now; he was mortified to have dedicated a hundred days to it.

The train stopped at a silent loading station. Lönnrot got off. It was one of those deserted afternoons that seem like dawns. The air of the turbid, puddled plain was damp and cold. Lönnrot began walking along the countryside. He saw dogs, he saw a car on a siding, he saw the horizon, he saw a silver-colored horse drinking the crapulous water of a puddle. It was growing dark when he saw the rectangular belvedere of the villa of Triste-le-Roy, almost as tall as the black eucalypti which surrounded it. He thought that scarcely one dawning and one nightfall (an ancient splendor in the east and another in the west) separated him from the moment long desired by the seekers of the Name.

A rusty wrought-iron fence defined the irregular perimeter of the villa. The main gate was closed. Lönnrot, without much hope of getting in, circled the area. Once again before the insurmountable gate, he placed his hand between the bars almost mechanically and encountered the bolt. The creaking of the iron surprised him. With a laborious passivity the whole gate swung back.

Lönnrot advanced among the eucalypti treading on confused generations of rigid, broken leaves. Viewed from anear, the house of the villa of Triste-le-Roy abounded in pointless symmetries and in maniacal repetitions: to one Diana in a murky niche corresponded a second Diana in another niche; one balcony was reflected in another balcony; double stairways led to double balustrades. A two-faced Hermes projected a monstrous shadow. Lönnrot circled the house as he had the villa. He examined everything; beneath the level of the terrace he saw a narrow Venetian blind.

He pushed it; a few marble steps descended to a vault. Lönnrot, who had now perceived the architect's preferences, guessed that at the opposite wall there would be another stairway. He found it, ascended, raised his hands and opened the trap door.

A brilliant light led him to a window. He opened it: a yellow, rounded moon defined two silent fountains in the melancholy garden. Lönnrot explored the house. Through anterooms and galleries he passed to duplicate patios, and time after time to the same patio. He ascended the dusty stairs to circular antechambers; he was multiplied infinitely in opposing mirrors; he grew tired of opening or half-opening windows which revealed outside the same desolate garden from various heights and various angles; inside, only pieces of furniture wrapped in yellow dust sheets and chandeliers bound up in tarlatan. A bedroom detained him; in that bedroom, one single flower in a porcelain vase; at the first touch the ancient petals fell apart. On the second floor, on the top floor, the house seemed infinite and expanding. *The house is not this large*, he thought. *Other things are making it seem larger: the dim light, the symmetry, the mirrors, so many years, my unfamiliarity, the loneliness.*

By way of a spiral staircase he arrived at the oriel. The early evening moon shone through the diamonds of the window; they were yellow, red and green. An astonishing, dizzying recollection struck him.

Two men of short stature, robust and ferocious, threw themselves on him and disarmed him; another, very tall, saluted him gravely and said:

"You are very kind. You have saved us a night and a day."

It was Red Scharlach. The men handcuffed Lönnrot. The latter at length recovered his voice.

"Scharlach, are you looking for the Secret Name?"

Scharlach remained standing, indifferent. He had not participated in the brief struggle, and he scarcely extended his hand to receive Lönnrot's revolver. He spoke; Lönnrot noted in his voice a fatigued triumph, a hatred the size of the universe, a sadness not less than that hatred.

"No," said Scharlach. "I am seeking something more ephemeral and perishable, I am seeking Erik Lönnrot. Three years ago, in a gambling house on the rue de Toulon, you arrested my brother and had him sent to jail. My men slipped me away in a coupé from the gun battle with a policeman's bullet in my stomach. Nine days and nine nights I lay in agony in this desolate, symmetrical villa; fever was demolishing me, and the odious two-faced Janus who watches the twilights and the dawns lent horror to my dreams and to my waking. I came to abominate my body, I came to sense that two eyes, two hands, two lungs are as monstrous as two faces. An Irishman tried to convert me to the faith of Jesus; he repeated to me the phrase of the *goyim*: All roads lead to Rome. At night my delirium nurtured itself on that metaphor; I felt that the world was a labyrinth, from which it was impossible to flee, for all roads, though they pretend to lead to the north or south, actually lead to Rome, which was also the quadrilateral jail where my brother was dying and the villa of Triste-le-Roy. On those nights I swore by the God who sees with two faces and by all the gods of fever and of the mirrors to weave a labyrinth around the man who had imprisoned my brother. I have woven it and it is firm: the ingredients are a dead heresiologist, a compass, an eighteenth-century sect, a Greek word, a dagger, the diamonds of a paint shop.

"The first term of the sequence was given to me by chance. I had planned with a few colleagues—among them Daniel Azevedo—the robbery of the Tetrarch's sapphires. Azevedo betrayed us: he got drunk with the money that we had advanced him and he undertook the job a day early. He got lost in the vastness of the hotel; around two in the morning he stumbled into Yarmolinsky's room. The latter, harassed by insomnia, had started to write. He was working on some notes, apparently, for an article on the Name of God; he had already written the words: *The first letter of the Name has been uttered*. Azevedo warned him to be silent; Yarmolinsky reached out his hand for the bell which would awaken the hotel's forces; Azevedo countered with a single stab in the chest. It was almost a reflex action; half a century of violence had taught him that the easiest and surest thing is to kill . . . Ten days later I learned through the *Yidische Zaitung* that you were seeking in Yarmolinsky's writings the key to his death. I read the *History of the Hasidic Sect*; I learned that the reverent fear of uttering the Name of God had given rise to the doctrine that that Name is all powerful and recondite. I discovered that some Hasidim, in search of that secret Name, had gone so far as to perform human sacrifices . . . I knew that you would make the conjecture that the Hasidim had sacrificed the rabbi; I set myself the task of justifying that conjecture.

"Marcel Yarmolinsky died on the night of December third; for the second 'sacrifice' I selected the night of January third. He died in the north; for the second 'sacrifice' a place in the west was suitable. Daniel Azevedo was the necessary victim. He deserved death; he was impulsive, a traitor; his apprehension could destroy the entire plan. One of us stabbed him; in order to link his corpse to the other one I wrote on the paint shop diamonds: *The second letter of the Name has been uttered*.

"The third murder was produced on the third of February. It was, as Treviranus guessed, a mere sham. I am Gryphius-Ginzberg-Ginsburg; I endured an interminable week (supplemented by a tenuous fake beard) in the perverse cubicle on the rue de Toulon, until my friends abducted me. From the footboard of the cab, one of them wrote on a post: *The last of the letters of the Name has been uttered*. That sentence revealed that the series of murders was *triple*. Thus the public understood it; I, nevertheless, interspersed repeated signs that would allow you, Erik Lönnrot, the reasoner, to understand that the series was quadruple. A portent in the north, others in the east and west, demand a fourth portent in the south; the Tetragrammaton—the name of God, JHVH—is made up of *four* letters; the harlequins and the paint shop sign suggested *four* points. In the manual of Leusden I underlined a certain passage: that passage manifests that Hebrews compute the day from sunset to sunset; that passage makes known that the deaths occurred on the *fourth* of each month. I sent the equilateral triangle to Treviranus. I foresaw that you would add the missing point. The point which would form a perfect rhomb, the point which fixes in advance where a punctual death awaits you. I have premeditated everything, Erik Lönnrot, in order to attract you to the solitudes of Triste-le-Roy."

Lönnrot avoided Scharlach's eyes. He looked at the trees and the sky subdivided into diamonds of turbid yellow, green and red. He felt faintly cold, and he felt, too, an impersonal—almost anonymous—sadness. It was already night; from the dusty garden came the futile cry of a bird. For the last time, Lönnrot considered the problem of the symmetrical and periodic deaths.

"In your labyrinth there are three lines too many," he said at last. "I know of one Greek labyrinth which is a single straight line. Along that line so many philosophers have lost themselves that a mere detective might well do so, too. Scharlach, when in some other incarnation you hunt me, pretend to commit (or do commit) a crime at A, then a second crime at B, eight kilometers from A, then a third crime at C, four kilometers from A and B, half-way between the two. Wait for me afterwards at D, two kilometers from A and C, again halfway between both. Kill me at D, as you are now going to kill me at Triste-le-Roy."

"The next time I kill you," replied Scharlach, "I promise you that labyrinth, consisting of a single line which is invisible and unceasing."

He moved back a few steps. Then, very carefully, he fired.

For Mandie Molina Vedia   *Translated by Donald A. Yates*

Nicholas in Exile

Herbert Gold

With our first meeting on the terrace of the Grand Hotel Oloffson at its station on a tropical hillside rising from Port-au-Prince, Nicholas greeted me as his long-lost, long-mourned, spiritual brother. "A white man—man of culture," he explained in his rapid, slightly stilted, peculiarly idiomatic English: "a man who knows the score in literature, music, and art. These monkeys, it's not their color, there are a few clever ones—they just don't have thousands of years of civilization behind them. Naturally there are always the clever ones. Gladly I so stipulate."

I didn't argue the point. Infected by the traveler's loneliness, welcoming an offer of pleasure or distraction, I allowed Nicholas to take over with his energetic thrust of sudden intimacy. I had no friends in this steaming Caribbean corner of oblivion. Nicholas deManheim, manager of the hotel, knew everybody, everything that was going on. He was short, stocky, jolly, with a shock of sun-bleached hair falling over merry blue eyes; he was French—"well, not entirely, *mais quand même j'ai fait mes études à Paris*"—he seemed French anyway, and he had that gift of instantaneous sympathy. I accepted his petition to be my brother. I sighed with relief. I was ready to let him help me settle into my year at the Université d'Haiti. Charm may have been a commodity he sold, but he really had it to sell.

He also gave me a rate at the hotel and an elegant room, away from the noises of rum and fun, drink and quarrel, with a painting of a cockfight on one wall. The room had a little flowered porch of its own, propped up against the hillside on stilts, and a view of the swimming pool just below, half hidden by banana and mango trees; and further on, blue hills and mountains, blue bay, the smoky city spread out along the curve of sea. The original buildings of the hotel had been the residence of a President of Haiti who had insulted his people and had consequently been torn limb from limb by a mob. It is said that parts of his body were eaten by his enemies. His son was still alive, in his eighties, elegant in a white suit and carrying a white cocomacaque, the traditional aristocrat's walking stick. The Son strolled about mostly at dawn, to breathe unbreathed air, he explained; he wore green catskin shoes to preserve his virility. Emaciated and haughty, in a white suit and a celluloid collar, he occasionally crossed over from his own little house nearby to visit the scene of his father's martyrdom. His rage had been converted to amiable smiles. He was determined to be virile forever.

Nicholas gave me the gossip about my new home. He entertained me with the shrewdness of a European flung upon this alien heap of coral and mountain, amid an alien people, neither African nor French, crippled by poverty, stubborn, undependable. They always answered "yes," no matter what he asked them. It was the traditional resistance of the slave. "Is this the way to the Magloire house?" "Yes." "Will you do this job?" "Yes." No matter which way it really was; no matter what the servant's real intentions about the job. Nicholas suffered much trouble in the kitchen with waiters and cooks, and with the maids, and with porters, shoeshine boys, everybody. It was such a pleasure, he declared, to find an intelligent person at last. And sweaty but relaxed, he hustled me into his blue 4-CV Renault to carry me up the mountain to the little house in Petionville where he lived with his wife and child. "I have amended the Mosaic law," he said. "Honor Thy Wife and Son!"

While Nicholas was almost French, a former student in France, "*français de coeur,*" as he said, his wife was really French. She had orange hair, freckled skin, and pale green eyes, washed paler by the sun; she spoke with the hard *r* of the Parisienne. Their child, eighteen months old, already knew how to swim, paddling for dear life in their tiny pool, while his mother waded alongside, keeping her hand cautiously beneath the straining, protuberant baby belly. Later we ate a tropical salad by the pool of their house. Nicholas smiled and smiled and nodded modestly over the earnest compliments I offered him on his family. Occasionally his face would cloud and become distracted, as for example, when the barefooted servant forgot to serve an item of the menu in its proper order.

"*De la crème fraîche! La crème fraîche, espèce de putain!*"

The country girl, who spoke Creole, not French, was confused by her master's anger. Since she ate mostly rice and beans and, on special occasions, pork, mangoes, and bananas, and little else, the variety and complexity of a foreigner's meal was beyond easy unraveling. Nicholas paid her about six dollars a month while she was learning. Later she might earn eight dollars a month. But not until she understood to bring the fresh cream along with the fruit salad.

"I don't take cream on fruit," I said.

"Neither do I," he said, "but that animal has to learn to present it. Do you know this was a rich country when the French were still here? And now look." He raised his chin and I looked at that instead. "They call this freedom. They are enslaved to their nature—nothing higher."

I had trouble finding the evidence for Haitian progress. The country is the most depressed in the Western Hemisphere. The French should not have left in 1804, Nicholas said. Toussaint l'Ouverture, the slave leader who brought freedom, was thought to be a great man, but what is his legacy? Misery, torture, corruption, and cynicism. The barefoot servants being cursed by mulatto and black masters instead of French ones. Abandon, incomprehension, and failure. "You don't like it? Look at it anyway, my friend."

But he was my host and this was not a time for debate. He made a soft little shrug. Smiling at my discomfort, he handed me his son to hold in my lap. He cooed at the wriggling child with the adoration of a man given a firstborn after crossing the middle of the journey of his life. We admired it together. His wife, Aurore, smiled, laughed, said little. She didn't participate in the excited warmth which Nicholas radiated in my direction, his shortcuts to friendship—flattery, intense listening, joking.

Nicholas and I disagreed about some matters. He was scornful of

Haitians; his sunbruised, perpetually peeling face folded in on itself when he thought he was lowering his voice—it was actually a penetrating tenor: "Fresh out of the jungle, *mon vieux*. What else can you expect?" I didn't reply and he seldom pushed it any further. But he winked in my direction when a servant put the silver down with too great a clatter, before he began his *"engueulade,"* the good hard-mouthing he believed they needed. When he lost his temper, his wife took their son in her arms and held him until the gust was past. Then, subsiding, Nicholas apologized to Madame and me for his shouting and the meal continued.

Nicholas enjoyed one frequent Haitian companion. Roussan Garou was six feet, four inches tall, almost blue in color, emaciated by cirrhosis of the liver, furious-eyed, very intelligent—a poet. He had the lofty look of those tribesmen who can stand motionless, like cranes, one leg folded against the other at the knee. He was a racist who hated whites, hated mulattoes, except during the rare days when he was sober. Then he would sit with Nicholas and me on the terrace of the Grand Hotel Oloffson, drinking canned fruit juice and describing how France must provide the third force of mediation between the Soviet Union and the United States. This task could only be accomplished with the aid of its sister republic, Haiti. And of course, first it would be necessary to wash Port-au-Prince in the blood of the exploiters, whoever they might be. He grinned and lifted his glass to toast me in Dole pineapple juice. "A citizen of the republic of letters like yourself has no other nationality. Let us assume . . ."

Nicholas beamed.

"Like our friend Nicholas, also, a European gentleman cast upon these distant shores."

Nicholas threw his arms across our shoulders in a rush of happy feeling. He had brought the three of us together, dear companions from three different worlds, united. What miracles of pleasure the world, in its fullness, offers! He ordered another can of chilled juice. He cursed out the waiter, who had brought the can on a plate instead of pouring the juice into a pitcher. When Nicholas put his arm around Roussan's shoulder, clutching it, the poet gazed at me from the yellowish whites of his eyes with a measuring, challenging stare. He did not return the ebullient European gesture. He was a poet from Port-de-Paix, not a Quartier Latin student.

The three of us went on sipping pineapple juice and discussing world politics at a table on the terrace of the hotel perched on its little slope up from the steaming port city. Down the hill a bit, the National Palace glittered in the sunlight, its cellars filled with the President's personal stock of munitions. Farther down, near the open-air markets, there was the "Boulevard des Millionaires," where people were born and died in the street, sold their goods, begged, survived in a corner of the universe designed to prove nothing, not even that hell exists. Beyond, under the perfect sky, the harbor glittered and the cruise ships lay at anchor.

When Roussan left us, stepping precariously on his stilt legs, Nicholas waved goodbye and even blew a kiss from his fingertips. The poet revolved slowly as if a flying kiss had hit him on the neck. Gravely he saluted, turned, walked on, stopped, and bowed to the ancient doctor-lawyer in his green catskin shoes, taking an unusual late-afternoon stroll, risking his virility in the breathed air of the Port-au-Prince afternoon.

As Roussan disappeared down the winding road, Nicholas said: "Decent chap. Drunkard like any Haitian with a brain in his head. Of course, that poetry of his is just addled brains. The cerebral matter must be like ratatouille—scrambled, what? with Rhum Barbancourt."

"He spoke rationally enough just now."

"Sick, that's why. They can't stand up under thinking, have to drink—must. It's the emotions break down, not just the brain. Come on up the hill, a bit of dinner at home. My son recognizes you. Refresh the chappie. At this age they have short memories, you know?"

And he urged me into his little blue 4-CV. I was homesick and susceptible to the flattery of his attention, the baby smiles of his son, the undemanding cheerfulness of his orange-haired wife. We clattered up the two-lane mountain highway to Petionville, dodging in and out of traffic, and I studied fatalism with my eyes shut. On the steep side of the highway, in the ravine, the wrecks of automobiles sank among refuse, grasses, and windfall rocks in the dry trickle of mountain water. Along the road, peasant women, balancing on their heads their loads of produce for market, walked downhill in a steady procession, talking softly or silent, following each other in a ceaseless line. Others, empty baskets on their heads, made the long climb back up the mountain on skinny legs with a scale of dust covering them. Occasionally they scrambled into the ravine to bathe in the stream. They carried away whatever was useful in the destroyed automobiles, but there was not very much they could use.

"Animals," Nicholas said. He gave me the traditional Haitian elite advice for an automobile accident involving peasants: *Make sure they're dead.* Back up if necessary. If the pedestrian is injured, you must pay hospital expenses; if killed, seventy dollars for the funeral. "The doctors are thieves. The hospitals are rackets. The whole family lives on what you give them for medicine. *Back up*," he repeated, grinning.

Then, as if this reminded him, he reported a bit of gossip about Roussan Garou. Roussan had been in charge of supplying foreign women to the previous President of the Republic. On his shopping trips to Cuba and Jamaica, he had diplomatic accreditation. "Now of course," said Nicholas, "he is confined to poetry, drastically limited to his alcoholic *delire verbale*, since the new regime has made other arrangements. Naturally he favors reform—immediate turnover."

The charm of my new friend may be hard to discover in this chronicle. But malice about others does not immediately put us off; we think ourselves immune when we see the sparkling eyes of the friend. You have to imagine the melancholy of a traveler far from home, his pleasure in a gregarious tropical evening after the blistering day, the power of smiles, winks, and random assumptions of complicity to bring a coziness into life among strangers. And there was more than malice to Nicholas. He loved music, he had written a novel, he spoke languages. He reacted vivaciously. He was in touch. It was hard to make severe judgment of a man who so obviously wanted to be liked.

We sat in the cool of the evening and discussed student days in Paris. His nostalgia for the Left Bank was contagious. Once, deep in rum, we spontaneously began singing "Le Quartier Latin" together, traditional among the medical students of Paris; we talked about Bergson and the school of Bergson, the cafés Le Dôme and the Select, the magic of French women. "A French girl who doesn't love him," Nicholas said, "is better to a man than a girl of any other nationality who might happen to adore him. Yes? You agree?"

We had found several grounds for friendship. I wondered if his wife loved him or was merely good to him.

Then one evening it happened that we were exploring the bars of the Boulevard Harry-Truman, the one attempt at a spacious avenue in Port-au-Prince, designed for elegance upon the leveled debris of a waterfront slum. It had been built for the Exposition by President Estimé; there were palm trees, cafés, and medieval ruins which dated back to 1949. It took only a few years to produce crumbling walls and picturesque ramparts worthy of ancient Rome, or at least of Cinecitta. Thick-leaved plants followed in the path of smaller weeds; soon whole trees were pushing through the cracks of the luxurious halls and galleries. Among the desolation of the wide boulevard, the broken pipes and breached foundations, several bars—Whiskey à Gogo, the Casino Italien, and a few others—kept afloat with their bit of neon, their tourists, and the nightly crop of celebrating Haitian men with their patient women.

We drank in the Whiskey à Gogo. At about midnight Nicholas began speaking of his wife and son. This reminded him of things beautiful, things eternal. The piano! he decided. He had been a child prodigy of the Seventh Arondissement. Right now, at this very moment, we would go home for a concert. He would play for me, for me alone, and for his wife and child, too. In the cool of the Haitian night, in the hot of the bar, it seemed a fine idea. We emerged from the bar and made our way, sideways and distracted, down the walk past the Casino. Nicholas wore the look, both happy and worried, of a man without a job who has suddenly, unexpectedly, found a bottle of rum in a paper bag. He believed his luck, but doubted it. He staggered a little.

The evening made me ridiculous, too. I was not used to the jolt of rum-soda, the drink of choice in Port-au-Prince. I was taken by a pointless whimsicality as we passed the little pack of black Buicks and Cadillacs which surrounded the Casino, the usual sign that the President of the Republic, plus cronies, bodyguards, and ladyfriends, was busy relaxing from the cares of state. Sleepy policemen with submachine guns leaned against the black fenders, fighting off their yawns. They blinked at us in the dark and wondered when the President would relieve them from long duty. Overhead, a tropical sky with blinking stars; at eye level, ruins, palm trees, bodyguards with black weapons, the Boulevard Harry-Truman. We were encircled in the dark as we uncertainly strolled past the police cars.

A dizzy joke possessed me. One of the black police cars had its door swung open. Like a cop, I took Nicholas by the shoulder and shoved him toward it. "Get in there!"

He stiffened. He turned cold as ice, and sober, his lank hair fallen over his forehead and his eyes enraged. *"Don't you touch me."*

It was as if we were different beings in another time and place. The evening was abruptly over. The violence of his anger and revulsion set us both out of gear. We had nothing to say to each other. We parted within a few minutes.

During the next days something peculiar and incomplete kept nagging at me. My friend's fear and rage reminded me of something.

At last I went to an American police officer, a black sergeant from the New York City department, who had been assigned to the Port-au-Prince police to help them develop a department of scientific fingerprint investigation. I asked him to find what he could about the history of Nicholas deManheim. "For a pal, why not?" he said. "It's strictly illegal, but one thing you learn quick around here is they don't have any laws."

That evening he drove up to the Hotel Oloffson. On his way to my room he passed the cheery time of day with Nicholas, who was getting ready to speed up the mountain in his little blue 4-CV toward his red-haired wife and his son. The policeman sat in my chair, fanned himself, and said: "It's easy. Your buddy's under a charge of accomplice to murder in France."

International criminals can make a comfortable home in Haiti if they keep up their payments to the proper officials. Haitian politicians are less demanding than most. "But it's only politics," the sergeant assured me. "He was a student in Paris. He was only a student. They say he was a Gestapo informer, but he didn't wait around for the trial, jumped right on the rat railway."

I'm not sure I thanked the smiling NYPD sergeant. A man responsible for torture and death during the Nazi time should have been identifiable by some clear marking, like a tattoo. That he could have a pretty wife, a baby son upon whom he doted, an interest in music and art, a normal taste for gossip—in theory, why not? We all know this. But the fact of Nicholas, grinning and ingratiating, now horrified me. There was also a kind of shame for not recognizing him. I felt unsafe. The world was filled with secret enemies. I didn't speak with him in the days that followed.

And yet Nicholas was not my enemy, not any longer, not in this altered world.

Nicholas understood that something had interrupted our friendship, perhaps that tipsy evening on the Boulevard Harry-Truman. But one night he again came to my room in the hotel, knocked, and waited till I opened. He brought a bottle of rum, glasses, ice, little bottles of soda. He sat at my table and served us both. His face was red and congested with the effort he was making. It had been worked out in his imagination; all he had to do was speak the rehearsed words. He pronounced the conclusion of an imaginary discussion he had been having with me. He knew my lines and hoped to give me the cue as rapidly as possible. "I cannot bear living in this place any longer," he said. "I must leave. I can write, translate, many jobs. I need your help. Help me get to New York. In New York I can find work fit for a man of my education." He talked rapidly, disjointedly, never saying "America" or "The United States." "I know New York well, though I have never been there. I have studied. A grid system, except for Greenwich Village. Aurore must not stay here any longer. She insists. You can recommend me. An affidavit. I need a little help, a signature, a letter. I have helped you here, have I not? My son must be raised among civilized people. It's for him, too—you like my son, don't you? In New York you must have friends, family. Do it."

I was foundering in the rush of desire sent my way. Whether I was fond of his child, whether I resented his contempt for Haitians, even whether or not I could do anything for him at the U.S. Embassy if he had been charged by a French court—this was irrelevant. *Merely political*, the American policeman had said.

"No, Nicholas. I won't do it."

He stood up and an empty bottle of soda somersaulted to the floor. It bounced without breaking. He looked at me with eyes which were suddenly very thoughtful and considerate. His mouth was still moving slightly, as if, with the sound turned off, he was continuing a lecture about how much he needed to go live in New York. His tongue was working on the inside of his lips and the muscles of his cheeks. He spoke wearily, pitifully, not wanting to; he spoke because it was expected of him; he uttered the word as if asking in still another way a favor of me: "*Jew*," and waited for me to hit him.

Captain Blood

Donald Barthelme

When Captain Blood goes to sea, he locks the doors and windows of his house on Cow Island personally. One never knows what sort of person might chance by, while one is away.

When Captain Blood, at sea, paces the deck, he usually paces the foredeck rather than the afterdeck—a matter of personal preference. He keeps marmalade and a spider monkey in his cabin, and four perukes on stands.

When Captain Blood, at sea, discovers that he is pursued by the Dutch Admiral Van Tromp, he considers throwing the women overboard. So that they will drift, like so many giant lotuses in their green, lavender, purple and blue gowns, across Van Tromp's path, and he will have to stop and pick them up. Blood will have the women fitted with life jackets under their dresses. They will hardly be in much danger at all. But what about the jaws of sea turtles? No, the women cannot be thrown overboard. Vile, vile! What an idiotic idea! What could he have been thinking of? Of the patterns they would have made floating on the surface of the water, in the moonlight, a cerise gown, a silver gown . . .

Captain Blood presents a façade of steely imperturbability.

He is poring over his charts, promising everyone that things will get better. There has not been one bit of booty in the last eight months.

Should he try another course? Another ocean? The men have been quite decent about the situation. Nothing has been said. Still, it's nerve-racking.

When Captain Blood retires for the night (leaving orders that he be called instantly if something comes up) he reads, usually. Or smokes, thinking calmly of last things.

His hideous reputation should not, strictly speaking, be painted in the horrible colors customarily employed. Many a man walks the streets of Panama City, or Port Royal, or San Lorenzo, alive and well, who would have been stuck through the gizzard with a rapier, or smashed in the brain with a boarding pike, had it not been for Blood's swift, cheerful intervention. Of course, there are times when severe measures are unavoidable. At these times he does not flinch, but takes appropriate action with admirable steadiness. There are no two ways about it: when one looses a seventy-four-gun broadside against the fragile hull of another vessel, one gets carnage.

Blood at dawn, a solitary figure pacing the foredeck.

No other sail in sight. He reaches into the pocket of his blue velvet jacket trimmed with silver lace. His hand closes over three round, white objects: mothballs. In disgust, he throws them over the side. One *makes* one's luck, he thinks. Reaching into another pocket, he withdraws a folded parchment tied with ribbon. Unwrapping the little packet, he finds that it is a memo that he wrote to himself ten months earlier. "*Dolphin*, Captain Darbraunce, 120 tons, cargo silver, paprika, bananas, sailing Mar. 10 Havana. *Be there!*" Chuckling, Blood goes off to seek his mate, Oglethorpe—that laughing blond giant of a man.

Who will be aboard this vessel which is now within cannon-shot? wonders Captain Blood. Rich people, I hope, with pretty gold and silver things aplenty.

"Short John, where is Mr. Oglethorpe?"

"I am not Short John, sir. I am John-of-Orkney."

"Sorry, John. Has Mr. Oglethorpe carried out my instructions?"

"Yes, sir. He is forward, crouching over the bombard, lit cheroot in hand, ready to fire."

"Well, fire then."

"Fire!"

BAM!

"The other captain doesn't understand what is happening to him!"

"He's not heaving to!"

"He's ignoring us!"

"The dolt!"

"Fire again!"

BAM!

"That did it!"

"He's turning into the wind!"

"He's dropped anchor!"

"He's lowering sail!"

"Very well, Mr. Oglethorpe. You may prepare to board."

"Very well, Peter."

"And Jeremy—"

"Yes, Peter?"

"I know we've had rather a thin time of it these last few months."

"Well it hasn't been so bad, Peter. A little slow, perhaps—"

"Well, before we board, I'd like you to convey to the men my appreciation for their patience. Patience and, I may say, tact."

"We knew you'd turn up something, Peter."

"Just tell them for me, will you?"

Always a wonderful moment, thinks Captain Blood. Preparing to board. Pistol in one hand, naked cutlass in the other. Dropping lightly to the deck of the engrappled vessel, backed by one's grinning, leering, disorderly, rapacious crew who are nevertheless under the strictest buccaneer discipline. There to confront the little band of fear-crazed victims shrinking from the entirely possible carnage. Among them, several beautiful women, but one really spectacular beautiful woman who stands a bit apart from her sisters, clutching a machete with which she intends, against all reason, to—

When Captain Blood celebrates the acquisition of a rich prize, he goes down to the galley himself and cooks *tallarínes a la Catalana* (noodles, spare ribs, almonds, pine nuts) for all hands. The name of the captured vessel is entered in a little book along with the names of all the others he has captured in a long career. Here are some of them: the *Oxford*, the *Luis*, the *Fortune*, the *Lambe*, the *Jamaica Merchant*, the *Betty*, the *Prosperous*, the *Endeavor*, the *Falcon*, the *Bonadventure*, the *Constant Thomas*, the *Marquesa*, the *Señora del Carmen*, the *Recovery*, the *Maria Gloriosa*, the *Virgin Queen*, the *Esmerelda*, the *Havana*, the *San Felipe*, the *Steadfast* . . .

The true buccaneer is not persuaded that God is not on his side, too—especially if, as is often the case, he turned pirate after some monstrously unjust thing was done to him, such as being press-ganged into one or another of the Royal Navies when he was merely innocently having a drink at a waterfront tavern, or having been confined to the stinking dungeons of the Inquisition just for making some idle, thoughtless, light remark. Therefore, Blood feels himself to be devout *in his own way*, and has endowed candles burning in churches in most of the great cities of the New World. Although not under his own name.

Captain Blood roams ceaselessly, making daring raids. The average raid yields something like 20,000 pieces-of-eight, which is apportioned fairly among the crew, with wounded men getting more according to the gravity of their wounds. A cut ear is worth two pieces, a cut-*off* ear worth ten to twelve. The scale of payments for injuries is posted in the forecastle.

When he is on land, Blood is confused and troubled by the life of cities, where every passing stranger may, for no reason, assault him, if the stranger so chooses. And indeed, the stranger's mere presence, multiplied many times over, is a kind of assault. Merely having to *take into account* all these hurrying others is a blistering occupation. This does not happen on a ship, or on a sea.

An amusing incident: Captain Blood has overhauled a naval vessel, has caused her to drop anchor (on this particular voyage he is sailing with three other ships under his command and a total enlistment of nearly one thousand men) and is now interviewing the arrested captain in his cabin full of marmalade jars and new perukes.

"And what may your name be, sir? If I may ask?"

"Jones, sir."

"What kind of a name is that? English, I take it?"

"No, it's American, sir."

"American? What is an American?"

"America is a new nation among the nations of the world."

"I've not heard of it. Where is it?"

"North of here, north and west. It's a very small nation, at present, and has only been a nation for about two years."

"But the name of your ship is French."

"Yes it is. It is named in honor of Benjamin Franklin, one of our American heroes."

"*Bon Homme Richard?* What has that to do with Benjamin or Franklin?"

"Well it's an allusion to an almanac Dr. Franklin published called—"

"You weary me, sir. You are captured, American or no, so tell me—do you surrender, with all your men, fittings, cargo and whatever?"

"Sir, I have not yet begun to fight."

"Captain, this is madness. We have you completely surrounded. Furthermore there is a great hole in your hull below the waterline where our warning shot, which was slightly miscalculated, bashed in your timbers. You are taking water at a fearsome rate. And still you wish to fight?"

"It is the pluck of us Americans, sir. We are just that way. Our tiny nation has to be pluckier than most if it is to survive among the bigger, older nations of the world."

"Well, bless my soul. Jones, you are the damnedest goatsucker I ever did see. Stab me if I am not tempted to let you go scot-free, just because of your amazing pluck."

"No sir, I insist on fighting. As founder of the American naval tradition, I must set a good example."

"Jones, return to your vessel and be off."

"No, sir, I will fight to the last shred of canvas, for the honor of America."

"Jones, even in America, wherever it is, you must have encountered the word 'ninny.' "

"Oh. I see. Well then. I think we'll be weighing anchor, Captain, with your permission."

"Choose your occasions, Captain. And God be with you."

Blood, at dawn, a solitary figure pacing the foredeck. The world of piracy is wide, and at the same time, narrow. One can be gallant all day long, and still end up with a spider monkey for a wife. And what does his mother think of him?

The favorite dance of Captain Blood is the grave and haunting Catalonian *sardana*, in which the participants join hands facing each other to form a ring which gradually becomes larger, then smaller, then larger again. It is danced without smiling, for the most part. He frequently dances this with his men, in the middle of the ocean, after lunch, to the music of a single silver trumpet.

Mirror Girl

William Bayer

Always on those rainy nights when she decided to drive into the city in search of a mark, she would first revisit the Mirror Maze . . .

All that afternoon, warm rain danced against the tin roof of the loft, and the faint howling of a dog, somewhere on the fringes of the park, made her think of pain.

With darkness, light from the neon "Mirror Maze" sign, cut by the blinds, cast harsh stripes across the walls and floor. She sat on her hard wooden chair listening to the patter on the roof and the squeak of the ceiling fan as it thrashed the humid air.

When, finally, she made her decision, she moved with swift resolve. She rolled up the little blue rug beside her bed, opened the trapdoor beneath, then made her way by memory and touch down the wooden ladder to the catwalks.

These she crossed with the elegant grace of an aerialist, moving skillfully between the wires that held up the background drapes of black velour. When she reached the switchboard, she turned on all the lights. Then she lowered herself deftly to the floor down a soft thick gym rope. Finally she stripped off all her clothes and walked out to face the mirrors.

The ones in the sharply angled "Corridor of Distortion" met her like angry sentinels—fattening, elongating, disproportioning her body. She strode rapidly down this corridor, crossed "The Fragmentation Chamber," then made her way via the sinuous "Mirror Serpent" to "The Great Hall of Infinite Deceptions." Here, in the middle of the room, she stopped, then slowly turned like a skater cutting a figure on a patch of virgin ice.

Her glossy tresses of dark brown hair, so dark they looked almost black in the mirrors, cascaded down her neck, broke upon her shoulders and edged her pale back. Pausing to regard her high cheekbones and sculpted lips, she smiled gently at her likeness. Fair skin, brown irises, dark brows, modeled chin—she basked before the multiple images. The reflections ravished her eyes. Then she began to look beyond herself, searching out corners and crevices in the silvered glass. There was secrecy in mirror-space, places to hide and to conceal, corridors of sparkling light, endless shimmering passages and tunnels.

She positioned her image in one of these, stared hard at her eyes, willed herself entry. Then, in an instant which, no matter how often she experienced it, would always seem magical, she passed through to become her dream-sister—the one she'd known since girlhood, the one who lived in mirrorworld.

She felt safe then, in a place where so many amazing things were possible, where the rules and laws that governed the world outside were null and void. Here, in the land of mirror-reverse, normally forbidden acts could be performed without fear or guilt and to degrees of intensity undreamt of even in deepest sleep.

Later, wigged blond, dressed smart, artfully made up, she drove into Manhattan through the rain-slick streets. She kept all her car windows shut. Only the whoosh of the air-conditioning and music from the tape deck, dizzying arias sung by great divas—Sutherland, Callas, Caballé—reached her ears.

Cruising the avenues of the Upper East Side, she raised her eyes from the herd of taxis to gaze into her rear-view mirror. Glimpsing the reflection of her dream-sister, she shivered at the sight. What if she were trapped? What if the mirrors turned cruel and refused to let her out? *Then I will be lost forever*, she whispered to herself, smiling contentedly, her dread dissolving in the vision of streetlamps reflected in the gleaming wet black avenue ahead.

She was searching for a bar, one she'd never been in before. She would know it when she saw it. There would be an aura: a sports car angled jauntily in front, a rich warm glow, laughter and conversation spilling out, perhaps a handsome well-dressed man entering alone, ironic smile on his lips.

Marks were always to be found in such places. Diana had taught her that. And, for the first months after she left Diana, she continued to follow her old mentor's rules. But she had always been better at it than Diana's other girls—subtler, slicker, far more credible. Diana had told her she had a gift for it, was a "natural," that with concentration she could outgross the others ten-to-one. Now, a year and a half after striking out on her own, she had begun to rely on her instincts. Now too she only played on rainy nights, employing methods, taught by Diana as a business, in an activity she now regarded as a game.

She chose a place called Aspen, a preppy jock-type hangout with an "*après* ski" look: glowing yellow lamps, glistening U-shaped bar, fireplace converted into a pizza oven in the rear. The decorations defined it: tarnished athletic trophies, crossed ski poles and lacrosse sticks, framed amateur team photos crowding the walls. Each adornment was calculated to create instant nostalgia for some nameless generic school, distinguished by its love of competitive sports played hard and fair and true.

She was standing just inside the doorway, listening to the hum, inhaling the aroma of smoke, perfume and beer, when she noticed a man glancing up at her from the bar. Late thirties, athletic build, expensive plaid tweed jacket, thinning light brown hair. He appraised her briefly, met her gaze, grinned in welcome, then turned back shyly to his drink.

In the instant when their eyes met and locked she recognized him as her mark—not the flashy type of salesman or conventioneer Diana had taught her to seek out, but someone better and less gullible than that. A superior man with cultural interests, perhaps moderately successful with women. A well-educated man, possibly divorced, who most likely owned an apartment in the neighborhood.

Plaid Jacket looked up, grinned at her again. Already she felt regret; this conquest, it seemed, would not be difficult. She turned slowly, a signal she noticed him but chose not to recognize his interest. Spotting an empty table, she moved toward it, knowing he was watching to see if she sat alone. She was careful to avoid glancing at her watch, her way of telling him she was not waiting for someone else.

The waiter was a puppy: bright eyes, cute polka-dot bow tie, a tail of frizzy hair tied back with a rubber band. He flirted with her ("How're *you* tonight?"), then asked what she'd like to drink.

She squinted at him. "Have I seen you in something?"

He smiled. "You a casting agent?" She shook her head. "Well," he admitted shyly, "I've been in a print ad in *M*. Maybe you saw me there."

They chatted briefly about his career. He was looking to break through with a TV commercial. "Just in case you know someone in the biz . . ." he added, wandering off to fetch her drink.

When he returned he told her she had an admirer.

"Plaid Jacket. Over there," he said, gesturing. "He picked up your check."

"That's nice," she said, "but I like to pay for myself."

"Sorry, I rang it up. But if you wanna make things even, you can always . . . you know . . . re-cip-ro-cate." He enunciated each syllable to show he felt reciprocation would be absurd.

She smiled, shook her head. "We know what that means, don't we?"

The waiter smiled too, then turned sincere. "Actually, he's a pretty nice guy. Comes in couple times a week. Works for a network, or maybe it's a magazine. Anyway, never heard any complaints."

She glanced at the bar. Plaid Jacket was grinning at her again. She nodded her thanks. He raised his glass in acknowledgment.

"Well?" asked the waiter.

"What's his name?"

"Roger something." He paused. "A girl could do worse." He gave her his best kid-brother look.

"Oh, I'm sure of that. But this girl usually does a lot better."

The waiter beamed. "Want me to tell him that?"

She laughed. "Sure, why not?"

Plaid Jacket appeared two minutes later, hovering at a respectful distance.

"Hi. I'm Roger. Welcome to the pub." He gestured to the empty chair. "May I?" She shrugged. He sat down carefully.

"What's your name?"

"Gelsey."

"Hi again." He stuck out his hand. She looked at it, hesitated, then shook it casually.

"Thanks for the drink. But I wish you hadn't—" She reached into her bag, pulled out her wallet.

His face fell. "Please don't. I'm sorry, I know I should have asked."

She noted his wounded pride. "Okay." She shrugged again. "This once."

He sighed his gratitude. "That would have been really humiliating." She smiled to show she understood. "I haven't seen you in here before."

"I haven't been in here before."

"Well, that figures." He was floundering. "What made you decide—?"

"I was out walking. It was raining and I started feeling thirsty. I saw the glow and decided to come in. Guess I was looking for a . . . refuge."

"Glad you chose Aspen. It's a friendly place. I know most of the regulars." He hesitated, then took the plunge. "That's why I can say you're the most attractive woman to drop in here in quite a while."

She pondered his compliment before accepting it. She wanted him to know she could not be won so easily. Finally she smiled, a signal she would allow him to warm her up. Encouraged, he set eagerly to work.

He was a staff writer at *Fortune*. She told him she worked in publicity at Simon & Schuster.

He was from St. Louis and had gone to Dartmouth. She told him she was from Oakland and had attended Cal.

He was thirty-six, divorced, an excellent skier, an earnest if fumbling tennis player, also interested in art. She told him she was twenty-six, had broken up with a live-in boyfriend two months before, belonged to a health club, and as for tennis—if they ever played he'd better watch out!

They discussed some of the concerns of people in their cohort: how difficult it was to live in the city with so much crime, homelessness, and AIDS; how hard it was to meet nice people outside of work; the relative virtues and drawbacks of the alternate coast.

They talked about their jobs. He told her he'd been thinking about recycling himself as a TV correspondent. But the truth was that he believed in print.

She did too, she said, which was the only reason she stayed in publishing, where the workload was heavy and the pay disgracefully low. Still, she was thinking of moving on. There'd been some sexual harassment by her boss. Subtle, not enough yet to substantiate a complaint, but still unnerving, and, in its own way, insidious. In fact, the reason she'd gone out walking in the rain that evening was to try and figure out what to do.

Now there was a bond. He turned compassionate. He knew exactly what she meant, he said, because he too had suffered something similar a couple of years back from a female superior.

"And it *was* insidious, because I knew if I complained I'd look like a total jerk. What could I say? That she made comments about my clothes, my build, told me I played 'a major role' in her 'fantasies'? I should have been flattered, right? Thing was, physically speaking, she was a fairly desirable woman. Under normal circumstances I might have been interested. But not in the workplace. Not for me anyway. There's a time and place for everything, don't you think? A place to work and a time to play . . ."

Gelsey picked up a half dozen signals from that little monologue. She made her eyes gleam, so he would know she'd become aroused.

He stared at her. There was silence between them. They listened to a little burst of laughter from a table in the rear.

"Are you comfortable here?" he asked.

"Tell you the truth—the smoke's kinda getting me down."

"Well," he said smoothly, "I hope this doesn't sound pushy. But I was wondering—you see I practically live around the corner."

This was it: the bar pickup endgame. She stared at him, noncommittal. She wanted him to work for it.

He swallowed. "Like I said, I don't want to sound pushy. But I've got an interesting idea."

She leaned forward slightly. "Tell me about it."

He grinned to diffuse any intimation of aggression. "I was thinking we might mosey out of here, go over to my place, and, you know," he grinned again, "have another drink. A nightcap."

She reached across the table, took hold of his hands, lightly played her fingers along his wrists. "Is that all you were thinking we might do?" she asked.

He tried not to show too much excitement. "That, of course, would be up to you," he said carefully.

She met his gaze, then lowered her eyes demurely. "I might decide that you should take off your pants," she said. She gazed at him again. "What would you think about that?"

"I'd think you were the most . . . intriguing girl I'd met in a very long time."

His building was what she expected, a fifteen-story white-brick-with-doorman, constructed as a rental in the sixties, converted to a co-op in the eighties. There were several mirrors in the lobby, one nice one between the elevators. They entered one of the cabs. Roger pushed the button for the penthouse floor. They leaned against opposite sides and smiled at one another as they rode up.

"Let's hurry and get these wet raincoats off," he said, fumbling with his keys.

Once inside, he switched on a set of track lights, then dimmed them down. There was a classic Manhattan penthouse view: squared-off apartment buildings against soaring midtown towers, a hundred thousand lit-up windows, golden cages hanging in the night.

She looked around. The sparse furnishings were expensive. Soft black leather couches faced one another across an elegant glass cocktail table. Smooth white walls served as background for a small collection of contemporary prints. She knew the look: downtown gallery. Now she peered about more carefully, hoping to be surprised. But she could find nothing personal, nothing except the artwork, and that spoke to her of risklessness. Yet Roger had taken a major risk: he had invited her into his home.

"Drink?"

"Sure. Let me make it."

He grinned at her. "I bet you can mix up something pretty mean."

" 'Gelsey's Special.' "

"Sounds interesting."

"It is, Roger. I promise . . ."

He led her to the kitchen, showed her where he kept his booze, glasses, bar tools, and blender, then excused himself. He had to dry his hair.

"Just call if you need me." His voice trailed off.

She set up a pair of highball glasses, quickly marked one with a slight smudge of lipstick against the rim. Then she set to work creating her potion. As she was finishing she heard music. He had put an album of Mabel Mercer on the stereo.

Drinks made, she carried them into the living room. He was slouched on one of the couches, jacket off, hair engagingly tousled.

She handed him his glass, sat down on the opposite couch and took a little sip from hers.

He grinned at her. "Starting to mellow out?"

"Very much so." She leaned back, flicked her hair, then casually stuck out her legs. She looked around. "I imagined you'd have a place like this."

"Really? Like what?"

"Cool. Hard-edged."

Perplexed by her analysis, he did the only thing he could under the circumstances: he laughed. "Am I really so predictable?"

"We'll soon find out, won't we?" she asked in a throaty whisper. Then she lightly touched her breasts.

It was a fine moment, the kind she tried to create every time she played, full of the promise of lust—tastes, aromas, moves and caresses that could not be predicted and would therefore surprise and delight.

They drank in silence, matching one another sip for sip. When, finally, he had drained his glass, she excused herself.

"Don't get up," she said. "I'll find it on my own."

As she passed close by him she studied his eyes. They were beginning to glaze. Unaware of how tired he was, he broke his yawn with a grin. She paused behind, approached him from the rear, laid her hands on his shoulders and bent her head down to his ear:

"I think it's getting time to take off those pants," she whispered. Then she patted his head and retired to the bathroom, where she studied herself in the mirror.

It was her dream-sister who stared back.

She spent three minutes examining the contents of his medicine cabinet, then flushed the toilet and wandered back to the living room. He was dozing. His pants were down, caught around his ankles. She knelt before him, placed a hand beneath his chin and carefully raised his head.

"Roger?"

He opened his eyes. "Sorry. I was feeling . . ." He stared at her. "Maybe too much to drink."

"Maybe," she said.

He gestured toward his glass, now resting on the cocktail table. "What did you—?"

She gazed at him. Her voice turned stern. "What did I *what*, Roger?"

"I dunno . . ." He slurred his words.

"You lied to me back at the bar. I know you did," she said.

He blinked. "Huh?"

"That little story about sexual harassment at the office—that never happened. Did it?"

He blinked again. "What's your problem? I don't get—"

"Get what, Roger?" she asked kindly.

He glanced at his glass again. "Did you put something—?"

"In your drink? As a matter of fact, I did." She nodded sweetly, then watched carefully as the realization struck and the terror filled his eyes.

"*Why?* What are you—?"

"Don't panic. Relax and go to sleep." She cooed at him like a pigeon from the park: "Sleep, Roger . . . sleep . . . sleep . . ."

He tried to strike out at her. She pulled back, but his thrust was too feeble in any case. After that he drooped; the effort had wasted what little energy he had left. She watched as he tried to fight off exhaustion the way they always did, shaking his head, fluttering his eyes. She peered at him closely. He was totally terrified, probably wondering whether she had poisoned him, whether he would ever wake up.

"Please . . ." he begged.

She waited until he closed his eyes and slumped, his heavy rhythmic breathing telling her he was out. "Goodnight, sweet prince," she whispered as she rose from her knees, then hurried to the kitchen, where she had left her purse.

The first thing, always, was to put on a fresh pair of surgical gloves, thoroughly wash out the highball glasses, then clean every place she had touched with her bare fingertips. There weren't many such places—a few spots in the kitchen, the refrigerator and freezer doors, the bathroom doorknob and medicine cabinet. When she finished with her chores she checked again on Roger. He was snoring deeply, lost in sleep. She nodded and began her search.

She removed his wallet from his fallen pants and emptied all his pockets. She took the cash (over four hundred dollars—*surprise!*), but left the credit cards and ID's arranged neatly on the cocktail table. The point, as Diana had always taught, was to rob the mark, not enrage him to the point at which he'd feel obliged to go to the police. She also removed his watch. It wasn't anything special, but it was in the nature of her game that he be deprived of his way of marking time. Then, when she had finished searching his person, she began a methodical search of the entire apartment.

It took her five minutes to discover that everything of interest was concentrated in the bedroom. The front closets and drawers were virtually empty. The bedroom, however, offered all sorts of treasures: a pair of gold Cartier cuff links, two Krugerrands, a gold pocket watch (probably his grandfather's), and, in the bottom of a drawer filled with commercially ironed shirts, an airmail envelope containing various denominations of foreign currency and five hundred-dollar bills.

All of this she took. She discovered and rapidly rearranged a good deal more. There was a trove of personal letters, which she laid out, like cards dealt for solitaire, neatly on the living room floor. And a collection of photographs, which she separated and then propped up in various places around the apartment—on top of the bureau, on the bedside tables, and then along the windowsills.

She uncovered a small cache of ho-hum sex toys—a box of condoms, a vibrator with attachments, and a pair of domino masks. She partially superimposed the masks in the middle of the bed, to suggest the classic symbols of comedy and tragedy. Then she unraveled the condoms and arranged them symmetrically so that they radiated from the masks like the rays of the sun. She completed the design by circling the masks and condoms with the vibrator cord. Then she stepped back and squinted at her work.

It was fine as far as it went, but not, she decided, sufficiently bizarre. It could, she thought, use a little more embellishment. She looked around the room, then, recalling a tangle of jockstraps she'd seen in one of the drawers, thought of a way to have some fun. She withdrew a pair of surgical scissors from her purse, retrieved the jocks, snipped off the fronts of the pouches, then added them to the bed display.

Pausing then, she thought of inflicting similar damage on all his trousers and undershorts. But that, she decided, would require too much work, and would demonstrate too much hostility. She felt that in Roger's case she would make a deeper impression if she showed a certain restraint.

But there was one final assault upon his dignity she would not resist. The "inscribing," she called it. It sent a message to the mark and, at the same time, doubled as her signature.

She hurried back to the living room. Roger was still snoring. She knew from the dosage that he would remain unconscious for at least twelve hours. Now it was necessary to place him on his back. She lifted his legs, still bound by his dropped pants, pulled them around ninety degrees, then laid him out full length on the couch. Then she bent down, unbuttoned his shirt, and pulled it open so that his upper chest was exposed.

Indelible black marker in hand, she straddled him like an equestrienne and began to write in script upon his flesh. When she was finished she smiled at her handiwork. To an ordinary viewer it would appear an incoherent scrawl. But she could read it easily. And so would Roger, when, awakening, he stumbled into his bathroom and examined his groggy features in the mirror. Then the message she had written on his chest would leap out at him with diabolic force. And the fact that she had inscribed it as one long word in mirror-reverse would haunt him far longer than her robbery. "YOUAREATOTALJERK."

Down in the apartment-house lobby, she paused before the mirror between the elevators. Pretending to smooth her hair, she willed herself egress from the glass. Her dream-sister stared back at her, and then, in an instant, disappeared. *She had done it, stepped back into the world.* She was once again herself.

Smiling sweetly at the doorman, she strode out into the open air. It was 2 A.M. The rain had stopped. The sidewalk was still slick. The air smelled faintly of iron.

She walked the four blocks to her car, got in, then began to drive leisurely along the empty avenue. At an intersection, when she stopped for a red light, a homeless man approached with a squeegee. She nodded encouragement when he began to wash her windshield; before the light changed, she handed him a twenty-dollar bill.

As she drove out of the city, she did not think about what she had done. Rather she pulled off her blond wig and glanced at herself in her rear-view mirror. This time it was her true image who stared back.

"Hello, Mirror Girl," she said.

The Man Who Hated Books

Stuart M. Kaminsky

The bullet went through four hardcover books and one paperback before breaking Keefer's rib and thudding into his heart.

The hardcover books were *Our Hearts Were Young and Gay*, *The Bishop Murder Case*, *The Army Boys in French Trenches* and *Life with Mother*. The paperback was *Saturday Review Crossword Puzzles of 1949*.

When I had entered the bookshop, Keefer had been standing behind the dark wood counter, glasses perched on the end of his nose, dwindling dark hair wildly wisped. Suspenders, blue work shirt, sedentary belly, the American antiquarian with an almost appropriate quote from an obscure work by a major author for almost every occasion.

He was every ounce the folksy bookseller reluctantly looking up over the rims of his half-glasses, tearing his eyes from some beloved tome of poetry, probably by an unknown woman who died in Sandusky, Ohio, half a century ago. Martin Keefer would rediscover her, write a piece, a very short piece, in his newsletter, *But Not Forgotten*, and jack the price of the book up from a dime to a hundred dollars.

It was a few minutes after nine, closing time, but Keefer always stayed open till at least half past nine to show how much he loved dust and dead words. I knew that and much more about Martin Keefer from the many hours I had spent in this very shop with its smell of

243

dead words and yellowing pages, going home with my sweating fingers turned red with the cheap dyes from the covers of nineteenth-century romances.

Keefer's face was a fall catalog of clichés: suspense, contempt, dyspeptic resignation. He shook his head once and looked back down at the book before him as I closed the door behind me and locked it. He heard the lock click and looked up at me again with a deep annoyed sigh.

"Your mother said you had a part in something in Akron," he said.

"Detroit," I answered, "and I don't have it yet. I'm just up for it."

"Had a hard day, Burton," he said. "I'm not up for a chapter of what-you-owe-me or what-you-did-to-Louise."

Keefer looked down and shook his head again, took off his glasses, rubbed his nose, put the glasses back on and looked up to see the gun in my hand. Then he put the book aside and leaned over to write something on a yellow pad already covered with notes. He wrote slowly with an ancient Waterman fountain pen that went perfectly with the stale smell of dead leather and fragile crumbling pages.

"Go home," he said. "I don't want to argue, get my blood pressure up, have a hard time getting to sleep. No point in our crying anyway. Never gets us anywhere."

"I have a gun," I said.

"I see," he said, continuing to write. "I turned the coffee maker off but there might be a cup left. Take it and leave."

"What did you think when I came in?"

Keefer grunted.

"For an instant, just a wink, you thought I might be him."

"Him?" said Keefer with a sigh designed to show me how distasteful he found my continuing presence.

"The bookstore killer," I said, stepping closer.

"No," said Keefer, "not an instant."

He finished writing, screwed the cap back on his Waterman, placed it in the pocket of his blue work shirt, removed his glasses with the second sigh of our non-conversation and looked at me.

Two booksellers, both men, both with small shops specializing in what they called "rare" books, had been shot in the past week.

"I killed them," I said.

"Willinski and Thomas?" Keefer chuckled, indicating that his stepson's infantile fantasy deserved only a minimum of humoring.

"Willinski couldn't have weighed more than a hundred and twenty. I had to get very close to be sure I'd hit him with the first shot."

I took another step toward Keefer. I had his attention now, if not his belief.

"The *Tribune* said he was eighty-two," I went on. "He didn't look a day over eighty."

"Burton," Keefer said, "I'm going home."

"Thomas was a bigger target," I said. "Got him at lunchtime in the middle of a burrito. If I'd been as close to him as I'd been to Willinski, I'd have been covered in refried beans."

"You're developing a macabre sense of humor," Keefer said. "I gather you don't want coffee. So hit the light and close the door on your way out."

I was a few feet from him now, my thighs against the counter. My eyes fixed on his. I had practiced not blinking. People who saw us together assumed Keefer and I were father and son. There was a reason. Keefer looked like my dead father, which, I'm sure, had something to do with Louise marrying him.

"I've established a pattern," I said. "Willinski in the morning, Thomas at noon and you at night. Each with a different gun. The next one will be at midnight. I was considering Frances Fonseca. What do you think?"

Keefer backed away from the counter and reached for his frayed gray jacket and the battered wide-brimmed hat on the standing rack behind him. Keefer claimed the rack had once been the property of William Dean Howells.

"A woman?" he asked. "Break the pattern?"

"That's the beauty of it," I said as he pulled his sleeves down. One side of his collar was up and awkward. "Variation on the pattern."

"And," said Keefer, "what do you do for an encore?"

"Nothing. She'll be the last. I've killed the others just so I could kill you and not be suspected."

Keefer went rigid for just an instant and looked at me without contempt. Not quite fear, not quite respect, but no contempt.

"Mystery literature is full of that kind of thing: Ed McBain, William Bayer, Ardis . . ."

"Literature," I interrupted. "Not life. Real people don't do such things."

"Go home, Burton," he said. "We've got nothing to talk about."

Keefer started around the counter and glanced at the door behind me. The courtyard was empty. The other shops had closed at least an hour ago.

"I didn't come to talk," I said. "I came to scare the shit out of you and kill you."

He was looking at me seriously now and I could read him like the cheap remainders in the bin near the window. When he got home, he thought, or perhaps in the morning because he'd be too busy abusing Louise tonight, he'd call the police and suggest they pick up his armed and psychotic stepson.

"I'm going to shoot you now, Keefer," I said, raising the gun and taking a step back to block his way to the door. "It's put up or shut up time. I either shoot you or suffer humiliation, not to mention the unnecessary deaths of Willinski and Thomas."

"This is . . ." He began backing away. "Get out of here. Now."

"Too late," I said.

Keefer grabbed a random handful of books from the bargain bin to his left and clutched them to his chest. I aimed carefully and he cooperated by freezing. I fired and he went, his hat pitching forward, Robert Forster going down in *The Stalking Moon*. I moved to the door and hit the light switch. Keefer was making an unpleasant sound like Daffy Duck gargling. By the light from the courtyard I moved to him, got on my knees, took the books from his hand and waited. I didn't want to shoot him again. That's not quite true. I did want to shoot him again, but I didn't want to make any more noise and I didn't want to break the pattern.

You see, I hadn't killed Willinski and Thomas, but their murders had certainly inspired me. And if whoever had killed them did not strike again soon, I might actually have to kill Frances Fonseca.

I knelt next to Keefer till I was sure he was dead and marveled at how easy it had been to kill him. No great rush of adrenaline, no pounding of the heart. It was like a dress rehearsal in which everything goes as planned with, perhaps, a few last-minute variations. It was, in fact, quite a letdown. I'd planned, rehearsed, anticipated, prepared and now it was over.

For thirty years Keefer had abused, ridiculed and stolen from my mother. She had entered the marriage a young, troubled widow with a ten-year-old son and had gradually become a distracted recluse who lived on ice cream and dreaded her husband's footsteps at night. "I'm glad what I done to you, Johnny Friendly," I whispered to Keefer's corpse in my best Marlon Brando. I'm an actor.

My father had left my mother more than well off and I had hopes of devoting myself full-time to my profession instead of selling shoes. But each year Keefer's collection had grown larger; my mother's bankroll and mind had grown smaller; and my talent had ceased to grow.

I took the folded plastic bag from my pocket, opened it, dropped in the four books and my gun and rose. Quiet, quiet. Nearing the end of Act One. Curtain. Applause. Curiosity. Conversation over coffee and cigarettes during the intermission. "Wasn't that young man, Burton Tyler, wonderful?" "A young James Stewart."

Not quite so young, I thought, moving behind the counter. Lots of time. Hate to see the scene end? I knew I'd have to look at the penetrated books once more to remind myself it had really happened before I burned them.

I pulled Keefer's corpse behind the counter and crouched as I reached for the phone. I leaned over to catch enough light so I could dial Louise. She answered after three rings.

"Hello?"

Her voice was a challenge, an expectation that there would be no one on the other end.

"Hello, Louise," I said cheerfully, Cary Grant without an accent.

"Yes?"

"It's me, Burton."

"My son?"

"The same. I'm driving in from Detroit in the morning."

"That's nice. Drive carefully."

"I want to talk to you and Keefer when I get in."

"I don't think that's a good idea."

"I'll be charming. Tell him I'm coming. I'll see you in the morning."

"Do you still have the Cubs shirt?" she asked. "The one Martin gave you?"

"When I was twelve," I said, looking at Keefer's body.

"You might want to consider wearing it," she said. "Show you appreciate him."

"It's long, long gone, but I'll dress properly."

"And shave."

"And shave. Good night, Louise."

Well, it could have been worse. It would take most of the night to drive back to Detroit and get an hour or two of sleep; I'd check out of the motel and head back when it was fairly certain Keefer's body would have been discovered by Karen, his assistant. I'd actually gone to two auditions in Detroit and there was a chance I'd get the role of the sidekick in *The Music Man* at a dinner theater in Stansfield.

I wiped the phone with my shirt and stood up with a last long look at Keefer, who looked like the dummy in a version of *Oh Dad, Poor Dad* I did in Kenosha, Wisconsin, in 1981.

He was standing at the door peering in. He saw me. Not clearly perhaps, but he saw me. He knocked.

"Closed," I said, trying for Keefer's gruff weariness.

"Important," he said, straining to see me.

"Tomorrow," I said.

There was only one way out. I had to get him to leave.

"Just take a minute," he pleaded.

"Sorry," I said.

"One question," he said.

"Ask," I said.

"Are you Martin Keefer?"

"Yes," I said.

"It's late. I can't stand out here yelling. Give me a minute."

Shit. Shit. Shit. Shit. Damn.

Okay. You're an actor. Prove it. I reached down, found Keefer's hat, plunked it low over my eyes and put his glasses on near the end of my nose so I could look over them. I'd watched Martin Keefer for thirty years. I could play Martin Keefer.

I picked up my Waldenbooks bag, slouched and went to the door.

"Sorry I'm late," the man said when I let him in.

I stepped back into the shadows as he closed the door.

"You're too late," I said wearily. "Come back in the morning."

"I'll just take the books," he said. "I told you I'll pay cash. I can't come back in the morning."

He was about my age, maybe a year or two younger, a little guy in a nice suit carrying a briefcase.

"Look," I said in my best possible Keefer. "I've had a long busy day. I've lost a sale on a complete set of Clarence Mulford's and someone stiffed me on a first edition of *The Bishop Murder Case*. I don't remember your call or what book you . . ."

"*Our Hearts Were Young and Gay*," he said. "First edition autographed by Cornelia Otis Skinner."

It was sitting in my book bag reedited by Smith and Wesson.

"I remember," I said. "It's been damaged."

"Damaged?"

He moved toward me in distress.

"Fell in the toilet."

"Oh God," he said. "Let me see it. Maybe it . . . Maybe you can dry it out."

"I sent it out to see if it can be saved. Place in San Francisco. They'll let me know in a week. Give me a call."

"A week? No. Too long. Too damn long. I'll take something else. Another first edition autographed. You said you had others."

"It's late," I said.

"I came a long way for this," he said, pacing the shop.

"And you don't care as long as it's an autographed first edition?"

"Present for my mother," he said. "She's a collector. It's her birthday. Tonight."

"Just stand there," I said, pointing to where he stood to keep him from following me around the counter. He nodded and watched me. I stepped over Keefer's body and moved to the rare-book cabinet. It was locked. I knelt and went through Keefer's pocket till I found his keys. When I stood the man had moved but not much. There was only one skeleton key on the ring. It opened the cabinet door.

"I appreciate this," he said.

I grunted and pulled out the first book.

"Should I turn on the . . ."

"No," I said stopping him as he took a step toward the wall switch.

"I don't want any more customers and I know my inventory. These are all autographed first editions."

I opened the book, squinted and read *How to Win Friends and Influence People*. Signed, "To Sigrid, Dale Carnegie."

"No," he said.

"*Penguin Island*. Anatole France."

"No."

"*The Murder of Roger Ackroyd*. Agatha Christie."

"Nice."

"You want it?"

"No. I'll know when I hear it."

I went through Philip Wylie, Anita Loos, Phil Rizzuto, Edna Best and Will Cuppy before coming to *Peyton Place* by Grace Metalious.

"How is it inscribed?" he asked.

"To Georgette from Grace," I read.

"I'll take it," he said, moving to the counter.

If he'd been two inches taller, in good light, and paying attention, he would have seen Keefer's body.

"Here," I said, handing him the book. "I've got to get home now."

"How much?"

"Thirty dollars," I said.

"It's worth more," he said opening his briefcase on the counter.

"Fifty dollars."

"More."

"A hundred and four."

"Better," he said. "You take Master Card?"

"No."

"It says on the window."

"Machine's broken."

"It doesn't matter," he said. "I'll get it all back in a few minutes."

He removed a very large gun from his briefcase and aimed it at me over the counter.

I reached for the antique cash register Keefer claimed had once belonged to O. Henry. I was both relieved and frightened. Relieved because a thief wasn't likely to come forward and finger me after Keefer's body was discovered. Frightened because he was shaking and his gun was aimed about the same place I had shot Keefer.

"No," he said as I touched the No Sale button.

I didn't care for the "no." It suggested something I didn't want to consider. A man and woman laughed in the courtyard. I looked through the window in their direction. She was blond, and not so young. He was narrow and very young. They were doing a Beatles concert. The little man turned to them and then back to me.

"Don't," he whispered. "I'll shoot them too."

I didn't answer. I wasn't terribly concerned about the well-being of Grace Slick and Mumbles in the courtyard, but I could see nothing to gain by calling them.

To the ebbing strains of something that must have been *Lady Madonna*, the man with the gun said, "Come out here."

"The money's in the . . ."

"I've got plenty of money," he said. "Do you know who I am?"

"No," I said.

"My name is Jack Gionetti."

Telling me his name was not a good sign.

"I have trouble with names," I said.

"You'll be the third," he said. "Come out here. Hurry up."

"Shit," I said. "You're making a mistake. I'm not Martin Keefer."

"Come on," Gionetti said, glancing at the door.

I took off Keefer's hat.

"Look."

"At what?"

"I'm not Keefer. Keefer's older. I was lying."

"I don't care," he said. "You sell books. I hate books and the people who sell them. I hate places like this that smell of dead words. It was a place like this, a creature like you that killed her."

"Her?"

"Get out here," he said aloud. "Now."

"Wait," I said. "I hate books too. Look. In this bag. I'll show you. The book you wanted? Here. I shot it."

I held out the copy of *Our Hearts Were Young and Gay* with one hand and put my other hand on the gun in the bag. He reached over carefully, and took the book and held it out to examine it.

"You shoot books?"

"I hate books," I said, pulling out the two remaining hardcovers.

I pointed behind the counter and Gionetti moved forward, gun reasonably level in his quivering hand. He motioned me back and I slid the bag to the end of the counter as he leaned over and looked down at Keefer.

"That's Keefer," I said.

"You shot him?" Gionetti asked.

"Like the books."

"Why?"

It was a good question.

"Some feelings are too private to talk about," I said.

Something electrical on a timer went on in the small room at the back of the shop. It was loud. It gave Gionetti pause.

"And we picked the same place," he said suspiciously.

"There aren't too many old bookshops in this town."

"Three more after this one," he said.

"You must be counting MacLean's," I said. "That's a remainder store. Big, bright. A family business."

"Two then," he said. "I believe you, but I'm going to have to shoot you. You're very crazy and you know my name. If they catch you . . . You know my name. Where is it?"

"What?"

"The gun you shot him with," he said.

"Oh, right here," I said lifting the weapon from the Waldenbook bag and leveling it at him.

It could have ended there. I would have been happy to let him walk. He fired as I moved to my right to get around Keefer's body. Something, it felt like an ax, wielded into my chest. I fell back over Keefer's corpse and shot. A window broke. I shot again, tasting blood. Jack Gionetti fired again but I was leaning in the darkness against the shelves. His bullet hit Keefer's body. I could see the startled corpse convulse. I was passing out as I pulled the trigger again and again and . . .

I woke up two nights and a day later in a hospital room. Someone had forgotten to take the ax from my chest. I tried to breathe.

"It's all right," Louise said.

"Slow, shallow breaths, Burton," an unfamiliar woman's voice said.

I obeyed. The ink slowly oozed away and I opened my eyes. My mother, in her party dress with the print of pink roses, sat on a chair next to me. Standing over me was a nurse in white, a chunky blond nurse with a round pretty face. Her name, unless she was wearing someone else's silver plate, was Janet Darby. Behind Janet Darby was a man leaning against the wall. His brown suit needed pressing. His tie needed serious rethinking and his cropped military hair needed time to grow. He bit a thumbnail, examined his work and looked at me with no expression. He was a cop.

"Tired," I said, closing my eyes.

"Martin is dead, dear," my mother said cheerfully.

"Great," I said and quickly amended that to "I'm sorry."

When I opened my eyes again, nurse and mother were gone. Cop was still there but sitting in a chair against the wall.

"You're the killer," he said.

I moaned and closed my eyes.

"*Shot in the Dark*," he said. "Some dinner theater last year. You were the killer."

"I . . ."

He got out of the chair and handed me a glass with a straw. The water looked dusty. I drank.

"Slow," he said.

"Hurts," I said, pushing it away. "I didn't kill him."

He put the glass on the table. The room smelled like alcohol.

"In the play," I croaked. "I was the butler, not the killer."

"My name's Berman," he said. "I'm a cop."

"Yes," I said.

"You were shot in the chest. Collapsed a lung. Lucky to be a Yankee."

"Gionetti," I said.

"Dead. You know his name."

"He told me."

"I got a brother wants to be an actor," said Berman. "He's almost fifty. Got a good business. Rent-A-Junk over on Sixteenth is the original. Opened another one on Roosevelt. Good business, but when you got a bug, you know, writer, actor, stunt pilot."

I nodded.

"Want to tell me what happened?"

"He came into my stepfather's shop," I said softly, weakly playing the ailing man. "Gave his name and said he'd killed two others. Started shooting. My stepfather just bought a gun. When the other bookshop owners were killed. He showed it to me. I got it out, aimed it at Gionetti and . . . that's it."

Berman nodded.

"You look a little like that guy on TV. He's in lots of things. What's his name? John something. Or Mike. Irish last name but I don't think it's his real one. How you doing?"

"O.K.," I said.

"You want me to come back tomorrow?"

"I'm O.K.," I said.

Berman shifted and pulled a recorder out of his pocket.

"O.K.?" he asked.

I nodded and he turned it on.

"His name wasn't Gionetti," Berman said. "He lied. Don't ask me why. His name was Clark Simonson. Had a collection of small arms in his house including the guns that killed the other two dealers. No kids. Wife's dead, owned a bookshop in Cleveland. Overdosed on something a year ago. Don't have the details."

"Weird," I said.

"I've heard weirder," said Berman. "Mother says you called her from Detroit about an hour before Simonson shot you and Keefer."

"Called her from the shop," I said. "You talked to her. You know she can . . ."

He nodded.

"She gets a little confused," I explained.

"You were registered in a motel in Detroit and you weren't scheduled to check out till the next day. Key was in your pocket."

"Martin, my stepfather, called. Said he had to see me about Louise, my mother. More water, please."

He obliged. The water was warm.

"He said it was urgent," I went on. "I planned to drive back to Detroit after seeing my mother. I'm up for a part there."

"Keefer had two bullets in him," said Berman. "One from Simonson's weapon. One from yours."

"Not mine, Martin's. I must have shot him when I was shooting in the dark at Simonson. Horrible."

"Coroner says the gun you had killed Keefer. He was dead when Simonson shot him and Simonson's bullet hit his arm, wouldn't have killed him."

I put my left arm over my eyes and let out one hell of a sob.

"I killed Martin. Oh my God, I killed him."

"Looks that way to me," agreed Berman.

"He wasn't dead when Gionetti . . ."

"Simonson," Berman corrected.

"I never fired a gun before," I sobbed, moving my arm and looking at him with eyes I hoped were red.

"The books," said Berman. "Someone shot four books. They were on the counter. One of them had Keefer's blood on it."

I looked puzzled.

"You didn't get along with Keefer, Louise said. Why'd you come running when he called?"

"My mother. He said it was urgent, about Louise."

"Keefer had no permit for a gun. Why would he buy an illegal?"

"I don't know," I said. "He was afraid."

"Burt," Berman said standing with a sigh. "I'm gonna give you some advice. Your story is full of shit. I think you need a lawyer."

"I think so too," I agreed.

He moved to the door, putting the tape recorder in his pocket.

"One more question," he said. "Nothing to do with the case."

"What?"

"My brother looks a little like you. What was that play you were trying out for in Detroit?"

Pig Latin

Clarice Lispector

Maria Aparecida—Cidinha, as they called her at home—was an English teacher. Neither rich nor poor: just properly comfortable. But she dressed to perfection. She looked wealthy. Even her suitcases were of high quality.

She lived in Minas Gerais and was going by train to Rio, where she would spend three days, and then take a plane to New York.

She was much sought after as a teacher. She loved perfection and was friendly, though strict. She wanted to perfect her English in the United States.

She took the seven o'clock train to Rio. It was really cold. And she with her suede coat and three suitcases. The car was empty, just an old woman sleeping in a corner under her shawl.

At the next station two men got on and sat down in the seat in front of Cidinha's. The train began to move. One man was tall, thin, with a little mustache and a cold eye, the other was short, paunchy, and bald. They looked at Cidinha. She quickly turned her eyes away and looked out the window.

It was uncomfortable in the coach. As if it were too hot. The girl uneasy. The men on the alert. My God, thought the girl, what could they want from me? There was no answer. And on top of it all she was a virgin. But why, oh why, had she thought of her own virginity?

256

The two men began to talk to each other. At first Cidinha didn't understand a word. It seemed a game. They spoke very quickly. But the language seemed vaguely familiar to her. What language was it?

Suddenly she understood: they were speaking Pig Latin—to perfection. Like this:

"Idday ouyay eckchay touay atthay ettypray ickchay?"

"Iay uresay idday. Eshay's ay eautybay. Eshay's inay ethay agbay."

In other words: "Did you check out that pretty chick? I sure did. She's a beauty. She's in the bag."

Cidinha pretended not to understand: to understand would be dangerous for her. The language was the same one they had used as children to protect themselves from the grownups. The two went on:

"Iay antway otay crewsay atthay irlgay. Atwhay outabay ouyay?"

"Emay ootay. Enwhay eway etgay otay ethay unneltay."

In other words they were going to rape her in the tunnel . . . What could she do? Cidinha didn't know, and she trembled with fear. She hardly knew herself. At least she had never known herself deep down. As for knowing the others, that made it even worse. Help me, Virgin Mary! Help me, help me!

"Fiay eshay esistsray eway ancay illkay erhay."

If she tried to resist they might kill her. So that's how it was.

"Eway ancay abstay erhay. Danay obray erhay."

Stab her to death! And rob her!

How could she tell them that she wasn't rich? That she was fragile, that the merest touch would kill her. She got a cigarette out of her pocketbook in order to smoke and calm herself down. It didn't do any good. When would the next tunnel come? She had to think quickly, quickly, quickly.

Then the idea came to her: if I pretend that I am a prostitute, they'll give up, they wouldn't want a whore.

So she pulled up her skirt, made sensual movements—she didn't even know she knew how, so unknown was she to herself—and opened the top buttons on her blouse, leaving her breasts half exposed. The men suddenly in shock.

"Eshay's razycay."

In other words, "she's crazy."

And she undulated like no samba-dancer, down from the hills.

She took her lipstick out of her bag and lavishly painted her lips. And she began to sing, off-key.

So the men began to laugh at her. They found Cidinha's foolishness amusing. She was desperate. And the tunnel?

The conductor appeared. He saw it all. He didn't say a thing. But he went and told the engineer. The engineer said:

"Let's do something about it. I'll turn her over to the police at the next station."

And the next station came.

The engineer climbed down, spoke with a soldier named José Lindalvo. José Lindalvo didn't fool around. He climbed into the car, saw Cidinha, grabbed her brutally by the arm, gathered up the three suitcases as best he could, and they both got off.

The two men burst out laughing.

In the small station painted blue and pink there was a young lady with a suitcase. She looked at Cidinha with scorn. She mounted the train, and it left.

Cidinha didn't know what to say to the police. How could she explain Pig Latin? She was taken to jail and booked. They called her the worst names. And she stayed locked up for three days. They let her smoke. She smoked like mad, inhaling, crushing the cigarettes on the cement floor. There was a fat cockroach crawling along the floor.

Finally they let her go. She took the next train to Rio. She had washed her face, she wasn't a prostitute anymore. What was bothering her was the following: when the two had spoken of raping her, she had wanted to be raped. She was shameless. Danay Iay maay aay orewhay. That was what she had discovered. Humiliation.

She arrived in Rio exhausted. She went to an inexpensive hotel. She quickly realized that she had missed her plane. At the airport she bought a new ticket.

And she walked through the streets of Copacabana, desolate she, desolate Copacabana.

It was on the corner of Rua Figueiredo Magalhães that she saw a newsstand. And hanging there the newspaper *O Día*. She couldn't have said why she bought it.

In black headlines were the words: "Girl Raped and Killed in Train."

She trembled all over. It had happened, then. And to the girl who had despised her.

She began to cry there in the street. She threw away the damned newspaper. She didn't want to know the details. She thought:

"Atefay siay placableimay."

Fate is implacable.

Translated by Alexir Levitin

Devices and Desires*

P. D. James

The Whistler's fourth victim was his youngest, Valerie Mitchell, aged fifteen years, eight months and four days, and she died because she missed the 9:40 bus from Easthaven to Cobb's Marsh. As always, she had left it until the last minute to leave the disco, and the floor was still a packed, gyrating mass of bodies under the makeshift strobe lights when she broke free of Wayne's clutching hands, shouted instructions to Shirl about their plans for next week above the raucous beat of the music and left the dance floor. Her last glimpse of Wayne was of his serious, bobbing face bizarrely striped with red, yellow and blue under the turning lights. Without waiting to change her shoes, she snatched up her jacket from the cloakroom peg and raced up the road past the darkened shops towards the bus station, her cumbersome shoulder-bag flapping against her ribs. But when she turned the corner into the station she saw with horror that the lights on their high poles shone down on a bleached and silent emptiness and, dashing to the corner, was in time to see the bus already halfway up the hill. There was still a chance if the lights were against it, and she began desperately chasing after it, hampered by her fragile, high-heeled shoes. But the lights were green and she watched helplessly,

* From *Devices and Desires*.

gasping and bent double with a sudden cramp, as it lumbered over the brow of a hill and like a brightly lit ship sank out of sight. "Oh no!" she screamed after it. "Oh God! Oh no!" and felt the tears of anger and dismay smarting her eyes.

This was the end. It was her father who laid down the rules in her family, and there was never any appeal, any second chance. After protracted discussion and her repeated pleas, she had been allowed this weekly visit on Friday evenings to the disco run by the church Youth Club, provided she caught the 9:40 bus without fail. It put her down at the Crown and Anchor at Cobb's Marsh, only fifty yards from her cottage. From 10:15 her father would begin watching for the bus to pass the front room where he and her mother would sit half-watching the television, the curtains drawn back. Whatever the program or weather, he would then put on his coat and come out to walk the fifty yards to meet her, keeping her always in sight. Since the Norfolk Whistler had begun his killings, her father had had an added justification for the mild domestic tyranny which, she half-realized, he both thought right in dealing with his only child and rather enjoyed. The concordat had been early established: "You do right by me, my girl, and I'll do right by you." She both loved him and slightly feared him, and she dreaded his anger. Now there would be one of those awful rows in which she knew she couldn't hope to look to her mother for support. It would be the end of her Friday evenings with Wayne and Shirl and the gang. Already they teased and pitied her because she was treated as a child. Now it would be total humiliation.

Her first desperate thought was to hire a taxi and to chase the bus, but she didn't know where the cab rank was and she hadn't enough money; she was sure of that. She could go back to the disco and see if Wayne and Shirl and the gang between them could lend her enough. But Wayne was always skint and Shirl too mean, and by the time she had argued and cajoled it would be too late.

And then came salvation. The lights had changed again to red, and a car at the end of a tail of four others was just drawing slowly to a stop. She found herself opposite the open, left-hand window and looking directly at two elderly women. She clutched at the lowered glass and said breathlessly: "Can you give me a lift? Anywhere Cobb's Marsh direction. I've missed the bus. Please."

The final desperate plea left the driver unmoved. She stared ahead, frowned, then shook her head and let in the clutch. Her companion hesitated, looked at her, then leaned back and released the rear door.

"Get in. Quickly. We're going as far as Holt. We could drop you at the crossroads."

Valerie scrambled in and the car moved forward. At least they were going in the right direction, and it took her only a couple of seconds to think of her plan. From the crossroads outside Holt it would be less than half a mile to the junction with the bus route. She could walk it and pick it up at the stop before the Crown and Anchor. There would be plenty of time; the bus took at least twenty minutes meandering round the villages.

The woman who was driving spoke for the first time. She said: "You shouldn't be cadging lifts like this. Does your mother know that you're out, what you're doing? Parents seem to have no control over children these days."

Silly old cow, she thought, what business is it of hers what I do? She wouldn't have stood the cheek from any of the teachers at school. But she bit back the impulse to rudeness, which was her adolescent response to adult criticism. She had to ride with the two old wrinklies. Better keep them sweet. She said: "I'm supposed to catch the nine-forty bus. My dad'ud kill me if he thought I'd cadged a lift. I wouldn't if you was a man."

"I hope not. And your father's perfectly right to be strict about it. These are dangerous times for young women, quite apart from the Whistler. Where exactly do you live?"

"At Cobb's Marsh. But I've got an aunt and uncle at Holt. If you put me down at the crossroads, he'll be able to give me a lift. They live right close. I'll be safe enough if you drop me there, honest."

The lie came easily to her and was as easily accepted. Nothing more was said by any of them. She sat looking at the backs of the two gray, cropped heads, watching the driver's age-speckled hands on the wheel. Sisters, she thought, by the look of them. Her first glimpse had shown her the same square heads, the same strong chins, the same curved eyebrows above anxious, angry eyes. They've had a row, she thought. She could sense the tension quivering between them. She was glad when, still without a word, the driver drew up at the crossroads and she was able to scramble out with muttered thanks and watch while they drove out of sight. They were the last human beings, but one, to see her alive.

She crouched to change into the sensible shoes which her parents insisted she wear to school, grateful that the shoulder-bag was now lighter, then began trudging away from the town towards the junction where she would wait for the bus. The road was narrow and unlit, bordered on the right by a row of trees, black cutouts pasted against the star-studded sky, and on the left, where she walked, by a narrow fringe of scrub and bushes at times dense and close enough to over-shadow the path. Up till now she had felt only an overwhelming relief that all would be well. She would be on that bus. But now, as she walked in an eerie silence, her soft footfalls sounding unnaturally loud, a different, more insidious anxiety took over and she felt the first prickings of fear. Once recognized, its treacherous power acknowl-edged, the fear took over and grew inexorably into terror.

A car was approaching, at once a symbol of safety and normality and an added threat. Everyone knew that the Whistler must have a car. How else could he kill in such widely spaced parts of the county, how else make his getaway when his dreadful work was done? She stood back into the shelter of the bushes, exchanging one fear for another. There was a surge of sound and the cat's-eyes momentarily gleamed before, in a rush of wind, the car passed. And now she was alone again in the darkness and the silence. But was she? The thought of the Whistler took hold of her mind, rumors, half-truths fusing into a terrible reality. He strangled women, three so far. And then he cut off their hair and stuffed it in their mouths, like straw spilling out of a Guy on November 5th. The boys at school laughed about him, whistling in the bicycle sheds as he was said to whistle over the bodies of his victims. "The Whistler will get you," they called after her. He could be anywhere. He always stalked by night. He could be here. She had an impulse to throw herself down and press her body into the soft rich-smelling earth, to cover her ears and lie there rigid until the dawn. But she managed to control her panic. She had to get to the crossroads and catch the bus. She forced herself to step out of the shadows and begin again her almost silent walk.

She wanted to break into a run but managed to resist. The creature, man or beast, crouching in the undergrowth was already sniffing her fear, waiting until her panic broke. Then she would hear the crash of the breaking bushes, his pounding feet, feel his panting breath hot on her neck. She must keep walking, swiftly but silently, holding her bag tightly against her side, hardly breathing, eyes fixed ahead. And as she walked she prayed: "Please, God, let me get safely home and I'll never lie again. I'll always leave in time. Help me to get to the crossroads safely. Make the bus come quickly. O God, please help me."

And then, miraculously, her prayer was answered. Suddenly, about thirty yards ahead of her, there was a woman. She didn't question how, so mysteriously, this slim, slow-walking figure had materialized. It was sufficient that she was there. As she drew nearer with quickening step, she could see the swath of long blond hair under a tight-fitting beret, and what looked like a belted trench coat. And at the girl's side, trotting obediently, most reassuring of all, was a small black-and-white dog, bandy-legged. They could walk together to the crossroads. Perhaps the girl might herself be catching the same bus. She almost cried aloud, "I'm coming, I'm coming," and, breaking into a run, rushed towards safety and protection as a child might to her mother's arms.

And now the woman bent down and released the dog. As if in obedience to some command, he slipped into the bushes. The woman took one swift backward glance and then stood quietly waiting, her back half-turned to Valerie, the dog's lead held drooping in her right hand. Valerie almost flung herself at the waiting back. And then, slowly, the woman turned. It was a second of total, paralysing terror. She saw the pale, taut face which had never been a woman's face, the simple, inviting, almost apologetic smile, the blazing and merciless eyes. She opened her mouth to scream, but there was no chance, and horror had made her dumb. With one movement the noose of the lead was swung over her head and jerked tight and she was pulled from the road into the shadow of the bushes. She felt herself falling through time, through space, through an eternity of horror. And now the face was hot over hers and she could smell drink and sweat and a terror matching her own. Her arms jerked upwards, impotently flailing. And now her brain was bursting and the pain in her chest, growing like a great red flower, exploded in a silent, wordless scream of "Mummy, Mummy." And then there was no more terror, no more pain, only the merciful, obliterating dark.

Martyrdom

Yukio Mishima

A diminutive Demon King ruled over the dormitory. The school in
question was a place where large numbers of sons of the aristocracy
were put through their paces. Equipped by the age of thirteen or
fourteen with a coldness of heart and an arrogance of spirit worthy
of many a grown-up, they were placed in this dormitory in their first
year at middle school in order to experience communal life; this was
one of the traditions of the spartan education devised several decades
earlier by the principal of the school, General Ogi. The members of
any one year had all been to the same primary school, so that their
training in mischief had taken thorough effect in the six years before
entering the dormitory, and facilitated an astonishing degree of col-
laboration among them. A "graveyard" would be arranged in a corner
of the classroom with a row of markers bearing the teachers' names;
a trap would be set so that when an elderly, bald teacher came into
the room a blackboard duster fell precisely onto his bald patch, coating
it with white; on a winter morning, a lump of snow would be flung
to stick on the ceiling, bright in the morning sun, so that it dripped
steadily onto the teacher's platform; the matches in the teachers' room
would be mysteriously transformed into things that spouted sparks
like fireworks when struck; a dozen drawing pins would be introduced
into the chair where the teacher sat, with their points just showing

above the surface—these and a host of other schemes that seemed the work of unseen elves were all in fact carried out by two or three masterminds and a band of well-trained terrorists.

"Come on—let's see it! What's wrong with showing me anyway?"

The older boy who had turned up in the lunch break lounged astride the broken dormitory chair. He could sense the itching curiosity in himself that crawled vaguely, like soft incipient beard, right up to his ears, but in trying to conceal it from the other, his junior by a year, he was only making his face turn all the pinker. At the same time, it was necessary to sit in as slovenly a way as possible in order to show his independence of the rules.

"I'll show you, don't worry. But you'll have to wait another five minutes. What's up, K?—it's not like you to be so impatient."

The Demon King spoke boldly, gazing steadily at the older boy with mild, beautiful eyes. He was well developed for a mere fourteen, and looked in fact at least sixteen or seventeen. He owed his physique to something called the "Danish method" of child rearing—which involved among other things dangling the baby by one leg and kneading its soft, plump body like so much dough—and to the fact that he'd been brought up in a Western house with huge plate-glass windows standing on high ground in the Takanawa district of Tokyo, where breezes borne on bright wings from the distant sea would occasionally visit the lawn. Naked, he had the figure of a young man. During physical checkups, when the other boys were pale with dire embarrassment, he was a Daphnis surveying his nanny goats with cool, scornful eyes.

The dormitory was the farthest from the main school buildings, and the Demon King's room on the second floor looked out over the shimmering May woods covering the gentle slope of the school grounds. The long grass and undergrowth seemed almost tipsy as it swayed in the wind. It was morning, and the chirping of the birds in the woods was particularly noisy. Now and again, a pair of them would take off from the sea of young foliage and fly up like fish leaping from its surface, only to produce a sudden, furious twittering, turn a somersault, and sink down again between the waves of greenery.

When K, his senior, came to see him in his room bearing sandwiches and the like, it had been instantly apparent to the Demon

King—young Hatakeyama—that the motive was a desire to see the book that everyone found so fascinating. To tease a senior pupil over something of this sort gave him a sweet sense of complicity, as though he too were being teased.

"Five minutes is up."

"No it isn't—it's only three minutes yet."

"It's five minutes!"

Quite suddenly, Hatakeyama gave him an almost girlish smile, the vulnerable smile of someone who had never yet had anyone be rude to him.

"Oh well, I suppose it can't be helped," he said. "I'll let you see it."

With his left hand thrust in his trouser pocket, as was his usual habit (in imitation of a cousin, a college student, whom he'd much admired for the way he let his shiny metal watchstrap show between the pocket and his sweater), he went lazily to open the bookcase. There, among the textbooks that he'd never once laid hands on after returning to the dorm, and the books his parents had bought for him—a grubby *Collected Boys' Tales*, the *Jungle Book*, and *Peter Pan* in paperback editions—there ought to have stood a volume with "*Plutarch's Lives*" inscribed in immature lettering on its spine. This book, whose red cover he had wrapped in uninviting brown paper and labeled with a title that he had memorized from a work of about the same thickness seen in the library, was constantly being passed from hand to hand, during classes and in recess alike. People would have been startled to find, on the page that should have portrayed a statue of Alexander the Great, an odd, complex sectional diagram in color.

"It's no use suddenly pretending you can't find it!" Gazing at the Demon King's rear view as he ferreted through the contents of the bookshelves, K was less concerned with the desire to see the book as such than with making sure, first, that he wasn't cheated by this formidable younger schoolmate, and then that he didn't put himself at a disadvantage by clumsy bullying.

"Somebody's stolen it!" shouted Hatakeyama, standing up. He'd been looking down as he searched, and his face was flushed, his eyes gleaming. Rushing to his desk, he frantically opened and closed each drawer in turn, talking to himself all the while:

"I made a point of getting everyone who came to borrow that book to sign for it. I mean, I couldn't have people taking my stuff out without my permission, could I? That book was the class's special secret. It meant a lot to everybody. I was particularly careful with it—I'd never have let anyone I didn't like read it. . . ."

"It's a bit late to get so angry about it, surely," said K with an assumed maturity, then, noticing the brutal glint in Hatakeyama's eye, suddenly shut up. More than anything, the look reminded him of a child about to kill a snake.

"I'm *sure* it's Watari," said his crony Komiyama, writing the name "Watari" twice in small letters on the blackboard and pointing to the bright-lit doorway through which the boy in question, by himself as usual, had just gone out into the school yard. Beyond the doorway a cloud was visible, smooth and glossy, floating in the sky beyond the spacious playground. Its shadow passed ponderously across the ground.

"Watari? Come off it! What does a kid like him understand about a book like that?"

"A lot—you wait and see! Haven't you ever heard of the quiet lecher? It's types with saintly expressions like him who're most interested in that kind of thing. Try barging in on him in his room tonight before supper, when all the rest have gone for exercise and there's nobody in the dorm. You'll see!"

Alone of their group, Watari had come to them from another primary school, and was thus a comparative outsider. There was something about him that kept others at a distance. Although he was particular about his clothes—he changed his shirt every day—he would go for weeks without cutting his nails, which were always an unhealthy black. His skin was a yellowish, lusterless white like a gardenia. His lips, in contrast, were so red that you wanted to rub them with your finger to see if he was wearing lipstick. Seen close to, it was an astonishingly beautiful face, though from a distance quite unprepossessing. He reminded you of an art object in which excessive care over detail has spoiled the effect of the whole; the details were correspondingly seductive in a perverse way.

He had begun to be bullied almost as soon as he appeared at the school. He gave the impression of looking disapprovingly on the tendency, common to all boys, to worship toughness as a way of making up for their awareness of the vulnerability peculiar to their age. If anything, Watari sought to preserve the vulnerability. The young man who seeks to be himself is respected by his fellows; the boy who tries to do the same is persecuted by other boys, it being a boy's business to become something else just as soon as he can.

Watari had the habit, whenever he was subjected to particularly vile treatment by his companions, of casting his eyes up at the clear blue sky. The habit was itself another source of mockery.

"Whenever he's picked on, he stares up at the sky as if he was Christ," said M, the most persistent of his tormentors. "And you know, when he does it, his nose tips back so you can see right up his nostrils. He keeps his nose so well blown, it's a pretty pink color round the edges inside. . . ."

Watari was, of course, banned from seeing *"Plutarch's Lives."*

The sun had set on all but the trees in the woods. The dark mass of foliage, minutely catching the lingering rays of the setting sun, trembled like the flame of a guttering candle. As he stealthily opened the door and went in, the first thing Hatakeyama saw was the wavering trees through the window directly ahead. The sight of Watari registered next; he was seated at his desk, gazing down with his head in his delicate white hands, intent on something. The open pages of the book and the hands stood out in white relief.

He turned around at the sound of footsteps. The next instant, his hands covered the book with an obstinate strength.

Moving swiftly and easily across the short space that separated them, Hatakeyama had seized him by the scruff of the neck almost before he realized it himself. Watari's large, expressionless eyes, wide open like a rabbit's, were suddenly close to his own face. He felt his knees pressing into the boy's belly, eliciting a strange sound from it as he sat on the chair; then he knocked aside the hands that tried to cling to him, and dealt a smart slap to his cheek. The flesh looked soft, as though it might stay permanently dented. For one moment, indeed, Watari's face seemed to tilt in the direction in which it had been struck, assuming an oddly placid, helpless expression. But then the cheek rapidly flooded with red and a thin, stealthy trickle of blood ran from the finely shaped nostrils. Seeing it, Hatakeyama felt a kind of pleasant nausea. Taking hold of the collar of Watari's blue shirt, he dragged him toward the bed, moving with unnecessarily large strides as though dancing. Watari let himself be dragged, limp as a puppet; curiously, he didn't seem to grasp the situation he was in, but gazed steadily at the evening sky over the woods with their lingering light. Or perhaps those big, helpless eyes simply let in the evening light quite passively, taking in the sky without seeing anything. The blood from his nose, though, cheerfully seemed to flaunt its glossy brightness as it dribbled down his mouth and over his chin.

"You thief!"

Dumping Watari on the bed, Hatakeyama climbed onto it himself and started trampling and kicking him. The bed creaked, sounding like ribs breaking. Watari had his eyes shut in terror. At times, he bared his over-regular teeth and gave a thin wail like a small sick bird. Hatakeyama thumped him in the side for a while, then, seeing that he had turned toward the wall and gone still, like a corpse, jumped down from the bed in one great leap. As a finishing touch, he remembered to thrust one guilty hand elegantly into the pocket of his narrow slacks and tilt himself slightly to one side. Then, whisking up *"Plutarch's Lives"* from the desk with his right hand, he tucked it stylishly under his arm and ran up the stairs to his second-floor room.

He had read the dubious book in question quite a few times. Each time, the first frenzied excitement seemed to fade a little. Recently in fact he had begun to get more pleasure, if anything, out of observing the powerful spell the book exerted over his friends as they read it for the first time. But now, reading it again himself after getting it back and roughing up Watari in the process, the original, wild excitement emerged as a still fiercer pleasure. He couldn't get through a single page at a time. Each appearance of one of those words of almost mystic power brought a myriad associations crowding, plunged him into an ever deeper intoxication. His breath grew shallower, his hand trembled, the bell for supper that happened just then to resound through the dormitory almost made him panic: how could he appear before the others in this state? He had entirely forgotten Watari.

That night, a dream woke Hatakeyama from a troubled sleep. The dream had led him to the lairs of various illnesses that he had suffered from in childhood. In actual fact, few children could have been healthier than he: the only illnesses he'd succumbed to were of the order of whooping cough, measles, and intestinal catarrh. Nevertheless, the diseases in his dream were all acquainted with him, and greeted him accordingly. Whenever one of them approached him, there was a disagreeable smell; if he tried to shove it away, "disease" transferred itself stickily to his hand like oil paint. One disease was even tickling his throat with its finger. . . .

When he awoke, he found himself staring, wide-eyed like a rabbit, in just the way that Watari had done earlier that day. And there, floating above the covers, was Watari's startled face, a mirror of his own. As their eyes met, the face rose slowly into the air.

Hatakeyama let out a high-pitched yell. At least, he thought he did: in fact his voice rose only as far as his throat.

Something was pressing down steadily, with cold hands, on his throat; yet the pressure was slight enough to be half pleasant. Deciding that it was a continuation of his dream after all, he extracted a hand unhurriedly from the bedclothes and stroked himself experimentally around the neck. It appeared that something like a cloth sash, about two inches wide, had been wrapped snugly around it.

He had the courage and good sense to fling it off without further ado. He sat up in bed, looking much older than he was, more like a young man of twenty. A chain of ivory clouds, lit up by the moon, was passing across the window outside, so that he was silhouetted against it like the statue of some god of old.

The thing that crouched like a dog at the foot of the bed had a white, human face turned resolutely toward him. It seemed to be breathing heavily, for the face as a whole appeared to swell and shrink; the eyes alone were still, overflowing with a shining light as they gazed, full of hostility (or was it longing?), at Hatakeyama's shadowed features.

"Watari. You came to get even, didn't you?"

Watari said nothing, the lips that were like a rose in the dark night quivering painfully. Finally, he said as though in a dream:

"I'm sorry."

"You wanted to kill me, I suppose."

"I'm sorry." He made no attempt to run away, simply repeating the same phrase.

Without warning, Hatakeyama flew at him and, propelled by the bedsprings, carried him face down onto the floor. There, kneeling astride him, he subjected him to a full twenty minutes' violence. "I'm going to make sure you feel ashamed in front of everyone in the bath!" he promised, then splashed his bare buttocks with blue-black ink; prodded them with the points of a pair of compasses to see their reaction; reared up, hauling the boy up by the ears as he did so. . . . He was brilliantly methodical, as though everything had been thought out in advance. There was no chance, even, for Watari to look up at the sky this time. He lay still, his cheek pressed against a join in the linoleum.

Two boys were allotted to each room in the dormitory, but Hatakeyama's roommate was home on sick leave. So long as he was careful not to be overheard downstairs, Hatakeyama could do as he wished.

Eventually, both of them began to tire. Before they realized it they were dozing, sprawled on the floor; Watari had even forgotten to cover his pale behind.

Their nap lasted no more than a moment. Hatakeyama awoke first. Pillowing his chin on clasped hands, he gazed at the moonlit window. All that was visible from the floor where he lay was the sky. The moon was below the frame of the window, but two or three clouds could be seen in the sky's fullness of limpid light. The scene had the impersonal clarity, precision, and fineness of detail of a scene reflected in the polished surface of a piece of machinery. The clouds seemed stationed as immovably as some majestic man-made edifice.

An odd desire awoke in Hatakeyama, taking him by surprise. It wasn't so much a break with the mood of tranquillity as a natural transition from it, and in a strange way it was linked with the terrifying sensation of the cord around his neck that he'd experienced a while before. This, he thought, is the fellow who tried to kill me. And suddenly a peculiar sense of both superiority and inferiority, a nagging humiliation at not in fact having been killed, made it impossible for him to stay still.

"You asleep?" he said.

"No," said Watari. As he replied, his eyes turned to look straight at Hatakeyama. He began to stretch out his thin right arm, then drew it in again and pressed it to his side, saying,

"It hurts here."

"Really? Does it *really* hurt?"

Hatakeyama rolled over twice. It brought him a little too close, so that he was lying half on top of Watari. Just as this happened, the latter gave a faint little chuckle, a sound—like the cry of a shellfish —he had never heard before. The Demon King sought out the sound, then pressed his whole face against Watari's lips and the soft down around them.

There was something going on between Hatakeyama and Watari: their classmates passed on the rumor in hushed voices. The scandal possessed a mysterious power; thanks to it, Hatakeyama became increasingly influential, and even Watari was taken into their circle. The process was similar to that whereby a woman so far generally ignored suddenly acquires value in everyone's eyes if the dandy of the group takes a fancy to her. And it was totally unclear how Hatakeyama himself responded to this general reaction.

Before long, it was felt that his authority as Demon King required some kind of strict legal system. They would draft the necessary laws during their English and spelling lessons. The criminal code, for example, must be an arbitrary one, based on the principle of intimidation. A strong urge to self-regulation had awoken in the boys. One morning in the dormitory, the gang insisted that their leader pick out someone for them to punish. They were sitting in their chairs in a variety of bizarre postures; some were not so much seated in them as clinging to them. One first-grader had turned his chair upside down and was sitting holding on to two projecting legs.

"Hatakeyama—you've got to name somebody. You name him, and the rest of us'll deal with him. Isn't there anyone who's been getting above himself lately?"

"No, no one." He spoke in a surly voice, his mature-looking back turned to them.

"You sure? Then we'll choose the person ourselves."

"Wait a minute! What I said wasn't true. Listen: I'll name someone. But I won't say why."

They waited breathlessly; there wasn't one of them who didn't want to hear his own name mentioned.

"Where's Watari?"

"Watari?—he went off somewhere just now."

"OK, it's him. He's been getting uppish. If we don't put a stop to it, he'll get completely out of hand."

This was pure imitation of fifth-grader talk. Even so, having got it out, Hatakeyama looked cheerfully relieved, like someone remembering something till then forgotten. It provoked a happy clamor among the others:

"Let's fix the time—the lunch break!"

"And the place—by Chiarai Pond."

"I'll take my jackknife."

"And I'll bring a rope. If he struggles we can tie him up."

On a pond already green with slime the surrounding trees spread an even reflection of lush young foliage, so that anyone who walked beside it was steeped in its green light. They were all privately enjoying the important sound of their own feet tramping through the bamboo grass, and the party with Hatakeyama and Watari at its center exchanged no words. Watari showed no sign of fear as he walked, a fact that had a disturbing effect on his classmates, as though they were watching a very sick man, supposedly on his last legs, suddenly striding along. From time to time, he glanced up at the sky visible through the new leaves of the treetops. But the others were all too sunk in their own thoughts for anyone to remark on his behavior. Hatakeyama walked with long strides, head bent, left hand in pocket. He avoided looking at Watari.

Halting, Hatakeyama raised both arms in their rolled-up sleeves above his head:

"Stop! Quiet!"

An elderly gardener was pushing a wheelbarrow along the path above them toward the flower beds.

"Well, well—up to some mischief, I suppose," he said, seeing them.

"Dirty old scrounger!" someone replied. It was rumored that the old man lived off free dormitory leftovers.

"He's gone." M gave a signal with his eyes.

"Right. Here, Watari—"

For the first time, Hatakeyama looked straight into his eyes. Both Watari and his companions had unusually grave expressions.

"You've been getting too big for your boots."

No more was said: the sentence was passed; but nothing was done to carry it out. The judge stood with bare arms folded, slowly stroking them with his fingertips. . . . At that moment, Watari seemed to see his chance. Quite suddenly, he lunged toward Hatakeyama as though about to cling to him. Behind the latter lay the pond. As he braced his legs, stones and soil rolled down into it with a faint splashing. That was the only sound; to those around them, the two seemed locked in an embrace, silently consoling each other. But in steadying himself to avoid falling backward, Hatakeyama had exposed his arms to an attack already planned. Watari's teeth—regular and sharp as a girl's, or perhaps a cat's—sank into his young flesh. Blood oozed out along the line between teeth and skin, yet biter and bitten remained still. Hatakeyama didn't even groan.

A slight movement separated them. Wiping his lips, more crimson than ever with the blood, Watari stood still, his eyes fixed on Hatakeyama's wound. A second or two before the members of the group had grasped what had happened, Watari had started running. But his pursuers were six tough boys. He lost his footing on the clay by the pond. He resisted, so that his blue shirt tore to give a glimpse of one shoulder, almost pathologically white. The boy with the rope tied his hands behind his back. His trousers, soiled by the red clay, were an oddly bright, shiny color.

Hatakeyama had made no move to chase him. His left hand was thrust casually into his pocket, with no care for his wound. The blood dripped down steadily, making a red rim around the glass of his wristwatch, then seeping from his fingertips into the bottom of his pocket. He felt no pain, aware only of something that hardly seemed like blood, something warm and familiar and intensely personal, caressing the surface of his skin as it went. But he had made up his mind on one thing: in his friends' faces when they brought Watari back, he would see nothing but an embodiment of his own decision, inviting him to proceed.

After that, he didn't look at Watari but gazed steadily at the long rope to which he was tied, with the slack wound round and round him and its end held in the hand of one of his classmates.

"Let's go somewhere quiet," he said. "The little wood behind the pigeon lofts."

Prodded, Watari began walking. As they filed along the red clay path, he staggered again and fell to his knees. With a coarse "heave-ho," they yanked him to his feet. His shoulder stood out so white in the light reflected from the foliage that it was as though the bone was sticking out of the rent in his blue shirt.

All the time as Watari walked, the incorrigible M hung about him, tickling him under the arms, pinching his backside, roaring with laughter because the boy, he said, had looked up at the sky. What if he had known that only two things in the whole world were visible to Watari's eyes: the blue sky—the eye of God, forever striking down into men's eyes through the green leaves of the treetops—and the precious blood spilled on his own account down here on earth, the lifeblood staining Hatakeyama's arm? His gaze went continually from one to the other of these two things. Hatakeyama was looking straight ahead, walking with a confident step more adult than any adult's. On his left arm, just in front of Watari, the blood was slowly drying, showing up a bright purple whenever it passed through the sun's rays.

The grove behind the pigeon lofts was a sunny patch of widely spaced trees, little frequented, where the pigeons often came to pass the time. An undistinguished collection of smallish deciduous trees, it had, at its very center, one great pine with gently outstretched branches on which the birds were fond of lining up to coo at one another. The rays of the afternoon sun picked out the trunk of the pine in a bright, pure light so that the resin flowing from it looked like veins of agate.

Hatakeyama came to a halt and said to the boy holding the rope:

"All right—this'll do. Take the rope off Watari. But don't let him get away. Throw the thing up like a lasso and put it over that big branch on the pine tree."

The rich jest of this sent the others into ecstasies. Watari was being held down by two of them. The remaining four danced like little demons on the grass as they helped hitch up the rope. One end of it was tied in a loop. Then one of the boys mounted a handy tree stump, poked his head through the noose, and stuck out his tongue.

"That's no good—it'll have to be higher."

The boy who'd stuck his tongue out was the shortest of them all. Watari would need at least another two or three inches.

They were all scared, scared by the occasional, shadowy suggestion that their prank might possibly be in earnest. As they led Watari, pale and trembling slightly, to the waiting noose, one waggish youth delivered a funeral address. All the while, Watari continued to gaze up at the sky with his idiotically wide-open eyes.

Abruptly, Hatakeyama raised a hand by way of a signal. His eyes were shut tight.

The rope went up.

Startled by the sudden beating of many pigeons' wings and by the glow on Watari's beautiful face, astonishingly high above them, they fled the grove, each in a different direction, unable to bear the thought of staying at the scene of such dire murder.

They ran at a lively pace, each boyish breast still swelling with the pride of having killed someone.

A full thirty minutes later, they reentered the wood as though by agreement and, huddling together, gazed up fearfully at the branch of the great pine.

The rope was dangling free, the hanged corpse nowhere to be seen.

Fathers and Daughters

Laura Grimaldi

When she was ten, Maria was happy one Sunday a month when she went out with her mother and sister to visit her grandma at the cemetery. They bought flowers from the vendor in front of the big iron gates and then walked along the drive to the tomb with the stone slab. Grandma watched Maria from the oval picture on the tomb and spoke to her, but only Maria could hear her voice. Grandma called her "darling" and told her what to do, and Maria waited for the occasion to follow her advice.

During the other days of the month Maria squatted in a corner of the kitchen as soon as she was back from school and she stayed there with her eyes closed, so other people couldn't see her, her father above all.

But during the night she kept her eyes wide open, listening to the snores from her parents' room, and as soon as the snoring diminished or stopped for a second, she began to shiver and to wait for her father to come into the room where she slept with her sister. And the times when her father arrived, with his naked feet slapping on the corridor's tile floor, she hid her head under the pillow not to hear her sister sobbing and her father whispering to her to be good. Maria preferred him to be angry, as he was sometimes when her sister didn't stop crying and he said he would kill her.

At school, Maria had begun to stutter and to get bad marks and to wee in her pants, but at home nobody worried about it. Her mother kept polishing furniture and the floors and shrieked a lot when her daughters messed up the house. When she didn't polish furniture, she cooked, but for some time Maria hadn't eaten much and she vomited the little she did eat.

It also happened that Maria, coming back home from school, fell down and was unable to stand up again because her legs were as stiff as a board. People carried her home and her father began to massage her and to look at her in a funny way, saying that it might be better if that night she slept in the big bed with him and her mother. Maria got up and fled from him with legs that had suddenly become alive again.

One morning Maria's sister spoke with their mother. Maria didn't understand all the words, but felt that her sister was speaking about the thing that happened with her father during the night. Their mother began to shriek like mad and grabbed Maria's sister by the hair, shouting that she had a dirty mind and shouldn't say things like that, otherwise she would be locked up in an asylum. But Maria could tell that her mother had tears in her voice.

That evening her mother was her usual self.—Go comb your hair and wash your hands. Daddy will be back soon.

And they sat as always around the table, with Daddy who ate and smacked his lips to let them understand that he liked the food.

Sometimes her father hit her mother, and Maria was glad. She came out of her corner and opened her eyes to look at him hitting his wife against the wall and punching her on her head and face. Maria hoped that he would kill her, so her mother would die and the police would come to take him away. But it never happened. Her mother would hide in the bathroom, putting a wet cloth over a blue eye, and during the night her father would come into the room and whisper to her sister.

The teacher had sent a social assistant to see why Maria didn't study anymore and lost weight and was almost unable to speak, but the assistant found a clean house and her mother very calm.

"My oldest daughter was also like that," her mother said. "When she was ten, nearly ten, she stopped eating and began to stutter. But after she started to menstruate she was herself again."

She didn't say that they had to take her sister away from school and since then her sister had that ugly twitch that deformed her face.

Maria thought that the assistant would have asked many questions and that her mother would have told her what happened at night in their home. She was breathless from hope and shame and fear as well, but the social assistant didn't ask any questions, and when her mother noticed that Maria was staring at her, Maria thought that she was angry and would have her sent to an asylum, and she shut her eyes so as not to see her mother's face.

—You love your Mum, do you? the social assistant asked with an inattentive voice, and Maria nodded, keeping her eyes closed.

In the same instant her father arrived, and he was very kind with the assistant and with Maria and her mother as well. He asked if the lady had been offered something to drink and told her how difficult it was to raise two daughters.

At dinner time, with her father already sitting at the table after having put his guard's gun on top of the cupboard and taken his jacket off because he was always hot, they noticed that Maria's sister was not at home. Her mother called her from the window and went up-stairs to see if she was in her girlfriend's flat, but she could not find her. Maria ran to hide in the bedroom. She understood that her sister had gone away and would never come back. She heard her father cursing and hitting her mother, with a great crash of chairs falling on the floor. Then her mother went in the bathroom and she stayed there for a long time, but when she came out at last, she grabbed Maria's wrist, ordering her to go and sit at the dining table.

That night her father didn't eat. He kept touching the spoon and the fork and muttering. He was pale, and Maria felt he was afraid. It was a great discovery. The terror she had had disappeared, and she saw only an ugly man with swollen eyes.

—What are we going to do? What are we going to do? her mother kept wailing.

—Let's wait until tomorrow morning, her father said.

Maria didn't want to get up from the table, because she knew that the fear would come back. She grabbed a bowl full of pasta and began to stuff her mouth. Her mother looked at her with sad, reproachful eyes. —How can you eat? she asked.

Maria felt she had been betrayed by her sister and hated her because she had gone away. When she was in her room, the bed near hers looked like a great, flat, deserted plain. She waited to hear the snoring from her parents' room, but a lot of time passed and the silence stayed compact, uninterrupted, as if their bed too was empty and her parents had left her forever alone. But she knew her father was there and that this time he would come to her.

She was stiff, listening, and when the bed in the other room creaked in the dark she imagined her father coming to her, with his big feet whispering on the corridor's tiles. She stayed with her head half up, her hands grabbing the cover, until daylight began to come in from the window and the snoring in the adjoining room had a regular rhythm. Then she left the bed and went into the kitchen.

She pushed a chair against the cupboard and crawled on it to take the gun. The day her father had found a job as a private guard and had come back home with the gun, he showed it to her and her sister, saying it was dangerous and that they should not touch it, even if he always left it with the safety-bolt on, and anyway here was the safety-bolt and that was how it worked, in case thieves would come when he wasn't at home. But when he wasn't at home the gun wasn't there either, Maria thought, and she understood that her father was just showing off the importance the gun gave him.

The gun was heavy, and Maria had to put it on the seat of the chair in order to climb down. Then she seized it again and took the safety-bolt off, as her father had shown them that day. Carrying it with both hands, she went into her parents' room.

Her father slept with his face buried in the pillow, a hairy arm dangling outside the bed, fat and dark shoulders interrupted by the white of the undershirt. Maria put the barrel against his ear and pulled the trigger. The noise deafened her, and she stayed for a long moment with the gun dancing in her hands, eyes fixed on her father's body, which had had a long shiver and then was completely motionless, with blood dripping on the linen, a dark patch that looked black in the weak light.

Maria's mother sat up, her eyes like pits of fear, her mouth wide open. She thrust her hands toward her daughter. She tried to shout but couldn't, and her throat contracted like it was being strangled by invisible fingers. She pushed herself across her husband's body to reach Maria, her open mouth near the gun's barrel.

Maria pulled the trigger again and again, shooting inside her mother's mouth, and kept pulling it until the gun made a click.

Then she went to bed and for the first time in years she fell asleep immediately and had a long sleep.

The Werewolf

Angela Carter

It is a northern country; they have cold weather, they have cold hearts.

Cold; tempest; wild beasts in the forest. It is a hard life. Their houses are built of logs, dark and smoky within. There will be a crude icon of the virgin behind a guttering candle, the leg of a pig hung up to cure, a string of drying mushrooms. A bed, a stool, a table. Harsh, brief, poor lives.

To these upland woodsmen, the Devil is as real as you or I. More so; they have not seen us nor even know that we exist, but the Devil they glimpse often in the graveyards, those bleak and touching townships of the dead where the graves are marked with portraits of the deceased in the naïf style and there are no flowers to put in front of them, no flowers grow there, so they put out small votive offerings, little loaves, sometimes a cake that the bears come lumbering from the margins of the forest to snatch away. At midnight, especially on Walpurgisnacht, the Devil holds picnics in the graveyards and invites the witches; then they dig up fresh corpses, and eat them. Anyone will tell you that.

Wreaths of garlic on the doors keep out the vampires. A blue-eyed child born feet first on the night of Saint John's Eve will have second sight. When they discover a witch—some old woman whose cheeses ripen when her neighbors' do not, another old woman whose black

283

cat, oh, sinister! *follows her about all the time*—they strip the crone, search for her marks, for the supernumerary nipple her familiar sucks. They soon find it. Then they stone her to death.

Winter and cold weather.

Go and visit grandmother, who has been sick. Take her the oat cakes I've baked for her on the hearthstone and a little pot of butter.

The good child does as her mother bids—five miles' trudge through the forest; do not leave the path because of the bears, the wild boar, the starving wolves. Here, take your father's hunting knife; you know how to use it.

The child had a scabby coat of sheepskin to keep out the cold; she knew the forest too well to fear it but she must always be on her guard. When she heard that freezing howl of a wolf, she dropped her gifts, seized her knife and turned on the beast.

It was a huge one, with red eyes and running, grizzled chops; any but a mountaineer's child would have died of fright at the sight of it. It went for her throat, as wolves do, but she made a great swipe at it with her father's knife and slashed off its right forepaw.

The wolf let out a gulp, almost a sob, when it saw what had happened to it; wolves are less brave than they seem. It went lolloping off disconsolately between the trees as well as it could on three legs, leaving a trail of blood behind it. The child wiped the blade of her knife clean on her apron, wrapped up the wolf's paw in the cloth in which her mother had packed the oat cakes and went on towards her grandmother's house. Soon it came on to snow so thickly that the path and any footsteps, track or spoor that might have been upon it were obscured.

She found her grandmother was so sick she had taken to her bed and fallen into a fretful sleep, moaning and shaking so that the child guessed she had a fever. She felt the forehead, it burned. She shook out the cloth from her basket, to use it to make the old woman a cold compress, and the wolf's paw fell to the floor.

But it was no longer a wolf's paw. It was a hand, chopped off at the wrist, a hand toughened with work and freckled with old age. There was a wedding ring on the third finger and a wart on the index finger. By the wart, she knew it for her grandmother's hand.

She pulled back the sheet, but the old woman woke up at that, and began to struggle, squawking and shrieking like a thing possessed.

But the child was strong, and armed with her father's hunting knife; she managed to hold her grandmother down long enough to see the cause of her fever. There was a bloody stump where her right hand should have been, festering already.

The child crossed herself and cried out so loud the neighbors heard her and came rushing in. They knew the wart on the hand at once for a witch's nipple; they drove the old woman, in her shift as she was, out into the snow with sticks, beating her old carcass as far as the edge of the forest, and pelted her with stones until she fell down dead.

Now the child lived in her grandmother's house; she prospered.

Missionary Stew

Ross Thomas

He flew into Paris, the city of his birth, on a cold wet November afternoon. He flew in from Equatorial Africa wearing green polyester pants, a white T-shirt that posed the suspect question "Have You Eaten Your Honey Today?" and a machine-knitted cardigan whose color, he had finally decided, was mauve.

The articles of clothing, possibly Oxfam castoffs, had been handed to him out of a green plastic ragbag by Miss Cecily Tettah of Amnesty International, who had apologized neither for their quality nor their fit. The mauve sweater must have belonged to a fat man once—an extremely tall fat man. Morgan Citron was a little over six-one, but the sweater almost reached mid-thigh and fitted his emaciated 142-pound frame like a reversed hospital gown. Still, it was wool and it was warm and Citron no longer cared greatly about his appearance.

It was in a cheap hotel room near the Gare du Nord that Citron had been born forty-one years ago, the son of a dead-broke twenty-year-old American student from Holyoke and a twenty-nine-year-old French army lieutenant who had been killed in May during the fighting at Sedan. Citron's mother, obsessed with her poverty, had named her son Morgan after a distant cousin who was vaguely connected to the banking family. Citron was born June 14, 1940. It was the same day the Germans rolled into Paris.

Now on that wet, cold November afternoon in 1981, Citron went through customs and immigration at Charles de Gaulle Airport, found a taxi, and settled into its rear seat. When the driver said, "Where to?" Citron replied in French: "Let's say you have a cousin who lives in the country."

"Ah. My country cousin. A Breton, of course."

"He's coming to Paris."

"But my cousin is poor."

"Unfortunately."

"Yet he would like a nice cheap place to stay."

"He would insist upon it."

"Then I would direct him to the Seventh Arrondissement, in the Rue Vaneau, number 42—Le Bon Hotel."

"I accept your suggestion."

"You've made a wise choice," the driver said.

When they reached the Périphérique, Citron confided further in the driver. "I have a diamond," he said.

"A diamond. Well."

"I wish to sell it."

"It is yours to sell, of course."

"Of course."

"You know anything of diamonds?"

"Almost nothing," Citron said.

"Still, you have no wish to be cheated."

"None."

"Then we shall try Bassou and you will tell him that I sent you. He will give me a commission. A small one. He will also give you a fair price. Low, but fair."

"Good," Citron said. "Let's try Bassou."

Three days before, Citron had watched in the early-morning African hours, already steaming, as Gaston Bama, the sergeant-warder, brought in and ladled out the famous meal that eventually was to help drive the Emperor-President from his ivory throne.

Bama was then an old man of fifty-three, corpulent, corrupt, and slow-moving, with three chevrons on his sleeve that testified to his rank, the same rank he had held for seventeen years. For nearly all of the past decade he had been chief warder in the *section d'étranger* of the old prison the French had built back in 1923, long before the country was an empire, or even a republic, and still then only a territory of French Equatorial Africa.

The foreigners' section was in the small, walled-off east wing of the prison. That November it held not only Morgan Citron, but also four failed smugglers from Cameroon; a handful of self-proclaimed political refugees from Zaire; six Sudanese reputed to be slavers; one mysterious Czech who seldom spoke; and an American of twenty-two from Provo, Utah, who insisted he was a Mormon missionary, although nobody believed him. There were also three rich young Germans from Düsseldorf who had tried to cross Africa on their BMW motorcycles only to break down and run out of money a few miles outside the capital. Because no one had quite known what to do with them, they were clapped into prison and forgotten. The rich young Germans wrote home every week begging for money and UN intervention. Their letters were never mailed.

It was largely because he was bilingual in French and English that Morgan Citron had been elected or perhaps thrust into the position of spokesman for the foreign prisoners. His only other qualification was his gold wrist watch, a costly Rolex, that he had bought in Zurich in 1975 on the advice of a knowledgeable barkeep who felt that gold might be looking up as an investment. Just before the Emperor-President's secret police had come for him in his room at the Inter-Continental, Citron had slipped the watch from his left wrist and onto his right ankle beneath his sock.

That had been nearly thirteen months ago. Since then he had traded the gold links in the expansion band one by one to Sergeant Bama for supplementary rations of millet and cassava and fish. Infrequently, no more than once a month, there might also be some red meat. Goat, usually. Elderly goat. Citron shared everything with the other prisoners and consequently was not murdered in his bed.

There had been thirty-six links in the watch's gold expansion band originally. In thirteen months, Citron had parted with thirty-four of them. He knew that soon he would have to part with the watch itself. With his gold all gone, Citron was confident that his term as spokesman would also end. If not drummed out of office, he would abdicate. Citron was one of those for whom political office had never held any attraction.

Sergeant Bama watched as the skinny young private soldier put the immense black ironstone pot down near the bench on which Citron sat in the shade just outside his cell.

"There," Sergeant Bama said. "As I promised. Meat."

Citron sniffed and peered into the pot. "Meat," he agreed.

"As I promised."

"What kind of meat?"

"Goat. No, not goat. Four young kids, tender and sweet. Taste, if you like."

Citron yawned hugely, both to express his indifference and to commence the bargaining. "Last night," he said, "I could not sleep."

"I am desolate."

"The screams."

"What screams?"

"The ones that prevented me from sleeping."

"I heard no screams," Sergeant Bama said and turned to the private soldier. "Did you hear screams in the night? You are young and have sharp ears."

The private soldier looked away and down. "I heard nothing," he said and drew a line in the red dirt with a bare toe.

"Then who screamed?" Citron said.

Sergeant Bama smiled. "Perhaps some pederasts with unwilling partners?" He shrugged. "A lovers' quarrel? Who can say?"

"They went on for half an hour," Citron said. "The screams."

"I heard no screams," Sergeant Bama said indifferently and then frowned. "Do you want the meat? Four kilos."

"And the price?"

"The watch."

"You grow not only deaf in your old age, but senile."

"The watch," Sergeant Bama said. "I must have it."

Citron swallowed most of the saliva that had been created by the smell of the meat. "I will give you two links—the last two—provided there're two kilos of rice to go with the meat."

"Rice! Rice is very dear. Only the rich eat rice."

"Two kilos."

Sergeant Bama scowled. It was an excellent bargain, far better than he had expected. He changed his scowl into a smile of sweet reasonableness. "The watch."

"No."

Sergeant Bama turned to the private soldier. "Fetch the rice. Two kilos."

After the private soldier left, Sergeant Bama squatted down beside the ironstone pot. He dipped his right hand into its lukewarm contents and removed a small piece of meat. He offered the piece to Citron. For a moment, Citron hesitated, then accepted the meat and popped it into his mouth. He chewed slowly, carefully, and then swallowed.

"It is not goat," Citron said.

"Did I say it was goat? I said kid—young and tender. Does it not dissolve in your mouth?"

"It is not kid either."

Sergeant Bama peered suspiciously into the pot, fished out another small piece of meat that swam in the brownish liquid, and sniffed it. "Pork perhaps?" He offered the piece to Citron. "Taste and determine. If it is pork, you will not have to share with the Sudanese, who are Muslim."

Citron took the meat and chewed it. "It is not pork. I remember pork."

"And this?"

"This is sweet and tough and stringy."

Sergeant Bama giggled. "Of course. How stupid of me." He clapped a hand to his forehead—a stage gesture. "It could only be monkey. A rare delicacy. Sweet, you said. Monkey tastes sweet. There is nothing sweeter to the tongue than fresh young monkey."

"I've never tasted monkey."

"Well, now you have." The sergeant smiled complacently and looked around. The other prisoners were seated or squatting in the shade, none of them nearer than six meters, awaiting the outcome of the negotiations. When the sergeant turned back to Citron, the scowl was again in place and a harsh new urgency was in his tone. "I must have the watch," he said.

"No," Citron said. "Not for this."

Sergeant Bama nodded indifferently and looked off into the hot distance. "There will be a visitor this afternoon at fifteen hundred," he said. "A black woman from England who is a high functionary in a prisoners' organization with a rare name."

"You lie, of course," Citron said, wiping a thin film of grease from his mouth with the back of his hand.

Sergeant Bama looked at him and shrugged. "Believe what you wish, but she will be here at fifteen hundred to interview the other foreign scum. It is all arranged. You, of course, will be transferred to the isolation block and thus will miss the black Englishwoman. A pity. I am told she is a marvelous sight. Of course . . ." The sergeant's unspoken offer trailed off into an elaborate Afro-Gallic shrug.

"The watch," Citron said, understanding now.

"The watch."

Citron studied Sergeant Bama for several seconds. Over the sergeant's left shoulder he could see the private soldier approaching with a big pot of rice. "All right," Citron said. "You get the watch—but only after I see the black Englishwoman."

He was surprised when the sergeant agreed with a single word: "Good." Sergeant Bama rose then and turned toward the other prisoners. "Come and eat," he called in near English, adding in rapid French, which not all of them could follow: "We want you fat and sleek for when the black Englishwoman arrives."

The prisoners rose and started filing past the pots of meat and rice. The sergeant presided over the meat, the private soldier over the rice. The sergeant used a gourd ladle to dish meat into the prisoners' plastic bowls.

"What's this shit?" the young Mormon missionary asked.

"Monkey," Citron said.

"Oh," the Mormon said, hurried away with his food, sat down in some shade, and ate it quickly with his fingers.

Miss Cecily Tettah, who worked out of the London headquarters of Amnesty International, had been born on a large plantation in Ghana just outside Accra forty-two years before, when Ghana was still called the Gold Coast. After the war she had been sent by her cocoa-rich father to London to be educated. She had never returned to Ghana, never married, and, when asked, usually described herself in her splendid British accent as either a maiden lady or a spinster. Many thought her to be hopelessly old-fashioned. The few men lucky enough to find their way into her bed over the years discovered not only a magnificent body, but also an acerbic wit and an excellent mind.

Still a handsome woman, quite tall with graying hair, Miss Tettah, as she rather primly introduced herself to almost everyone, had been granted the use of Sergeant Bama's tiny office to interview the foreign prisoners. She sat behind the plain wooden table, a thick file open before her. Citron sat in the chair opposite. Cecily Tettah tapped the open file with a pencil and looked up at Citron with wide-spaced, bitter-chocolate eyes. She made no effort to keep the suspicion out of either her tone or gaze.

"There is no record of you," she said, giving the papers in the file a final tap with her pencil. "There're records of all the others, but none of you."

"No," Citron said. "I'm not surprised."

"They claim you're a spy, either French or American. They're not sure which."

"I'm a traveler," Citron said.

"I had an audience with the Emperor-President this morning." She sniffed. "I suppose that's what one should call it—an audience. He has agreed to release all of the foreign nationals—all except you."

"Why not me?"

"Because he thinks you're a spy, as I said. He wants to see you. Privately. Will you agree?"

Citron thought about it and shrugged. "All right."

"Not to worry," Cecily Tettah said. "We'll get it sorted out. Now then. How've they been treating you?"

"Not bad. Considering."

"What about food? You look thin."

"There was enough—just barely."

"Today, for instance. What did they feed you today?"

"Meat and rice."

"What kind of meat?"

"Monkey."

Cecily Tettah pursed her lips in approval, nodded, and made a note. "Monkey's not bad," she said. "Quite nutritious. Almost no fat. Did they feed you monkey often?"

"No," Citron said. "Only once."

The Emperor-President's anteroom was an immense hall with no chairs or benches and a once magnificent parquet floor now ruined by cigarette burns and boot scars. The room was crowded with those who wanted to petition the Emperor-President, and with those whose job it was to prevent his assassination.

There were at least two dozen uniformed armed guards, plus another dozen secret police. The secret police all wore wide gaudy ties and peered suspiciously out at the world over tinted Ben Franklin glasses. The guards and the secret police stood. The threadbare petitioners sat on the floor along with a host of preening sycophants, a squad of sleepy-looking young messengers, and a pair of Slav businessmen in boxy suits who spoke Bulgarian to each other and tried to look forbidding, but whose wet friendly eyes betrayed their optimistic salesmen souls.

Citron also sat on the floor, his back to the wall, guarded by Sergeant Bama, who amused himself by shooting out his left wrist to admire his new gold Rolex. The sergeant smiled at his watch, then scowled at Citron.

"You will be alone with him."

"Yes."

"Do not lie about me."

"No."

"If you lie, then I might have to reveal what was in the morning pot. There are those who would pay well to learn its contents."

"Monkey," Citron said, knowing it wasn't.

The sergeant smiled a quite terrible smile that Citron felt he might remember for years. "It was not monkey," Sergeant Bama said.

"Last night," Citron said. "The screams. They sounded like children's screams."

Sergeant Bama shrugged and gave his new watch another admiring glance. "Some got carried away."

"Who?"

"I will not say." He glanced around quickly, then leaned closer to Citron. The smile reappeared, even more awful than before. "But you helped destroy the evidence," he whispered and then giggled. "You ate up all the evidence."

Citron stood throughout his audience with the Emperor-President, who sat slumped on the throne that had been cleverly crafted in Paris out of ebony and ivory. Citron thought it looked uncomfortable. He also thought the Emperor-President looked hung over.

"So," the Emperor-President said. "You are leaving us."

"I hope so."

"Some say you are French; some say American. What do you say?"

"I was both for a time. Now I'm American."

"How could you be both?"

"A matter of papers."

"Documents?"

"Yes."

"Ahhh."

The Emperor-President closed his eyes and seemed to nod off for a moment or so. He was a chunky man in his early fifties with a big stomach that bounced and rolled around underneath a long white cotton robe. The robe resembled a nightgown, and Citron thought it looked both cool and eminently practical. The Emperor-President opened his eyes, which seemed a bit inflamed, picked his nose, wiped his finger somewhere on the throne, and then beckoned Citron. "Come closer."

Citron moved closer.

"Closer still."

Citron took two more steps. The Emperor-President looked around suspiciously. They were alone. He beckoned Citron with a single finger. Citron leaned forward until he could smell last night's gin. Or today's.

"I wish to send a secret message to the Presidents of France and the United States," the Emperor-President whispered. "No one must know. No one." He waited for Citron's reply.

"I'm not sure," Citron said carefully, "how soon I will be seeing them."

The Emperor-President nodded his big head, as if that were exactly what he would expect a spy to say. "My message is brief. Tell them—tell them both that I am ready for reconciliation—on their terms."

"I see."

"Can you remember that?"

"Yes. I believe so."

"Here." The Emperor-President fumbled into the folds of the long white gown, found the pocket, and brought out a clenched fist. "Hold out your hand."

Citron held out his hand.

"Palm up."

Citron turned his palm up. The Emperor-President unclenched his fist. A two-carat diamond dropped into Citron's open palm. He automatically wrapped a fist around it.

"A token," the Emperor-President said. "A gesture."

"A token gesture."

"Yes. For your trouble."

"I see."

"You are free to go."

"Yes. Well. Thank you."

Citron turned and started toward the tall double doors, but stopped at the sound of the Emperor-President's voice. "Wait." Citron turned.

"I understand they fed you monkey today."

Citron only nodded.

"Did you like it?"

"I ate it."

"So did I," the Emperor-President said and began to chuckle—a deep bass chuckle that seemed to rumble up from his belly. "We both ate monkey today," the Emperor-President said and then went back to his chuckling. He was still at it when Citron walked through the tall double doors.

Miss Cecily Tettah counted three hundred French francs onto the plain table, picked them up, and handed them to Citron. He put them into the envelope that contained his Air France ticket to Paris and his American passport.

"How was he?" she asked. "You never said."

"He laughed a lot."

"Nothing else?"

"He still thinks I'm a spy."

"Really? I thought we'd got that all sorted out. Are you still quite certain there is no one you wish us to notify in the States?"

"No. No one."

"Not even your mother?"

Citron shook his head. "Especially not her."

The Moment Before
the Gun Went Off

Nadine Gordimer

Marais Van der Vyver shot one of his farm laborers, dead. An accident, there are accidents with guns every day of the week—children playing a fatal game with a father's revolver in the cities where guns are domestic objects, nowadays, hunting mishaps like this one, in the country—but these won't be reported all over the world. Van der Vyver knows his will be. He knows that the story of the Afrikaner farmer—regional Party leader and Commandant of the local security commando—shooting a black man who worked for him will fit exactly *their* version of South Africa, it's made for them. They'll be able to use it in their boycott and divestment campaigns, it'll be another piece of evidence in their truth about the country. The papers at home will quote the story as it has appeared in the overseas press, and in the back-and-forth he and the black man will become those crudely drawn figures on anti-apartheid banners, units in statistics of white brutality against the blacks quoted at the United Nations—he, whom they will gleefully be able to call "a leading member" of the ruling Party.

People in the farming community understand how he must feel. Bad enough to have killed a man, without helping the Party's, the government's, the country's enemies, as well. They see the truth of that. They know, reading the Sunday papers, that when Van der

Vyver is quoted saying he is "terribly shocked," he will "look after the wife and children," none of those Americans and English, and none of those people at home who want to destroy the white man's power will believe him. And how they will sneer when he even says of the farm boy (according to one paper, if you can trust any of those reporters), "He was my friend, I always took him hunting with me." Those city and overseas people don't know it's true: farmers usually have one particular black boy they like to take along with them in the lands; you could call it a kind of friend, yes, friends are not only your own white people, like yourself, you take into your house, pray with in church and work with on the Party committee. But how can those others know that? They don't want to know it. They think all blacks are like the big-mouth agitators in town. And Van der Vyver's face, in the photographs, strangely opened by distress—everyone in the district remembers Marais Van der Vyver as a little boy who would go away and hide himself if he caught you smiling at him, and everyone knows him now as a man who hides any change of expression round his mouth behind a thick soft mustache, and in his eyes by always looking at some object in hand, leaf of a crop fingered, pen or stone picked up, while concentrating on what he is saying, or while listening to you. It just goes to show what shock can do; when you look at the newspaper photographs you feel like apologizing, as if you had stared in on some room where you should not be.

There will be an inquiry; there had better be, to stop the assumption of yet another case of brutality against farm workers, although there's nothing in doubt—an accident, and all the facts fully admitted by Van der Vyver. He made a statement when he arrived at the police station with the dead man in his bakkie. Captain Beetge knows him well, of course; he gave him brandy. He was shaking, this big, calm, clever son of Willem Van der Vyver, who inherited the old man's best farm. The black was stone dead, nothing to be done for him. Beetge will not tell anyone that after the brandy Van der Vyver wept. He sobbed, snot running onto his hands, like a dirty kid. The Captain was ashamed, for him, and walked out to give him a chance to recover himself.

Marais Van der Vyver left his house at three in the afternoon to cull a buck from the family of kudu he protects in the bush areas of his farm. He is interested in wildlife and sees it as the farmers' sacred duty to raise game as well as cattle. As usual, he called at his shed workshop to pick up Lucas, a twenty-year-old farmhand who had shown mechanical aptitude and whom Van der Vyver himself had taught to maintain tractors and other farm machinery. He hooted, and Lucas followed the familiar routine, jumping onto the back of the truck. He liked to travel standing up there, spotting game before his employer did. He would lean forward, braced against the cab below him.

Van der Vyver had a rifle and .300 ammunition beside him in the cab. The rifle was one of his father's, because his own was at the gunsmith's in town. Since his father died (Beetge's sergeant wrote "passed on") no one had used the rifle and so when he took it from a cupboard he was sure it was not loaded. His father had never allowed a loaded gun in the house; he himself had been taught since childhood never to ride with a loaded weapon in a vehicle. But this gun was loaded. On a dirt track, Lucas thumped his fist on the cab roof three times to signal: look left. Having seen the white-ripple-marked flank of a kudu, and its fine horns raking through disguising bush, Van der Vyver drove rather fast over a pothole. The jolt fired the rifle. Upright, it was pointing straight through the cab roof at the head of Lucas. The bullet pierced the roof and entered Lucas's brain by way of his throat.

That is the statement of what happened. Although a man of such standing in the district, Van der Vyver had to go through the ritual of swearing that it was the truth. It has gone on record, and will be there in the archive of the local police station as long as Van der Vyver lives, and beyond that, through the lives of his children, Magnus, Helena and Karel—unless things in the country get worse, the example of black mobs in the towns spreads to the rural areas and the place is burned down as many urban police stations have been. Because nothing the government can do will appease the agitators and the whites who encourage them. Nothing satisfies them, in the cities: blacks can sit and drink in white hotels, now, the Immorality Act has gone, blacks can sleep with whites . . . It's not even a crime any more.

Van der Vyver has a high barbed security fence round his farmhouse and garden which his wife, Alida, thinks spoils completely the effect of her artificial stream with its tree-ferns beneath the jacarandas. There is an aerial soaring like a flagpole in the backyard. All his

vehicles, including the truck in which the black man died, have aerials
that swing their whips when the driver hits a pothole: they are part
of the security system the farmers in the district maintain, each farm
in touch with every other by radio, twenty-four hours out of twenty-
four. It has already happened that infiltrators from over the border
have mined remote farm roads, killing white farmers and their families
out on their own property for a Sunday picnic. The pothole could
have set off a land-mine, and Van der Vyver might have died with
his farm boy. When neighbors use the communications system to call
up and say they are sorry about "that business" with one of Van der
Vyver's boys, there goes unsaid: it could have been worse.

It is obvious from the quality and fittings of the coffin that the
farmer has provided money for the funeral. And an elaborate funeral
means a great deal to blacks; look how they will deprive themselves
of the little they have, in their lifetime, keeping up payments to a
burial society so they won't go in boxwood to an unmarked grave.
The young wife is pregnant (of course) and another little one, wearing
red shoes several sizes too large, leans under her jutting belly. He is
too young to understand what has happened, what he is witnessing
that day, but neither whines nor plays about; he is solemn without
knowing why. Blacks expose small children to everything, they don't
protect them from the sight of fear and pain the way whites do theirs.
It is the young wife who rolls her head and cries like a child, sobbing
on the breast of this relative and that.

All present work for Van der Vyver or are the families of those
who work; and in the weeding and harvest seasons, the women and
children work for him, too, carried—wrapped in their blankets, on a
truck, singing—at sunrise to the fields. The dead man's mother is a
woman who can't be more than in her late thirties (they start bearing
children at puberty) but she is heavily mature in a black dress between
her own parents, who were already working for old Van der Vyver
when Marais, like their daughter, was a child. The parents hold her
as if she were a prisoner or a crazy woman to be restrained. But she
says nothing, does nothing. She does not look up; she does not look
at Van der Vyver, whose gun went off in the truck, she stares at the
grave. Nothing will make her look up; there need be no fear that she
will look up; at him. His wife, Alida, is beside him. To show the
proper respect, as for any white funeral, she is wearing the navy-blue-

and-cream hat she wears to church this summer. She is always supportive, although he doesn't seem to notice it; this coldness and reserve—his mother says he didn't mix well as a child—she accepts for herself but regrets that it has prevented him from being nominated, as he should be, to stand as the Party's parliamentary candidate for the district. He does not let her clothing, or that of anyone else gathered closely, make contact with him. He, too, stares at the grave. The dead man's mother and he stare at the grave in communication like that between the black man outside and the white man inside the cab the moment before the gun went off.

The moment before the gun went off was a moment of high excitement shared through the roof of the cab, as the bullet was to pass, between the young black man outside and the white farmer inside the vehicle. There were such moments, without explanation, between them, although often around the farm the farmer would pass the young man without returning a greeting, as if he did not recognize him. When the bullet went off what Van der Vyver saw was the kudu stumble in fright at the report and gallop away. Then he heard the thud behind him, and past the window saw the young man fall out of the vehicle. He was sure he had leapt up and toppled—in fright, like the buck. The farmer was almost laughing with relief, ready to tease, as he opened his door, it did not seem possible that a bullet passing through the roof could have done harm.

The young man did not laugh with him at his own fright. The farmer carried him in his arms, to the truck. He was sure, sure he could not be dead. But the young black man's blood was all over the farmer's clothes, soaking against his flesh as he drove.

How will they ever know, when they file newspaper clippings, evidence, proof, when they look at the photographs and see his face —guilty! guilty! they are right!—how will they know, when the police stations burn with all the evidence of what has happened now, and what the law made a crime in the past. How could they know that *they do not know*. Anything. The young black callously shot through the negligence of the white man was not the farmer's boy; he was his son.

Soft Monkey

Harlan Ellison

At twenty-five minutes past midnight on 51st Street, the wind-chill factor was so sharp it could carve you a new asshole.

Annie lay huddled in the tiny space formed by the wedge of locked revolving door that was open to the street when the document copying service had closed for the night. She had pulled the shopping cart from the Food Emporium at First Avenue near 57th into the mouth of the revolving door, had carefully tipped it onto its side, making certain her goods were jammed tightly in the cart, making certain nothing spilled into her sleeping space. She had pulled out half a dozen cardboard flats—broken-down sections of big Kotex cartons from the Food Emporium, the half dozen she had not sold to the junkman that afternoon—and she had fronted the shopping cart with two of them, making it appear the doorway was blocked by the management. She had wedged the others around the edges of the space, cutting the wind, and placed the two rotting sofa pillows behind and under her.

She had settled down, bundled in her three topcoats, the thick woolen merchant marine stocking cap rolled down to cover her ears, almost to the bridge of her broken nose. It wasn't bad in the doorway, quite cozy, really. The wind shrieked past and occasionally touched her, but mostly was deflected. She lay huddled in the tiny space, pulled out the filthy remnants of a stuffed baby doll, cradled it under her chin, and closed her eyes.

She slipped into a wary sleep, half in reverie and yet alert to the sounds of the street. She tried to dream of the child again. Alan. In the waking dream she held him as she held the baby doll, close under her chin, her eyes closed, feeling the warmth of his body. That was important: his body was warm, his little brown hand against her cheek, his warm, warm breath drifting up with the dear smell of baby.

Was that just today or some other day? Annie swayed in reverie, kissing the broken face of the baby doll. It was nice in the doorway; it was warm.

The normal street sounds lulled her for another moment, and then were shattered as two cars careened around the corner off Park Avenue, racing toward Madison. Even asleep, Annie sensed when the street wasn't right. It was a sixth sense she had learned to trust after the first time she had been mugged for her shoes and the small change in her snap-purse. Now she came fully awake as the sounds of trouble rushed toward her doorway. She hid the baby doll inside her coat.

The stretch limo sideswiped the Caddy as they came abreast of the closed repro center. The Brougham ran up over the curb and hit the light stanchion full in the grille. The door on the passenger side fell open and a man scrabbled across the front seat, dropped to all four on the sidewalk, and tried to crawl away. The stretch limo, angled in toward the curb, slammed to a stop in front of the Brougham, and three doors opened before the tires stopped rolling.

They grabbed him as he tried to stand, and forced him back to his knees. One of the limo's occupants wore a fine navy blue cashmere overcoat; he pulled it open and reached to his hip. His hand came out holding a revolver. With a smooth stroke he laid it across the kneeling man's forehead, opening him to the bone.

Annie saw it all. With poisonous clarity, back in the V of the revolving door, cuddled in darkness, she saw it all. Saw a second man kick out and break the kneeling victim's nose. The sound of it cut against the night's sudden silence. Saw the third man look toward the stretch limo as a black glass window slid down and a hand emerged from the back seat. The electric hum of opening. Saw the third man go to the stretch and take from the extended hand a metal can. A siren screamed down Park Avenue, and kept going. Saw him return to the group and heard him say, "Hold the motherfucker. Pull his head back!" Saw the other two wrench the victim's head back, gleaming white and pumping red from the broken nose, clear in the sulfurous light from the stanchion overhead. The man's shoes scraped and scraped the sidewalk. Saw the third man reach into an outer coat pocket and pull out a pint of scotch. Saw him unscrew the cap and begin to pour booze into the face of the victim. "Hold his mouth open!" Saw the man in the cashmere topcoat spike his thumb and index fingers into the hinges of the victim's jaws, forcing his mouth open. The sound of gagging, the glow of spittle. Saw the scotch spilling down the man's front. Saw the third man toss the pint bottle into the gutter where it shattered; and saw him thumb press the center of the plastic cap of the metal can; and saw him make the cringing, crying, wailing victim drink the Drano. Annie saw and heard it all.

The cashmere topcoat forced the victim's mouth closed, massaged his throat, made him swallow the Drano. The dying took a lot longer than expected. And it was a lot noisier.

The victim's mouth was glowing a strange blue in the calcium light from overhead. He tried spitting, and a gobbet hit the navy blue cashmere sleeve. Had the natty dresser from the stretch limo been a dunky slob uncaring of what *GQ* commanded, what happened next would not have gone down.

Cashmere cursed, swiped at the slimed sleeve, let go of the victim; the man with the glowing blue mouth and the gut being boiled away wrenched free of the other two, and threw himself forward. Straight toward the locked revolving door blocked by Annie's shopping cart and cardboard flats.

He came at her in fumbling, hurtling steps, arms wide and eyes rolling, throwing spittle like a racehorse; Annie realized he'd fall across the cart and smash her flat in another two steps.

She stood up, backing to the side of the V. She stood up: into the tunnel of light from the Caddy's headlights.

"The nigger saw it all!" yelled the cashmere.

"Fuckin' bag lady!" yelled the one with the can of Drano.

"He's still moving!" yelled the third man, reaching inside his topcoat and coming out of his armpit with a blued steel thing that seemed to extrude to a length more aptly suited to Paul Bunyan's armpit.

Foaming at the mouth, hands clawing at his throat, the driver of the Brougham came at Annie as if he were spring-loaded.

He hit the shopping cart with his thighs just as the man with the long armpit squeezed off his first shot. The sound of the .45 magnum tore a chunk out of 51st Street, blew through the running man like a crowd roar, took off his face and spattered bone and blood across the panes of the revolving door. It sparkled in the tunnel of light from the Caddy's headlights.

And somehow he kept coming. He hit the cart, rose as if trying to get a first down against a solid defense line, and came apart as the shooter hit him with a second round.

There wasn't enough solid matter to stop the bullet and it exploded through the revolving door, shattering it open as the body crashed through and hit Annie.

She was thrown backward, through the broken glass, and onto the floor of the document copying center. And through it all, Annie heard a fourth voice, clearly a fourth voice, screaming from the stretch limo, "Get the old lady! Get her, she saw everything!"

Men in topcoats rushed through the tunnel of light.

Annie rolled over, and her hand touched something soft. It was the ruined baby doll. It had been knocked loose from her bundled clothing. *Are you cold, Alan?*

She scooped up the doll and crawled away, into the shadows of the reproduction center. Behind her, crashing through the frame of the revolving door, she heard men coming. And the sound of a burglar alarm. Soon police would be here.

All she could think about was that they would throw away her goods. They would waste her good cardboard, they would take back her shopping cart, they would toss her pillows and the hankies and the green cardigan into some trash can; and she would be empty on the street again. As she had been when they made her move out of the room at 101st and First Avenue. After they took Alan from her . . .

A blast of sound, as the shot shattered a glass-framed citation on the wall near her. They had fanned out inside the office space, letting the headlight illumination shine through. Clutching the baby doll, she hustled down a hallway toward the rear of the copy center. Doors on both sides, all of them closed and locked. Annie could hear them coming.

A pair of metal doors stood open on the right. It was dark in there. She slipped inside, and in an instant her eyes had grown acclimated.

There were computers here, big crackle-gray-finish machines that lined three walls. Nowhere to hide.

She rushed around the room, looking for a closet, a cubbyhole, anything. Then she stumbled over something and sprawled across the cold floor. Her face hung over into emptiness, and the very faintest of cool breezes struck her cheeks. The floor was composed of large removable squares. One of them had been lifted and replaced, but not flush. It had not been locked down; an edge had been left ajar; she had kicked it open.

She reached down. There was a crawlspace under the floor.

Pulling the metal-rimmed vinyl plate, she slid into the empty square. Lying face-up, she pulled the square over the aperture, and nudged it gently till it dropped onto its tracks. It sat flush. She could see nothing where, a moment before, there had been the faintest scintilla of filtered light from the hallway. Annie lay very quietly, emptying her mind as she did when she slept in the doorways; making herself invisible. A mound of rags. A pile of refuse. Gone. Only the warmth of the baby doll in that empty place with her.

She heard the men crashing down the corridor, trying doors. *I wrapped you in blankets, Alan. You must be warm.* They came into the computer room. The room was empty, they could see that.

"She *has* to be here, dammit!"

"There's gotta be a way out we didn't see."

"Maybe she locked herself in one of those rooms. Should we try? Break 'em open?"

"Don't be a bigger asshole than usual. Can't you hear that alarm? We gotta get out of here!"

"He'll break our balls."

"Like hell. Would he do anything else than we've done? He's sittin' on the street in front of what's left of Beaddie. You think he's happy about it?"

There was a new sound to match the alarm. The honking of a horn from the street. It went on and on, hysterically.

"We'll find her."

Then the sound of footsteps. Then running.

Annie lay empty and silent, holding the doll.

It was warm, as warm as she had been all November. She slept there through the night.

The next day, in the last Automat in New York with the wonderful little windows through which one could get food by insertion of a token, Annie learned of the two deaths.

Not the death of the man in the revolving door; the deaths of two black women. Beaddie, who had vomited up most of his internal organs, boiled like Chesapeake Bay lobsters, was all over the front of the *Post* that Annie now wore as insulation against the biting November wind. The two women had been found in midtown alleys, their faces blown off by heavy-caliber ordnance. Annie had known one of them; her name had been Sooky and Annie got the word from a good Thunderbird worshipper who stopped by her table and gave her the skinny as she carefully ate her fish cakes and tea.

She knew who they had been seeking. And she knew why they had killed Sooky and the other street person: to white men who ride in stretch limos, all old nigger bag ladies look the same. She took a slow bite of fish cake and stared out at 42nd Street, watching the world swirl past; what was she going to do about this?

They would kill and kill till there was no safe place left to sleep in midtown. She knew it. This was mob business, the *Post* inside her coats said so. And it wouldn't make any difference trying to warn the women. Where would they go? Where would they *want* to go? Not even she, knowing what it was all about . . . not even she would leave the area: this was where she roamed, this was her territorial imperative. And they would find her soon enough.

She nodded to the croaker who had given her the word, and after he'd hobbled away to get a cup of coffee from the spigot on the wall, she hurriedly finished her fish cake and slipped out of the Automat as easily as she had the document copying center this morning.

Being careful to keep out of sight, she returned to 51st Street. The area had been roped off, with sawhorses and green tape that said *Police Investigation—Keep Off*. But there were crowds. The streets were jammed, not only with office workers coming and going, but with loiterers who were fascinated by the scene. It took very little to gather a crowd in New York. The falling of a cornice could produce a *minyan*.

Annie could not believe her luck. She realized the police were unaware of a witness: when the men had charged the doorway, they had thrown aside her cart and goods, had spilled them back onto the sidewalk to gain entrance; and the cops had thought it was all refuse, as one with the huge brown plastic bags of trash at the curb. Her cart and the good sofa pillows, the cardboard flats and her sweaters . . . all of it was in the area. Some in trash cans, some amid the piles of bagged rubbish, some just lying in the gutter.

That meant she didn't need to worry about being sought from two directions. One way was bad enough.

And all the aluminum cans she had salvaged to sell, they were still in the big Bloomingdale's bag right against the wall of the building. There would be money for dinner.

She was edging out of the doorway to collect her goods when she saw the one in navy blue cashmere who had held Beaddie while they fed him Drano. He was standing three stores away, on Annie's side, watching the police lines, watching the copy center, watching the crowd. Watching for her. Picking at an ingrown hair on his chin.

She stepped back into the doorway. Behind her a voice said, "C'mon, lady, get the hell outta here, this's a place uhbizness." Then she felt a sharp poke in her spine.

She looked behind her, terrified. The owner of the haberdashery, a man wearing a bizarrely cut gray pinstripe worsted with lapels that matched his ears, and a passion flame silk hankie spilling out of his breast pocket like a crimson afflatus, was jabbing her in the back with a wooden coat hanger. "Move it on, get moving," he said, in a tone that would have gotten his face slapped had he used it on a customer.

Annie said nothing. She *never* spoke to anyone on the street. Silence on the street. *We'll go, Alan; we're okay by ourselves. Don't cry, my baby.*

She stepped out of the doorway, trying to edge away. She heard a sharp, piercing whistle. The man in the cashmere topcoat had seen her; he was whistling and signaling up 51st Street to someone. As Annie hurried away, looking over her shoulder, she saw a dark blue Oldsmobile that had been double-parked pull forward. The cashmere topcoat was shoving through the pedestrians, coming for her like the number 5 uptown Lexington express.

Annie moved quickly, without thinking about it. Being poked in the back, and someone speaking directly to her . . . that was frightening: it meant coming out to respond to another human being. But moving down her streets, moving quickly, and being part of the flow, that was comfortable. She knew how to do that. It was just the way she was.

Instinctively, Annie made herself larger, more expansive, her raggedy arms away from her body, the dirty overcoats billowing, her gait more erratic: opening the way for her flight. Fastidious shoppers and suited businessmen shied away, gave a start as the dirty old black bag lady bore down on them, turned sidewise praying she would not brush a recently Martinized shoulder. The Red Sea parted miraculously, permitting flight, then closed over instantly to impede navy blue cashmere. But the Olds came on quickly.

Annie turned left onto Madison, heading downtown. There was construction around 48th. There were good alleys on 46th. She knew a basement entrance just three doors off Madison on 47th. But the Olds came on quickly.

Behind her, the light changed. The Olds tried to rush the intersection, but this was Madison. Crowds were already crossing. The Olds stopped, the driver's window rolled down and a face peered out. Eyes tracked Annie's progress.

Then it began to rain.

Like black mushrooms sprouting instantly from concrete, Totes blossomed on the sidewalk. The speed of the flowing river of pedestrians increased; and in an instant Annie was gone. Cashmere rounded the corner, looked at the Olds, a frantic arm motioned to the left, and the man pulled up his collar and elbowed his way through the crowd, rushing down Madison.

Low places in the sidewalk had already filled with water. His wing-tip cordovans were quickly soaked.

He saw her turn into the alley behind the novelty sales shop (*Nothing over $1.10!!!*); he *saw* her; turned right and ducked in fast; *saw* her, even through the rain and the crowd and half a block between them; *saw* it!

So where was she?

The alley was empty.

It was a short space, all brick, only deep enough for a big Dempsey Dumpster and a couple of dozen trash cans; the usual mounds of rubbish in the corners; no fire escape ladders low enough for an old bag lady to grab; no loading docks, no doorways that looked even remotely accessible, everything cemented over or faced with sheet steel; no basement entrances with concrete steps leading down; no manholes in the middle of the passage; no open windows or even broken windows at jumping height; no stacks of crates to hide behind.

The alley was empty.

Saw her come in here. *Knew* she had come in here, and couldn't get out. He'd been watching closely as he ran to the mouth of the alley. She was in here somewhere. Not too hard figuring out where. He took out the .38 Police Positive he liked to carry because he lived with the delusion that if he had to dump it, if it were used in the commission of a sort of kind of felony he couldn't get snowed on, and if it were traced, it would trace back to the cop in Teaneck, New Jersey, from whom it had been lifted as he lay drunk in the back room of a Polish social club three years earlier.

He swore he would take his time with her, this filthy old porch monkey. His navy blue cashmere already smelled like soaked dog. And the rain was not about to let up; it now came sheeting down, traveling in a curtain through the alley.

He moved deeper into the darkness, kicking the piles of trash, making sure the refuse bins were full. She was in here somewhere. Not too hard figuring out where.

Warm. Annie felt warm. With the ruined baby doll under her chin, and her eyes closed, it was almost like the apartment at 101st and First Avenue, when the Human Resources lady came and tried to tell her strange things about Alan. Annie had not understood what the woman meant when she kept repeating *soft monkey, soft monkey*, a thing some scientist knew. It had made no sense to Annie, and she had continued rocking the baby.

Annie remained very still where she had hidden. Basking in the warmth. *Is it nice, Alan? Are we toasty; yes, we are. Will we be very still and the lady from the City will go away? Yes, we will.* She heard the crash of a garbage can being kicked over. *No one will find us. Shh, my baby.*

There was a pile of wooden slats that had been leaned against a wall. As he approached, the gun leveled, he realized they obscured a doorway. She was back in there, he knew it. Had to be. Not too hard figuring that out. It was the only place she could have hidden.

He moved in quickly, slammed the boards aside, and threw down on the dark opening. It was empty. Steel-plate door, locked.

Rain ran down his face, plastering his hair to his forehead. He could smell his coat, and his shoes, oh god, don't ask. He turned and looked. All that remained was the huge dumpster.

He approached it carefully, and noticed: the lid was still dry near the back side closest to the wall. The lid had been open just a short time ago. Someone had just lowered it.

He pocketed the gun, dragged two crates from the heap thrown down beside the Dempsey, and crawled up onto them. Now he stood above the dumpster, balancing on the crates with his knees at the level of the lid. With both hands bracing him, he leaned over to get his fingertips under the heavy lid. He flung the lid open, yanked out the gun, and leaned over. The dumpster was nearly full. Rain had turned the muck and garbage into a swimming porridge. He leaned over precariously to see what floated there in the murk. He leaned in to see. *Fuckin' porch monk—*

As a pair of redolent, dripping arms came up out of the muck, grasped his navy blue cashmere lapels, and dragged him head-first into the metal bin. He went down, into the slime, the gun going off, the shot spanging off the raised metal lid. The coat filled with garbage and water.

Annie felt him struggling beneath her. She held him down, her feet on his neck and back, pressing him face-first deeper into the goo that filled the bin. She could hear him breathing garbage and fetid water. He thrashed, a big man, struggling to get out from under. She slipped, and braced herself against the side of the dumpster, regained her footing, and drove him deeper. A hand clawed out of the refuse, dripping lettuce and black slime. The hand was empty. The gun lay at the bottom of the bin. The thrashing intensified, his feet hitting the metal side of the container. Annie rose up and dropped her feet heavily on the back of his neck. He went flat beneath her, trying to swim up, unable to find purchase.

He grabbed her foot as an explosion of breath from down below forced a bubble of air to break on the surface. Annie stomped as hard as she could. Something snapped beneath her shoe, but she heard nothing.

It went on for a long time, for a time longer than Annie could think about. The rain filled the bin to overflowing. Movement under her feet lessened, then there was hysterical movement for an instant, then it was calm. She stood there for an even longer time, trembling and trying to remember other, warmer times.

Finally, she closed herself off, buttoned up tightly, climbed out dripping and went away from there, thinking of Alan, thinking of a time after this was done. After that long time standing there, no movement, no movement at all in the bog beneath her waist. She did not close the lid.

When she emerged from the alley, after hiding in the shadows and watching, the Oldsmobile was nowhere in sight. The foot traffic parted for her. The smell, the dripping filth, the frightened face, the ruined thing she held close to her.

She stumbled out onto the sidewalk, lost for a moment, then turned the right way and shuffled off.

The rain continued its march across the city.

No one tried to stop her as she gathered her goods on 51st Street. The police thought she was a scavenger, the gawkers tried to avoid being brushed by her, the owner of the document copying center was relieved to see the filth cleaned up. Annie rescued everything she could, and hobbled away, hoping to be able to sell her aluminum for a place to dry out. It was not true that she was dirty; she had always been fastidious, even in the streets. A certain level of dishevelment was acceptable, but this was unclean.

And the blasted baby doll needed to be dried and brushed clean. There was a woman on East 60th, near Second Avenue; a vegetarian who spoke with an accent; a white lady who sometimes let Annie sleep in the basement. She would ask her for a favor.

It was not a very big favor, but the white woman was not home; and that night Annie slept in the construction of the new Zeckendorf Towers, where S. Klein-On-The-Square used to be, down on 14th and Broadway.

The men from the stretch limo didn't find her again for almost a week.

She was salvaging newspapers from a wire basket on Madison near 44th when he grabbed her from behind. It was the one who had poured the liquor into Beaddie, and then made him drink the Drano.

He threw an arm around her, pulled her around to face him, and she reacted instantly, the way she did when the kids tried to take her snap-purse.

She butted him full in the face with the top of her head, and drove him backward with both filthy hands. He stumbled into the street, and a cab swerved at the last instant to avoid running him down. He stood in the street, shaking his head, as Annie careened down 44th, looking for a place to hide. She was sorry she had left her cart again. This time, she knew, her goods weren't going to be there.

It was the day before Thanksgiving.

Four more black women had been found dead in midtown doorways.

Annie ran, the only way she knew how, into stores that had exits on other streets. Somewhere behind her, though she could not figure it out properly, there was trouble coming for her and the baby. It was so cold in the apartment. It was always so cold. The landlord cut off the heat, he always did it in early November, till the snow came. And she sat with the child, rocking him, trying to comfort him, trying to keep him warm. And when they came from Human Resources, from the City, to evict her, they found her still holding the child. When they took it away from her, so still and blue, Annie ran from them, into the streets; and she ran, she knew how to run, to keep running so she could live out here where they couldn't reach her and Alan. But she knew there was trouble behind her.

Now she came to an open place. She knew this. It was a new building they had put up, a new skyscraper, where there used to be shops that had good throwaway things in the cans and sometimes on the loading docks. It said Citicorp Mall and she ran inside. It was the day before Thanksgiving and there were many decorations. Annie rushed through into the central atrium, and looked around. There were escalators, and she dashed for one, climbing to a second story, and then a third. She kept moving. They would arrest her or throw her out if she slowed down.

At the railing, looking over, she saw the man in the court below. He didn't see her. He was standing, looking around.

Stories of mothers who lift wrecked cars off their children are legion.

When the police arrived, eyewitnesses swore it had been a stout, old black woman who had lifted the heavy potted tree in its terracotta urn, who had manhandled it up onto the railing and slid it along till she was standing above the poor dead man, and who had dropped it three stories to crush his skull. They swore it was true, but beyond a vague description of old, and black, and dissolute looking, they could not be of assistance. Annie was gone.

On the front page of the *Post* she wore as lining in her right shoe, was a photo of four men who had been arraigned for the senseless murders of more than a dozen bag ladies over a period of several months. Annie did not read the article.

It was close to Christmas, and the weather had turned bitter, too bitter to believe. She lay propped in the doorway alcove of the Post Office on 43rd and Lexington. Her rug was drawn around her, the stocking cap pulled down to the bridge of her nose, the goods in the string bags around and under her. Snow was just beginning to come down.

A man in a Burberry and an elegant woman in a mink approached from 42nd Street, on their way to dinner. They were staying at the New York Helmsley. They were from Connecticut, in for three days to catch the shows and to celebrate their eleventh wedding anniversary.

As they came abreast of her, the man stopped and stared down into the doorway. "Oh, Christ, that's awful," he said to his wife. "On a night like this, Christ, that's just awful."

"Dennis, *please!*" the woman said.

"I can't just pass her by," he said. He pulled off a kid glove and reached into his pocket for his money clip.

"Dennis, they don't like to be bothered," the woman said, trying to pull him away. "They're very self-sufficient. Don't you remember that piece in the *Times?*"

"It's damned near Christmas, Lori," he said, taking a twenty-dollar bill from the folded sheaf held by its clip. "It'll get her a bed for the night, at least. They can't make it out here by themselves. God knows, it's little enough to do." He pulled free of his wife's grasp and walked to the alcove.

He looked down at the woman swathed in the rug, and he could not see her face. Small puffs of breath were all that told him she was

alive. "Ma'am," he said, leaning forward. "Ma'am, please take this."
He held out the twenty.

Annie did not move. She never spoke on the street.

"Ma'am, please, let me do this. Go somewhere warm for the night,
won't you . . . please?"

He stood for another minute, seeking to rouse her, at least for a
go away that would free him, but the old woman did not move. Finally,
he placed the twenty on what he presumed to be her lap, there in
that shapeless mass, and allowed himself to be dragged away by his
wife.

Three hours later, having completed a lovely dinner, and having
decided it would be romantic to walk back to the Helmsley through
the six inches of snow that had fallen, they passed the Post Office and
saw the old woman had not moved. Nor had she taken the twenty
dollars. He could not bring himself to look beneath the wrappings to
see if she had frozen to death, and he had no intention of taking back
the money. They walked on.

In her warm place, Annie held Alan close up under her chin,
stroking him and feeling his tiny black fingers warm at her throat and
cheeks. *It's all right, baby, it's all right. We're safe. Shhh, my baby. No
one can hurt you.*

Psychologists specializing in ethology know of the soft monkey experiment. A mother
orangutan, whose baby has died, given a plush toy doll, will nurture it as if it were alive, as if
it were her own. Nurture and protect and savage any creature that menaces the surrogate.
Given a wire image, or a ceramic doll, the mother will ignore it. She must have the soft monkey.
It sustains her.

The Casebook of Dr. Billingsgate

Eric Wright

Every doctor sees himself as both artist and scientist. The perfect doctor holds the two in balance, but most doctors lean in one direction or the other. The greater the angle of lean, the worse the doctor.

The nearly purely scientific practitioner views the body as an arrangement of bones, muscles, nerves and sinews, cooking in blood. The artist sees these elements as under the control of the mind and spirit. The scientist dispenses in an attempt to readjust the chemical and mechanical imbalances he finds through examination, analysis, and laboratory tests. The artist listens, hoping to hear voices from the interior which, if properly answered, will make much physical tampering unnecessary.

Dr. Billingsgate was an artist; he even fancied himself a writer. His heroes were those doctors who had achieved best-sellerdom with accounts of curious and brilliantly treated patients who had come under their care. Some of these doctors were scientists, detectives who had sifted the evidence to find the causes of a mysterious affliction, usually affecting a group. But the ones Dr. Billingsgate admired were the psychologists and the psychiatrists, artists who had seen through the physical world to the disturbed soul beneath.

As a physician, Billingsgate retained enough science to check the physical symptoms and recognize influenza, jaundice, anemia, and so on when he found them. But even in the most obvious cases he remained suspicious as to why this patient and not his spouse or his children had contracted a disease, always on the lookout for the psychological answer. His interest manifested itself as the attitude of a deeply caring man. His patients felt properly listened to, and Billingsgate enjoyed a large practice as he asked his apparently irrelevant questions that seemed to have their origin in a medical knowledge so vast that no layman could hope to understand why he was asking them. Patients who complained about tiredness, for example, fearing they had contracted the latest fatigue syndrome, found themselves answering questions about their children, their jobs, even their sex lives, as Billingsgate burrowed for the truth.

The case of Jack Worsfold was almost too easy. Worsfold came to him, not on his own behalf, but, unknown to her, on behalf of his sister. He was worried about her, he said. She woke in the small hours, sometimes crying, and hardly ever went out of the house when the day's work was done. In general, she seemed to have lost interest in life.

Helena Worsfold was also his patient, and although he had not seen her for some time, Billingsgate was immediately on the alert as Worsfold rattled off the classical symptoms of depression. In the doctor's mind, there was no doubt from the start that Worsfold was talking about himself. It was a favorite device, not restricted to medicine, when someone was seeking advice about something he felt very private about.

While Worsfold talked, Billingsgate studied his history. The doctor's records were admirable, because they began with as much as he could find out about the patient's life and world and continued the narrative through every visit. They also included the patient's medical history. Other doctors might filter out the patient's peripheral chat, believing that to appear to be listening to the patient's troubles was to provide some form of therapy, while they stayed alert to hear the facts that could help them with the medical problem. Billingsgate did the reverse. Very often he taped the interviews, then wrote up the record, shaping it into a miniature biography. One day a selected dozen or fifteen of the most interesting might be worked up into a little book.

As he read Worsfold's history, he saw the whole background of the man's situation. Worsfold was fifty, and had lived with his sister for five years. She was two years older than he, so he probably invested her with a maternal role. Their parents had been killed in a car crash when the children were in their early twenties and must have left them a good deal of money, because Helena had retained a fair-sized house in Deer Park, belonged to the Granite Club, and maintained a Mercedes. Worsfold, though, had gone through his inheritance in a series of bad business ventures, all of which had ended in bankruptcy and quarrels with his partners. In the end he had been reduced to working for a living: he had failed to hold for long each of a series of jobs and now he was reduced to being on call as the backup driver for a limousine company.

Helena had taken him in and made a home for him, so Worsfold did not have to worry about his bed and board. In spite of his failures, all of which he could account for, he was still full of ideas for new business schemes. All he needed was a bit of capital, but the only source of capital, Helena, could not help because their parents had left her money in a trust and she required the approval of her lawyers to spend any major sum.

It was obvious now to Billingsgate that Worsfold was describing his own depression. He was going through a midlife crisis more severe than that of most people who felt they had somehow failed, because he really was a failure. Until now, his only physical problem had been a mild heart condition, probably congenital, which might at some time require an operation, but Worsfold had refused to see a specialist, and Billingsgate had not pressed him. The condition was mild enough so that if Worsfold lived a quiet life, emotionally and physically, he could live out his span without surgical interference. It occurred to Billingsgate now that Worsfold's heart might have been acting up lately, or rather, he thought, that the symptoms had man-ifested themselves psychosomatically, which would increase his anx-iety. He let his patient rattle on about his sister's purported condition, then said, "I'll talk to her. Ask her to come in."

Worsfold looked alarmed. "How? You can't tell her I've been worried about her. Anyway, she'll deny that there's anything wrong. She's like that. She's terrified of doctors and hospitals."

Now Billingsgate was sure of his man. Worsfold didn't want his story contradicted by a cheerful and optimistic Helena. "Tell her it's time for her flu shot. From what you've told me her symptoms are clear. I think I'll be able to tell if she's covering them up. Now what about you? No irregularity? Anything like that. The ticker behaving itself?"

"I've never felt better. Haven't been aware of my heart in months." He paused. "I do have a bit of a problem with insomnia, though. Could I get a prescription for that?"

Billingsgate nodded. Insomnia was a classical symptom of depression. He looked at Worsfold's record. "You already have a prescription for Zephyr, I think. Not working?"

"I need something different. I borrowed a Seconal from a man I know last week, and it worked perfectly."

"No problem. Take your shirt off and let me listen in a bit."

Heart, lungs, blood pressure—all about what he expected. He took his time examining Worsfold as he decided what to do. Worsfold almost certainly knew he was depressed—by the way he had chimed the symptoms off he had been looking them up somewhere and diagnosed himself, and Billingsgate suspected he was slightly ashamed of his condition. The doctor had often noticed that people over the age of fifty tended to regard nervous conditions in the first instance as self-inflicted, as though they should be able to cheer themselves up without inflicting their misery on everyone else. Probably the last traces of being taught as children to be self-reliant. He had considered doing a paper on the subject.

He finished examining Worsfold, then gave him a flu shot.

"A prescription?" Worsfold asked, as Billingsgate appeared to be waiting for him to go.

"Of course. Must get you a decent night's sleep." Billingsgate disappeared into his other office and returned with a small tube of capsules. "This is a sample," he said. "There's twenty-four here. Try half a one once a week to see if you can get yourself into a rhythm. These are better than Seconal; they won't leave you groggy, but they are just as strong. Stronger."

"How many?"

"Only half a one. A whole one if you absolutely have to, getting over jet lag, for example. Never more."

"So what about Helena? What can I do to help her get over this thing she has?"

Billingsgate considered the problem. Worsfold wanted him to give him some advice about his sister that he could take himself, of course. "Does she ever admit that she's depressed?" he asked.

"She has done sometimes, yes."

"When she does, don't try to jolly her out of it. Encourage her to bring her fears—because that's what they are—to the surface, to talk about them. If she can admit that she is afraid of something, even if it's something that is true, like"—here Billingsgate paused—"a sense of lack of accomplishment, even failure in some way, then she can begin to sort out the reality from her fears. Apart from that, try to provide regular diversions for her, and a regular life. Buy a season ticket for you both to the symphony, or a film club, something like that. Take a cooking course—get *her* to, I mean. Invite some people to dinner."

Billingsgate paused. He seemed to have said enough; Worsfold was nodding and buttoning his coat. "Come back in a couple of weeks and let me know how she is."

Helena came in for her flu shot the following week. She was a slightly untidy woman with a kind and silly look about her, as plump as her brother was lean. As he expected, she displayed none of the symptoms her brother had described. The only other thing he could discuss to provide an entry to his real interest was her ongoing hiatus hernia.

"Any attacks lately?"

"A small one, but it cleared up immediately. When I feel anything now I just take a few swigs from the bottle and that's that."

"What are you using?"

She reminded him of the particular brand of magnesium hydroxide she kept in the medicine cabinet. "Does it matter if it's mint-flavored?"

"Whatever tastes nicest. Don't be afraid of it. Just keep drinking it until the symptoms go. Remember it just *feels* like a heart attack. Your heart is as sound as a bell, so don't worry."

"Unlike Jack's," she said. "I worry about him."

It was a perfect opening. "He behaving . . . oddly?" he asked, leading her slightly.

"He's very morose. Bitter. He thinks the world sees him as a failure. I try to make a nice, cheerful home for him, but a man needs

his independence. I hope that they make him permanent at the limousine company. That'll give him a boost."

Now Billingsgate confronted the delicate question of patient con-
fidentiality. She was not entitled to his information about her brother,
but he thought of a clever way of getting her to talk. He told her of
Jack's worry about her.

"But that's not true," she cried. "I've never been happier. Before
Jack moved in I was beginning to wonder if I wasn't becoming a bit
eccentric, living alone, and so on . . ."

"If you wondered that, then you are in no danger," he cut in,
smiling. "Eccentrics think they are normal."

". . . but I have him to talk to and take care of now. He isn't very
forthcoming, but I can talk enough for two. We never quarrel."

Then Billingsgate told her of his diagnosis.

"Oh, poor Jack. What can I do to cheer him up?"

"Nothing," Billingsgate warned quickly. "On no account are you
to tell him of this conversation. He would never confide in me again,
even at second hand. If you see the symptoms becoming more pronounced, give me a call. But he and I will have to work this out."

Billingsgate had no doubt that he would hear from one of them
again soon, but a month went by before Helena made another ap-
pointment. When she arrived, he saw immediately that something
had happened.

"I simply wanted to tell you that whatever you said to him, whatever you did, he's a changed man. Much, much better. He's cheerful
and quite chatty—for him. And they've made him permanent at the
car company."

"Perhaps that did it."

"No, no. He was made permanent because he had changed. Don't
you see? The credit is all yours."

"His insomnia?"

"Completely gone. Of course I never noticed it in the first place."

When she left, Billingsgate got out Worsfold's chart and tried to
reconstruct the conversation he had had with the man for which
Helena was giving him such credit. Evidently his prescription was
working. The power of suggestion. Billingsgate wondered if a little
account of the case might be worked up for the next medical conven-

tion that was scheduled to take place aboard a cruise ship in January, something about treating a patient at second hand.

Six A.M. calls Billingsgate normally left to the answering service but they had discretion to wake him if the matter was urgent. There was a death at the Worsfold house. Could he go immediately?

It's not possible, Billingsgate thought, but fear got him to the house in ten minutes. Jack Worsfold was lying at the foot of the stairs, his neck broken, and there were signs that he had suffered a heart attack. Helena was hysterical. Billingsgate called for an ambulance and gave her a sedative. She was in a shocking condition, distraught with grief, her dressing gown smeared with blood from a cut on Worsfold's forehead, and with her white hair standing out like a fright wig. The ambulance left and Billingsgate got her to make some tea.

"I was having a bad night," she said. "Right after I went to bed at eleven, I had a hernia attack that persisted. I couldn't find the magnesia at first and I had to wake Jack, and he found an old bottle in the back of the medicine cabinet that still had enough left in it so I drank it all down. It did the trick eventually and I went back to sleep. Then, about five, I heard him try the handle of my door, but he never came in and I realized he was having one of those depressed mornings you mentioned, so I thought I'd get up and comfort him, make him some tea. He'd been so kind the night before.

"I went to the door and saw him just at the end of the hall. I switched on the light and called to him, just his name, not loud. Jack, I called, and he turned and screamed as if I were a ghost, then something funny happened to his face and he put his hand up to his chest and fell backwards. I killed him."

"It was an accident."

"No, I killed him. I frightened him."

"He'd seen you before, ready for bed, hadn't he?"

She was something of an apparition, though. In the corridor, with the light behind her, illuminating her hair, she would have been quite a sight. But enough to make Worsfold drop dead? "It was an accident, Miss Worsfold. He was depressed, and trying to go downstairs in the dark."

She shook her head. "There's something else. He was coming to me for help. Look." She held out the vial of sleeping pills that Billingsgate had given Worsfold. It was empty. "He must have swallowed them all then changed his mind, and he came to me and I didn't answer."

Billingsgate looked with horror at the empty tube. "It's not possible," he began. He stopped, then searched for some meaningless chat that would give him time to think. Finally he said, "Even if that were the case, what is the point of telling the world about it?"

"It'll come out in the autopsy, won't it?"

Committed now, he said, firmly, "There will be no autopsy. He died of a broken neck, in a fall, probably brought on by a heart attack. I imagine there will be an inquest, but the case is very clear."

"I suppose that's best. Anyway, they might blame you, mightn't they?"

"Me?"

"For prescribing the pills in his condition. That wouldn't be fair. You acted as you thought best, I know."

Billingsgate struggled with this one, then accepted it as the lesser of the two grim alternatives facing him. "I did, yes. One can never know everything. Now let's get you to bed."

She was very hard to console but eventually he got her back into bed and quietened down. If a policeman came, he told her, on no account was she to use silly phrases about killing her brother. They would be extremely suspicious, take her literally, and it could only upset her more. And on no account was she to mention the pills. She saw the point of what he was saying and subsided into misery.

Billingsgate searched Worsfold's room, and found, between two winter shirts, the bottle of magnesia that Helena had lost. He put that back in the medicine cabinet and made sure the empty vial of sleeping pills was in his pocket. In the bathroom he found the bottle of magnesia that Helena had finished, empty, but with enough left to be easily analyzed, and with traces of powder around the neck. He considered taking this, then put it back, realizing she might miss it and blurt out something about it when someone else was present. Then he sat on Worsfold's bed and thought about what would happen next. There was no question that it was an accident, but a coroner would certainly be involved. Without the vial of sleeping pills, there would be no need for an autopsy. If the vial were discovered, they would need to look at the contents of Worsfold's stomach, and finding nothing, would take the first step along the chain of inquiry that would discover that Worsfold had intended to murder his sister. Billingsgate had made an utter fool of himself. As a consequence, Worsfold was dead and his sister was alive, but how would Billingsgate come out? He could see himself giving evidence at the inquiry:

"I believed that he was depressed and might do himself some harm so I gave him a placebo, flavored chalk, instead of the sleeping pills he asked for. (I also wanted to conduct a little experiment with a placebo, just for the fun of it.)"

"I see," the coroner would say. "Now, the laboratory has established that this chalk was introduced into Miss Worsfold's medicine, which she drank the night before. Worsfold went to her room at five A.M., evidently with the idea of checking up on her, but lost his nerve, no doubt. However, she heard him in the corridor and went to the door, switched on the light, and called to him down the hall. Knowing the dose she had ingested, he assumed she was dead and he was seeing a ghost—I believe she might have looked extraordinary enough. He had a seizure and fell to his death. The verdict is clear: accidental death. But there is the matter of this practice of yours, Doctor Billingsgate, the practice of manipulating your patients' drugs without their knowledge, based in this case on an entirely false diagnosis. It's true that this time it had as happy a result as if you had divined Worsfold's mind accurately. But I think you'll have to stop it, and I shall inform your Association that they have a possible case for admonishment."

Oh, no. He could see the stories in the press now. Billingsgate went back to his office and sat staring out the window, knowing there was no real danger (he had edited Worsfold's record as soon as he returned), but appalled by the near miss. Gradually, though, his instinct for self-justification took over. He *had* seen through Worsfold's story, had he not? He had just misinterpreted what he saw. Could have happened to anybody. Hardly malpractice. After all, if he were just a pill-dispenser, Helena would be dead now, wouldn't she? One day he would tell the story, perhaps as a story he had heard from someone else.

Within a very short time he saw that he had just been unlucky. Then, in a very little more time, he was trying to think of another topic for a paper for the medical convention.

Imagine This

George C. Chesbro

" 'Imagine this,' " the pudgy FBI agent reads aloud, holding the open book very close to his face. I wonder if he is nearsighted, and if so, why he doesn't wear eyeglasses. I wonder if FBI agents, like fighter pilots, are supposed to have 20-20 vision. Perhaps he's vain. But then, why not wear contact lenses? Perhaps dry eyes, or an allergy? If he is nearsighted *and* vain, it would serve as description as well as characterization. These are matters of concern to me. " 'Here are words that can kill; this story is your death warrant, complete with a list of particulars giving the reasons you have been chosen to die.' " Now he lowers the book slightly, squints at me over the top of the page. "Did you write that?"

The police chief, having given up his desk to the FBI agent, sits in a straight-backed chair set against the mauve wall to my left. How to describe the office? Cluttered? Too trite. Except for a score of bowling trophies in a dusty case, which somehow look incongruous in a police chief's office, there just isn't much worth describing, certainly nothing to advance the cause of a piece of short fiction. The FBI agent interests me because he's overweight and nearsighted. He doesn't much look like an FBI agent, which could be a problem. I've never read of an FBI agent, or seen one depicted in films or on television, who didn't look the part as it had originally been cast by

J. Edgar Hoover. Would I dare to try to describe him as he is, against type, or would it be better to make him up? He's got even, improbably white teeth, probably capped, which means the FBI must have a good dental plan, but who cares? Technique. What to put in and what to leave out is always the problem; you want to create atmosphere, but not slow down the story. I wonder if a writer could ever get away with a story in which there was virtually no characterization or description of physical surroundings. It might be interesting to try. If worse came to worse, I could always call it an experiment in minimalism. "What?" I ask.

"I asked if you wrote the words I just read."

I desperately want to ask him if it's a trick question, but I restrain myself. "Of course I wrote them," I reply, making an effort to keep my tone civil so as not to sound snide or condescending. It's not that I fear the consequences of offending an FBI agent, it's just that I have a polite nature. "The story has my name on it, and I assume that has something to do with why I was called down here. So why do you ask if I wrote it? You know I wrote it."

"Why did you write those particular words?"

"It's the opening paragraph of a short story."

"Why did you write the story?"

"I was asked to. Or invited."

"You were asked to write *this* story?"

"I was invited to submit a story to be considered for inclusion in that collection you're holding. I did, and it was accepted. I don't understand what you're getting at."

"Why?"

"Why don't I understand what you're getting at?"

"Why were you asked to submit a story for this collection?"

"The editor knows me personally, and I have to assume he likes my work. We're both members of the International Association of Crime Writers, under whose aegis the anthology was published. All of the contributors are IACW members." I try to resist, but I can't. I add: "I hope I wasn't called down here just so you could tell me you don't like the piece. What are you, a literary critic?"

A bit of color appears high on the agent's cheekbones as he stares at me; I suppose I could even describe his look as a "hard" stare if I was feeling lazy. He appears to be trying not to squint, and I wonder if my features look fuzzy to him. I glance over at the police chief, who I'm not certain is even paying attention. For the first time I notice that he's wearing a toupee. It embarrasses me, and I quickly look away. The toupee on the man's head seems as out of place as the bowling trophies. It just seems wrong to me that a man wielding such authority should be wearing such a transparent and weak symbol of . . . symbol of what? Of what is a toupee a symbol? Nothing. It simply means that the chief of police here feels self-conscious about his baldness, so he wears the best toupee he can afford on a police chief's salary. Why should that make me feel uncomfortable? That probably gets too complicated, so I wouldn't use the toupee in any description of him. At the moment, I'm rather amused. I've always wondered what it would be like to be questioned by the FBI or CIA, wondered what kinds of questions they would ask. So far it's nothing to write home, or anywhere else, about. I would definitely have to make up a charged atmosphere and crisp dialogue, with dark, threatening undertones.

The FBI agent seems to sense that his stare—his hard stare—is not having its desired effect, that my thoughts are wandering, for he finally looks back at the book and resumes reading from my story. " 'But then, you have no imagination. You have no empathy, which forms the critical mass of both imagination and conscience, which are probably the same thing. A story cannot transport you into other people's minds. No story can make you feel anybody's anguish or anger but your own, for you lack imagination. You shed tears for no one but yourself. Like a dark sun, your egocentricity is sucking the life out of all the rest of us. You are a perfect example of the tenet that a sociopath who manages to stay out of prison and avoids becoming a serial killer can achieve great success in law or business, and especially in politics—however, in order to defend my deniability (Oh, how you've always loved that word!) in what is about to happen, I must hasten to add that I'm not stating here that you, the object of my profound hatred, necessarily practice any of these professions. I don't have to say what you do, or what you've done. You know who you are.' Who?"

Since I wrote, rewrote, edited and rewrote again what he's reading before I submitted it, I'm well aware of the text. My thoughts have been wandering again, but the second "who" gets my attention. I only wrote one "who" in that sentence. When I glance up and find him again squinting at me over the top of the book, I realize that the second "who" is a question directed at me. I ask, "What?"

"Who?" he repeats. "Who are you calling a sociopath? Who are you talking about?"

"Nobody in particular. Don't you understand that it's just a story? To *me*, the person referred to is a symbol, a composite of the kinds of monsters who rise to positions of power in our society and then proceed to wreak havoc in the lives of people all over the planet. But the writer of that death warrant is seriously pissed at a particular person. The writer actually intends to kill that person, after publicly announcing his intention in print for all the world to see, and get away with it."

"*You're* the writer."

"No. I'm the *author* of a story in which a writer writes a story which is actually a warning and an announcement of an intention to kill. I don't know who it is the writer's pissed at. I don't even know the sexes of the writer and the intended victim. It's not important. Don't you get it? Writing fiction means that you can make it up."

"You claim you just made all this up?"

What am I feeling here? A twinge of exasperation? "Of *course* I made it all up. That book you're holding in your hand is a collection of *fiction*, for Christ's sake! Are you putting me on? What is it you want to *know*? I'll be happy to sit here all day and have you read my own words to me, but I would think that a big FBI agent like yourself would have more important work to do."

"You're beginning to sound snide and condescending," the FBI agent says after a pause. There is a definite change in tone.

"I don't mean to. Actually, I have a polite nature."

"It would be a big mistake to treat me lightly."

"There's no doubt in my mind."

He again stares at me—yes, hard—for a few seconds before turning his attention back to the book. His voice rises slightly as he resumes reading my story, and he begins emphasizing certain words, occasionally bobbing his head up and down in a curious, bird-like motion. " 'Fiction has nothing to say to people like you, men and women without soul or imagination, and you're probably reading this only because you recognize my name, and you're curious. Perhaps you wonder what's become of me, although you don't really care. You may wonder how I can bear to continue living after what you did to

me. Most of all, you must wonder why someone should have anon-
ymously sent you a copy of an anthology with one of my stories in
it. I may have sent it to you—but not necessarily; you're not the only
murderous, thieving bastard who deserves to die, not the only soul-
crushing monster who will receive this sentence of execution cloaked
as a short story. I would dearly love to actually shove these pages
down your throat and watch you choke to death, but I'm not certain
I'll be able to manage that.' " The FBI agent slams the book down—
hard—on the police chief's desk. "See?"

"See what?"

"You *admit* that it's not really a story. You actually *are* threatening
to kill somebody!"

"Don't be absurd."

"It's all *written down*! How can you deny it?"

"Read the next paragraph."

Asking him to continue reading what he so obviously thinks is my
own indictment seems to catch him off guard. He hesitates, but then
picks up the volume and leafs through it until he finds the page where
he left off. Squinting, he runs his index finger down the page until
he finds his place, then resumes reading. " 'But enough of this self-
referencing. Let me cut right to the chase, as it were, since I only
have three to five thousand words in which to demonstrate that, yes,
it is *you* I'm writing to, *you* whose life I am going to end in retribution
for all the lives you have ended or blighted. Fear, I know, is one
emotion you are capable of feeling.' " He pauses and looks at me. If
I could find a fresh way of describing uncertainty reflected in a man's
eyes, that is what I would proceed to do. "What the hell is 'self-
referencing'?"

"The story purposely calls attention to the fact that it's a story."

"But it's *not* a story. You come right out and *admit* that it's not a
story."

"You're missing the point. It *is* a story—that refers to itself. I
mean, can't you—?"

I stop in mid-sentence when I realize that the agent is no longer
squinting at me; his pale green eyes are clearly in focus as he stares
at me. I have written hundreds of times about characters reflecting
some emotion or another in their eyes, but it has always been just a
literary device. Now I actually do see anger in this man's eyes. Worse,
I see contempt, and that bothers me. In fact, I now wonder if he was

ever actually squinting, or whether I just imagined it as a kind of protective distancing device. Also, he no longer appears to be over-weight. I wonder if I focused in on the police chief's cheap toupee because he is a man who can take away my freedom. Fiction means you can make it up, imagine any kind of bizarre, dangerous situation, and then walk away from it unscathed simply by putting down your pen. It is imagined danger. The FBI agent, I realize, really believes that I have done harm, and he means to do me harm. He is my enemy, and I cannot make him go away, cannot erase, tear up, or unimagine him.

Now he reads even more slowly, emphasizing almost every word. " 'To describe you in too much detail could expose me to prosecution after your death, especially in the likely event that this volume is found near your corpse, perhaps on your end table next to the bed. Above all else I must be able to maintain the fiction that this is just another of my fictions, and carries no weight beyond itself. This story must appear to be as insular as your mind. To my knowledge, you have never actually been physically present when any of your victims were murdered, as I may not be present when you are murdered. Like you, I will have someone else perform the actual killing. But you are not only a killer of people, but a destroyer of hope, which is to say the slayer of imagination: thus it is only fitting that an imaginer should kill you. At the risk of mixing my metaphors, I ask: Are you beginning to get the picture? Can you see yourself in it? Is your executioner entering your home or place of business, or coming up behind you now, even as you read this? You'd best take a look over your shoulder.' " Now the FBI agent, my enemy, slowly closes the book and sets it to one side before saying to me quietly, "What you've written makes you, at the least, an accomplice to murder."

"Whose murder?"

"The person to whom this was written. I want you to tell me that person's name."

"It was written at the request of the editor of that crime fiction anthology. His name's on the jacket, and he's still alive."

He is silent for some time. When he does finally speak, it is to quote more of my own words to me, from memory. " 'After all, who is better suited to commit a perfect crime, a perfect murder, than a professional imaginer? I just want you to know that I am the one planning your murder, although I will be far away, in possession of

a perfect alibi, when another professional imaginer, who has no personal link to you, takes your life. As you can see, I don't mind con-
fessing this in public, because the fact that I am a professional imaginer
will enable me to get away with it.' "

"It's just a story."

"What the hell would make you even *think* of writing something
like this if you weren't serious about actually doing what you say
you're going to do?"

All of this time I have been assuming that the FBI is merely
interested in harassing me because of what I had to say about America
and Americans, Republicans in general and Ronald Reagan and
George Bush in particular, Oliver North, James Watt, religion in
general and fundamentalists in particular. Now it strikes me that the
man may actually think I've killed somebody, and I'm uncertain how
to respond to such monumental stupidity.

"Look," I say, no longer making any effort to hide my impatience
and growing disdain. "Let me try to make it really simple for you.
I've already told you that I was invited to contribute a story to an
anthology of crime fiction; the working title for the collection was *The
New Mystery*. Stories were to be three to five thousand words long,
and contributors were encouraged to be 'innovative' and 'explosive.'
Well, what's 'explosive'? Violence? Gore? I didn't think so. I think
that fiction has largely exhausted itself in the past twenty years. How
can you out-fantasize the headlines in the daily newspaper? *Ideas*
can still be explosive, but the most explosive ideas can't—maybe
shouldn't—be written about. You have to be careful. 'Explosive'?
What was I supposed to write about? The fact that the masses are
asses, as witnessed by the absolute, roaring stupidity of the majority
of the American people in electing Republicans whose Holy Grail is
to redistribute ever-increasing amounts of wealth into the bank accounts of people who are already the wealthiest in the nation? How
about the irritation a lot of non-Jews feel when some Jews act like
they want to claim an exclusive franchise on suffering? I mean, how
many people does a government have to kill before the slaughter can
properly be called a 'holocaust'? Human history is one long holocaust.
Should I write about self-pitying blacks who use slavery as an excuse
for every failure? What about the insanity of religious belief? Maybe
I should have done a piece on demonic possession. Should I have

written about the madness and mischief of Cardinal O'Connor in New York spooking an untold number of good Roman Catholic kids by warning them that they might wake up some morning and find that they've caught a demon like they might have caught a cold? Hey, you can't make this stuff up. How's a fiction writer supposed to compete? You think I'm going to try to write fiction about any of those topics? No way. I'd be labeled antisemitic, racist, and anti-American. That's bad for business, and it would serve no purpose. This country has been destroyed by a succession of leaders who've corrupted language and substituted symbols for thought, as witness George Bush clowning around in a flag factory. Ronald Reagan was a cartoon character, Roger Rabbit running this country for eight years. Hey, how about James Meredith, of all people, going to work as a PR flack for Jesse Helms, of all people? Can you top this? Garry Trudeau is the only successful and serious fiction writer working in America today, because he had the prescience to realize that our entire society has become the equivalent of a cartoon strip. And I'm supposed to write something 'explosive' in a short story? Give me a break."

"You're a very angry man," the FBI agent says in an even tone. Now I imagine he's squinting again, although it could merely be a thoughtful expression.

"Not really. I'm more baffled than angry. I'm just amazed at the incredible fantasies the American people will believe are the truth when a story is told by a man in a flag factory, or tales spun by a megalomaniac in a uniform testifying before Congress. I'm baffled by the lack of imagination in people who slaughter women and children and call it a battle for freedom, and the people who allow such a thing to be done in their name. As George Bush would say, there's no 'vision thing' left in America. Now *these* things are 'explosive,' but there's no way to write fiction about them. If you want to send a message, you should use Western Union."

"But you did send a message," the agent says quietly. "And you were angry enough to kill."

"No. I wrote a story. If I couldn't think of anything explosive to write about, then I decided that I would at least try to be innovative. I imagined—and imagined *is* the operative word—a group of fiction writers joining in a conspiracy to remove some of the more destructive sociopaths and murderers from our midst. These writers would form a kind of star chamber to select appropriate victims, people who were overwhelmingly deserving of death, and then pool their imaginations to think up ways to kill the victims, and get away with it. One of these writers who had been invited to submit a story for an anthology would use the occasion to write a general indictment, a sort of calling card that would be sent to each victim just before he or she was killed by a member or members of the conspiracy—but never including the writer who had written the story. The name of the story would be 'Imagine This.' It's an exercise in self-referencing, an experiment in exploring the line between what is real and what is not, between fact and fiction. But there is no reality to the piece itself. It's just a story. Get it?"

"You've killed twenty-three people with that damn story."

"I've killed nobody. I'm a writer, not a murderer."

"Since this book with your story in it was published, copies have been found next to the corpses of twenty-three murder victims in eleven states. One victim was found with the pages of 'Imagine This' pinned to his heart with a foot-long butcher knife. Another victim was found with the pages of your story crammed down his throat— just as you suggested might, or even should, happen. What you've written has become a murder weapon."

How to describe my reaction? I do actually get a chill, but am I startled? Surprised? I really shouldn't be surprised. I should have realized that the FBI wouldn't be questioning me about the story if some crime hadn't been committed in connection with it. I had been rather enjoying my interrogation, but no more; now reality has indeed intruded upon my fiction. Although what has happened *was* the actual premise of the story, I had never imagined that people would actually die as a result of my having written it. Explosive, indeed. I need time to think about this, away from this police station. It's time to go home or go to jail.

"If you're going to charge me with something, do it," I say as I rise from my chair. "If not, I'm leaving."

"Just a minute!"

Despite my intention to keep walking straight out of the office, I do not. I turn back to face the FBI agent.

"Maybe you didn't have anything to do with the actual killing of these people," the man says, his voice trembling slightly. "It may be true that the victims did some pretty nasty things that destroyed other people's lives. But what was *their* side of the story? We'll never know now, will we? These killers are clever people; all of the murders were meticulously planned and executed. Still, we'll catch them. But what are we supposed to do with you? You *incited* those people to murder. First you romanticized vigilante acts of murder, and then you gave people with grievances permission to murder. You fired their imaginations. You killed with those words you wrote. You caused other people to kill, and that makes you responsible."

"It does not make me responsible. There are a great many angry people in our society. Whoever committed those murders had their own reasons; they didn't need me to give them permission, or to fire their imaginations. Leaving my story beside the corpses was just their way of trying to be clever."

"Like you were trying to be clever by writing it in the first place."

"I'm a fiction writer. I write stories for a living, and I hope some of them are clever."

"You're a coward. You write something that gives people ideas about murder, and when they do murder you hide behind the claim that what you wrote is just fiction."

" 'Imagine This' is just fiction."

"But it's *killed* people!"

"No."

"If I have my way, you'll be indicted for *something*, mister! Or maybe someday you, or someone you love, will have that story delivered to you, or them, as a prelude to being murdered."

"Is that a threat?"

"Of course not."

"Wishful thinking?"

"I'm trying to get you to accept responsibility for what you've *done!*"

"All I've done is write a piece of fiction," I say before I turn around and walk out of the office. I'm upset, but the confrontation with the FBI agent has also stimulated me. I have an idea, and I'm eager to get on with it. I imagine I will go home and write a story, complete with the appropriate fictional devices of adequate description and colorful characterization, about being questioned about the story I have written.

A Boy and His Dog

Manuel Vásquez Montalbán

For some time the minister of commerce had been saying that the
modernization of industry was having a generally positive impact,
effecting lasting change. Our country's industries, Señor Croissier
claimed, are being completely transformed by runaway change. The
intelligent, the progressive reaction is not to try to brake this motion,
but to do just the opposite, "to take advantage of the gathering mo-
mentum to assume our rightful place among the world's most advanced
countries." His message had no way to reach the boy: neither by the
direct route, reading—he couldn't read—nor by an indirect route,
oral transmission, through friend or family. His family came and went
like flickering shadows; the steadiest might have been his mother,
always between two drunken sprees or two crazy love affairs. His
mother maintained a drawn-out silence punctuated by an occasional
look of surprise at the way he kept popping up from time to time, as
if demanding time and space in the life of a woman without a sense
of space and time. His older brothers prowled the farthest corners of
the city while his younger brothers peed softly in the corners of their
room, gumming the same chunk of bread as yesterday or fighting over
the chocolate bars the boy brought them from time to time. The
candy bars were the product of a pact he'd made with a shopkeeper
he'd tried to rob, waving a penknife at her. "How old are you?"

"Seven." "Put that knife away and I'll give you a thousand pesetas." They ended up agreeing that he would come by now and then and she'd have something for him, but never money. "No money, you'd just spend it on nasty habits." And he did have a nasty habit, which he indulged in basements that had been left to water and rats, or between old factories and stores that were in the final throes of disintegration. He shot up with the help of Superhands, a twelve-year-old pickpocket who stood head and shoulders above his competition in the Clot slum; but the boy wasn't "hooked," the needle was just a diversion when he was low, when he was too tired to run the city streets breaking into cars and sticking up shabby little stores that were mostly run by slow-moving old ladies who couldn't find their voices or their feet when they saw the point of his knife like a tongue sticking out from a snake with hooded eyes. A neutral observer—the minister of commerce, for example, or the managers of the Bank of Spain who were responsible for raising the interest rate—might have remarked that the boy would be perfect as a beggar in a neorealist film, except that his miserable beauty was diminished a little by his lifeless eyes, which did not light up for the more stimulating aspects of reality. This would be no more than a literary device to get across the fact that the boy's eyes held no illusions, neither in them nor behind them.

And in this respect he was like the dog. The misfortunes of the animal had begun the day that the children of an insurance inspector, a man at the top of his field, had accepted their father's criticisms of the dog's eyes. Not only was he a mutt, but his eyes were two different colors besides, and the inspector, when he got tired of watching television, inevitably found his glance wandering to the little dog, huddled in one corner of the living room, and he couldn't suppress a grimace of disgust. "Don't look at me, Russky," he commanded in an irritable voice, and the dog hid his head between his paws so he couldn't be seen or be forced to see the displeasure that surrounded him. He wasn't a puppy anymore, and he sometimes felt the need—very very rarely, it's true—to pee on the corner of an imitation Persian rug that marked the twenty square yards of lawn that the inspector tended over and over outside his second-floor flat, which faced the sea in a development with a swimming pool, a tennis court, and a social club where they played cards and ate paella in summer and wild boar civets

in winter. If there wasn't any other reason to break the old tie the
family felt to the dog, the veterinarian charged five thousand pesetas
for removing a sebaceous cyst that had grown on one leg, and he
couldn't promise that there wouldn't be others. That's right, this one
is benign. All that was left to do was convince the kids that dogs are
a lot happier running free than cooped up in apartments, and as
fawning as Russky could be when he wanted to, he wouldn't have
any trouble finding a new owner. And so he was set loose in a park:
the tiniest push made him jump from the car, Russky taking off fast,
starting a mad dash in pursuit of the nature that had been offered him
like the unexpected gift of a May afternoon. It had been the youngest
boy's express condition that Russky be abandoned when the weather
was nice, because the dog had thin skin and not much fat on his bones,
and he was a little sensitive to cold, maybe a little over-sensitive.

He survived for some time playing Snoopy off the generosity of
the same neighborhood where he'd been abandoned, and he learned
to climb up the big square plastic garbage bins, tip them over, and
pick out the few morsels that were left by citizens who had learned
the principle of letting no food go to waste and even finding a use for
the bones. Yes he had bones, but Russky had a liver that was not
really equipped for so many leftover treats, contradicting the popular
belief, apparently false and malicious, that bones are the ideal food
for dogs. A popular belief, like so many, dreamt up by men over the
centuries to not only keep the best part of the spoils for themselves,
but to maintain the virtues of the scraps they left. Poorly fed, mangy,
his frame warped and maimed after he was hit by a Peugeot 505
Turbo, Russky had become an ugly-looking, foul-smelling dog; a dog
who couldn't even inspire pity among ugly-looking, foul-smelling people, themselves bony and dog-tired. Just the opposite. They were
probably the hardest on him, and that's why, when the boy and the
dog first met, Russky sensed he would be attacked and, being smart
and well aware that the best defense is a good offense, he beat the
boy to the punch.

The bite lingered on the thin calf of the street urchin like a purple
kiss of death. Superhands said the dog could be rabid and that he'd
been foolish not to catch it and bring it to the park so they could
observe it. "Stray dogs have really bad bites, and you could die of

rabies, which is a terrible way to die." His mother—summoned between absences by the boy's anguished cry—was of the same opinion.
As soon as she saw the bite and found out how he had gotten it, she
set up a howl like a hired mourner and invited their ghostly neighbors
to witness it with their own eyes. "You have to bring back the dog,
dead or alive" was the diagnosis, and the boy went back out in the
street, this time not to try to sell ballpoint pens or papers to motorists
trapped in the nets of red lights, not to steal the purses of little old
ladies, not to crack the side windows of cars looking for digital radios
or other less high-tech booty. This time he was obsessively searching
for the dog, scattering shouts and stories in every direction, in the
belief that such a revolting dog would be easy to spot and hard to
forget. This was where he got some invaluable help from Fizz, so
called because whether the boy was talking or not, there were always
bubbles of foam between his lips, which had lost him more than one
client after he'd been picked out and identified from the initial line-
up and the sometime lover had had time to take in a little more visual
detail. Fizz spent the day leaning against a lamppost that Russky
sometimes approached to fool himself. Not from an urge to pee, but
to pretend that he was still a dog with the instinct and authority to
mark out his own territory.

It was Fizz who said that Russky had just gone by; he had seen
him two blocks away sniffing at a wad of paper plates, to smell out
whether its core contained any pitiful scrap of food. The boy crept
up on him with every attempt at stealth, but not enough so that the
animal didn't lift his head and look at him with his green eye, though
keeping the blue eye more or less glued to the potential treasure. And
although the boy used a friendly voice to call him and pretended to
have something for him in the hand he extended, Russky backed off
and broke into a run up the sidewalk when he saw a kick coming from
Fizz, and to elude him he ran into a doorway that had no other exit
than a stairway that rose high above the insignificance of his bony
frame and mangy fur. Hobbling, he went up the stairway, sniffing
every side and turning his head to verify that Fizz and the boy were
sticking to their pursuit. And he kept this up till he got to the last
landing and offered his pursuers the surrender of a helpless animal,
a desperate parody of Snoopy that had won him a few kind words,

a few extra tidbits in the past. With his back on the ground, his feet in the air, and his head tilted to one side to offer his throat, while his tail wagged from east to west, uncertain of the proper directions, he didn't see or didn't wish to see the knife the boy held in his hand, while he pushed Fizz off with the other. "Leave him to me, it's my business." And he stabbed him twice in the neck, and when the dog leapt up as if he wanted to hang from his own howl of anguish, he was stabbed twice more in the body, and then twice more, and a final four times that were just to get the blood flowing, while his pointy snout turned like the needle of a compass and the skin stretched back over his teeth in a posthumous display of ferocity.

The boy put his quarry in a garbage bag and took him to analyze whether he had had rabies. Russky had had runaway cirrhosis, but not rabies. The boy went back to his streets and to our indifference, while the dog became food for the tiger in the zoo, who though he was born in captivity has the sense to roar now and again with the accent of Punjab, distant home of his ancestors. As for Señor Croissier, minister of commerce, he announced in the Twentieth Century Club that adapting to the pace of the technological revolution was a simple matter, but the agents of social power must monitor its progress carefully, and the Bank of Spain, for its part, yesterday responded by raising the price of money lent to financial institutions, banks, and savings and loans, continuing its policy of restricting the supply of money to accelerate the attainment of the goals of monetary growth that have been set for the current year.

Translated by Carol Christensen and Thomas Christensen

A Good Man Is Hard to Find

Flannery O'Connor

The grandmother didn't want to go to Florida. She wanted to visit some of her connections in east Tennessee and she was seizing every chance to change Bailey's mind. Bailey was the son she lived with, her only boy. He was sitting on the edge of his chair at the table, bent over the orange sports section of the *Journal*. "Now look here, Bailey," she said, "see here, read this," and she stood with one hand on her thin hip and the other rattling the newspaper at his bald head. "Here this fellow that calls himself The Misfit is aloose from the Federal Pen and headed toward Florida and you read here what it says he did to these people. Just you read it. I wouldn't take my children in any direction with a criminal like that aloose in it. I couldn't answer to my conscience if I did."

Bailey didn't look up from his reading so she wheeled around then and faced the children's mother; a young woman in slacks, whose face was as broad and innocent as a cabbage and was tied around with a green headkerchief that had two points on the top like rabbit's ears. She was sitting on the sofa, feeding the baby his apricots out of a jar. "The children have been to Florida before," the old lady said. "You all ought to take them somewhere else for a change so they would see different parts of the world and be broad. They never have been to east Tennessee."

The children's mother didn't seem to hear her, but the eight-year-old boy, John Wesley, a stocky child with glasses, said, "If you don't want to go to Florida, why dontcha stay at home?" He and the little girl, June Star, were reading the funny papers on the floor.

"She wouldn't stay at home to be queen for a day," June Star said without raising her yellow head.

"Yes, and what would you do if this fellow, The Misfit, caught you?" the grandmother asked.

"I'd smack his face," John Wesley said.

"She wouldn't stay at home for a million bucks," June Star said. "Afraid she'd miss something. She has to go everywhere we go."

"All right, Miss," the grandmother said. "Just remember that the next time you want me to curl your hair."

June Star said her hair was naturally curly.

The next morning the grandmother was the first one in the car, ready to go. She had her big black valise that looked like the head of a hippopotamus in one corner, and underneath it she was hiding a basket with Pitty Sing, the cat, in it. She didn't intend for the cat to be left alone in the house for three days because he would miss her too much and she was afraid he might brush against one of the gas burners and accidentally asphyxiate himself. Her son, Bailey, didn't like to arrive at a motel with a cat.

She sat in the middle of the back seat with John Wesley and June Star on either side of her. Bailey and the children's mother and the baby sat in the front and they left Atlanta at eight forty-five with the mileage on the car at 55890. The grandmother wrote this down because she thought it would be interesting to say how many miles they had been when they got back. It took them twenty minutes to reach the outskirts of the city.

The old lady settled herself comfortably, removing her white cotton gloves and putting them up with her purse on the shelf in front of the back window. The children's mother still had on slacks and still had her head tied up in a green kerchief, but the grandmother had on a navy blue straw sailor hat with a bunch of white violets on the brim and a navy blue dress with a small white dot in the print. Her collar and cuffs were white organdy trimmed with lace and at her neckline she had pinned a purple spray of cloth violets containing a sachet. In case of an accident, anyone seeing her dead on the highway would know at once that she was a lady.

She said she thought it was going to be a good day for driving, neither too hot nor too cold, and she cautioned Bailey that the speed limit was fifty-five miles an hour and that the patrolmen hid themselves behind bill-boards and small clumps of trees and sped out after you before you had a chance to slow down. She pointed out interesting details of the scenery: Stone Mountain; the blue granite that in some places came up to both sides of the highway; the brilliant red clay banks slightly streaked with purple; and the various crops that made rows of green lace-work on the ground. The trees were full of silver-white sunlights and the meanest of them sparkled. The children were reading comic magazines and their mother had gone back to sleep.

"Let's go through Georgia fast so we won't have to look at it much," John Wesley said.

"If I were a little boy," said the grandmother, "I wouldn't talk about my native state that way. Tennessee has the mountains and Georgia has the hills."

"Tennessee is just a hillbilly dumping ground," John Wesley said, "and Georgia is a lousy state too."

"You said it," June Star said.

"In my time," said the grandmother, folding her thin veined fingers, "children were more respectful of their native states and their parents and everything else. People did right then. Oh look at the cute little pickaninny!" she said and pointed to a Negro child standing in the door of a shack. "Wouldn't that make a picture, now?" she asked and they all turned and looked at the little Negro out of the back window. He waved.

"He didn't have any britches on," June Star said.

"He probably didn't have any," the grandmother explained. "Little niggers in the country don't have things like we do. If I could paint, I'd paint that picture," she said.

The children exchanged comic books.

The grandmother offered to hold the baby and the children's mother passed him over the front seat to her. She set him on her knee and bounced him and told him about the things they were passing. She rolled her eyes and screwed up her mouth and stuck her leathery thin face into his smooth bland one. Occasionally he gave her a faraway smile. They passed a large cotton field with five or six graves fenced in the middle of it, like a small island. "Look at the graveyard!" the grandmother said, pointing it out. "That was the old family burying ground. That belonged to the plantation."

"Where's the plantation?" John Wesley asked.

"Gone With the Wind," said the grandmother. "Ha. Ha."

When the children finished all the comic books they had brought, they opened the lunch and ate it. The grandmother ate a peanut butter sandwich and an olive and would not let the children throw the box and the paper napkins out the window. When there was nothing else to do they played a game by choosing a cloud and making the other two guess what shape it suggested. John Wesley took one the shape of a cow and June Star guessed a cow and John Wesley said, no, an automobile, and June Star said he didn't play fair, and they began to slap each other over the grandmother.

The grandmother said she would tell them a story if they would keep quiet. When she told a story, she rolled her eyes and waved her head and was very dramatic. She said once when she was a maiden lady she had been courted by a Mr. Edgar Atkins Teagarden from Jasper, Georgia. She said he was a very good-looking man and a gentleman and that he brought her a watermelon every Saturday afternoon with his initials cut in it, E.A.T. Well, one Saturday, she said, Mr. Teagarden brought the watermelon and there was nobody at home and he left it on the front porch and returned in his buggy to Jasper, but she never got the watermelon, she said, because a nigger boy ate it when he saw the initials, E.A.T.! This story tickled John Wesley's funny bone and he giggled and giggled but June Star didn't think it was any good. She said she wouldn't marry a man that just brought her a watermelon on Saturday. The grandmother said she would have done well to marry Mr. Teagarden because he was a gentleman and had bought Coca-Cola stock when it first came out and that he had died only a few years ago, a very wealthy man.

They stopped at The Tower for barbecued sandwiches. The Tower was a part-stucco and part-wood filling station and dance hall set in a clearing outside of Timothy. A fat man named Red Sammy Butts ran it and there were signs stuck here and there on the building and for miles up and down the highway saying, TRY RED SAMMY'S FAMOUS BARBECUE. NONE LIKE FAMOUS RED SAMMY'S! RED SAM! THE FAT BOY WITH THE HAPPY LAUGH. A VETERAN! RED SAMMY'S YOUR MAN!

Red Sammy was lying on the bare ground outside The Tower with his head under a truck while a gray monkey about a foot high, chained to a small chinaberry tree, chattered nearby. The monkey sprang back into the tree and got on the highest limb as soon as he saw the children jump out of the car and run toward him.

Inside, The Tower was a long dark room with a counter at one end and tables at the other and dancing space in the middle. They all sat down at a broad table next to the nickelodeon and Red Sam's wife, a tall burnt-brown woman with hair and eyes lighter than her skin, came and took their order. The children's mother put a dime in the machine and played "The Tennessee Waltz," and the grandmother said that tune always made her want to dance. She asked Bailey if he would like to dance but he only glared at her. He didn't have a naturally sunny disposition like she did and trips made him nervous. The grandmother's brown eyes were very bright. She swayed her head from side to side and pretended she was dancing in her chair. June Star said play something she could tap to so the children's mother put in another dime and played a fast number and June Star stepped out onto the dance floor and did her tap routine.

"Ain't she cute?" Red Sam's wife said, leaning over the counter. "Would you like to come be my little girl?"

"No, I certainly wouldn't," June Star said. "I wouldn't live in a broken-down place like this for a million bucks!" and she ran back to the table.

"Ain't she cute?" the woman repeated, stretching her mouth politely.

"Aren't you ashamed?" hissed the grandmother.

Red Sam came in and told his wife to quit lounging on the counter and hurry up with these people's order. His khaki trousers reached just to his hip bones and his stomach hung over them like a sack of meal swaying under his shirt. He came over and sat down at a table nearby and let out a combination sigh and yodel. "You can't win," he said. "You can't win," and he wiped his sweating red face off with a gray handkerchief. "These days you don't know who to trust," he said. "Ain't that the truth?"

"People are certainly not nice like they used to be," said the grandmother.

"Two fellers come in here last week," Red Sammy said, "driving a Chrysler. It was an old beat-up car but it was a good one and these boys looked all right to me. Said they worked at the mill and you know I let them fellers charge the gas they bought? Now why did I do that?"

"Because you're a good man!" the grandmother said at once.

"Yes'm, I suppose so," Red Sam said as if he were struck with this answer.

His wife brought the orders, carrying the five plates all at once without a tray, two in each hand and one balanced on her arm. "It isn't a soul in this green world of God's that you can trust," she said. "And I don't count nobody out of that, not nobody," she repeated, looking at Red Sammy.

"Did you read about that criminal, The Misfit, that's escaped?" asked the grandmother.

"I wouldn't be a bit surprised if he didn't attack this place right here," said the woman. "If he hears about it being here, I wouldn't be none surprised to see him. If he hears it's two cent in the cash register, I wouldn't be a tall surprised if he. . . ."

"That'll do," Red Sam said. "Go bring these people their Co'Colas," and the woman went off to get the rest of the order.

"A good man is hard to find," Red Sammy said. "Everything is getting terrible. I remember the day you could go off and leave your screen door unlatched. Not no more."

He and the grandmother discussed better times. The old lady said that in her opinion Europe was entirely to blame for the way things were now. She said the way Europe acted you would think we were made of money and Red Sam said it was no use talking about it, she was exactly right. The children ran outside into the white sunlight and looked at the monkey in the lacy chinaberry tree. He was busy catching fleas on himself and biting each one carefully between his teeth as if it were a delicacy.

They drove off again into the hot afternoon. The grandmother took cat naps and woke up every few minutes with her own snoring. Outside of Toombsboro she woke up and recalled an old plantation that she had visited in this neighborhood once when she was a young lady. She said the house had six white columns across the front and that there was an avenue of oaks leading up to it and two little wooden trellis arbors on either side in front where you sat down with your suitor after a stroll in the garden. She recalled exactly which road to turn off to get to it. She knew that Bailey would not be willing to lose any time looking at an old house, but the more she talked about it, the more she wanted to see it once again and find out if the little twin arbors were still standing. "There was a secret panel in this house," she said craftily, not telling the truth but wishing that she were, "and the story went that all the family silver was hidden in it when Sherman came through but it was never found. . . ."

"Hey!" John Wesley said. "Let's go see it! We'll find it! We'll poke all the wood work and find it! Who lives there? Where do you turn off at? Hey Pop, can't we turn off there?"

"We never have seen a house with a secret panel!" June Star shrieked. "Let's go to the house with the secret panel! Hey, Pop, can't we go see the house with the secret panel!"

"It's not far from here, I know," the grandmother said. "It wouldn't take over twenty minutes."

Bailey was looking straight ahead. His jaw was as rigid as a horseshoe. "No," he said.

The children began to yell and scream that they wanted to see the house with the secret panel. John Wesley kicked the back of the front seat and June Star hung over her mother's shoulder and whined desperately into her ear that they never had any fun even on their vacation, that they could never do what THEY wanted to do. The baby began to scream and John Wesley kicked the back of the seat so hard that his father could feel the blows in his kidney.

"All right!" he shouted and drew the car to a stop at the side of the road. "Will you all shut up? Will you all just shut up for one second? If you don't shut up, we won't go anywhere."

"It would be very educational for them," the grandmother murmured.

"All right," Bailey said, "but get this. This is the only time we're going to stop for anything like this. This is the one and only time."

"The dirt road that you have to turn down is about a mile back," the grandmother directed. "I marked it when we passed."

"A dirt road," Bailey groaned.

After they had turned around and were headed toward the dirt road, the grandmother recalled other points about the house, the beautiful glass over the front doorway and the candle lamp in the hall. John Wesley said that the secret panel was probably in the fireplace.

"You can't go inside this house," Bailey said. "You don't know who lives there."

"While you all talk to the people in front, I'll run around behind and get in a window," John Wesley suggested.

"We'll all stay in the car," his mother said.

They turned onto the dirt road and the car raced roughly along in a swirl of pink dust. The grandmother recalled the times when there were no paved roads and thirty miles was a day's journey. The dirt road was hilly and there were sudden washes in it and sharp curves on dangerous embankments. All at once they would be on a hill, looking down over the blue tops of trees for miles around, then the next minute, they would be in a red depression with the dust-coated trees looking down on them.

"This place had better turn up in a minute," Bailey said, "or I'm going to turn around."

The road looked as if no one had traveled on it in months.

"It's not much farther," the grandmother said and just as she said it, a horrible thought came to her. The thought was so embarrassing that she turned red in the face and her eyes dilated and her feet jumped up, upsetting her valise in the corner. The instant the valise moved, the newspaper top she had over the basket under it rose with a snarl and Pitty Sing, the cat, sprang onto Bailey's shoulder.

The children were thrown to the floor and their mother, clutching the baby, was thrown out the door onto the ground; the old lady was thrown into the front seat. The car turned over once and landed right-side-up in a gulch on the side of the road. Bailey remained in the driver's seat with the cat—gray-striped with a broad white face and an orange nose—clinging to his neck like a caterpillar.

As soon as the children saw they could move their arms and legs, they scrambled out of the car, shouting, "We've had an ACCIDENT!" The grandmother was curled up under the dashboard, hoping she was injured so that Bailey's wrath would not come down on her all at once. The horrible thought she had had before the accident was that the house she had remembered so vividly was not in Georgia but in Tennessee.

Bailey removed the cat from his neck with both hands and flung it out the window against the side of a pine tree. Then he got out of the car and started looking for the children's mother. She was sitting against the side of the red gutted ditch, holding the screaming baby, but she only had a cut down her face and a broken shoulder. "We've had an ACCIDENT!" the children screamed in a frenzy of delight.

"But nobody's killed," June Star said with disappointment as the grandmother limped out of the car, her hat still pinned to her head but the broken front brim standing up at a jaunty angle and the violet spray hanging off the side. They all sat down in the ditch, except the children, to recover from the shock. They were all shaking.

"Maybe a car will come along," said the children's mother hoarsely.

"I believe I have injured an organ," said the grandmother, pressing her side, but no one answered her. Bailey's teeth were clattering. He had on a yellow sport shirt with bright blue parrots designed in it and his face was as yellow as the shirt. The grandmother decided that she would not mention that the house was in Tennessee.

The road was about ten feet above and they could see only the tops of the trees on the other side of it. Behind the ditch they were sitting in there were more woods, tall and dark and deep. In a few minutes they saw a car some distance away on top of a hill, coming slowly as if the occupants were watching them. The grandmother stood up and waved both arms dramatically to attract their attention. The car continued to come on slowly, disappeared around a bend and appeared again, moving even slower, on top of the hill they had gone over. It was a big black battered hearselike automobile. There were three men in it.

It came to a stop just over them and for some minutes, the driver looked down with a steady expressionless gaze to where they were sitting, and didn't speak. Then he turned his head and muttered something to the other two and they got out. One was a fat boy in black trousers and a red sweat shirt with a silver stallion embossed on the front of it. He moved around on the right side of them and stood staring, his mouth partly open in a kind of loose grin. The other had on khaki pants and a blue striped coat and a gray hat pulled down very low, hiding most of his face. He came around slowly on the left side. Neither spoke.

The driver got out of the car and stood by the side of it, looking down at them. He was an older man than the other two. His hair was just beginning to gray and he wore silver-rimmed spectacles that gave him a scholarly look. He had a long creased face and didn't have on any shirt or undershirt. He had on blue jeans that were too tight for him and was holding a black hat and a gun. The two boys also had guns.

"We've had an ACCIDENT!" the children screamed.

The grandmother had the peculiar feeling that the bespectacled man was someone she knew. His face was as familiar to her as if she had known him all her life but she could not recall who he was. He moved away from the car and began to come down the embankment, placing his feet carefully so that he wouldn't slip. He had on tan and white shoes and no socks, and his ankles were red and thin. "Good afternoon," he said. "I see you all had you a little spill."

"We turned over twice!" said the grandmother.

"Oncet," he corrected. "We see it happen. Try their car and see will it run, Hiram," he said quietly to the boy with the gray hat.

"What you got that gun for?" John Wesley asked. "Whatcha gonna do with that gun?"

"Lady," the man said to the children's mother, "would you mind calling them children to sit down by you? Children make me nervous. I want all you all to sit down right together there were you're at."

"What are you telling us what to do for?" June Star asked.

Behind them the line of woods gaped like a dark open mouth. "Come here," said their mother.

"Look here now," Bailey began suddenly, "we're in a predicament! We're in. . . ."

The grandmother shrieked. She scrambled to her feet and stood staring.

"You're The Misfit!" she said. "I recognized you at once!"

"Yes'm," the man said, smiling slightly as if he were pleased in spite of himself to be known, "but it would have been better for all of you, lady, if you hadn't of reckernized me."

Bailey turned his head sharply and said something to his mother that shocked even the children. The old lady began to cry and The Misfit reddened.

"Lady," he said, "don't you get upset. Sometimes a man says things he don't mean. I don't reckon he meant to talk to you thataway."

"You wouldn't shoot a lady, would you?" the grandmother said and removed a clean handkerchief from her cuff and began to slap at her eyes with it.

The Misfit pointed the toe of his shoe into the ground and made a little hole and then covered it up again. "I would hate to have to," he said.

"Listen," the grandmother almost screamed, "I know you're a good man. You don't look a bit like you have common blood. I know you must come from nice people!"

"Yes mam," he said, "finest people in the world." When he smiled he showed a row of strong white teeth. "God never made a finer woman than my mother and my daddy's heart was pure gold," he said. The boy with the red sweat shirt had come around behind them and was standing with his gun at his hip. The Misfit squatted down on the ground. "Watch them children, Bobby Lee," he said. "You know they make me nervous." He looked at the six of them huddled together in front of him and he seemed to be embarrassed as if he couldn't think of anything to say. "Ain't a cloud in the sky," he remarked, looking up at it. "Don't see no sun but don't see no cloud neither."

"Yes, it's a beautiful day," said the grandmother. "Listen," she said, "you shouldn't call yourself The Misfit because I know you're a good man at heart. I can just look at you and tell."

"Hush!" Bailey yelled. "Hush! Everybody shut up and let me handle this!" He was squatting in the position of a runner about to sprint forward but he didn't move.

"I pre-chate that, lady," The Misfit said and drew a little circle in the ground with the butt of his gun.

"It'll take a half a hour to fix this here car," Hiram called, looking over the raised hood of it.

"Well, first you and Bobby Lee get him and that little boy to step over yonder with you," The Misfit said, pointing to Bailey and John Wesley. "The boys want to ask you something," he said to Bailey. "Would you mind stepping back in them woods there with them?"

"Listen," Bailey began, "we're in a terrible predicament! Nobody realizes what this is," and his voice cracked. His eyes were as blue and intense as the parrots in his shirt and he remained perfectly still.

The grandmother reached up to adjust her hat brim as if she were going to the woods with him but it came off in her hand. She stood staring at it and after a second she let it fall on the ground. Hiram pulled Bailey up by the arm as if he were assisting an old man. John Wesley caught hold of his father's hand and Bobby Lee followed. They went off toward the woods and just as they reached the dark edge, Bailey turned and supporting himself against a gray naked pine trunk, he shouted, "I'll be back in a minute, Mamma, wait on me!"

"Come back this instant!" his mother shrilled but they all disappeared into the woods.

"Bailey Boy!" the grandmother called in a tragic voice but she found she was looking at The Misfit squatting on the ground in front of her. "I just know you're a good man," she said desperately. "You're not a bit common!"

"Nome, I ain't a good man," The Misfit said after a second as if he had considered her statement carefully, "but I ain't the worst in the world neither. My daddy said I was a different breed of dog from my brothers and sisters. 'You know,' Daddy said, 'it's some that can live their whole life out without asking about it and it's others has to know why it is, and this boy is one of the latters. He's going to be into everything!' " He put on his black hat and looked up suddenly and then away deep into the woods as if he were embarrassed again. "I'm sorry, I don't have on a shirt before you ladies," he said, hunching his shoulders slightly. "We buried our clothes that we had on when we escaped and we're just making do until we can get better. We borrowed these from some folks we met," he explained.

"That's perfectly all right," the grandmother said. "Maybe Bailey has an extra shirt in his suitcase."

"I'll look and see terrectly," The Misfit said.

"Where are they taking him?" the children's mother screamed.

"Daddy was a card himself," The Misfit said. "You couldn't put anything over on him. He never got in trouble with the Authorities though. Just had the knack of handling them."

"You could be honest too if you'd only try," said the grandmother. "Think how wonderful it would be to settle down and live a comfortable life and not have to think about somebody chasing you all the time."

The Misfit kept scratching in the ground with the butt of his gun as if he were thinking about it. "Yes'm, somebody is always after you," he murmured.

The grandmother noticed how thin his shoulder blades were just behind his hat because she was standing up looking down on him. "Do you ever pray?" she asked.

He shook his head. All she saw was the black hat wiggle between his shoulder blades. "Nome," he said.

There was a pistol shot from the woods, followed closely by another. Then silence. The old lady's head jerked around. She could hear the wind move through the tree tops like a long satisfied insuck of breath. "Bailey Boy!" she called.

"I was a gospel singer for a while," The Misfit said. "I been most everything. Been in the arm service, both land and sea, at home and abroad, been twict married, been an undertaker, been with the railroads, plowed Mother Earth, been in a tornado, seen a man burnt alive oncet," and he looked up at the children's mother and the little girl who were sitting close together, their faces white and their eyes glassy; "I even seen a woman flogged," he said.

"Pray, pray," the grandmother began, "pray, pray. . . ."

"I never was a bad boy that I remember of," The Misfit said in an almost dreamy voice, "but somewheres along the line I done something wrong and got sent to the penitentiary. I was buried alive," and he looked up and held her attention to him by a steady stare.

"That's when you should have started to pray," she said. "What did you do to get sent to the penitentiary that first time?"

"Turn to the right, it was a wall," The Misfit said, looking up again at the cloudless sky. "Turn to the left, it was a wall. Look up it was a ceiling, look down it was a floor. I forget what I done, lady. I set there and set there, trying to remember what it was I done and I ain't recalled it to this day. Oncet in a while, I would think it was coming to me, but it never come."

"Maybe they put you in by mistake," the old lady said vaguely.

"Nome," he said. "It wasn't no mistake. They had the papers on me."

"You must have stolen something," she said.

The Misfit sneered slightly. "Nobody had nothing I wanted," he said. "It was a head-doctor at the penitentiary said what I had done was kill my daddy but I known that for a lie. My daddy died in nineteen ought nineteen of the epidemic flu and I never had a thing to do with it. He was buried in the Mount Hopewell Baptist churchyard and you can go there and see for yourself."

"If you would pray," the old lady said, "Jesus would help you."

"That's right," The Misfit said.

"Well then, why don't you pray?" she asked trembling with delight suddenly.

"I don't want no hep," he said. "I'm doing all right by myself."

Bobby Lee and Hiram came ambling back from the woods. Bobby Lee was dragging a yellow shirt with bright blue parrots in it.

"Throw me that shirt, Bobby Lee," The Misfit said. The shirt came flying at him and landed on his shoulder and he put it on. The grandmother couldn't name what the shirt reminded her of. "No, lady," The Misfit said while he was buttoning it up, "I found out the crime don't matter. You can do one thing or you can do another, kill a man or take a tire off his car, because sooner or later you're going to forget what it was you done and just be punished for it."

The children's mother had begun to make heaving noises as if she couldn't get her breath. "Lady," he asked, "would you and that little girl like to step off yonder with Bobby Lee and Hiram and join your husband?"

"Yes, thank you," the mother said faintly. Her left arm dangled helplessly and she was holding the baby, who had gone to sleep, in the other. "Hep that lady up, Hiram," The Misfit said as she struggled to climb out of the ditch, "and Bobby Lee, you hold onto that little girl's hand."

"I don't want to hold hands with him," June Star said. "He reminds me of a pig."

The fat boy blushed and laughed and caught her by the arm and pulled her off into the woods after Hiram and her mother.

Alone with The Misfit, the grandmother found that she had lost her voice. There was not a cloud in the sky nor any sun. There was nothing around her but woods. She wanted to tell him that he must pray. She opened and closed her mouth several times before anything came out. Finally she found herself saying, "Jesus. Jesus," meaning, Jesus will help you, but the way she was saying it, it sounded as if she might be cursing.

"Yes'm," The Misfit said as if he agreed. "Jesus thrown everything off balance. It was the same case with Him as with me except He hadn't committed any crime and they could prove I had committed one because they had the papers on me. Of course," he said, "they never shown me my papers. That's why I sign myself now. I said long ago, you get you a signature and sign everything you do and keep a copy of it. Then you'll know what you done and you can hold up the crime to the punishment and see do they match and in the end you'll have something to prove you ain't been treated right. I call myself The Misfit," he said, "because I can't make what all I done wrong fit what all I gone through in punishment."

There was a piercing scream from the woods, followed closely by a pistol report. "Does it seem right to you, lady, that one is punished a heap and another ain't punished at all?"

"Jesus!" the old lady cried. "You've got good blood! I know you wouldn't shoot a lady! I know you come from nice people! Pray! Jesus, you ought not to shoot a lady. I'll give you all the money I've got!"

"Lady," The Misfit said, looking beyond her far into the woods, "there never was a body that give the undertaker a tip."

There were two more pistol reports and the grandmother raised her head like a parched old turkey hen crying for water and called, "Bailey Boy, Bailey Boy!" as if her heart would break.

"Jesus was the only One that ever raised the dead," The Misfit continued, "and He shouldn't have done it. He thrown everything off balance. If He did what He said, then it's nothing for you to do but throw away everything and follow Him, and if He didn't then it's nothing for you to do but enjoy the few minutes you got left the best way you can—by killing somebody or burning down his house or doing some other meanness to him. No pleasure but meanness," he said and his voice had become almost a snarl.

"Maybe He didn't raise the dead," the old lady mumbled, not knowing what she was saying and feeling so dizzy that she sank down in the ditch with her legs twisted under her.

"I wasn't there so I can't say He didn't," The Misfit said. "I wisht I had of been there," he said, hitting the ground with his fist. "It ain't right I wasn't there because if I had of been there I would of known. Listen lady," he said in a high voice, "if I had of been there I would of known and I wouldn't be like I am now." His voice seemed about to crack and the grandmother's head cleared for an instant. She saw the man's face twisted close to her own as if he were going to cry and she murmured, "Why, you're one of my babies. You're one of my own children!" She reached out and touched him on the shoulder. The Misfit sprang back as if a snake had bitten him and shot her three times through the chest. Then he put his gun down on the ground and took off his glasses and began to clean them.

Hiram and Bobby Lee returned from the woods and stood over the ditch, looking down at the grandmother who half sat and half lay in a puddle of blood with her legs crossed under her like a child's and her face smiling up at the cloudless sky.

Without his glasses, The Misfit's eyes were red-rimmed and pale and defenseless-looking. "Take her off and throw her where you thrown the others," he said, picking up the cat that was rubbing itself against his leg.

"She was a talker, wasn't she?" Bobby Lee said, sliding down the ditch with a yodel.

"She would of been a good woman," The Misfit said, "if it had been somebody there to shoot her every minute of her life."

"Some fun!" Bobby Lee said.

"Shut up, Bobby Lee," The Misfit said. "It's no real pleasure in life."

The Parker Shotgun

Sue Grafton

The Christmas holidays had come and gone, and the new year was underway. January, in California, is as good as it gets—cool, clear, and green, with a sky the color of wisteria and a surf that thunders like a volley of gunfire in a distant field. My name is Kinsey Millhone. I'm a private investigator, licensed, bonded, insured; white, female, age thirty-two, unmarried, and physically fit. That Monday morning, I was sitting in my office with my feet up, wondering what life would bring, when a woman walked in and tossed a photograph on my desk. My introduction to the Parker shotgun began with a graphic view of its apparent effect when fired at a formerly nice-looking man at close range. His face was still largely intact, but he had no use now for a pocket comb. With effort, I kept my expression neutral as I glanced up at her.

"Somebody killed my husband."

"I can see that," I said.

She snatched the picture back and stared at it as though she might have missed some telling detail. Her face suffused with pink, and she blinked back tears. "Jesus. Rudd was killed five months ago, and the cops have done shit. I'm so sick of getting the runaround I could scream."

She sat down abruptly and pressed a hand to her mouth, trying

355

to compose herself. She was in her late twenties, with a gaudy pret-
tiness. Her hair was an odd shade of brown, like cherry Coke, worn
shoulder length and straight. Her eyes were large, a lush mink brown;
her mouth was full. Her complexion was all warm tones, tanned, and
clear. She didn't seem to be wearing makeup, but she was still as vivid
as a magazine illustration, a good four-color run on slick paper. She
was seven months pregnant by the look of her; not voluminous yet,
but rotund. When she was calmer, she identified herself as Lisa
Osterling.

"That's a crime lab photo. How'd you come by it?" I said when
the preliminaries were disposed of.

She fumbled in her handbag for a tissue and blew her nose. "I
have my little ways," she said morosely. "Actually I know the photographer and I stole a print. I'm going to have it blown up and hung
on the wall just so I won't forget. The police are hoping I'll drop the
whole thing, but I got news for *them*." Her mouth was starting to
tremble again, and a tear splashed onto her skirt as though my ceiling
had a leak.

"What's the story?" I said. "The cops in this town are usually
pretty good." I got up and filled a paper cup with water from my
Sparklett's dispenser, passing it over to her.

She murmured a thank-you and drank it down, staring into the
bottom of the cup as she spoke. "Rudd was a cocaine dealer until a
month or so before he died. They haven't said as much, but I know
they've written him off as some kind of small-time punk. What do
they care? They'd like to think he was killed in a drug deal—a double
cross or something like that. He wasn't, though. He'd given it all up
because of this."

She glanced down at the swell of her belly. She was wearing a
Kelly green T-shirt with an arrow down the front. The word "Oops!"
was written across her breasts in machine embroidery.

"What's your theory?" I asked. Already I was leaning toward the
official police version of events. Drug dealing isn't synonymous with
longevity. There's too much money involved and too many amateurs
getting into the act. This was Santa Teresa—ninety-five miles north
of the big time in L.A., but there are still standards to maintain. A
shotgun blast is the underworld equivalent of a bad annual review.

"I don't have a theory. I just don't like theirs. I want you to look
into it so I can clear Rudd's name before the baby comes."

I shrugged. "I'll do what I can, but I can't guarantee the results. How are you going to feel if the cops are right?"

She stood up, giving me a flat look. "I don't know why Rudd died, but it had nothing to do with drugs," she said. She opened her handbag and extracted a roll of bills the size of a wad of socks. "What do you charge?"

"Thirty bucks an hour plus expenses."

She peeled off several hundred-dollar bills and laid them on the desk.

I got out a contract.

My second encounter with the Parker shotgun came in the form of a dealer's appraisal slip that I discovered when I was nosing through Rudd Osterling's private possessions an hour later at the house. The address she'd given me was on the Bluffs, a residential area on the west side of town, overlooking the Pacific. It should have been an elegant neighborhood, but the ocean generated too much fog and too much corrosive salt air. The houses were small and had a temporary feel to them, as though the occupants intended to move on when the month was up. No one seemed to get around to painting the trim, and the yards looked like they were kept by people who spent all day at the beach. I followed her in my car, reviewing the information she'd given me as I urged my ancient VW up Capilla Hill and took a right on Presipio.

The late Rudd Osterling had been in Santa Teresa since the sixties, when he migrated to the West Coast in search of sunshine, good surf, good dope, and casual sex. Lisa told me he'd lived in vans and communes, working variously as a roofer, tree trimmer, bean picker, fry cook, and forklift operator—never with any noticeable ambition or success. He'd started dealing cocaine two years earlier, apparently netting more money than he was accustomed to. Then he'd met and married Lisa, and she'd been determined to see him clean up his act. According to her, he'd retired from the drug trade and was just in the process of setting himself up in a landscape maintenance business when someone blew the top of his head off.

I pulled into the driveway behind her, glancing at the frame and stucco bungalow with its patchy grass and dilapidated fence. It looked like one of those households where there's always something under construction, probably without permits and not up to code. In this case, a foundation had been laid for an addition to the garage, but the weeds were already growing up through cracks in the concrete. A wooden outbuilding had been dismantled, the old lumber tossed in an unsightly pile. Closer to the house, there were stacks of cheap pecan wood paneling, sun-bleached in places and warped along one edge. It was all hapless and depressing, but she scarcely looked at it.

I followed her into the house.

"We were just getting the house fixed up when he died," she remarked.

"When did you buy the place?" I was manufacturing small talk, trying to cover my distaste at the sight of the old linoleum counter, where a line of ants stretched from a crust of toast and jelly all the way out the back door.

"We didn't really. This was my mother's. She and my stepdad moved back to the Midwest last year."

"What about Rudd? Did he have any family out here?"

"They're all in Connecticut, I think, real la-di-dah. His parents are dead, and his sisters wouldn't even come out to the funeral."

"Did he have a lot of friends?"

"All cocaine dealers have friends."

"Enemies?"

"Not that I ever heard about."

"Who was his supplier?"

"I don't know that."

"No disputes? Suits pending? Quarrels with the neighbors? Family arguments about the inheritance?"

She gave me a no on all four counts.

I had told her I wanted to go through his personal belongings, so she showed me into the tiny back bedroom, where he'd set up a card table and some cardboard file boxes. A real entrepreneur. I began to search while she leaned against the doorframe, watching.

I said, "Tell me about what was going on the week he died?" I was sorting though canceled checks in a Nike shoe box. Most were written to the neighborhood supermarket, utilities, telephone company.

She moved to the desk chair and sat down. "I can't tell you much because I was at work. I do alterations and repairs at a dry cleaner's up at Presipio Mall. Rudd would stop in now and then when he was out running around. He'd picked up a few jobs already, but he really wasn't doing the gardening full time. He was trying to get all his old business squared away. Some kid owed him money. I remember that."

"He sold cocaine on *credit?*"

She shrugged. "Maybe it was grass or pills. Somehow the kid owed him a bundle. That's all I know."

"I don't suppose he kept any records."

"Un-uhn. It was all in his head. He was too paranoid to put anything down in black and white."

The file boxes were jammed with old letters, tax returns, receipts. It all looked like junk to me.

"What about the day he was killed? Were you at work then."

She shook her head. "It was a Saturday. I was off work, but I'd gone to the market. I was out maybe an hour and a half, and when I got home, police cars were parked in front, and the paramedics were here. Neighbors were standing out on the street." She stopped talking, and I was left to imagine the rest.

"Had he been expecting anyone?"

"If he was, he never said anything to me. He was in the garage, doing I don't know what. Chauncey, next door, heard the shotgun go off, but by the time he got here to investigate, whoever did it was gone."

I got up and moved toward the hallway. "Is this the bedroom down here?"

"Right. I haven't gotten rid of his stuff yet. I guess I'll have to eventually. I'm going to use his office for the nursery."

I moved into the master bedroom and went through his hanging clothes. "Did the police find anything?"

"They didn't look. Well, one guy came through and poked around some. About five minutes' worth."

I began to check through the drawers she indicated were his. Nothing remarkable came to light. On top of the chest was one of those brass and walnut caddies, where Rudd apparently kept his watch, keys, loose change. Almost idly, I picked it up. Under it there was a folded slip of paper. It was a partially completed appraisal form from a gun shop out in Colgate, a township to the north of us. "What's a Parker?" I said when I'd glanced at it. She peered over the slip.

"Oh. That's probably the appraisal on the shotgun he got."

"The one he was killed with?"

"Well, I don't know. They never found the weapon, but the homicide detective said they couldn't run it through ballistics, anyway— or whatever it is they do."

"Why'd he have it appraised in the first place?"

"He was taking it in trade for a big drug debt, and he needed to know if it was worth it."

"Was this the kid you mentioned before or someone else?"

"The same one, I think. At first, Rudd intended to turn around and sell the gun, but then he found out it was a collector's item so he decided to keep it. The gun dealer called a couple of times after Rudd died, but it was gone by then."

"And you told the cops all this stuff?"

"Sure. They couldn't have cared less."

I doubted that, but I tucked the slip in my pocket anyway. I'd check it out and then talk to Dolan in Homicide.

The gun shop was located on a narrow side street in Colgate, just off the main thoroughfare. Colgate looks like it's made up of hardware stores, U-Haul rentals, and plant nurseries; places that seem to have half their merchandise outside, surrounded by chain-link fence. The gun shop had been set up in someone's front parlor in a dinky white frame house. There were some glass counters filled with gun paraphernalia, but no guns in sight.

The man who came out of the back room was in his fifties, with a narrow face and graying hair, gray eyes made luminous by rimless glasses. He wore a dress shirt with the sleeves rolled up and a long gray apron tied around his waist. He had perfect teeth, but when he talked I could see the rim of pink where his upper plate was fit, and it spoiled the effect. Still, I had to give him credit for a certain level of good looks, maybe a seven on a scale of ten. Not bad for a man his age. "Yes, ma'am," he said. He had a trace of an accent, Virginia, I thought.

"Are you Avery Lamb?"

"That's right. What can I help you with?"

"I'm not sure. I'm wondering what you can tell me about this appraisal you did." I handed him the slip.

He glanced down and then looked up at me. "Where did you get this?"

"Rudd Osterling's widow," I said.

"She told me she didn't have the gun."

"That's right."

His manner was a combination of confusion and wariness. "What's your connection to the matter?"

I took out a business card and gave it to him. "She hired me to look into Rudd's death. I thought the shotgun might be relevant since he was killed with one."

He shook his head. "I don't know what's going on. This is the second time it's disappeared."

"Meaning what?"

"Some woman brought it in to have it appraised back in June. I made an offer on it then, but before we could work out a deal, she claimed the gun was stolen."

"I take it you had some doubts about that."

"Sure I did. I don't think she ever filed a police report, and I suspect she knew damn well who took it but didn't intend to pursue it. Next thing I knew, this Osterling fellow brought the same gun in. It had a beavertail fore-end and an English grip. There was no mistaking it."

"Wasn't that a bit of a coincidence? His bringing the gun in to you?"

"Not really. I'm one of the few master gunsmiths in this area. All he had to do was ask around the same way she did."

"Did you tell her the gun had showed up?"

He shrugged with his mouth and a lift of his brows. "Before I could talk to her, he was dead and the Parker was gone again."

I checked the date on the slip. "That was in August?"

"That's right, and I haven't seen the gun since."

"Did he tell you how he acquired it?"

"Said he took it in trade. I told him this other woman showed up with it first, but he didn't seem to care about that."

"How much was the Parker worth?"

He hesitated, weighing his words. "I offered him six thousand."

"But what's its value out in the marketplace?"

"Depends on what people are willing to pay."

I tried to control the little surge of impatience he had sparked. I could tell he'd jumped into his crafty negotiator's mode, unwilling to tip his hand in case the gun showed up and he could nick it off cheap.

"Look," I said, "I'm asking you in confidence. This won't go any further unless it becomes a police matter, and then neither one of us will have a choice. Right now, the gun's missing anyway, so what difference does it make?"

He didn't seem entirely convinced, but he got my point. He cleared his throat with obvious embarrassment. "Ninety-six."

I stared at him. "Thousand dollars?"

He nodded.

"Jesus. That's a lot for a gun, isn't it?"

His voice dropped. "Ms. Millhone, that gun is priceless. It's an A-1 Special 28-gauge with a two-barrel set. There were only two of them made."

"But why so much?"

"For one thing, the Parker's a beautifully crafted shotgun. There are different grades, of course, but this one was exceptional. Fine wood. Some of the most incredible scroll-work you'll ever see. Parker had an Italian working for him back then who'd spend sometimes five thousand hours on the engraving alone. The company went out of business around 1942, so there aren't any more to be had."

"You said there were two. Where's the other one, or would you know?"

"Only what I've heard. A dealer in Ohio bought the one at auction a couple years back for ninety-six. I understand some fella down in Texas has it now, part of a collection of Parkers. The gun Rudd Osterling brought in has been missing for years. I don't think he knew what he had on his hands."

"And you didn't tell him."

Lamb shifted his gaze. "I told him enough," he said carefully. "I can't help it if the man didn't do his homework."

"How'd you know it was the missing Parker?"

"The serial number matched, and so did everything else. It wasn't a fake, either. I examined the gun under heavy magnification, checking for fill-in welds and traces of markings that might have been over-stamped. After I checked it out, I showed it to a buddy of mine, a big gun buff, and he recognized it, too."

"Who else knew about it besides you and this friend?"

"Whoever Rudd Osterling got it from, I guess."

"I'll want the woman's name and address if you've still got it. Maybe she knows how the gun fell into Rudd's hands."

Again he hesitated for a moment, and then he shrugged. "I don't see why not." He made a note on a piece of scratch paper and pushed it across the counter to me. "I'd like to know if the gun shows up," he said.

"Sure, as long as Mrs. Osterling doesn't object."

I didn't have any other questions for the moment. I moved toward the door, then glanced back at him. "How could Rudd have sold the gun if it was stolen property? Wouldn't he have needed a bill of sale for it? Some proof of ownership?"

Avery Lamb's face was devoid of expression. "Not necessarily. If an avid collector got hold of that gun, it would sink out of sight, and that's the last you'd ever see of it. He'd keep it in his basement and never show it to a soul. It'd be enough if he knew he had it. You don't need a bill of sale for that."

I sat out in my car and made some notes while the information was fresh. Then I checked the address Lamb had given me, and I could feel the adrenaline stir. It was right back in Rudd's neighborhood.

The woman's name was Jackie Barnett. The address was two streets over from the Osterling house and just about parallel; a big corner lot planted with avocado trees and bracketed with palms. The house itself was yellow stucco with flaking brown shutters and a yard that needed mowing. The mailbox read "Squires," but the house number seemed to match. There was a basketball hoop nailed up above the two-car garage and a dismantled motorcycle in the driveway.

I parked my car and got out. As I approached the house, I saw an old man in a wheelchair planted in the side yard like a lawn ornament. He was parchment pale, with baby-fine white hair and rheumy eyes. The left half of his face had been disconnected by a stroke, and his left arm and hand rested uselessly in his lap. I caught sight of a woman peering through the window, apparently drawn by the sound of my car door slamming shut. I crossed the yard, moving toward the front porch. She opened the door before I had a chance to knock.

"You must be Kinsey Millhone. I just got off the phone with Avery. He said you'd be stopping by."

"That was quick. I didn't realize he'd be calling ahead. Saves me an explanation. I take it you're Jackie Barnett."

"That's right. Come in if you like. I just have to check on him," she said, indicating the man in the yard.

"Your father?"

She shot me a look. "Husband," she said. I watched her cross the grass toward the old man, grateful for a chance to recover from my gaffe. I could see now that she was older than she'd first appeared. She must have been in her fifties—at that stage where women wear too much makeup and dye their hair too bold a shade of blond. She was buxom, clearly overweight, but lush. In a seventeenth-century painting, she'd have been depicted supine, her plump naked body draped in sheer white. Standing over her, something with a goat's rear end would be poised for assault. Both would look coy but excited at the prospects. The old man was beyond the pleasures of the flesh, yet the noises he made—garbled and indistinguishable because of the stroke—had the same intimate quality as sounds uttered in the throes of passion, a disquieting effect.

I looked away from him, thinking of Avery Lamb instead. He hadn't actually told me the woman was a stranger to him, but he'd certainly implied as much. I wondered now what their relationship consisted of.

Jackie spoke to the old man briefly, adjusting his lap robe. Then she came back and we went inside.

"Is your name Barnett or Squires?" I asked.

"Technically it's Squires, but I still use Barnett for the most part," she said. She seemed angry, and I thought at first the rage was directed at me. She caught my look. "I'm sorry," she said, "but I've about had it with him. Have you ever dealt with a stroke victim?"

"I understand it's difficult."

"It's impossible! I know I sound hard-hearted, but he was always short-tempered and now he's frustrated on top of that. Self-centered, demanding. Nothing suits him. Nothing. I put him out in the yard sometimes just so I won't have to fool with him. Have a seat, hon."

I sat. "How long has he been sick?"

"He had the first stroke in June. He's been in and out of the hospital ever since."

"What's the story on the gun you took out to Avery's shop?"

"Oh, that's right. He said you were looking into some fellow's death. He lived right here on the Bluffs, too, didn't he?"

"Over on Whitmore."

"That was terrible. I read about it in the papers, but I never did hear the end of it. What went on?"

"I wasn't given the details," I said briefly. "Actually, I'm trying to track down a shotgun that belonged to him. Avery Lamb says it was the same gun you brought in."

She had automatically proceeded to get out two cups and saucers, so her answer was delayed until she'd poured coffee for us both. She passed a cup over to me, and then she sat down, stirring milk into hers. She glanced at me self-consciously. "I just took that gun to spite *him*," she said with a nod toward the yard. "I've been married to Bill for six years and miserable for every one of them. It was my own damn fault. I'd been divorced for ages and I was doing fine, but somehow when I hit fifty, I got in a panic. Afraid of growing old alone, I guess. I ran into Bill, and he looked like a catch. He was retired, but he had loads of money, or so he said. He promised me the moon. Said we'd travel. Said he'd buy me clothes and a car and I don't know what all. Turns out he's a penny-pinching miser with a mean mouth and a quick fist. At least he can't do that anymore." She paused to shake her head, staring down at her coffee cup.

"The gun was his?"

"Well, yes, it was. He has a collection of shotguns. I swear he took better care of them than he did of me. I just despise guns. I was always after him to get rid of them. Makes me nervous to have them in the house. Anyway, when he got sick, it turned out he had insurance, but it only paid eighty percent. I was afraid his whole life savings would go up in smoke. I figured he'd go on for years, using up all the money, and then I'd be stuck with his debts when he died. So I just picked up one of the guns and took it out to that gun place to sell. I was going to buy me some clothes."

"What made you change your mind?"

"Well, I didn't think it'd be worth but eight or nine hundred dollars. Then Avery said he'd give me six thousand for it, so I had to guess it was worth at least twice that. I got nervous and thought I better put it back."

"How soon after that did the gun disappear?"

"Oh, gee, I don't know. I didn't pay much attention until Bill got out of the hospital the second time. He's the one who noticed it was gone," she said. "Of course, he raised pluperfect hell. You should have seen him. He had a conniption fit for two days, and then he had another stroke and had to be hospitalized all over again. Served him right if you ask me. At least I had Labor Day weekend to myself. I needed it."

"Do you have any idea who might have taken the gun?"

She gave me a long, candid look. Her eyes were very blue and couldn't have appeared more guileless. "Not the faintest."

I let her practice her wide-eyed stare for a moment, and then I laid out a little bait just to see what she'd do. "God, that's too bad," I said. "I'm assuming you reported it to the police."

I could see her debate briefly before she replied. Yes or no. Check one. "Well, of course," she said.

She was one of those liars who blush from lack of practice.

I kept my tone of voice mild. "What about the insurance? Did you put in a claim?"

She looked at me blankly, and I had the feeling I'd taken her by surprise on that one. She said, "You know, it never even occurred to me. But of course he probably would have it insured, wouldn't he?"

"Sure, if the gun's worth that much. What company is he with?"

"I don't remember offhand. I'd have to look it up."

"I'd do that if I were you," I said. "You can file a claim, and then all you have to do is give the agent the case number."

"Case number?"

"The police will give you that from their report."

She stirred restlessly, glancing at her watch. "Oh, lordy, I'm going to have to give him his medicine. Was there anything else you wanted to ask while you were here?" Now that she'd told me a fib or two, she was anxious to get rid of me so she could assess the situation. Avery Lamb had told me she'd never reported it to the cops. I wondered if she'd call him up now to compare notes.

"Could I take a quick look at his collection?" I said, getting up.

"I suppose that'd be all right. It's in here," she said. She moved toward a small paneled den, and I followed, stepping around a suitcase near the door.

A rack of six guns was enclosed in a glass-fronted cabinet. All of them were beautifully engraved, with fine wood stocks, and I wondered how a priceless Parker could really be distinguished. Both the cabinet and the rack were locked, and there were no empty slots. "Did he keep the Parker in here?"

She shook her head. "The Parker had its own case." She hauled out a handsome wood case from behind the couch and opened it for me, demonstrating its emptiness as though she might be setting up a magic trick. Actually, there was a set of barrels in the box, but nothing else.

I glanced around. There was a shotgun propped in one corner, and I picked it up, checking the manufacturer's imprint on the frame. L. C. Smith. Too bad. For a moment I'd thought it might be the missing Parker. I'm always hoping for the obvious. I set the Smith back in the corner with regret.

"Well, I guess that'll do," I said. "Thanks for the coffee."

"No trouble. I wish I could be more help." She started easing me toward the door.

I held out my hand. "Nice meeting you," I said. "Thanks again for your time."

She gave my hand a perfunctory shake. "That's all right. Sorry I'm in such a rush, but you know how it is when you have someone sick."

Next thing I knew, the door was closing at my back and I was heading toward my car, wondering what she was up to.

I'd just reached the driveway when a white Corvette came roaring down the street and rumbled into the drive. The kid at the wheel flipped the ignition key and cantilevered himself up onto the seat top. "Hi. You know if my mom's here?"

"Who, Jackie? Sure," I said, taking a flyer. "You must be Doug."

He looked puzzled. "No, Eric. Do I know you?"

I shook my head. "I'm just a friend passing through."

He hopped out of the Corvette. I moved on toward my car, keeping an eye on him as he headed toward the house. He looked about seventeen, blond, blue-eyed, with good cheekbones, a moody, sensual mouth, lean surfer's body. I pictured him in a few years, hanging out in resort hotels, picking up women three times his age. He'd do well. So would they.

Jackie had apparently heard him pull in, and she came out onto the porch, intercepting him with a quick look at me. She put her arm through his, and the two moved into the house. I looked over at the old man. He was making noises again, plucking aimlessly at his bad hand with his good one. I felt a mental jolt, like an interior tremor shifting the ground under me. I was beginning to get it.

I drove the two blocks to Lisa Osterling's. She was in the backyard, stretched out on a chaise in a sunsuit that made her belly look like a watermelon in a laundry bag. Her face and arms were rosy, and her tanned legs glistened with tanning oil. As I crossed the grass, she raised a hand to her eyes, shading her face from the winter sunlight so she could look at me. "I didn't expect to see you back so soon."

"I have a question," I said, "and then I need to use your phone. Did Rudd know a kid named Eric Barnett?"

"I'm not sure. What's he look like?"

I gave her a quick rundown, including a description of the white Corvette. I could see the recognition in her face as she sat up.

"Oh, him. Sure. He was over here two or three times a week. I just never knew his name. Rudd said he lived around here somewhere and stopped by to borrow tools so he could work on his motorcycle. Is he the one who owed Rudd the money?"

"Well, I don't know how we're going to prove it, but I suspect he was."

"You think he killed him?"

"I can't answer that yet, but I'm working on it. Is the phone in here?" I was moving toward the kitchen. She struggled to her feet and followed me into the house. There was a wall phone near the back door. I tucked the receiver against my shoulder, pulling the appraisal slip out of my pocket. I dialed Avery Lamb's gun shop. The phone rang twice.

Somebody picked up on the other end. "Gun shop."

"Mr. Lamb?"

"This is Orville Lamb. Did you want me or my brother, Avery?"

"Avery, actually. I have a quick question for him."

"Well, he left a short while ago, and I'm not sure when he'll be back. Is it something I can help you with?"

"Maybe so," I said. "If you had a priceless shotgun—say, an Ithaca or a Parker, one of the classics—would you shoot a gun like that?"

"You could," he said dubiously, "but it wouldn't be a good idea, especially if it was in mint condition to begin with. You wouldn't want to take a chance on lowering the value. Now if it'd been in use previously, I don't guess it would matter much, but still I wouldn't advise it—just speaking for myself. Is this a gun of yours?"

But I'd hung up. Lisa was right behind me, her expression anxious. "I've got to go in a minute," I said, "but here's what I think went on. Eric Barnett's stepfather has a collection of fine shotguns, one of which turns out to be very, very valuable. The old man was hospitalized, and Eric's mother decided to hock one of the guns in order to do a little something for herself before he'd blown every asset he had on his medical bills. She had no idea the gun she chose was worth so much, but the gun dealer recognized it as the find of a lifetime. I don't know whether he told her that or not, but when she realized it was more valuable than she thought, she lost her nerve and put it back."

"Was that the same gun Rudd took in trade?"

"Exactly. My guess is that she mentioned it to her son, who saw a chance to square his drug debt. He offered Rudd the shotgun in trade, and Rudd decided he'd better get the gun appraised, so he took it out to the same place. The gun dealer recognized it when he brought it in."

She stared at me. "Rudd was killed over the gun itself, wasn't he?" she said.

"I think so, yes. It might have been an accident. Maybe there was a struggle and the gun went off."

She closed her eyes and nodded. "Okay. Oh, wow. That feels better. I can live with that." Her eyes came open, and she smiled painfully. "Now what?"

"I have one more hunch to check out, and then I think we'll know what's what."

She reached over and squeezed my arm. "Thanks."

"Yeah, well, it's not over yet, but we're getting there."

When I got back to Jackie Barnett's, the white Corvette was still in the driveway, but the old man in the wheelchair had apparently been moved into the house. I knocked, and after an interval, Eric opened the door, his expression altering only slightly when he saw me.

I said, "Hello again. Can I talk to your mom?"

"Well, not really. She's gone right now."

"Did she and Avery go off together?"

"Who?"

I smiled briefly. "You can drop the bullshit, Eric. I saw the suitcase in the hall when I was here the first time. Are they gone for good or just for a quick jaunt?"

"They said they'd be back by the end of the week," he mumbled. It was clear he looked a lot slicker than he really was. I almost felt bad that he was so far outclassed.

"Do you mind if I talk to your stepfather?"

He flushed. "She doesn't want him upset."

"I won't upset him."

He shifted uneasily, trying to decide what to do with me.

I thought I'd help him out. "Could I just make a suggestion here? According to the California penal code, grand theft is committed when the real or personal property taken is of a value exceeding two hundred dollars. Now that includes domestic fowl, avocados, olives, citrus, nuts, and artichokes. Also shotguns, and it's punishable by imprisonment in the county jail or state prison for not more than one year. I don't think you'd care for it."

He stepped away from the door and let me in.

The old man was huddled in his wheelchair in the den. The rheumy eyes came up to meet mine, but there was no recognition in them. Or maybe there was recognition but no interest. I hunkered beside his wheelchair. "Is your hearing okay?"

He began to pluck aimlessly at his pant leg with his good hand, looking away from me. I've seen dogs with the same expression when they've done pottie on the rug and know you've got a roll of newspaper tucked behind your back.

"Want me to tell you what I think happened?" I didn't really need to wait. He couldn't answer in any mode that I could interpret. "I think when you came home from the hospital the first time and found out the gun was gone, the shit hit the fan. You must have figured out that Eric took it. He'd probably taken other things if he'd been doing cocaine for long. You probably hounded him until you found out what he'd done with it, and then you went over to Rudd's to get it. Maybe you took the L. C. Smith with you the first time, or maybe you came back for it when he refused to return the Parker. In either case, you blew his head off and then came back across the yards. And then you had another stroke."

I became aware of Eric in the doorway behind me. I glanced back at him. "You want to talk about this stuff?" I asked.

"Did he kill Rudd?"

"I think so," I said. I stared at the old man.

His face had taken on a canny stubbornness, and what was I going to do? I'd have to talk to Lieutenant Dolan about the situation, but the cops would probably never find any real proof, and even if they did, what could they do to him? He'd be lucky if he lived out the year.

"Rudd was a nice guy," Eric said.

"God, Eric. You *all* must have guessed what happened," I said snappishly.

He had the good grace to color up at that, and then he left the room. I stood up. To save myself, I couldn't work up any righteous anger at the pitiful remainder of a human being hunched in front of me. I crossed to the gun cabinet.

The Parker shotgun was in the rack, three slots down, looking like the other classic shotguns in the case. The old man would die, and Jackie would inherit it from his estate. Then she'd marry Avery and they'd all have what they wanted. I stood there for a moment, and then I started looking through the desk drawers until I found the keys. I unlocked the cabinet and then unlocked the rack. I substituted the L. C. Smith for the Parker and then locked the whole business up again. The old man was whimpering, but he never looked at me, and Eric was nowhere in sight when I left.

The last I saw of the Parker shotgun, Lisa Osterling was holding it somewhat awkwardly across her bulky midriff. I'd talk to Lieutenant Dolan all right, but I wasn't going to tell him everything. Sometimes justice is served in other ways.

I Spy

Graham Greene

Charlie Stowe waited until he heard his mother snore before he got out of bed. Even then he moved with caution and tiptoed to the window. The front of the house was irregular, so that it was possible to see a light burning in his mother's room. But now all the windows were dark. A searchlight passed across the sky, lighting the banks of cloud and probing the dark deep spaces between, seeking enemy airships. The wind blew from the sea, and Charlie Stowe could hear behind his mother's snores the beating of the waves. A draft through the cracks in the window-frame stirred his night-shirt. Charlie Stowe was frightened.

But the thought of the tobacconist's shop which his father kept down a dozen wooden stairs drew him on. He was twelve years old, and already boys at the County School mocked him because he had never smoked a cigarette. The packets were piled twelve deep below, Gold Flake and Player's, De Reszke, Abdulla, Woodbines, and the little shop lay under a thin haze of stale smoke which would completely disguise his crime. That it was a crime to steal some of his father's stock Charlie Stowe had no doubt, but he did not love his father; his father was unreal to him, a wraith, pale, thin, indefinite, who noticed him only spasmodically and left even punishment to his mother. For his mother he felt a passionate demonstrative love; her large boisterous presence and her noisy charity filled the world for him; from her speech he judged her the friend of everyone, from the rector's wife to the "dear Queen," except the "Huns," the monsters who lurked in Zeppelins in the clouds. But his father's affection and dislike were as indefinite as his movements. Tonight he had said he would be in Norwich, and yet you never knew. Charlie Stowe had no sense of safety as he crept down the wooden stairs. When they creaked he clenched his fingers on the collar of his night-shirt.

At the bottom of the stairs he came out quite suddenly into the little shop. It was too dark to see his way, and he did not dare touch the switch. For half a minute he sat in despair on the bottom step with his chin cupped in his hands. Then the regular movement of the searchlight was reflected through an upper window and the boy had time to fix in memory the pile of cigarettes, the counter, and the small hole under it. The footsteps of a policeman on the pavement made him grab the first packet to his hand and dive for the hole. A light shone along the floor and a hand tried the door, then the footsteps passed on, and Charlie cowered in the darkness.

At last he got his courage back by telling himself in his curiously adult way that if he were caught now there was nothing to be done about it, and he might as well have his smoke. He put a cigarette in his mouth and then remembered that he had no matches. For a while he dared not move. Three times the searchlight lit the shop, as he muttered taunts and encouragements. "May as well be hung for a sheep," "Cowardy, cowardy custard," grown-up and childish exhortations oddly mixed.

But as he moved he heard footfalls in the street, the sound of several men walking rapidly. Charlie Stowe was old enough to feel surprise that anybody was about. The footsteps came nearer, stopped; a key was turned in the shop door, a voice said: "Let him in," and then he heard his father, "If you wouldn't mind being quiet, gentlemen. I don't want to wake up the family." There was a note unfamiliar to Charlie in the undecided voice. A torch flashed and the electric globe burst into blue light. The boy held his breath; he wondered whether his father would hear his heart beating, and he clutched his night-shirt tightly and prayed, "O God, don't let me be caught." Through a crack in the counter he could see his father where he stood, one hand held to his high stiff collar, between two men in bowler hats and belted mackintoshes. They were strangers.

"Have a cigarette," his father said in a voice dry as a biscuit. One of the men shook his head. "It wouldn't do, not when we are on duty. Thank you all the same." He spoke gently, but without kindness: Charlie Stowe thought his father must be ill.

"Mind if I put a few in my pocket?" Mr. Stowe asked, and when the man nodded he lifted a pile of Gold Flake and Players from a shelf and caressed the packets with the tips of his fingers.

"Well," he said, "there's nothing to be done about it, and I may as well have my smokes." For a moment Charlie Stowe feared discovery, his father stared round the shop so thoroughly; he might have been seeing it for the first time. "It's a good little business," he said, "for those that like it. The wife will sell out, I suppose. Else the neighbors'll be wrecking it. Well, you want to be off. A stitch in time. I'll get my coat."

"One of us'll come with you, if you don't mind," said the stranger gently.

"You needn't trouble. It's on the peg here. There, I'm all ready."

The other man said in an embarrassed way, "Don't you want to speak to your wife?" The thin voice was decided, "Not me. Never do today what you can put off till tomorrow. She'll have her chance later, won't she?"

"Yes, yes," one of the strangers said and he became very cheerful and encouraging. "Don't you worry too much. While there's life . . ." and suddenly his father tried to laugh.

When the door had closed Charlie Stowe tiptoed upstairs and got into bed. He wondered why his father had left the house again so late at night and who the strangers were. Surprise and awe kept him for a little while awake. It was as if a familiar photograph had stepped from the frame to reproach him with neglect. He remembered how his father had held tight to his collar and fortified himself with proverbs, and he thought for the first time that, while his mother was boisterous and kindly, his father was very like himself, doing things in the dark which frightened him. It would have pleased him to go down to his father and tell him that he loved him, but he could hear through the window the quick steps going away. He was alone in the house with his mother, and he fell asleep.

About the Authors

Isaac Babel: Ukrainian, 1894–1941. Babel, whose writing career was encouraged by Maxim Gorky, is best known for *Red Cavalry*, stories about his experiences during the Civil War of 1918–1920, when he rode with the Cossacks. Babel stopped writing in the 1930s and observed what he called "the genre of silence" as his country fell victim to the Stalinist terror. He was arrested and sent to a camp in 1939, where he disappeared. His Odessa stories, featuring Benya Krik, a gangster in orange pants, are marvelously funny and cruel.

Donald Barthelme: American, 1931–1989. Considered one of the most influential writers of short fiction since Faulkner and Hemingway, Barthelme has received many awards, including the National Book Award for *The Slightly Irregular Fire Engine*. Among his works are *City Life*, *Sixty Stories*, *Paradise*, and *The Dead Father*.

William Bayer: American, born 1939. Educated at Harvard, Bayer has been a Foreign Service officer, filmmaker, screenwriter, and photographer. Among his crime novels are *Tangier*, *Peregrine* ("Best Novel" Edgar Award), *Switch*, *Pattern Crimes*, *Blind Side*, and *Wallflower*. He currently serves as president of the International Association of Crime Writers North American Branch.

Pieke Biermann: German, born 1950. A former postwoman (she never rang twice, she says) and prostitute, she writes essays and documentary film scripts and translates from Italian and English. She has written a series of novels featuring a Berlin homicide squad. Her most recent novel, *Violetta*, won the Klagenfurt Lieteraturpries award. She is considered by many critics the most important new voice in German crime fiction.

Lawrence Block: American, born 1938. Recipient of an Edgar for the short story and Japan's Maltese Falcon Award. He is best known for his Matt Scudder novels, featuring an alcoholic ex-cop working the mean streets of New York. His most recent novel is *A Dance at the Slaughterhouse*. Block is also a prolific short story writer. He is currently a member of the Executive Council of IACW's North American Branch. He lives in New York.

Jorge Luis Borges: 1899–1986. Poet, essayist, and short story writer. Borges found an international audience in 1961 when he won the Prix Formentor for *Ficciones*. Borges's stories are so incredibly compact, they are like little Madame Bovarys, written in five or ten pages.

Italo Calvino: Italian, born in Cuba, 1923–1985. Calvino is known for his novels, fables, and folk tales. His works include *T-Zero*, *Invisible Cities*, and *If on a Winter's Night a Traveler*. A master of prose fiction, Calvino builds invention upon invention, dream upon dream, to create a universe that echoes with its own sinister delight.

Angela Carter: British, 1940–1992. Carter's works have been called a cross between Edgar Allan Poe and Roman Polanski, with their combination of Gothic themes, violence, and perverse eroticism. She wrote novels—*War of Dreams*, *The Passion of the New Eve*—short stories, juvenile fiction, and radio plays.

Raymond Carver: American, 1938–1988. Recipient of the National Book Award for *Will You Please Be Quiet, Please?* *Cathedral* was nominated for both a National Book Critics Circle award and a Pulitzer. Carver's stories, always muscular and terse, have their own essential mystery and sense of some hidden crime.

Jerome Charyn: American, born 1937. His novels include *Paradise Man*, *Elsinore*, and *Maria's Girls*. Charyn has devoted seven books to the Pink Commish, Isaac Sidel, a murderously romantic police chief.

Charyn lives in Paris and New York. He serves on the Executive Council of IACW's North American Branch.

George C. Chesbro: American, born 1940. Chesbro writes about Dr. Robert Frederickson, Ph.D., a criminologist and former circus headliner who happens to be a dwarf. Chesbro's novels include *The Language of Cannibals*, *The House of Secret Enemies*, and most recently *The Fear in Yesterday's Rings*. He lives in Nyack, New York.

Didier Daeninckx: French, born 1941. Daeninckx worked for many years as a printer and a journalist before writing his first crime novel, *Meurtre Pour Memoire*, in 1984. He is universally considered the best crime writer in France.

Don DeLillo: American, born 1936. Recipient of the American Book Award for *White Noise*. His most recent novel is *Mao II*. DeLillo's short stories have appeared in *The New Yorker*, *Esquire*, and *The Atlantic*. He lives in New York. He has created a body of work that dissects the American dream and all its murderous myths.

Harlan Ellison is the author of 58 books, more than 1,200 stories, essays, reviews, articles, motion picture scripts and teleplays. He has won the Hugo award eight times, the Nebula three times, the Edgar Allan Poe award of Mystery Writers of America twice, the Bram Stoker award of Horror Writers of America twice, the World Fantasy Award, the British Fantasy Award, the Silver Pen award for journalism from P.E.N., and is the only scenarist in Hollywood ever to have won the Writers Guild of America award for Most Outstanding Teleplay *four* times for solo work. His latest books are *The Harlan Ellison Hornbook*, a thirty-five-year retrospective of his work, *The Essential Ellison*, and forthcoming this year are *The City on the Edge of Forever*, the first book publication of his famous *Star Trek* script in its original (not the aired) version . . . and a new collection of stories, *Slippage*. He lives with his wife, Susan, in the Lost Aztec Temple of Mars, somewhere in the Los Angeles area.

James Ellroy: American, born 1948. One of America's masters of the *noir* genre, Ellroy is known for his gritty realism and high-intensity prose. His books include a series of novels set in an hallucinatory Hollywood of the 1940s and 1950s, *The Black Dahlia*, *The Big Nowhere*, and *L.A. Confidential*. He lives in Eastchester, New York.

Mickey Friedman: American, born 1944. A former *San Francisco Examiner* reporter/columnist, Friedman turned to crime fiction in 1983 with *Hurricane Season*, followed by *Paper Phoenix*, *The Fault Tree*, and *Venetian Mask*. In 1988, she started a series of novels featuring Georgia Lee Maxwell, a free-lance writer based in Paris. Friedman's most recent work is *A Temporary Ghost*. She lives in New York.

Herbert Gold: American, born 1924. Gold, who is considered one of the chief chroniclers of modern American life, writes novels, short stories, and nonfiction. Among his novels are *Salt*, *Fathers*, *He/She*, *Family*, and *A Girl of Forty*. He lives in San Francisco.

Nadine Gordimer: South African, born 1923. Winner of many awards, including the Booker Prize and the Nobel Prize for Literature. Gordimer's novels and short stories often deal with apartheid and its brutal effects on both blacks and whites. She lives in Johannesburg.

Joe Gores: American, born 1931. Recipient of Edgar Awards for his novels, short stories, and teleplays. Gores is a former private eye. His first novel, *A Time of Predators*, dealt with the impact of rape on a man and his family, and is considered a classic of the hard-boiled genre. He also writes a series featuring the DKA Agency of San Francisco. Gores was formerly on the Executive Council of IACW's North American Branch. He lives near San Francisco.

Sue Grafton: American, born 1940. Along with Sara Paretsky, Grafton is one of the pioneering authors of the hard-boiled female private-eye novel. Grafton's heroine, Kinsey Millhone, got her start in *"A" Is for Alibi*, followed by *"B" Is for Burglar* and most recently *"I" Is for Innocent*. Grafton also writes short stories. She lives in Santa Barbara, California.

Graham Greene: British, 1904–1991. Greene's novels are fierce and melancholic at the same time. *Brighton Rock*, a morality tale about a young "bad boy" on the beaches of Brighton, is among the best crime novels of the twentieth century. Other works include *The Heart of the Matter, Ministry of Fear, The Power and the Glory*, and *A Burnt Out Case*.

Laura Grimaldi: Grimaldi is considered Italy's finest living crime writer for her best-selling fiction and nonfiction, essays, and scripts. She is also a translator and an owner of the publishing house Interno Giallo. Grimaldi has won numerous awards, among them the SILA Literary Award and the Selezione Bancarella. Her most recent novels are *Suspicion, The Guilt, The Noose*, and *Monsieur Bovary*. Grimaldi has been active in IACW since its founding and has served as European president. She lives in Milan.

Patricia Highsmith: American, born 1921. Recipient of the Grand Prix de Littérature (1957) and the British Crime Writers Association's Silver Dagger Award (1964). Highsmith is best known for a series of quirky suspense novels featuring Tom Ripley, a murderer with passive-aggressive traits. Her novel *Strangers on a Train* was filmed by Alfred Hitchcock. Her latest work is *Ripley Underwater*. She lives in Switzerland. Highsmith has revolutionized crime writing with a merciless poetics that never judges or intrudes upon her characters.

Tony Hillerman: American, born 1925. Recipient of an Edgar and the Mystery Writers of America's Grandmaster Award for lifetime achievement. Hillerman is best known for his mysteries set among Native Americans in the Southwest, featuring two Navajos, Jim Chee and Joe Leaphorn. Hillerman lives in Albuquerque, New Mexico.

P. D. James: British, born 1920. Her awards include the Order of the British Empire, as well as several "Daggers" from the British Crime Writers Association. A former hospital administrator, James later worked as a senior civil servant in the criminal department of the Home Office. James is one of the most honored crime writers in the world, and her protagonist, Chief Superintendent Adam Dalgliesh, is perhaps the most sympathetic character in modern crime fiction. Her works include *An Unsuitable Job for a Woman, Black Tower, A Taste for Death*, and most recently, *Devices and Desires*.

Stuart M. Kaminsky: American, born 1934. Recipient of an Edgar for *A Cold Red Sunrise*. Kaminsky is best known for two widely different series: the Porfiry Rostnikov novels (influenced by Julian Semionov's *Petrovka 38*), feature a Moscow police inspector; the Toby Peters books focus on a detective in the golden years of Hollywood. Kaminsky is Professor and Director of the Florida State University Conservatory of Motion Picture, Television and Recording Arts, and is on the Executive Council of IACW's North American Branch. He lives in Sarasota, Florida.

Clarice Lispector: Born in the Ukraine, lived in Brazil, 1925–1977. Lispector was among the best Brazilian writers. Her works include *Close to the Savage Heart*, *Family Ties*, and *The Apple in the Dark*.

Gabriel García Márquez: Colombian, born 1928. Recipient of numerous international awards, including the Nobel Prize for Literature. Among his best-known novels are *One Hundred Years of Solitude*, *Chronicle of a Death Foretold*, and *Love in the Time of Cholera*. He currently lives and works in Mexico City.

Yukio Mishima: Japanese, 1925–1977. One of the most influential writers in postwar Japan, Mishima was known for his novels, plays, essays, and short stories, as well as his devotion to the arts of the samurai. Author of *Thirst for Love* and *The Sailor Who Fell from Grace with the Sea*, he delivered the final pages of his *Sea of Futility* tetralogy on the day he committed ritual suicide.

Manuel Vásquez Montalbán: Spanish, born 1939. Montalbán's works have been widely published in Europe, and he has won crime writing awards in France, Germany, and Italy, as well as in Spain. His popular Pepe Carvalho novels, featuring a Barcelona detective who is an ex-CIA agent, have been adapted for television and film. Montalbán's novels include *The Pianist*, *The Southern Seas* (which has been published in the United States), *Assassination in the Central Committee*, and most recently *The Greek Labyrinth*.

Walter Mosley: American, born 1952. Highly acclaimed author of a series of novels set in post-World War II Los Angeles, featuring the black part-time detective "Easy" Rawlins, an ex-serviceman. Mosley's books include *Devil in a Blue Dress*, *A Red Death*, and *White Butterfly*. He lives in New York. Mosley is one of the most original new voices in American crime fiction.

Joyce Carol Oates: American, born 1938. Winner of numerous awards, including the National Book Award for *Them*. Oates's works include novels, short stories, essays, and nonfiction, ranging from literary criticism to a metaphysical study of boxing. She also writes under the pseudonym Rosamund Smith (*Lives of the Twins* and most recently *Snake Eyes*). Her other works include *Because It Is Bitter and Because It Is My Heart*, *Heat and Other Stories*, and *The Rise of Life on Earth*. Oates teaches creative writing at Princeton University, where she is the Roger S. Berlind Distinguished Professor in the Humanities. She has created her own sense of the neo-Gothic novel, where crime exists under the surface of things, like some impossible lullaby.

Flannery O'Connor: American, 1924–1964. Winner of numerous awards, including the National Book Award. O'Connor's works are filled with "tender" violence and grim Gothic humor. Her books include the novels *Wise Blood* and *The Violent Bear It Away* and the collections *A Good Man Is Hard to Find* and *Everything That Rises Must Converge*.

Sara Paretsky: American, born 1947. Her Chicago private eye, V. I. Warshawski, was a pioneer among hard-boiled female detectives. Paretsky's most recent work, the best-seller *Guardian Angel*, is the sixth in the Warshawski series. Paretsky was one of the founders of Sisters-in-Crime and is the editor of the anthology *A Woman's Eye*. She lives in Chicago.

Leonardo Sciascia: Italian, 1921–1989. One of Italy's finest novelists, Sciascia wrote "metaphysical mysteries" about his own Sicilian landscape. Among Sciascia's works that have appeared in translation are *Mafia Vendetta*, *A Man's Blessing*, *Equal Danger*, *One Way or Another*, and most recently *Open Doors*.

Julian Semionov: Russian, born 1931. Considered the former Soviet Union's most popular crime writer. Semionov's novels in English translation include *Petrovka 38*, *17 Moments of Spring*, and *Tass Is Authorized to Announce*. Semionov is the founding president of IACW. He lives in Moscow and Yalta.

Roger L. Simon: American, born 1943. Author of the popular Moses Wine series featuring a hip L.A. private eye, an orphan of the sixties. Simon's novels include *The Big Fix*, *California Roll*, *Wild Turkey*, and most recently *Raising the Dead*. He is also a screenwriter whose work has won an Edgar and was also nominated for an Academy Award. He is one of the founders of IACW and served as the first president of the North American Branch. He lives in Hollywood.

Paco Ignacio Taibo II: Spanish, born 1949. Recipient of numerous awards in Mexico, Latin America, and Spain, including most recently the Planeta/Mortiz Prize. Taibo's novels, including *An Easy Thing*, *Calling All Heroes*, *The Shadow of the Shadow*, and *Some Clouds*, have all been published in the United States. Taibo is one of the founders of the IACW and currently serves as president of the organization-at-large. He lives in Mexico City.

Ross Thomas: American, born 1926. Thomas won the Edgar for his first novel, *The Cold War Swap*, and another Edgar for *Briarpatch*. Among his other novels are *The Fools in Town Are on Our Side*, *The Eighth Dwarf*, *Missionary Stew*, and most recently *Twilight at Mac's Place*. Thomas is a member of the Executive Council of IACW and lives in Malibu.

Andrew Vachss: American, born 1942. An attorney specializing in the problems of abused children, he is also the author of a gritty series of novels set in Manhattan's underworld of sexual exploitation, featuring the ex-con/private eye Burke and his extraordinary companions, among them a mute Mongolian, a transsexual prostitute, and Mama Wong, whose restaurant provides both cover and comfort for Burke and his friends. Vachss's novels include *Flood*, *Strega*, *Hard Candy*, and most recently *Sacrifice*. He lives in New York.

Donald E. Westlake: American, born 1933. Recipient of three Edgars and an Academy Award nomination for his screenplay for *The Grifters*. Under the pseudonym Richard Stark, Westlake started his career as a tough-guy writer, but today he is better known for his wacky, funny novels, including a series that features the rogue thief Dortmunder. His most recent work is *Humans*. He lives in New York.

Eric Wright: British, born 1929. Wright emigrated to Canada as a young man and currently lives in Toronto. He has won awards from the Crime Writers of Canada and the British Crime Writers Association for his novels featuring Charlie Salter, a Toronto police inspector. His works include *A Death in the Old Country*, *A Sensitive Case*, *Final Cut*, and most recently *A Fine Italian Hand*. Wright has been active in IACW since its inception and currently serves as North American regional director.

385